Misplaced Trust

An Alexis Parker novel

G.K. Parks

Copyright © 2018 G.K. Parks

A Modus Operandi imprint

All rights reserved.

ISBN: 1942710089
ISBN-13: 978-1-942710-08-0

For my mom and dad

ONE

"Aren't you forgetting something?" I asked.

James Martin checked his pockets, ensuring he had his phone and wallet. He adjusted his sleeves and regarded his cufflinks to make sure they were fastened. He glanced back at me, confused. Scanning his reflection, he ran a hand through his dark brown hair, straightened his tie, and smoothed the creases on his jacket. I snorted, making my annoyance known.

"What?" he asked.

"You forgot to say *thank you, ma'am.*"

He smirked. "You don't like being called ma'am."

"That's not the point."

"Alexis," he sighed, "not this again. You know I have an early morning meeting, and I need to spend tonight preparing."

"In a three-piece suit?"

"Luc and I are meeting over drinks to discuss strategy."

"Fine." I rolled onto my side, so I didn't have to look at him. "Lock the door on your way out."

"Sweetheart," he cooed, "I wanted to see you, but I don't have a lot of spare time."

"You never do," I muttered. "Just go. You don't want to

keep Luc waiting."

He hesitated for a brief moment. Then without another word, he walked out of the bedroom. Once I heard the door slam, I climbed out of bed. Something shiny caught my eye, and I picked up the engagement ring that sat on top of my dresser. His proposal had been magical and all the things most girls would want, except I wasn't most girls. What followed were numerous freakouts amidst mortal peril and the events that turned us into this. We weren't exactly Sid and Nancy, probably more Nick and Nora, but then again, I might be remembering Hammett wrong. The only thing I knew for certain was I deserved this—the cold indifference, the emptiness, the hurt.

Most men would have walked away a long time ago, but Martin was different. Perhaps he was a masochist, or he had the world's worst savior complex. Either way, I had lied to him and betrayed him, but my deception had been for his own good. Or so I told myself.

My work had always been dangerous. Even when I went on sabbatical from the Office of International Operations, a branch of the FBI, trouble always found me. Occasionally, that meant his life was also in jeopardy, and I would be damned if I'd let anyone hurt him. Somehow, that insistence had strained our relationship to the point that I was once again living alone in my apartment. We had taken a huge step backward, which I wouldn't have minded if some things were the same, but everything was different. It was true what they say. You never appreciate what you have until it's gone.

The phone rang, and relief washed over me. Finally, something to derail this pity party. Checking the caller ID, I chuckled and answered the phone.

"Did you forget how to catalog evidence?" I asked.

"Parker," my partner, Eddie Lucca, said, "where the hell are you?"

"At home."

"Not for long. Jablonsky wants your ass back in the office. He's on a tear. Again."

"What happened this time?"

Under normal conditions, Lucca would have gone home

several hours earlier. It was nearly ten p.m. Most federal agents ducked out at five if they could get away with it. On the days that we didn't have an ongoing op in play, even I'd occasionally leave early. Today was an excellent case in point.

"We're overloaded with the sheer volume of connected cases, and the DEA requested our assistance with something. Director Kendall has everyone assisting OCU, and Jablonsky thinks you should be here to help out."

"I'm on my way." I had a love-hate relationship with the job. Most of the time, I hated it and the things I'd done, but I had to admit, I loved working cases. And at the moment, I needed the distraction.

Arriving at the federal building, I took the elevator to the OIO level and stepped into the corridor. A few agents were in one of the larger conference rooms. Mark Jablonsky's office door was ajar, but he wasn't inside. Lucca was holed up at his desk with folders stacked higher than his head. My desk had a few items piled up, but it looked like I might have been the only one who wasn't behind on work.

"What's the latest?" I took a seat and hit the computer's power button.

Lucca rolled his eyes, picking up half the folders and placing them in front of me. "Here. Thanks for volunteering to help." He returned to his side of the aisle and leaned back in his chair. "Where do you want me to start?"

"At the beginning. When I left three hours ago, you said you'd be finished in twenty minutes. I've heard of performance anxiety, but this is ridiculous. Your wife must be a very patient woman."

Glaring, he chose to ignore the dig. Although I suspected he might file a sexual harassment complaint at some point. "I would have left on time, except we received a request from the DEA for a full workup on a group of individuals they're investigating."

"Are they part of a cartel?" I asked, unsure why this was our problem.

"They might be. The FBI didn't possess any info on

these individuals, but according to the IRS, they've filed for a religious exemption."

"So we're talking about a cult."

"I didn't say that." Lucca liked playing the politically correct card. "Maybe they are a co-op of like-minded individuals who believe in the same higher power."

"Do we know the cult leader's name?"

"Tax forms were filed by Timothy Wilde. I've run a complete background. He has a record, accused of sexual assault and possession with intent."

"Lovely." Opening the top folder, I skimmed the pages. "Question," I held up one of the forms, "what does that have to do with these files?"

"While I was busy running Mr. Wilde and his cohorts through the database, Jablonsky dropped off a dozen cases that need review. Since I was the one assigned to repair the internal leak, our boss thinks I should also be in charge of double-checking our recent case work for any bias or compromise."

"In other words, none of this is actually my problem." Turning the screws was one of my favorite pastimes when it came to dealing with the boy scout.

"Parker, you owe me."

"Actually, I don't. That debt has been repaid, but I'll help anyway." I keyed in the first case in the stack. "Does the DEA think Wilde is importing drugs and selling them on behalf of our friends south of the border?"

"I don't know what they think. They didn't say why they needed the intel. They just wanted our assessment. I assume they must have an operative in play or are planning some sort of infiltration. Why else would they send us the request? They could have gotten the intel on their own."

"We do have more funding, but it is strange they asked. Something else must be going on." Getting distracted by the more interesting possibilities, I opened a second browser window and read the most recent intelligence reports. However, there was no mention of Wilde or updated cartel activity. "Whatever. As long as they don't make this our issue, I guess it doesn't matter." I went back to analyzing the stack of OIO cases. "How many more all-nighters do you think we'll have to pull before we're back on solid ground?"

"This should be the last one. It's been a couple of months. There can't be that many more cases to evaluate after this." Lucca shook his head. "Next week, the AG hands down the rest of the indictments. They just want to make sure everything will hold up in court since our compromised agent and the data breach nearly destroyed everything."

"By the way, you said Jablonsky wanted me back here. Where is he?"

"He'll be back soon. He's coordinating a raid." Lucca gestured obliquely to the area behind him. "I'm surprised we weren't tasked with assisting." For several minutes we worked in silence until Lucca let out a confused grunt. "Come to think of it, we haven't been tasked with any field work at all."

"So?" I didn't bother to look up. I was aware of that fact and had my suspicions as to the reason why.

"Did you request desk duty?"

"No."

"How's your wrist?" Lucca asked, unwilling to drop this line of questioning. The boy scout must have been yearning to conduct an interrogation.

"It's fine." Without turning, I picked up the nearest coffee cup and held it in the air. "No shakes. Would you prefer if I aim my firearm at you?"

"That won't be necessary. So it isn't because you're injured. Is it because you haven't shaken the fear of dying yet?"

"Lucca, do you want my help or not? I'll leave if the only reason you called was to bust my chops."

"I just don't get it, and I don't get why you aren't chomping at the bit to get back in the field. You hate this office. You hate being stuck behind a desk. You like being out there, so why are you acting perfectly content to conduct analyses and reviews?"

"That's part of the job, and unlike you, I can keep up with the workload." Giving him an icy glare, I went back to tackling the files for which he was responsible.

"Parker," Mark Jablonsky bellowed, "my office. Now."

"Sounds like someone's in trouble," Lucca teased, but I couldn't help but wonder how true those words might be.

I finished what I was doing and went down the corridor to Mark's office. Stepping inside, I found my mentor pouring a shot of whiskey into a glass. Drinking on the job was typically frowned upon, but it was late. So he could take a creative license to a few of the rules.

"Alex," he jerked his chin toward the sofa in the corner, "why don't you have a seat? Do you want a drink?"

"No."

"Right." He nodded, remembering my aversion to liquor. "Is there anything I should know?"

Swallowing, I was suddenly filled with apprehension. I'd been harboring a deep dark secret for a while now. I always suspected Mark knew but thought better than to ask. However, I wasn't entirely sure how true that was.

"I don't know." I slumped onto the sofa, squelching my ingrained desire to pace. "What are we talking about?"

"I was at Marty's the other day," he said casually, leaning back in his chair and swiveling to face me. "Do you know what I discovered?"

"That he's building a robot army in the basement?"

Mark chuckled politely, but he wasn't amused. "No." He eyed me. "You don't live there anymore."

"I don't?"

"Cut the bullshit. Are you okay?"

"I'm fine. He needed space. Maybe we both did. I don't know."

"The two of you will figure it out." He took another sip, bolstering his courage. "That's not the problem."

"There's a problem?"

"I asked what led to your changing living arrangements." He emptied the glass and put it on the desk, crossed the room, and sat next to me, making sure the door was closed. "You never went to London. You were here when the club caught fire and when seven bodies were pulled out of the back room." He held up a hand before I could say anything. "I don't blame you. You didn't have a choice, but I do not want to know any details. Speculation doesn't mean shit, and I have no reason to speculate. That wasn't our case. Murder and arson are dealt with by the police department, not the OIO. Is there any way this will bounce back on you?"

"I hope not. Nothing has so far."

"Good. Let's keep it that way. Does anyone know about this?"

"Not exactly."

"Marty doesn't know what happened?"

"Not in any specific terms. That's not why he kicked me out. At least, I don't think it is. Then again, who would want to live with a killer?"

"Alex," Mark warned, but his voice held that fatherly quality, like he wanted to provide comfort and tell me everything would be okay instead of chastising me, "this job comes with some really shitty possibilities. You're not a killer. Do you remember what I told you after your very first field assignment?"

"Never use that word because it's loaded."

"That's right. Plus, we stop killers through any means necessary. That doesn't mean we are killers."

"Tomato, tomato," I pronounced the word differently.

"Just know, if something pops up concerning this, I'll take care of it." Clearing his throat, he went back to his desk. "Now on to other matters, we need to talk about Lucca."

"What about him? Did he file a complaint against me? I swear, that man can't take a joke."

"That's not it."

"Is this about his sudden desire to be out in the field?"

"He noticed the two of you have been benched?"

"It has been pretty obvious. We're the only active agents who haven't been assigned an op in a couple of months. Perhaps you should reassign him until you figure out what you're going to do with me."

"Actually, that's already been done."

TWO

"What?" I blinked a few times, failing to comprehend what I just heard.

"That's what I wanted to talk to you about." Mark sifted through the paperwork on his desk. "As you know, Lucca was assigned to the OIO from the D.C. office to ferret out our leak. His job's done. They want to recall him."

"I guess that makes sense."

"Director Kendall believes Eddie's an asset, and since he works under me, I'm to provide a thorough evaluation—strengths, weaknesses, the whole nine. I figured you'd be the best place to start. Do you want him to stay?"

Oddly enough, I did. It was a strange revelation since the last thing I ever wanted was a partner. Eddie Lucca had been forced upon me when I was reinstated. He'd inundated me with rules and regulations and had been a thorn in my side ever since we met. However, at some point, I put my trust in him. I didn't want to lose another partner. Honestly, I never wanted to lose anyone ever again.

"It shouldn't be up to me. He has a wife and daughter. You're in charge. You figure out if he's a good fit for our unit, and if he is, ask him if he wants to stay. Lucca had a life in D.C. that he was forced to leave. Maybe he'd like to go back to it."

"You're telling me you're okay with him staying here?"

I shrugged.

"You've gotta be shitting me. After I've had to listen to you moan and groan about how you never wanted a partner again and how annoying and incompetent he is, you're now telling me that you're fine letting him stick around? Are you feeling okay?" A dark, knowing look crossed Jablonsky's face. "How long are you planning to stay once he's gone?"

"I'll stay for as long as you want. I've already let you down so many times. I won't do it again. You have my word."

"Fine. I'll write up the evaluation and let Director Kendall make the call. Then we'll see what Lucca wants to do." He jerked his head toward the office door, and I pulled it open. "Hey, Parker, don't mention any of this to him."

"My lips are sealed."

Returning to my desk, I tackled the stack of files for the next several hours, casting furtive glances at Lucca. Granted, losing a partner to a transfer was much better than permanently losing one. I'd experienced that firsthand with the only other man with whom I'd worked, Michael Carver. His death had been devastating. It was the reason I left the OIO, how I ended up spending a couple of years in the private sector, and what led me to James Martin. Now that I was receiving a government paycheck again, my civilian life was quickly crumbling away. I always feared it was one or the other, and so far, I hadn't been proven wrong.

From an entirely selfish standpoint, I had no idea what would become of me if Lucca was reassigned. Perhaps I'd be shifted to another branch or office, or I'd be stuck as the OIO secretary. After everything I'd seen and done, being behind a desk might be the safest thing for everyone, including me.

"What?" Lucca asked, noticing my lingering gaze. "Did I spill teriyaki sauce on my tie?"

"No. I was just thinking about the DEA request."

"What brilliant fictional fabrication have you come up with this time?"

"They screwed up a bust and are hoping to cover their asses by passing the buck to us and saying we provided them with bogus intel."

"It could happen. Let's be honest, interagency politics always work that way." Having completed the final review, Lucca closed the folder and yawned. "If they call back, tell them to fuck off. I'm going home." He slipped on his jacket and made sure his computer was powered down. "You should do the same. We can at least get four or five hours of sleep before we start this entire process over again."

"Yeah, okay. I'll see you later."

After he was gone, I leaned back in my chair and looked around the nearly empty office. Mark's light was on, and two other agents were working on something in the conference room. The forensic experts and tech department were waiting for the results of the raid, but it was quiet. Too quiet.

Opening my bottom drawer, I pulled out a case I'd been researching privately. It was a murder investigation from across the pond, but I was too scatterbrained to concentrate on chasing down what continued to be unsubstantiated leads and dead ends. I wanted an escape from my internal torment, not a further infliction of additional anguish.

With nothing else to do, I went down a few floors to the gym, changed in the locker room, and went for a long run. By the time I was showered and back in regulation attire, it was six a.m. Obviously, there was no reason to leave now.

Brewing a pot of coffee, I filled two mugs and went to Mark's office. He never went home, but he was taking a catnap on the sofa. Lucky bastard. I left the mug on his desk and returned to mine. Frankly, I was tired and would have loved to get some sleep, but I didn't want to go home. It reminded me of Martin and the distance between us. Plus, I'd probably have to wash the sheets to get the smell of his cologne out of them. I used to find that comforting. Now it was just a reminder of our dying relationship. Something had to change. Martin had a right to be resentful and keep me at arm's length, but this couldn't go on forever. At some point, he'd have to forgive me or let me go. But until he came to a decision, I was determined to find some way to deal with it, like hiding out at work all night.

Using the time difference to my advantage, I made a few overseas phone calls, hoping to find some intel on that murder case to share with Julian Mercer, the man to which I owed a substantial debt. After being told I would get a call back, I moved on to other ways to waste the early morning hours.

I started my fifty-seventh game of Sudoku when Mark stepped out of his office. He grunted good morning to a few early birds who had just arrived and stumbled to my desk. Pulling a chair over, he sat down with his now cold cup of coffee.

"Did you leave this for me?" he asked.

I looked up from my game, nodding. "No wonder your clothes always look wrinkled. Didn't you tell me the federal government doesn't like it when we sleep on the job?"

"It's too early for this." He took a long sip. "You never went home last night."

"Yes, I did, but Lucca phoned and said you wanted me back. So like an obedient dog, I came running when you called." I glanced at him. "You never bothered to tell me to go home for the night, so I wasn't sure if I should."

"Definitely too early." Picking up my empty mug, he topped his off and refilled mine. Then he scooted the chair closer to see what I was doing. "You don't get paid to play computer games."

"My reports are finished. Analysis complete. No old cases left to review, at least not that I've been handed. DEA didn't give us enough information to waste our time running through Wilde and every person he's ever met, so this seemed like a good way to keep my mind active until something pressing crosses my desk."

"And it never occurred to you to pick a random cold case and solve it?"

"That would have involved choosing a cold case. I thought about going with the whole JFK thing since I'm fairly certain Oswald wasn't working alone, but the CIA would probably have me disappeared if I actually solved it. So filling in empty squares with numbers seemed much safer."

"You should have gone home when Lucca did."

"Martin won't let me go home, but that's not your problem." Picking up the mug, I took a sip. Clearing my throat, I clicked off the game. "So what's on the agenda today, boss?"

"You tell me."

"Usual morning memos don't have us flagging down any new or immediate threats. Lucca and I finished reviewing the last batch of potentially compromised FBI cases. The prosecutor's office hasn't sent over anything else to peruse. So that pretty much clears my day. As you know, I haven't done anything but analysis lately, so I don't have anywhere to be. Humdrum. That's my goal, right?"

"Why don't you get out of here? You sound like you're about to crack."

"No. This is me happy. This is me being safe and staying out of trouble."

"This is you bored out of your mind which is never safe for anyone. And you are far from happy. How much of this is about Marty, and how much is about what's been going on around here?"

"Honestly, I can't separate the two, and I can't talk to you about it for obvious reasons."

"So you're planning on spending the day working on number puzzles?"

"I'm waiting to receive a file from New Scotland Yard. I promised an acquaintance I'd look into a homicide from a few years ago. The police didn't perform their due diligence, so I want to see if there's anything I can do from here."

"New Scotland Yard? Where did this murder take place?"

"England."

"Makes sense on account of your recent trip." He gave me a look. "Fine, but don't piss anyone off. We have field agents and overseas operations that require international cooperation and assistance." He picked up his mug and pushed the chair back to its former location. "When you get bored with that, see if there's any work you can do on the raid from last night."

"Yes, sir."

"And, Parker, don't get too comfortable. Your talents are being wasted inside the office. I've heard whispers of several ops in the works. You'll be out there sooner than you like, so you might want to dust off those cobwebs."

"I'll get on that."

He threw another glance over his shoulder. "If they don't want your help cataloging anything from last night, call it quits. Being inside this building for long periods of time never agrees with you."

"Don't I know it."

Pressing my palms into my eyes, I leaned back in the chair and inhaled deeply. After a nice long stretch, I checked my e-mail a final time and surveyed the room. The nearby desks and offices were becoming populated. Phones were ringing. The clickety-clack of typing turned into white noise, and I realized just how numb I was.

Numb was better than how I typically felt while inside the federal building, but it was an unfamiliar sensation. Nothing was wrong exactly, but something wasn't right. Lucca slipped past my desk, taking a seat behind his and powering on his computer. He mumbled good morning, but he was already buried in catching up with the day's reports.

Without saying a word, I went into the conference room to speak to the agents assessing the evidence recovered from the raid. They appeared to have a handle on things, so I returned to my desk. Lucca was on the phone. I couldn't help but wonder what he was researching.

"Who was that?" I asked as soon as he placed the receiver down.

"Agent Decker," he practically rolled his eyes, "the DEA agent who requested additional intel on Timothy Wilde."

"Right." I nodded, hoping he'd get to the heart of the matter.

"He didn't believe the intel I passed along was

particularly helpful and decided to call personally to tell me that." Lucca sneered at the phone. "You'd think the DEA would have better things to do."

"I guess their jobs are just as boring as ours."

"Still no active assignments?"

"No. Jablonsky told me I could go home. It really doesn't pay to get ahead on work."

He studied me for a long moment. "You haven't slept yet. Did you stay here all night?"

I shrugged.

"Is everything okay?" Lucca had an annoying habit of showing genuine concern at the oddest of times.

"Fantastic."

"You're lying. Are you having trouble sleeping again?"

"God," I slammed my palms on the desk louder than I intended, "not everything is post-traumatic stress." Glancing around the room, I wondered if anyone heard me and realized I didn't care. "I'm just off my game right now. If you must know, my boyfriend kicked me out of his house."

"I thought you had your own apartment."

"I do."

Lucca thought for a moment, deciding not to ask any more questions. "I'm sorry."

"What? No quip like 'why'd it take him so long to do that' or 'who in their right mind would ever be with you?' Nothing?"

"No. The guy's an idiot. Do you want me to knock some sense into him? In case you don't remember, I know where he works. And if I forget, his name's on the building, right?"

"That won't be necessary." I smiled. "Thanks though."

"Sure, no problem."

"Can you do me one favor?"

"Damn, I walked right into that. What do you want?"

"I'm waiting for a few files to come in. If you happen to see them, can you put them in my desk drawer?"

He nodded. "Where are you going?"

"Home."

THREE

The rest of the week went by incredibly slowly. Slow was good. It meant lives weren't being jeopardized and the status quo was being maintained. For shits and giggles, Mark tasked me with dissecting everything I could find on Timothy Wilde. The DEA had issued a formal request for our assistance, and whatever intel I could piece together would be used to brief whoever was loaned to assist on the deep cover assignment.

Typically, one of the analysts would do this, but I had some free time. And I'd made it known long ago that I had a penchant for finding tidbits of valuable information that were occasionally overlooked. I always imagined it was because of my time in the field, but maybe every single person in the office possessed the same ability. After all, we'd been trained the same. Therefore, we should have the same skill set. We were interchangeable cogs in the machine.

Glancing down at the time, I decided to take a break from mapping Wilde's family tree and residential history. I'd done nothing but live and breathe Timothy Wilde for the last three days. At this rate, I probably knew him better than his followers or whatever they were calling themselves. If this kept up, in another few days, I might be ready to drink the Kool-Aid just to put an end to the misery.

The information from New Scotland Yard proved just as useless as everything else I'd gotten on the cold case. I slammed the drawer closed. Lucca chuckled, and I turned to him with a glare. He pretended not to notice, but the smile remained on his face.

"What?" I asked.

"You've done the exact same thing every single day. And to think, there was a time when I thought you were the most unpredictable agent I'd ever met. I might actually miss this little comedy routine."

"Why?" I stopped what I was doing, my focus entirely on him. "Am I going somewhere?"

"No." The smile fell from his face. "I am."

"You've been recalled?"

He nodded. "This was just a temporary assignment to clean house. My job here is done."

"When are you leaving?"

"In a few days."

"You must be happy." I brushed the hair out of my face for something to do.

"Eh, not particularly. My wife likes her job. She found a playgroup for our daughter. We were going to start looking at preschools, but it's cool. We knew this would be temporary. Plus, now I get to live close to my in-laws again. Yay." The sarcasm was undeniable.

"Did you talk to Jablonsky? Perhaps he could pull some strings."

"He tried, even Director Kendall tried, but my reassignment came from our boss's boss's boss. It's no biggie. Shouldn't you be over the moon elated by the news?" The smile returned. "You actually like me. Damn, wonders never cease to amaze."

"I don't like you. I'm thrilled that no one will be around to pester me or remind me of some antiquated regulation. Plus, you drive like a geriatric."

"What does that mean?"

"I don't know, grandma. Shouldn't you be smart enough to figure it out?"

He laughed. "It's okay. I understand. The bitchiness is to mask the pain. Do you need a hug?"

"Don't even." I pointed an accusing finger in his face. "That is an inappropriate sexual advance. Just for the hell of it, I should report you." Getting up from my desk, I went down the hall to Jablonsky's office. Without knocking, I entered to find him reading a report. "Why didn't you tell me?"

"Eddie wanted to tell you himself."

"He doesn't want to go."

"I know, but the orders came from above my paygrade. They need him back in D.C. to conduct some kind of oversight analysis. That's all I know. Kendall seems concerned about something. I imagine this links back to our office being compromised, but there's no way of knowing for certain."

"Great. This really is the gift that keeps on giving." I bit my bottom lip, temporarily lost in thought. "Any idea what the powers that be plan on doing with yours truly?"

"As far as I can tell, you're still my problem. Do you have any progress to report on the Wilde expedition?"

"How long did it take you to come up with that?"

"Probably longer than it should have." He folded his hands over his gut and leaned back in his chair, waiting for my response.

"Wilde grew up in the system, going from foster home to foster home. No juvie record. After he turned eighteen, he fell off the radar for a couple of years. Surfaced at age twenty-three when he was picked up for possession with intent to distribute. At twenty-five, he was arrested for sexual assault. The case fell apart, as so many of them do. It turned into a he said, she said with no definitive evidence. He stayed clean for the next ten years, or he got smart."

"Maybe he was just lucky."

"Probably. He has no tax records during that time. No employment history. He lived in halfway houses and homeless shelters. It's hard to follow his whereabouts without a money trail."

"Have you tried phone records?"

"Either he never had a phone, or he used burners and payphones. This guy lived on the fringes of society. He might be one of the few who managed to stay off the grid."

"Until now."

"Well, three years ago. He reappeared. Suddenly, he had a permanent address, a phone, utilities, credit cards, the whole nine. I'm trying to figure out where he got the money. It must have been liquid. He purchased the land that now houses his co-op with cash."

"I'm guessing he didn't win the lottery."

"There would be a record of that, and that would be too easy. I've been tracing his roots, hoping there's a rich dead relative somewhere, but honestly, we know the money came from some sort of illegal activity. Knowing the DEA's involved, it has to be drugs."

"But you're trying not to let that information cloud your judgment."

"Right."

"Why don't you ever do things the easy way? Life doesn't have to be as hard as you make it."

"I imagine Martin would agree with you." Sighing, I turned back toward the door. "Are we throwing Lucca a going away party?"

"Of course."

"At the usual place?"

"Yep."

"Okay."

"Alex," Mark called, halting my departure, "are you okay? I know it's different, but he's still your partner."

"It doesn't matter. We roll with the punches, right?"

"Yeah, except last time you got KO'ed. I don't want to see that happen again."

"Neither do I."

*　　*　　*

I rubbed my shoulder and stared at the blackboard behind the bar. When did they start listing daily cocktails? Apparently, I'd been on the wagon for some time. Ever since being force-fed an entire bottle of vodka, I'd been abstaining from liquor. Tonight, I couldn't imagine that spending the rest of the evening with my head in the toilet would make me feel much worse than I already did.

"Lemon drop." I smiled at the bartender who had been kind enough to keep my water glass filled.

"You sure about that, hun?" he asked, assuming I was a recovering alcoholic.

"Not really, but it'll be a nice accompaniment to this cocktail napkin. The two should coordinate splendidly."

"Whatever you say." Placing the contents in a shaker, he rimmed the glass, poured, and placed it on my napkin. Then he went and filled the tequila shots Agent Davis ordered.

"To Eddie," someone called out in the background. A round of cheers was followed by the clinking of glasses.

"Don't you want to join in the festivities?" Kate Hartley, FBI forensic accountant and my former Quantico roommate, asked.

"I'm here, aren't I?"

She rolled her eyes. "Alex, seriously, you know Eddie better than anyone else in this room. Shouldn't you give a toast or share some embarrassing story or something?"

"Nope." I picked up the martini, decided against drinking it, and placed it back on the napkin.

"But he got transferred. Did you at least sign the card?"

"Yes, Kate. I even pitched in on the gift."

She stared at me for a long moment, downing the rest of her rum and coke. "I remember a few months ago when the two of you got into a brawl. Is there still bad blood between you?" Kate had always been a good friend, but she was inquisitive by nature and believed our friendship gave her carte blanche to nag and wheedle all kinds of things out of me. She wouldn't stop until she was satisfied with the answer.

"It's not that. This just reminds me of that night right after Carver's memorial. Every single agent got trashed. It was story after story. One toast after another."

"God, I was so blitzed. I don't remember much of it. I'm surprised you do."

"I remember all of it."

"Oh, sweetie." She put her drink down and hugged me. "I never thought how this must feel to you."

"What?" I shrugged out of her arms. "It's a great relief. Lucca's favorite pastime is busting my balls. As of right now, he's no longer my problem. I'm fucking ecstatic he's leaving."

Sighing dramatically, she gave me an exaggerated eye roll. "You certainly have a funny way of showing it." She nudged my shoulder with hers. "I'm just a phone call away if you want to talk."

"Thanks, but I'm fine."

"You always say that." Picking up her refilled drink, she gave me an uncertain look before returning to her table.

Checking the time, I wondered if I had stayed long enough to duck out. These were my colleagues and friends, but I felt more isolated and alone in this crowded bar than I felt at my desk or at home. Wow, this was one hell of a pity party, and I didn't even have any real problems. Lucca was the one being uprooted. My life was just peachy. Damn, when did I turn into an ungrateful bitch?

"Hey," Lucca slid onto the stool next to mine and motioned for another beer, "I wasn't sure if I'd get a chance to talk to you." His eyes darted to the untouched cocktail. "Tough day?"

"I got stuck pulling double-duty. It sucks." I met his eyes. "And if you tell anyone what I'm about to say, I'll hunt you down. But I'm gonna miss you, Eddie. God knows I've put you through hell, but you've saved my ass more times than I care to admit. So thank you."

"Ditto." He held out his hand.

"Seriously?" I laughed. "I think I'd like to cash in on that hug now?"

"So you can report me to HR?"

"Shut up."

He embraced me. "Take care of yourself since I won't be around to do it for you."

Pulling away, I glared at him playfully. Before I could say anything else, I felt a hand on my shoulder. Turning, my boss had a serious expression on his face.

"Not to dampen the mood, but I thought the two of you

would want to know a body was found in the desert. The local police identified it as belonging to a woman who was reported missing six months ago. She was last seen in the company of Timothy Wilde. The DEA's undercover operative has no way of knowing how this happened, but the situation's escalated. We'll be sending our own people to help in the morning." He turned to face Lucca. "When you get to D.C., see if there's anything we might have overlooked and have it forwarded to the DEA. I know this isn't your responsibility anymore, but our people will need all the help they can get."

"What was the cause of death?" I asked.

Mark shook his head. "I'm not sure. I didn't get a copy of the report. I just received notification concerning the identification." He glanced down at my drink. "I don't want you back at the office tonight, but first thing in the morning, I want you ready to go. You can brief whoever volunteers for the assignment on the plane."

"You want me to fly out to the West Coast?"

"It'll just be for a day or two. Hell, maybe even a turnaround. Since you've been versed in the research, you might possess something valuable the DEA missed." Mark's gaze went back to Lucca. "I hate that you're leaving us now that things are heating up."

"I'm sorry, sir," Lucca replied.

"Kid, you don't work for me anymore, and we're at a fucking bar. It's Mark," Jablonsky insisted. Someone called to him from across the room, and he excused himself.

"I should get out of here. I promised my wife I'd help her pack. Do you think I can sneak out?" Lucca asked.

"You can try. If you get stopped, I'll provide a distraction. A striptease on top of the bar might work. Now if only I could find some way to get Jablonsky to take his clothes off."

"Okay, I'm out." Lucca bumped my forearm. "It really has been a pleasure working with you, Agent Parker."

"Go." I jerked my head at the door, afraid I might shed a tear or two. Apparently, I was no longer numb, but I wished I was.

Staring at the drink in front of me, I picked it up and

took a sip, forcing the sour-sweet liquid down my throat and swallowing again when it attempted to make a reappearance. Of course, I had work in the morning, and drinking myself into oblivion wasn't recommended, not that my body would have allowed it anyway. After fishing my phone from my purse, I dialed a familiar number.

"What are you doing?" I asked.

Martin sounded amused, perhaps even intrigued by my call. "Reading the quarterly financial reports and modifying the projections for the next fiscal year. I'm surprised you called on a school night. Are you sure you dialed the right number?"

"Don't be a smart ass."

"Is everything okay?"

"Yeah. I thought you might like to come over."

"Really?"

"I could use the company."

"I'll see you in an hour."

Hanging up, I gave the glass another look and threw it back in one gulp. Perhaps I could use it as an excuse for calling Martin. I really must be a glutton for punishment, and I didn't care. I missed him and the way things used to be. I wanted that back, particularly now that everything else was changing. Nothing in my life was the same anymore.

FOUR

My hand gently rested against Martin's obliques. It was the only connection between us. When I pulled away, he focused on the spot of lost contact for several moments before throwing his legs over the side of the bed. Closing my eyes, I knew this couldn't go on. It hurt too much.

"Leaving?" I asked, forcing my tone to remain neutral.

"In a few minutes." He glanced back at me while fastening the buttons on his shirt. "Like I said, it's a school night. We both have work in the morning."

"Right. Work comes first."

"Hey, you instigated this time. You called me, not that I mind, but something's up."

"Lucca's going away party was tonight."

"And you wanted to celebrate." Martin snickered.

"No." I sat up, pulling on my clothes. "I'm going to miss him."

His brow furrowed, and he scrutinized me for a long moment, eventually shaking it off while he went to work on his cufflinks. "That's a surprise. I thought you hated the guy. I guess I'll never really understand you or what you're thinking."

Tired of the backhanded remarks, I knew this had to

end. "Stop. We can't keep doing this. *I* can't do this. I thought I could. I hoped in time we'd go back to the way we were, but this isn't working. It hurts too much."

"Alex, I don't want to hurt you."

"Yes, you do. You probably never intended to, but that's what this is. Every time you come here, you use me like some brothel whore, and then you go home. You won't let me inside your house. We've barely done anything except screw. When's the last time we had dinner or coffee or took a walk?"

"What do you want from me?" The heartbreaking defeat covered his face. "Tell me what you want."

"For starters, you could kiss me."

"I'm pretty sure I lavished every part of your body with kisses an hour ago."

"I'm not talking about foreplay. You haven't kissed me for the sake of kissing me since the night you said you forgave me, which you haven't."

"Fine." He came around to my side of the bed, taking a seat on the edge. As slowly as possible, he leaned forward, pressing his lips against mine. It was gentle and full of promise and love. My hand went to his face, but he grabbed my wrist before I could touch him. Pulling away, he dropped my hand and faced the dresser. Squeezing his eyes closed, he let out a long exhale. "Perhaps it'll make you feel better to know you aren't the only one hurting."

"It doesn't." I reached for him again, but he stood abruptly, moving toward the foot of the bed as if my touch were scalding.

"Dammit, you could at least wait for me to turn around before twisting the knife in deeper. Don't you understand that this is torture? I want things to be the way they were too, but you destroyed everything, Alex. I'm doing my best, but I can't kiss you like that. I can't spend the night. I can't let you come home because whenever you do come home, I never want you to leave again." His voice was edgy and desperate. "I need to figure out how to trust you again."

"I'm sorry."

"Are you?" He turned on me like a rabid dog. "You lied to me. You manipulated the situation in order to send me away. I don't think you're sorry. In fact, I'm pretty fucking sure you'd do it again in a heartbeat, and that's the problem."

"I sent you away to protect you."

"Protect me from what?"

"The psycho who wanted me dead. That fucking crime lord who swore he would take his time and make you suffer. I needed you safe. I needed to know you'd be okay."

"While you went on a suicide mission." He shook his head and rubbed a hand through his hair. "How many times have I been there for you when you needed help? The reason you sent me away wasn't for my protection. It was for yours. You were being selfish. You'd rather die than risk losing someone else, but you still haven't figured out that your actions will cause you to lose me."

"Martin," I began, but he shushed me.

"No. I don't want to hear that you're sorry. You aren't. You can't be because you still don't understand why what you did was wrong." He clenched his fists and looked away. "I can't trust you, and until I can, I don't want you to come home. I don't want to wake up to you in the morning. I don't want to fall into our old patterns because when this happens again, I don't want to feel the way that I do right now. So yeah, maybe I want you to feel a little hurt too. And I know I shouldn't, but sweetheart, until I can find some way to wrap my mind around this, I need some distance to keep from going insane. I'll figure it out eventually. I just need time."

"No amount of time is going to make a difference." I swallowed, moving closer to him. "You know this is who I am. We've had this fight more times than we should have. It was your one nonnegotiable point to our relationship. You shouldn't have to compromise. I never should have expected you to." I blinked. "This is killing us." I gestured around the room. "I won't keep doing it."

"Dammit, Alexis. Don't. Please don't."

"You should be with someone who won't betray you, who will be absolutely overjoyed at the prospect of marriage, who doesn't do shit like this for a living, and who will make you insanely happy."

"But I love you."

"That's not enough." Inhaling to steady myself, I slid the ring box across the dresser. "I leave tomorrow for a deep cover assignment across the country. I don't know when I'll be back. Honestly, it could be years. The agent tasked with this has already been under for eight months, and there's no way of knowing how close he is to making a break in the case. I don't want you to wait for me. I want you to date and find that someone who will be amazing and incredible. You deserve incredible."

"No." He shook his head angrily, his eyes on fire. "I don't accept. Who left it up to you to decide when we break up? I sure as hell didn't." He rolled his eyes, scoffing. "You just want me to go screw someone, so when you do come back, you'll have a reason to leave me. I'm not that stupid. Don't tell me that we should break up because it's not fair to me. This isn't fair to me. You're the only one I want to be with."

"Wake up. You just said you won't be with someone you can't trust. And you don't trust me."

His face contorted, and he tried to back-pedal. "That's not what I said, and it certainly isn't what I meant. I trust you. I know you'd never cheat on me. You'd never willingly allow anything to happen to me. You'd die for me, Alex. And that's the problem. I'm a grown man. You don't get to treat me like a child and decide what's best for me. You don't get to dismiss my objections and make decisions on your own. We are in this together."

"Bullshit. You make unilateral decisions for everyone."

"When have I ever forced you to do something you legitimately refused to do?" He waited expectantly for an answer, knowing he was right. "Even now, you're trying to make a decision about us based on what's easiest for you. I'm not going to let you decide we should break up because we've hit a rough patch or because you'll be gone for work. Newsflash, your decisions suck."

"That's not how this works. You can be as deluded as you want, but that doesn't mean we aren't over. If we were already married, we'd have grounds for divorce over irreconcilable differences."

He scowled. "I don't believe that. We'll work through it. I will work through it. Lord knows there isn't a chance in hell you'll ever change, but I can. I'll come to terms with this, just don't go. Don't do this."

I couldn't help but think that the stages of grief were playing out in front of me. First, he was depressed, then angry; now he was bargaining. Hell, he'd probably hit acceptance by the time he made it to the front door.

"Martin, I don't want you to wait for some epiphany that'll never come. And there's no reason to wait for me to get back. I could legitimately be away for more than a year. It's too long. You should move on. Maybe afterward we'll see where we are, but I don't see a way through this mess. We can't change. At least, I can't. You said it yourself."

"Do you love me?"

"It doesn't matter."

"It's all that matters. Answer the question, Alex. Do you love me?"

"Yes."

"Then we'll figure this out. I will figure this out. Stay." He stared at me. "I'll stay the night. We can talk. We can rebuild. I don't know, just don't go on this assignment. Tell Jabber to find someone else. Don't leave me again."

I never heard him beg like this, and it broke my heart. "I have to go. There's nothing left for me here. Lucca's gone. I've lost you. I need a break. I need to make peace with the shit I've done and the people I've hurt. Going is for the best. Please don't make this harder than it already is."

"Sweetheart," he pulled me close, squeezing me hard, "I won't let you go. We're not done."

"Do it for me. I want you to be happy."

"Then stop ripping out my heart." He let go and rubbed his eyes. "Dammit." He picked up the ring box, popping it open before placing it back on my dresser. "You made a promise. I intend to hold up my end of it. You better do the same."

Thankfully, he left my apartment before the tears started to fall. I didn't want my sobs to manipulate him more than everything else. After taking some time to get myself under control, I picked up the phone and dialed

Mark. It didn't matter that it was late. I knew he'd answer.

"You can stop looking for volunteers," I declared. "I want the assignment."

"Are you sure? You'll be on loan to the DEA for god knows how long."

"I don't care."

"But you made me agree to no long-term deep cover gigs when you came back to the OIO. You said you didn't want to leave Marty."

"Things change. Martin and I broke up."

Suddenly, Mark sounded much more awake. "Shit. Are you okay? Is there anything I can do?"

"Just give me the assignment."

"Pack a bag. The plane leaves at ten a.m."

Hanging up, I looked around my apartment. I hadn't thought this through. I knew I needed to escape. I needed an out, and fortuitously, this opportunity happened to present itself in the nick of time. Opening my fridge, I stared inside at the contents for what felt like hours. Eventually, movement returned, and I chucked the leftovers into the trash can and boxed up whatever was in my pantry. The unopened items could be delivered to a local soup kitchen, and the rest met the same fate as the perishables.

Next, I packed a few bags with clothing and gear. I didn't even know in what capacity the DEA expected assistance. It could be anything from analyst to a secondary undercover operative. I had to prepare for all contingencies.

After filling two large suitcases, I looked around the room. The sparkle of the diamond caught my eye, and I slammed the lid down. "Dammit." I threw the velvet box across the room and into the wall. Truth be told, I wasn't mad at Martin. I was mad at myself.

"You fuck everything up," I growled, catching my reflection in the mirror. "You don't deserve him. You don't even deserve to be walking around free." Maybe I would have been better off letting some crime boss kill me. Perhaps that would have led to enough evidence to finally put him behind bars. Instead, I took matters into my own hands and put him and his cronies six feet under. There was no coming back from that. My relationship with Martin had become collateral damage.

Sucking in a shaky breath, I stared at the crumpled blankets on my bed. My room was a crime scene. It had been the location of the slaughter of the only decent romantic relationship I'd ever had. And I couldn't even deal with it. The walls were closing in, and I felt dizzy. Taking my bags, I went into the living room, collapsed on the couch, and didn't move again until Mark knocked on my door the next morning.

FIVE

"Are you sure about this?" Mark asked for what felt like the millionth time.

I nodded, too drained to answer. I'd spent the early morning filling out paperwork in the office and getting copies of the recent developments concerning the operation and the dead woman to take along for light reading on the plane. In five hours, I'd be three thousand miles away from my home and my problems. Whoever said you couldn't run away was an idiot.

"Do you want me to come with you?" Mark asked.

"Are you insane? I'm not a five-year-old heading off to my first day of kindergarten."

"No, but you're whoring yourself out to the DEA. Those guys are cowboys. They have a reputation for reckless behavior and going a little too dark, if you know what I mean."

"One, there will be no whoring, and two, don't you think I've gone dark lately?"

"That's not reassuring me." Jablonsky pulled into the parking garage at the airport, found a reserved space, and cut the engine. "If Lucca wasn't reassigned, would you still be volunteering for this?"

Staring out the windshield, I imagined a lot of things would have been different if Lucca wasn't leaving. None of last night would have happened. I would have continued to be miserable while waiting and hoping for something to change. "It was time to pull the trigger. I couldn't hide behind a desk forever. I hate that office. I hate being there. And now, I hate this city. I hate my apartment. I hate my life. I hate myself. I need to be someone else for a while."

"So you decided to volunteer to UC in order to become Becky Sue with a coke addiction or some shit like that?"

"Something like that."

"I can't say I blame you." He opened his door and headed for the trunk. He hefted the larger bag over his shoulder. "Do you want me to feed the cat or water the plants while you're gone?"

"I don't have a cat or plants, but there's a box of food to donate on the counter, unless you have a hankering for canned soup and cereal. Other than that, check my place every once in a while and make sure it's not flooded or infested. You can clear out the liquor cabinet."

"I thought I already did that."

"That was before Martin," saying his name felt like a punch to the gut, "started keeping some shit on hand. I don't think it's even opened. It's not like he stuck around long enough to drink any of it, so take it." I pulled out my credentials and passport while we made our way through the check-in line. "Will you make sure he's okay?"

Mark nodded solemnly. "Marty's my friend, but I swear I could break his legs for hurting you like this."

"Don't. This wasn't his fault." I didn't want to ask for another favor, but it needed to be done. "On the floor in my bedroom is a jewelry box. Can you make sure he gets that back? I tried giving it to him last night, but he's so damn stubborn sometimes."

"Okay."

I finished checking my bags, took my ticket, and headed for airport security. Jablonsky followed behind, probably planning to follow me through the checkpoint by flashing his credentials. Standing in the long line, I had an amusing thought.

"Shouldn't this trip warrant the use of a government jet? Doesn't the FBI have some Gulfstreams hanging around?"

"We're being fiscally responsible," Jablonsky said. "I probably could have gotten you a seat on some military aircraft, but you'd be stuck in the back of a cargo hold, clinging to the net and surrounded by recently deployed jarheads. This is a much better alternative." He glanced around as if someone might be eavesdropping on our conversation. "An agent will meet you when you land. He'll take you to their command center, and you'll be officially briefed. After that, call me. I'll be your unofficial handler. I expect updates weekly, more often if circumstances warrant it. I've already made this obvious to the DEA, and they've assured me they have regular check-ins with their undercover operative. I don't know the logistics or what they'll expect from you, but I assume you'll be providing backup in some capacity."

"No problem."

"It better not be. I want you to stay safe out there and keep a clear head. When you land, this shit stays on the plane. You can't be focused on Marty, Lucca, or your troubles. Do you hear me?"

"Yes, sir."

He hugged me hard. "I'll talk to you tonight. Don't make me regret sending you, or I will fly across the country and kick your ass."

"I know."

"You should." He smiled. "I taught you everything you know. Now get the hell out of here. The sooner you show these cowboys how to work an assignment, the sooner you can get back to doing actual OIO work." He saw the displeased look on my face. "We have deep cover assignments too, and they don't involve cult leaders on the US-Mexico border. Now go."

"I'll see you around, Mark." I hugged him one last time before flashing my credentials at the TSA agents and moving through the security checkpoint without as much muss or fuss as the average traveler.

*   *   *

"Agent Parker," my escort, DEA agent Matt Eckhardt, called my name, waiting impatiently for my jaw to close, "you'll get used to it. I take it the FBI doesn't have any command centers that look like this."

"None that I've seen. Is there a map or signs to point me in the right direction?"

He laughed politely. "You'll get the hang of this place soon enough. All you need to do is think like a rich, narcissistic drug dealer. Then the layout of the place is easy."

"Rich and narcissistic shouldn't be a problem," I muttered under my breath before following him through the vast compound and up a winding staircase. The crystal chandelier hanging over the steps was custom made with each crystal sculpted into an ornate nude. "Who the hell was this guy?"

"It doesn't matter. He'll be behind bars for the rest of his life." Eckhardt entered a code and pushed through to another secure section of the house. "To your left is our armory, in the event we need to conduct a raid or tactical recovery. In the basement, we have a shooting range and gym set up, should you require practice."

"I don't think that'll be necessary."

"We'll let our assistant director determine that." He tossed an apologetic smile over his shoulder. "Our standards might be different than the OIO's." He pointed to a room at the end of the corridor. "We have a fully functional lab and qualified medics on duty twenty-four seven. Mandatory drug testing is required and will continue at regular intervals for the duration of the assignment. Should the assignment require you to use drugs, we prefer advanced notification, if possible. There's also paperwork, but I'm sure you're familiar. The FBI has a similar procedure."

"Yep." I jerked my head to a room off the side where loud voices resonated. "What's in there?"

"Briefing room."

"Okay."

"Moving on." He ignored the confused look on my face.

"If you follow me back this way, I'll take you to meet the support team. We have some amazing analysts and computer whizzes working for us. They'll catch you up to speed on our op, and you can update them on the evaluation you conducted concerning Timothy Wilde."

Eckhardt opened the door, smiling brightly at a woman in the corner of the room. "Hey, Stella."

"Matt," she barely nodded in his direction while typing away at the keyboard, "you didn't include the date and time in your report. The judge nearly tossed out our request for a search warrant. How many times have I told you details are important? Even now, we have to worry that some shyster defense attorney will have the evidence ruled inadmissible."

He cleared his throat. "Can't that wait?" He glanced around at the other three people who hadn't acknowledged our presence. "Listen up," he clapped his hands together, "this is the FBI agent tasked with assisting on the Wilde op. She just arrived, so let's not scare her off. She might prove useful. And if she isn't, then we'll show her what we're really like."

"Fine," a guy with horn-rimmed glasses said, swiveling around, "let's hear what she has to say."

"And while that's happening, you and I can have a talk." Stella grabbed Eckhardt by the elbow and nodded to me. "Just think of me as in-house counsel. I keep these guys from breaking the rules. And you, Agent Eckhardt, have been a very bad boy. I need access to your notes and reports. Now."

Before I could say or do anything, they were gone. Turning, I found three sets of eyes staring at me. "I'm Alex Parker," I offered lamely.

"Yeah, we know," Mr. Horn-rimmed said. "I'm Carlo. That's Ben and Eve." He turned back to the computer, clicking a few keys and sending a projection of his screen to the large monitor mounted to the wall at the front of the room. "This is our target, Timothy Wilde."

"I know." I couldn't help but return the jab.

"This is the co-op he's been using." The screen changed to a collage of images. "There are a dozen different

- 34 -

permanent structures on the property. We haven't been able to keep an accurate headcount since someone is always coming or going, which explains how we missed the woman disappearing." He clicked again, and a blown-up copy of the ME's report filled half the screen while the other side displayed autopsy photos. "Cause of death was a drug overdose." He zoomed in on the photograph. "These incisions occurred post-mortem and appear to be surgical in nature. A tiny amount of latex was found in her GI tract." He turned to me. "Do you know what that means?"

"She was a mule, and one of the balloons ruptured. They probably cut out the rest to save the goods and hide the evidence."

"See, I told you the FBI isn't as dumb as you said," Ben said from his cubicle.

Eve rolled her eyes. "Agent Parker, have you spoken to Jace yet?"

"Jace?"

"Obviously not." She sighed. "Unless he signs off, this is a waste of time."

"He's running point on this," Carlo offered, casting a glance at Ben as if to say, *see, the FBI agent is an idiot.* "I'm sure he'll have plenty to say when you see him." Shaking his head, he pulled up a list of names, each linked with an autopsy photo. "As you can see, this recent death isn't the first. It's the sixth overdose. Three have happened since we began our operation, but Agent Decker hasn't had any contact with these women. They were all reported missing several months before their deaths. From our surveillance footage, we know each of them visited the co-op at least once. We've searched vehicles, conducted surveillance, but we still don't know how Wilde finds his recruits or where the drugs are coming from. We aren't even sure if they are coming in or being sent out. Decker hasn't found anything on the property, but we're certain Wilde's behind it."

"It doesn't matter, unless you can prove it," Stella said, stepping back into the room with Eckhardt behind her. In her arms were several notepads. Eckhardt carried a file box filled to the brim with manila folders. "No judge will issue a sweeping search warrant without probable cause. The deaths have all been miles away from the co-op with no clear connection between the deceased and Wilde. None of them were active members of the church at the time of their deaths. They didn't establish permanent residency within the co-op or provide a substantial donation, like many of the other followers, so we're hoping to find another angle to give us grounds to bust in there and get this done. Whatever's in plain sight or is willingly shared with our operative is fair game, but so far, it hasn't led to anything substantial."

"I guess that's where you come in," Ben said. "What have you found that I've missed?"

"Not much. My partner actually received the request, but since he was in the midst of a transfer, I did some digging. Wilde's record indicates he has a history with drug dealing which makes him a likely candidate to still be in the biz. However, aside from that one arrest, his only other offense was an unsubstantiated sexual assault. After that, he fell off the radar. Hell, he was always off the radar. He fell through the cracks in the system. Somehow, he managed to exist on the fringes without drawing attention to himself, but to go from nothing to having enough liquid assets to buy that property," I stepped closer to Carlo and reached for the mouse, clicking the minimized aerial image of the compound so it filled the screen again, "and the buildings on it, he has to be in bed with someone serious."

"Or he's a serious player," Ben said. "We don't know what he was doing for over a decade. He could have built an entire network since he wasn't under any scrutiny. Given that we know he's been recruiting and possibly kidnapping and brainwashing these women and has at least two dozen followers living at the compound, we can assume he knows how to keep his criminal activities under wraps. None of these supposed like-minded individuals have voiced any complaints. They leave the gates open. On weekends, they sell artisanal goods as if they are a millennial farmer's market. Everything appears to be on the up and up."

"And they have permits," Stella volunteered. "It looks

clean. Every move Wilde makes is aboveboard."

"Are you sure you have the right guy?" I asked, earning a searing gaze from everyone in the room. "Seriously, that was a joke." I shook my head, feeling as if I were tanking my first impression. "I'm on your side. I wouldn't have spent the last week researching everything about this guy and his cult if I didn't believe he was involved in something heinous." I stepped back, narrowing my eyes at the screen. "Have you investigated shipments going in and out? If there are that many people living on the grounds, they must have to transport certain supplies, especially if they are producing items to sell. Have you checked the shipments they send out?"

"Yep." Carlo made the word sound like condescension on steroids.

"This isn't our first rodeo," a voice said from behind. I spun to see who had joined the party. "Agent Parker, please come with me."

I followed the man out into the hallway. He wore a charcoal grey Henley over dark blue jeans. His light brown hair was slicked back, but I didn't believe the blond highlights or length were regulation. Neither was the light beard that covered his face. His eyes were bright blue, and his skin was perfectly tanned. He looked like a surfer dressed up like commando Ken.

"Jackson Decker," he extended his hand, and we shook. "Have those knuckleheads been giving you a hard time?"

"I just got here. They were updating me on the situation."

He smiled. "Sure, they were." He glanced around the corridor. "Walk with me. We have much to discuss."

SIX

"What were your first impressions of Timothy Wilde?" Decker asked.

"I haven't met the man."

"No, but you've read his jacket. You've researched him, studied him, his church, his beliefs, his followers. What do you think?"

"I think he's full of shit." I glanced at Decker from the corner of my eye. "His life started out rough. I don't imagine it miraculously improved by finding god or religion or whatever, nor do I believe that's why he decided to start his own church and share it with others."

"Isn't that cynical?" Decker smiled, leading me through the house at a leisurely pace. From the way we meandered through the hallways, I didn't think he had a destination in mind. "Have you always been so jaded, or did the job do that to you?"

"The job didn't help."

"But you were always jaded. Tough childhood?"

"Who has it easy these days? But I'm not about to run off and start a cult, so I guess it wasn't that tough."

Decker scratched at his beard, like it was something unfamiliar and itchy. "Are you able to empathize with

Wilde or the people who follow him?"

Stopping in my tracks, I waited for Decker to turn around and face me. "What kind of question is that?"

"An honest one." He narrowed his eyes. "Agent Parker, are you capable of empathizing with these people?"

"Shit happens. People do what they have to in order to survive. When they start preying on others, I tend to take issue with that. These so-called followers might very well be victims. I'm not in the business of ruining the lives of innocent people, but until I'm aware of the precise circumstances, I can't answer that question."

He snorted, turning back around and continuing down the corridor. "You're also not in the business of giving straight answers." He spun. "Keep up. We have lots to explore and more to discuss." Walking backward, he continued to study me. "What happened to Agent Lucca? He was tasked with the research. I spoke to him on the phone. Shouldn't he be here instead of you?"

"He was on loan to our office. He's back in D.C. now. And from what I heard, you weren't particularly happy with the intel he provided anyway."

"Sticking up for your partner." Decker nodded. "I like that. I didn't expect that, not after the physical altercation the two of you had a few months ago."

"How do you know about that?"

"I read your file." He slowed his pace, turning around so we were facing the same direction. "Wait one second." The door in front of us burst open, and six men in full tactical assault gear emptied out of the room, moving swiftly down the hallway and out the door. "Just like clockwork." He checked his watch. "Damn, it would absolutely drive me crazy." He poked his head into the room, watching some of the support staff clear up the paperwork. "Grab me that file when you get a chance," he called to someone inside before turning his attention back to me. "Does the OIO function with such precision? Our tac teams plan their assaults to the second. I don't get it. How can they pinpoint actionable intel that accurately? Like you said, shit happens, but they have no qualms about coordinating precision raids."

"Sometimes, it's necessary."

"Yeah, sorry, I'm not exactly a planner. I react to changing situations." He gestured at someone inside the room and checked his watch again. "Have you seen the backyard yet?" I shook my head, and he chuckled. "Come on, you at least ought to get to take a look before we exile you." He took a sharp right and led me past several more rooms filled with agents in the midst of briefings.

I must have seen at least twenty different agents fulfilling different roles. "How many people are tasked with cracking Wilde?"

Decker laughed, putting a gentle hand at the small of my back while he entered a code to unlock the door. "You met my team. There are six of us, Stella, Matt, Ben, Carlo, Eve, and me. Everyone else has another mission in play. You have to keep in mind we're incredibly close to LA, Nevada, and the Mexican border. This is prime real estate for the DEA, and given the size and magnitude of this place, we use it for pretty much everything. It's much better than the stuffy offices in the federal building with their outdated tech and facilities. Everything here is shiny, new, and state-of-the-art." He led me out onto the deck, overlooking two incredibly large and slightly pornographic hot tubs.

"Like the set of giant tits?" I nodded at the view from the top. The interior tiling was flesh colored with rose pink tiling in the center. "It coordinates great with the chandelier."

"I see you have an eye for detail." He leaned back against the railing, resting his elbows on the edge while he stared down at me. He was five ten, probably a hundred and sixty-five pounds of lean muscle. "Or you enjoy the female form, not that I would blame you."

"You mean to tell me my sexual orientation wasn't included in my file?" This guy appeared to be all over the place, but I knew enough to realize every question was part of some kind of test.

"It wasn't, but you know that." His eyes traveled the length of my body but didn't linger. "I'm also sure that I don't need you to answer the question. And for the record, I won't sleep with you, at least not during the mission." But despite the way he said it, I had just been greenlit for the operation.

"Trust me, that won't be an issue. In what capacity did you want my assistance on the Wilde case?"

Decker grinned. "You'll be joining me undercover. Have you UCed before?"

"I thought you read my file."

"I did. I just have one final question."

Nodding, I waited.

"Are you a recovering addict?"

"No. Jablonsky told me there were notes explaining that wonky drug test."

"There are." Decker moved away from me, opening the door and calling to someone inside the house. A moment later, he held out a folder. "I just wanted to gauge your response, see if it made you nervous." He leaned closer, narrowing his eyes. "Do I make you nervous?"

I practically scoffed at the notion, reaching for the folder. He pulled it away before I could grab it. His blue eyes found mine, searching for some kind of answer.

"You're not nervous to be here. Or anxious. You've been professional and tried to make a good impression, but you're not an ass-kisser either. And you don't take shit from anyone. Frankly, I'm having trouble figuring out if you volunteered for this or if someone forced you to take the assignment."

"I'm sure there's a note somewhere in my file that says I don't play well with others. After all, you know Lucca and I came to blows."

"And yet I feel like there's more to that story."

I looked away. "It doesn't matter, and for the record, I volunteered." I held out my hand for the file again. "What do you want me to do with this? Shred it? File it? Mail it back to the OIO?"

"It's not your file, Alexis. It's mine." Dropping it in my hand, he moved toward the staircase. "I've had an unfair advantage. I already know you on paper, and after talking to you these last few minutes, I think we can work together. But you get a say in the matter. I don't care if you volunteered. This is a shit assignment. I've been under for eight months already. I don't want to spend another eight with someone I don't trust and don't like. You should get to decide the same thing. Take your time, read my file, and when you're done, I'll be downstairs near the tit pools."

"Decker," I called, stopping him from leaving, "I'm here. I told my boss I was committed to this. I can get the job done. It doesn't matter what's in here." I held up the folder.

"Jablonsky's waiting for a call from my assistant director to make sure we want to keep you. Whatever you decide, it won't impact your career. This is just how I work, and my team knows it."

"I didn't realize you were in charge."

"I'm not, but I'm a valuable asset. And since I'm willing to go deep for the long haul, they grant me certain concessions. Now get to reading." He went down two steps before turning back around. "And my friends call me Jace, not Agent Decker."

"Is that your undercover handle?"

"It's a nickname, short for Jackson. Weren't you paying attention when I introduced myself?"

"I must have been too busy wondering how I'd lure you into bed."

Opening the file, I read his history. Immediately, I stopped on his academic background. Most FBI agents held advanced degrees, typically law or accounting, unless they specialized in foreign language or culture, had computer or technical backgrounds, or were skilled in some other manner. A lot also had military or law enforcement experience. I imagined the DEA had a similar set of requirements. However, Decker didn't fit the profile.

Decker's academic background was one of clinical psychology. He was top of his class, had his pick of fellowships and internships, and his pick of jobs. Unlike most who hung a shingle and opened their own practice, he worked as a prison counselor for several years in addition to working inside addiction rehabilitation centers.

While those were admirable qualities, I automatically reassessed every syllable I'd spoken to him. It was no secret I wasn't a fan of psychobabble. Mandated therapy sessions had been the most loathsome part of my career and a large factor that led to my brief resignation. How was I supposed to work in close quarters with someone who made me paranoid? Then again, he wasn't a shrink now. He was an undercover drug enforcement agent. And truth be told, I would rather pull out my own fingernails than go home.

Reading beyond his background, I scanned his commendations and evaluation reports, finding he was a very skilled individual. Maybe the background gave him the ability to read marks better or deescalate volatile situations. There were no blemishes on his record or any indication he was the impetuous cowboy Mark warned me about. It'd be okay. It had to be. I needed an out, and unless I wanted to beg for an OIO reassignment, this was the next best thing.

Going down the stairs, I dropped the file on the ground beside Jace. "Like I said, I flew all the way here. I'm not going home."

"Great." He picked up the file and stood up. "Do you have any questions, Alexis?"

"It's Alex. And plenty."

"Good. We'll get to them, but first, let's get you settled while they establish your undercover identity. You must be exhausted and hungry after the flight and the long day. You'll be kept at a safe house until everything's been ironed out. We don't want to risk putting you up in a hotel or exposing you to the public, just in case you end up crossing paths with someone in Wilde's flock. It'll probably be a few days. That should give you time to call Jablonsky, review our progress, and tie up whatever loose ends you might have left at home. Once you go under, communication with your old life will cease."

"I have done this before." I stared into the distance, feeling smothered beneath the open sky and oppressive heat. "And I already took care of personal matters."

"It sounds like there's a story there."

"None that concerns you."

"We'll see. Being undercover gets boring fast, especially after you've already watched everything on TV and read every book on the shelf twice. Talking might not seem so bad."

"Is that the shrink speaking?"

"I prefer the term headshrinker. It conjures images of witch doctors and actual shrunken heads. You have to admit that's pretty cool."

"I've never been a fan."

"Of witch doctors, shrunken heads, or psychology?" He stared at me for a moment. "I'll try not to take it personally."

"Great, just don't make me your pet project."

His blue eyes seemed to glint like the sun's reflection on the water. "Damn, now that just sounds like a challenge."

SEVEN

Agent Matt Eckhardt provided a ride to the safe house. It was a studio apartment at some out of the way roadside inn. From the musty smell, I didn't think it had been used recently. The room was depressing, despite the bright teal and coral décor that screamed welcome to the Southwest. It was nothing like I imagined. I expected more Venice Beach and less Albuquerque, but what did I know? Clearly, not much.

"Parker," Eckhardt said, drawing me out of my funk at the sight of the room, "I know you must have been expecting the Taj Mahal after seeing our command center, but this is only temporary. Until you receive the go-ahead, you're to remain here."

"You mean I can't hit the clubs and party until dawn?"

"Not yet. I imagine there will be a time and place for that. Carlo and Eve are creating your background as we speak. Ben will determine your best chance of introduction and entry into Wilde's world. Jace will drop by this evening with the preliminary dossier and some supplies. In the meantime, give me a list of what you need. I'll grab some food and anything else you require."

"Like a box of tampons?" I teased, watching him squirm. "Relax, Agent Eckhardt, that was a joke."

"Damn," he laughed, "did Stella ask you to say that?"

"No, Eve whispered that in my ear on our way out."

"That's my team." He looked at me for a moment. "Our team, I suppose. We're pretty close-knit. I guess I should apologize for Carlo and Ben. They aren't pleased about having an outsider intrude. They'll warm up to you eventually."

"It's fine. I don't like it when people step on my toes either."

"We've never had to ask for outside assistance before, but the nature of the situation warranted it." He glanced around the room, making it apparent he felt like he was speaking out of turn. "Human trafficking isn't uncommon, particularly in the drug trade. But given that we haven't seen Wilde use or distribute drugs, there is a chance we could be off base. If this is about selling women to be used as drug mules or sex slaves, it'd be best to let the FBI handle it."

"Glad I could be of service." I didn't like those prospects, particularly since no one had come out and said this until now. "Is that based solely on the bodies discovered?"

"Mostly. Jace never saw any of those women on the property, but there have been others who have come and gone. It's possible they left on their own volition and decided Wilde's brand of religion wasn't their scene, but we haven't been able to locate them either. When you arrived instead of Agent Lucca, we figured the OIO knew something we didn't." He waited expectantly for me to confess we had a hunch or an ongoing investigation concerning this matter, but I busied myself with unzipping my bag. "Agent Parker, is there anything we should know?"

"We couldn't find anything on Wilde or his religious order. My arrival is a fluke. My partner transferred, and I was stuck behind a desk. It made sense to volunteer for this assignment. Had I known ahead of time, maybe things would have been different."

"You wouldn't have come?"

"I didn't say that." I was itching to phone Mark with the

latest updates. "I would have made sure we had better intel and a damn good plan before I got on that plane." I went back to unpacking. "Can you grab me a sandwich, maybe some fries, and something with caffeine and sugar. It looks like I have a long night ahead of me."

"Sure, no problem." He pulled the door closed behind him.

After unzipping my bags, assembling my nine millimeter, and loading it, I fished out my cell phone and dialed Jablonsky. He wouldn't be pleased with the latest developments, but the heads-up might prove useful. If anything, there might be a connected case one of the FBI field offices or local police departments was investigating.

"Hey," I greeted, shouldering the phone while I unpacked some of my work attire and hung it in the closet, "it looks like I'll be here a while." I updated him on what I knew of the situation. "Agent Decker is supposed to stop by later with their case files and my cover identity."

"Any idea what they expect from you?"

"I'll be providing support to Decker. The rest of the team works in the office, except for Agent Eckhardt. I have a feeling he performs official field work. He's the badge and gun that will ride in and save the day should we need it."

"Why didn't they tell us they thought this might involve human trafficking? Have all the victims been women?"

"I believe so, but it's speculation. They aren't even positive if the deaths are related to Wilde and his organization."

"His cult." Mark sounded displeased and anxious. "The Followers of Perpetual Light. What the hell kind of name is that? Who does he think he is? ConEd?"

"Mark," I began, wanting to stop his annoyed tirade before it got worse, "how many times have you told me to play nice with other government agencies?"

"That was different. They didn't want to sell you into a life of prostitution or fill your belly with drugs. They should have informed me of the possibility before they took one of my best agents. I don't like that they're still keeping you in the dark."

"Ironic, isn't it? I guess they aren't buying into the

whole perpetual light thing either."

"Don't be cute. It's not too late. I can still pull you out."

"I'm good."

"Are you sure?" From the question, it sounded like he had an ace up his sleeve. "What did you think of Agent Decker?"

"I don't know. He plays games, but he seems decent. He has an impeccable record and a long history of deep cover assignments. He ought to know what he's doing."

"He's a psychologist, Alex. All he does is play mind games. He's trained to play mind games."

I laughed. "Like you're doing right now? Get off it, Mark. The only reason you told me that is because you're hoping it's enough to make me come home. It's not like this is some sort of forced therapy session. Decker won't be focused on me, and if he wants to use some psychobabble to talk some sense into some confused cult followers, then more power to him."

A long silence followed. I pulled the phone from my ear to make sure we hadn't lost the connection.

Finally, he cleared his throat. "You need to be very careful. Deep cover is dangerous, and the situation hasn't improved since we first heard about it."

"I'm always careful."

"Alex, I'm serious." He lowered his voice, even though I'd phoned him at home. "There's something else you need to know."

Panic gripped my insides. "What? Is Martin okay?" Squeezing my eyes closed at the knee-jerk reaction, I silently reminded myself that was no longer my business. I walked away. I broke us.

"Not really, but neither are you." Mark swallowed, returning to the actual topic. "Lucca called. He's okay, but D.C. has their sights set on our office. It's been going on for some time. Ever since the breach, they've been investigating our agents. I don't think they've found anything, but now's not the time to attract any unnecessary attention. Follow orders and don't color outside the lines. Anything that happens undercover needs to be on the up and up. I don't care what the DEA's regs say about drug use and appropriate undercover behavior. You need to stay clean. If any shit goes down, make sure your actions are by the book. I don't want your head to be on the chopping block. It's bad enough your reinstatement had been contingent on the breach." He sighed. "Be smart. I don't care if the bad guys get away or someone gets hurt, just as long as it isn't you. Do you hear me?"

"Roger that." I wasn't sure what to ask. "Who exactly are they investigating? What if something surfaces?"

"Every agent in this office is being evaluated. They're looking at financial records, unexplained or odd behaviors, and questionable ties or meetings. They're turning over the usual stones, looking for dirt, but there's nothing to find. You've never had any of those types of connections to any crime boss in this city. So it's not like you have reason to worry."

I laughed nervously. "Aside from the bounty some asshole had put on my head."

"That's not exactly the type of connection Washington is looking for. Just be careful, and for once, think before you act. I'll call in some favors with the DEA and make sure I'm read in on everything that transpires. Since they wanted our help, I fully intend to give it to them."

"Thanks."

"One last thing. This isn't my business, but I need to know something." He paused. "Y'know what, never mind. I don't want to know. It's probably for the best if I don't. I'll talk to you soon."

He hung up, and I dropped onto the bed. No news was good news. It was disconcerting to learn I had drawn scrutiny from D.C. when there was dirt to find. Perhaps I should come clean about what happened in that nightclub. It wasn't exactly by the book, but the man I killed would have killed me. He wanted to kill Martin, and he'd already murdered many others. Maybe I couldn't run from my problems, even though when I left home this morning that had been the plan.

The sound of the key in the door startled me. I shot up, poised to fire. Agent Eckhardt stepped inside, pulling the door closed behind him while balancing a bag in one hand

and a large drink in the other. He smiled as I put the gun on the table and attempted to play it cool.

"Jumpy?" he asked

"Force of habit."

"You'll need to break yourself of that. It's unlikely you'll be armed or encouraged to demonstrate that you're armed to a group of religious zealots."

"Don't you think the NRA is full of religious zealots? And what about al-Qaeda and ISIS? God and guns go hand in hand, which has always struck me as strange bedfellows."

"Regardless, pulling a," he cocked his head to the side to get a better glimpse of my handgun, "nine millimeter on someone while under as a broke heiress isn't particularly believable."

"A broke heiress? Tell me your techs didn't get the idea from a daytime soap opera."

"No, it was Ben's idea."

"Great, the analyst got the idea from a daytime soap. Unbelievable."

Eckhardt looked at my unpacked bags. "Y'know, I'll let you discuss this with Jace. He'll be able to share his personal insight on the matter. In the meantime, here's a chicken sandwich, fries, and a cherry coke. You aren't vegetarian or anything, right?"

Shaking my head at the question, I couldn't help but think these DEA agents had a bad habit of asking for relevant information after the fact. Then again, that made it easier to ask for forgiveness than permission. Too bad I was supposed to be operating by the book on this assignment. But I was stuck here for the next several months or however long. At some point, the internal investigation would end, and no one would care if we took a few liberties, just as long as it coincided with acceptable undercover protocols.

"Thanks, Agent Eckhardt."

"Matt," he corrected. "You might have noticed we're very much on a first name basis. Jace insists on it. It makes it easier to transition from debriefs and mission reports back to his undercover persona."

"What's his undercover handle?"

"Jason Ellis, that way he still gets to go by Jace."

"Brilliant."

"Isn't it?" He looked around the room. "I'll leave you to it. If you need anything, you have my cell."

After a few bites, I was done. My stomach was in knots. Wrapping what was left of the sandwich, I stuck the bag in the fridge and looked around the room. The only intel I had on the case were the documents I brought with me. At least it was a start. Now that there was a new angle to consider, perhaps I'd glean something useful that we'd missed.

I'd been jotting notes in the margins for the better part of two hours when there was a knock at the door. Getting up, I tucked the nine millimeter at the small of my back and went to the door. A quick glance through the peephole assured me it was safe, and I unlocked the door.

"I assumed you had a key." I stepped away from the door and went back to the table. "You didn't have to knock."

"It's the polite thing to do." Jace crossed the room and dropped a stack of files on the table, looking down to see what I was doing. "I'm sure we'll be in each other's face a lot. I don't want to start off on the wrong foot by invading your privacy."

"It's your house. I'm just the help."

He raised a questioning eyebrow. "Is everything okay?"

"Yep." I finished my final notation and shifted my attention to him. "Eckhardt informed me there's some question as to whether Wilde is involved with drugs. It seems your office failed to notify mine that this might be a case of human trafficking."

"Matt isn't entirely incorrect, but Timothy Wilde is doping his followers and dealing. I just have no fucking idea how." Jace dropped into a chair and leaned his head back. "I have to be back in two hours. We don't have much time. Are you okay to listen while I talk?"

"Please."

"Okay." Decker ran his hands down his face and leaned forward in the chair. "Wilde's a predator. He targets potential followers and creates seemingly random encounters and situations in order to gain their trust. Granted, a few individuals seem to discover him on their own, but those tend to be people who are already on the fringe of society. They confuse the mix, and for now, it's not important that we discuss them."

I nodded, picking up a pen. "Do you mind if I take notes?"

"Whatever." He swallowed. "His targets tend to be female, mid-twenties to early forties, with no real family ties. No husbands, no children, and estranged from their parents and siblings. They tend to be unemployed or work at places with high turnover rates. Oddly enough, they've all been educated, at least with some college experience. A few have masters degrees, but I haven't happened upon anyone beyond that. I don't know if it's worth mentioning, but that's the current profile."

"All right. What's the motivation?"

"It depends, doesn't it?" Abruptly, he stood and began to pace. "In some circumstances, Wilde targets wealth. He's claiming tax exemptions, but his co-op's reported financial returns are abysmal. There's no way he makes enough with his artisanal crafts and bake sales to keep the church functioning, let alone providing for those who reside on the property. His biggest source of income is through charitable donations made by well-endowed members."

"Does he charge his followers to join?"

"No, they willingly hand over the money because they are convinced the work being done is good and the church's need is great. It's manipulation, plain and simple. Frankly, it resembles a form of Stockholm syndrome." Jace retook his seat. "Tim makes people become dependent on him. He gives them everything. If they need a place to stay, he provides one. Meals are prepared for his entire community, and the kitchen is always open. If someone needs help to pay a bill or needs a ride, he makes it happen. All he asks is that they pay it forward."

"By giving to the church?"

Jace scrunched his face. "Yes and no." He rubbed at his beard again. "It's weird. I've been there for eight months. I came in as a drifter, and he's helped me find a job, a place to live, and has given me rides. Then he'll ask for tiny favors. The kinds of things you'd do for a friend, like help out with dinner or talk about my experiences with some prospective recruits. He's never asked for money directly."

"So it's like living with a sympathetic relative?"

"Yeah. He makes everyone feel welcomed. He doesn't turn people away, at least not that I've seen. It's supposed to be a safe environment. Tim has structured his commune with classes."

"Classes?"

"Meditation, yoga, stress-relief. Believe it or not, he even has an addiction group to help those who are dealing with cravings and urges. He's been very open within the group about his previous experiences and dealings, at least to the extent that we know he has a record. There's nothing he's said that we haven't uncovered by running him through the databases, so it's not helpful."

"Not to us, but I imagine it earns trust and encourages his followers to open up." A thought crossed my mind. "Do you think he uses whatever confessions people tell him as blackmail?"

"It's possible."

I leaned back, studying the man before me. "C'mon, it's been eight months. You must have seen or heard something by now."

"I haven't. Privacy is a weird thing at the compound. The church broadcasts openness leading to enlightenment, but what Wilde is told in confidence by his followers stays that way. He doesn't share, and gossip doesn't travel. It's a strange dichotomy."

"Is that because you're a guy?"

Jace looked completely confused. "I don't see the relevance."

"Wilde targets women. Are they treated differently? He was accused of sexual assault. Is he open about that? Does he sleep with his female followers, or does he just want their money? If he's manipulating them, he could convince them to do anything."

"It doesn't appear he has forced anyone into anything

they didn't want to do. We have equipment set up to monitor parts of the compound. I have no proof, but I gather he's slept with several of his followers. I haven't been invited into his chambers, so we don't have eyes inside, nor do I believe a court would allow it without some sort of valid reason. But none of the women he's had relations with have left. No one complains, and there have been no repeat performances." He jerked his chin up. "What are you thinking?"

"Women have left. He's lost followers. One of them is currently in the morgue. Others are six feet under. Maybe he attacked them, and they escaped. Perhaps he killed them."

Jace shook his head. "He didn't kill them, not personally. We monitor his movements. He rarely leaves the compound, and when he does, he typically stays in town. A surveillance unit tries to keep eyes on him. He has eluded us on occasion, but I still think we would have seen something."

"But you don't have audio or visual surveillance in parts of the compound. Things could happen right under your nose, and you might not know about it."

"It's a good thing there's two of us now." Jace stood, tapping the top folder in the stack. "This is your new identity. Get to know her. I won't be able to get away for the next few days. Matt will call when we're ready to put you into play. You'll move to a different location, and that morning, I'll bump into you at a coffee shop. It'll be purely accidental, but it'll get the ball rolling. We'll make sure your insertion goes as smoothly as possible. I have a good feeling about this. You and I have a nice rhythm. This partnership should work out well."

"I hope so."

He smiled. "I'll see you soon, Alex."

EIGHT

I couldn't remember the last time I'd slept or managed to choke down more than a few bites. I'd read and reread the files, spent hours on the phone with Mark, working through the intel and searching for new angles, taken meticulous notes, and requested profiles and background checks on Wilde's flock. Apparently, I was such a pain in the ass, the entire team was taking turns answering my calls. I was completely focused on work, probably to the point of obsession. Luckily, the resident shrink was deep undercover and nowhere near the safe house to pass judgment.

Rubbing my eyes, I grabbed a bottle of water from the fridge, took a sip, and put it down on the table. I stretched my arms and back, dropped to the ground and did a few dozen push-ups followed by some sit-ups. Getting up, I did some squats and lunges, thinking I'd gladly kill someone for the opportunity to go for a run and clear my head. If I had to stare at these sickening walls for another moment, I might crack. The little voice in my head chuckled. *You already cracked, Parker.*

"Knock, knock," Eve called. I straightened up and went to the door. "Sheets, fragrance-free detergent, a new pillow, and a fluffy throw." She dropped the bedding on the couch and looked around the apartment. "Damn. When I can't sleep, I watch TV. What do you call this style of decoration? Serial killer chic?"

"Bored OIO agent." I picked up the sheet set, unzipping the plastic. "Hopefully, this will help. The crap they have on the bed is scratchy and it smells."

"Are you anxious to get to work?"

"That's why I'm here." I finished unwrapping the items and crossed into the kitchenette where a small washing machine was hidden in the corner. "Y'know, it'd be nice to use the laundry room or breathe some fresh air."

"You can open the window," she teased.

"Thanks a lot."

She laughed, making herself comfortable on the couch. "Quiz time." She picked up the dossier on my undercover persona. "What's your name, and where are you from?"

"Alice Lexington. I was born in Springfield, but I don't remember much about it. My parents split up when I was a baby. My mom took us to stay with my grandparents in Florida. They were elderly." I blinked, looking up. The last time we'd run through this exercise I had been encouraged to sell it, so I was doing that now. "There was a fire. She got me out of the house but went back for them. They didn't make it. It took a while, but my dad finally came for me. He'd been abroad. We lived in Europe for a while, London and Paris mostly." I stopped. "You realize my foreign language skills suck, right? What if Wilde expects me to speak perfect French?"

"I don't believe he speaks French, and there's no indication any of these twenty-odd individuals we ran backgrounds on speak French either. You're familiar with the region, and you have basic conversational skills. Plus, Lexington said she lived there. Remember, she's from a wealthy background, so she had private American teachers."

I slammed the lid on the washing machine. "You don't get it. You want me to be some rich snob who moved to southern California because of a contested inheritance after being estranged from my father for several years."

"Over resentment concerning your mother," Eve

pointed out, attempting to demonstrate she knew the profile better than I did. "What's the problem?"

"Wealthy children are given a certain type of upbringing. They speak several languages, are forced to endure music lessons, and develop refined tastes." Suddenly, I couldn't stop wondering if Martin played any instruments. Why didn't I know the answer to that?

"Alex," Eve stood in front of me, "you zoned out. What's wrong?"

"I'm just tired." I shook it off. "The point I'm making is I don't believe I'll be convincing."

"You're nervous. It's natural, but Ben's really good at coming up with enticing personas. This will work. You have enough experience to make it realistic. Everything in that profile is based on skills and experiences we pulled from your personnel file. The things you know, Alice Lexington knows."

"Like how long it takes for a man to lose consciousness while in a chokehold?"

Eve held up her palms. "I get your point. Just do the best you can and follow Jace's lead. There are two things you need to know that you're not going to find in any report. One, Jace is harmless. He might tease and flirt, but he won't cross any lines." She fell silent, studying me.

"What's two?"

"You damn well better be on your game and have his back. He's been running himself ragged on this mission. Bringing in outside help is supposed to lighten his load, not make it worse. You're going to pick up the slack and give him a break. And you're going to make absolutely certain nothing happens to him. Do I make myself clear?"

I nodded.

"Good." She went back to the couch and picked up the file. When she looked up, her friendly smile was back in place. "Let's continue with the pop quiz."

"After some time, I was sent to boarding school back home. I lost touch with my dad, except for an occasional birthday card. He didn't even show up at my college graduation."

"Where'd you go to school?"

"NYU, graduated with a degree in English lit., which clearly is the way to go career wise. Since then, I've tried waitressing, working as a temp, and being a barista. By the way, you really should tip your baristas."

Eve laughed. "What brought you to the West Coast?"

"A lawyer." My face contorted, and I looked away. "I was the only heir, but there have been complications. Dad owed money, back taxes or something, I'm not entirely sure. It's a mess. Until things are sold and everything's straightened out, my trust fund is frozen. I have nothing."

"Bingo. That's exactly the type of story Wilde will go nuts over. You don't have the money yet, which means you need his help, but from the financial information we've planted, you're going to come into millions soon enough. Wilde needs you and the money, so he'll do anything to get you to join his church. That's why I don't think your lack of proper upbringing will be a problem." Her phone buzzed, and she dug it out of her purse. Checking the display, she typed a quick reply and placed it on the table. "We've been careful. He has no reason to believe he's even on our radar. No badges or uniforms have been poking around the co-op. We're in the clear for now."

"Great."

The phone buzzed again, and she gave it another glance. "Even better news, we'll start the insertion process in two days. Tonight, review whatever you want. Tomorrow, we'll be here to clear this place out. Your research will be taken to our command center, and I'll see about getting you an office for your check-ins. If there's anything Alex Parker needs to do, get it done between now and tomorrow." She went to the door. "My suggestion would be prioritize sleep. You need to be sharp. Jace needs you to be sharp." Her eyes flashed a warning, and then she was gone.

* * *

"Shit." I scrambled to wipe the hot coffee off my blouse. Following Decker's instructions, I'd arrived on time to the agreed upon coffeehouse and waited in line, not spotting him inside. When I got to the front, I had ordered the cheapest thing on the menu to sell my story. It wasn't like Alice Lexington had eight dollars to blow on a fancy unpronounceable concoction. As soon as I picked up the cup, someone bumped into my side.

"I'm sorry. Are you okay?" He held out a handful of napkins. I took a few while he wiped off the counter, apologizing to the barista and requesting a repeat of my order.

Glancing up, I almost didn't recognize Jace. He'd shaved since our last encounter, and his shaggy hair wasn't slicked back. Wilde wasn't inside, but Agent Decker was no amateur. He wouldn't risk any sort of compromise, especially not eight months into an active op.

"I'm fine. I'm just having a doozy of a day." My eyes flicked briefly to the man waiting outside the café before I shifted my focus back to Jace. Timothy Wilde watched us with bored curiosity. "Don't worry about it." I took the remaining napkin from Jace's hand, spotting a handwritten note on it. *Leave, go left down the street, and enter the clothing shop. Buy a new shirt.*

He raised his palms and took a step back toward the order window. "I'll have an herbal tea and a chai latte to go." He glanced back at me. "I'll stay over here until you're no longer in the splash zone."

I laughed. "Thanks."

As soon as the replacement drink was ready, I took my cup and went out the door, tossing the note in the trash. Pulling the wet material away from my skin, I looked down and sighed. Turning in the proper direction, I saw the boutique and continued walking. I felt eyes on me, but I didn't risk turning around. Jace had a plan.

Meandering through the racks, I searched for a white button-up blouse like the one I was wearing. It had been part of my regulation attire, but since Ben stipulated I was to dress as if going on an interview, I'd put on the blouse with a pair of dark jeans. No jacket. No gun. No badge. Admittedly, I felt naked.

Finding a suitable replacement in my size, I checked the price and fished out the credit card I'd been given. It contained the fake name that matched my fake ID. I guess it was time to see how things would play out. Smiling at the clerk, I handed her the item.

"If you need a place to change, you can use the dressing room after I ring you up," she said.

"Thanks."

After taking my credit card, she slid it through the machine. It beeped angrily, and she tried again. Then she looked at the name and the expiration date. She tried sliding it once more. "Do you have another card I can use? This one was declined."

"No problem." Flipping through the cards in my wallet, I pulled out another one, noticing two men lingering outside the shop. "Try this one." I handed her the card, but it was also declined.

"I'm sorry." She looked at me. "Do you want to pay cash?"

"No, I'll have to come back for it." Stuffing everything back inside my purse, I picked up my coffee, put on a pair of sunglasses, and went out the door.

"Miss," a voice called from behind, "wait." Spinning around, I came face-to-face with the clerk. She held out the blouse. "Take this with you. You can come back and pay when you have more cash on you."

"This is so embarrassing. Thank you so much. I'm already late. I have to go, but I will pay you back. I promise." Heading toward the parking lot where I left the rental, I couldn't help but wonder if the clerk was part of the plan.

As soon as I got inside the car, I slipped out of my shirt and into the new one, hoping there would be additional instructions. However, I didn't find any notes anywhere. Jace didn't make a reappearance, and when I pulled out of the lot and onto the road, he and Wilde were nowhere to be found. Without additional instructions, I had to fall back on my standing orders.

Navigating the streets took some getting used to, but I made it back to my cover apartment. It was a condo in one of the exclusive high-rise buildings. The valet waited for me to grab my bags before offering to park the car, and the doorman greeted me by name, asking if I needed help upstairs.

"No, thanks." At least it was an improvement over the roadside inn.

When I made it to the condo, I found flowers in a vase. Knowing the DEA had full access to the apartment and performed sweeps weekly, I correctly assumed they were responsible for the delivery. The note gave an address and a time. *Good luck on your second job interview of the day. I'm sorry you missed the first one. Dress accordingly and avoid clutzy coffee drinkers.*

The note had been typewritten. Jace had everything planned from the get-go. I was just rolling with the punches. I hated being out of the loop. Normally, I called the shots, so playing second chair wasn't particularly comfortable. How was I supposed to know what was in store for me this evening?

Taking a seat behind the computer, I entered the address and found the name of the business. It was a saloon, or rather, a recreation of an Old West saloon. It was a restaurant and bar that boasted dinner entertainment. It looked like a tourist trap with some kind of song and dance number. They had several openings for barmaids and servers. It was a good thing Alice Lexington had previous experience. Now all I had to do was show up on time, fill out an application, and wait for Jace to throw a wrench into the mix.

My eyes scanned the walls, but my intel was safely boxed up and inside the command center. There wasn't anything for me to do between now and then. I had my instructions, so I just had to wait. Looking at the walls of my new prison, I laughed and changed clothes. The luxury building had a gym, and while I had the chance, I planned to make use of it. I didn't imagine someone on the verge of eviction getting to hang out in a fancy condo too terribly long.

After my workout, I showered, changed back into the white blouse and dark jeans, and decided to do some sightseeing. I'd been cramped up in that tiny hovel for almost a week. I needed to do something to get out of my own head before I went crazy. Plus, it would help to have some familiarity with the area. We were positioned between the Nevada border and Los Angeles. It was less than an hour to the city. If we had to call in the cavalry, they'd arrive from there. The L.A. field office was massive and able to deal with every contingency. If this became an FBI matter, they'd take jurisdiction.

Somehow, I ended up driving farther west than I intended. My original plan was to stay in the suburban town and get a feel for the area, the people, and see if there were any hints of a criminal element. Instead, I ended up a few blocks from the Martin Technologies west coast offices. Grabbing some fish tacos from a food truck, I took a seat on a bench and stared at the skyline, seeing the MT logo in the distance.

I really fucked up, and there was no way to fix it. Coming here was just a means of preventing Martin and me from falling back into the destructive, painful pattern. This was for the best. By removing myself from the equation, he'd be able to move on.

I gave the building a final look, as if saying goodbye, threw out the uneaten tacos, and went back to the car. Alex Parker was gone for now. I was Alice Lexington, and I had a job interview in two hours. On the way back to the condo, I stopped at a big box store and picked up a couple of throwaway phones. It was best to be prepared, and I wanted to have an untraceable way of communicating with Jablonsky should the need arise. My phone was in a locker at the DEA command center, along with most of my personal belongings. I'd been given a phone for use that they could track, but if things went sideways, it was nice to have a plan B.

NINE

"Your internet listing says you're hiring barmaids and waitresses." I pointed emphatically at the printed page. "I have experience waitressing, and I worked as a barista. I'm good with complicated drink orders."

"I get that you're looking for a job, but that listing is old and outdated." The restaurant owner shrugged.

"But you have a help wanted sign out front." I spun, spotting Jace and Wilde at a booth near the bar. Ignoring them, I turned back to the owner. "Please, I need to find work. Maybe I could update your website?"

"Do you know how to do that?"

"I'm a fast learner." Alice didn't possess any overt computer skills, and since Alex Parker was great at the research and using government databases but no whiz at computer programming, it was best to stick with what I knew.

"Sorry." The owner turned away. He'd been behind the bar, filling orders and managing. It was a small, hands-on establishment.

Plopping down on a barstool, I sighed dramatically. The last thing I wanted was a drink, but given the circumstances, it would be the normal thing to do. "Can I at least get a glass of wine?"

He nodded, pouring from the nearest bottle of red. Placing it in front of me, he offered a reassuring smile. "On the house."

"I don't want charity." I swallowed. "Sir, I need a job. I'm about to lose my apartment. I don't have anywhere to go. I'm new here. I don't know anyone. I just need something to work out."

"I'll tell you what. I'll hold on to your application. If we have any openings in the future, I'll keep you in mind."

"That's not going to help. I need something now." The desperation in my tone carried, and a few of the people at the bar turned to look at me. I hoped Wilde was close enough to hear what was going on. However, I didn't think making two passes in one day was the best plan, but Decker and Ben orchestrated this. I had to trust their judgment, even if it seemed downright risky. "I'll do anything. I'll scrub the toilets, mop the floors, wash dishes, whatever you need. I'm at the end of my rope." With any luck, the owner wasn't going to prey on the situation, take me into the back, and ask for a blowjob, but I couldn't be sure.

He looked around the bar. "The only opening I have is for a dancer, and we only hire professionals."

"I can dance."

He gave me a 'yeah, right' look. "Nice try, hun."

"At least let me audition. Are you having an open call?"

His eyes narrowed, sizing me up. "You're serious? It's not listed on your application."

"So?" I wondered just how thoroughly the DEA had delved into my history. As a child, I'd been forced to endure ballet lessons for nearly ten years. I was never good enough to be admitted to a troupe, but I knew basic positions. However, I didn't think any of that would be relevant to the saloon's stage show. "Can't a girl have a hobby?"

"Why do I get the feeling you're going to pester me until I agree?"

I picked up the glass and took a tiny sip, eyeing him over the rim. "Is that a yes?"

"Fine. Come in tomorrow at three. Costumes are in the back. If you fit the costume, you can audition, but the choreographer will make the call. Is that understood?"

"Thank you. You won't be disappointed."

The owner rolled his eyes and went down the bar to serve some drinks. Standing up, I grabbed my bag and turned to leave. With insane precision, Jace collided with me at that exact moment. If this were to keep up, I'd start wearing football pads to the rest of our planned meets. He swept his foot behind mine, knocking me off balance and propelling me backward. But he caught me before I fell into the barstools.

"Whoa, I didn't see you there," he said. I searched his eyes for a clue as to how to proceed. "Do I know you?"

"Oh my god." I righted myself and shoved him backward. "You're the jerk from the coffee shop." I backed away, holding my palms up. "Stay away from me."

He laughed uncomfortably. "Maybe it's fate that we keep bumping into each other."

"Or maybe you're stalking me." I continued scooting backward. "Why don't you stay right there, and I'll go this way." I pointed behind me. "Let's not cross paths again."

"Come on," he turned up the flirtatious charm, "let me buy you a drink or dinner or something. It's the least I can do." He looked down at my shirt. "Shit, at least let me pay for your dry cleaning."

I followed his gaze, watching the wine drip down the front of my new blouse. Slumping onto the closest stool, I put my hands over my eyes and took a few unsteady breaths. Playing this wrong might be a disaster, but I was going with my gut. I shuddered, attempting to appear to be on the brink of a meltdown. A few tears sprang to my eyes, and I forced myself to calm down, fearing if the waterworks started, they wouldn't be entirely staged.

"Excuse me, miss," Wilde's smooth voice interrupted Jace's attempts at an apology, "my friend is very sorry for upsetting you." I removed my hands from my face and took a deep breath, focusing on Wilde. "Why don't you join us for dinner?" He pointed to the booth. "I don't mean to pry, but you look like you could use a meal and some friendly conversation."

"No, I...," I shook my head, knowing that jumping at the offer would seem suspicious, but protesting too much might force him to back off, "I should get this into the wash before it stains."

"Let me reimburse you," Jace offered from beside Wilde. "How much did you pay?" He reached into his pocket and pulled out his wallet.

Looking as sheepish as possible, I shook my head. "I haven't even paid for this yet. God, I'm such a mess." I shuddered again, forcing a few more tears to my eyes.

"That's it." Wilde put a cautious arm around my shoulders. "You're going to sit down and have something to eat. It'll make you feel better. It's our treat." My eyes darted around the busy restaurant, and he sensed my trepidation. "If you're worried about my friend spilling something else on you, you can sit at your own table, and we'll pick up the tab."

"No, that's just silly." I pressed my lips together in thought. "Just a quick bite and then I have to go."

"Okay." Wilde brightened, leading the way back to the booth. He and Jace sat together on one side, and I took the other. "I'm Tim." He held out his hand, and we shook. "This is Jason."

"Jace," Decker corrected, winking.

"Alice Lexington." I busied myself with picking up a menu from behind the napkin holder.

"Nice to meet you," Wilde cooed. "Alice's a lovely name."

"Thanks, but no one calls me that. I'm just Alex."

"Alex?" Tim asked.

"Yeah, our dorm assignments were first initial, last name. But since my last name was too long to fit on the sheet, I became A. Lex. And it stuck."

"Alex," Jace smiled, "I like that."

To avoid the awkwardness, I remained focused on the menu, hoping to find something small and cheap to order. Wilde kept asking personal questions, but they seemed innocent enough. He wanted to know if I was new to town, how long I'd been in the area, and if I liked it. Those were normal small talk questions, so I stuck to the script. Finally, the waitress arrived, took my order for half a steak sandwich and a side salad, and spoke to Tim about how much she enjoyed the honey butter she'd bought the previous week from his stand.

"Do you have a farm?" I asked.

"It's not solely mine. It's a co-op. We grow fruits and veggies, and we keep bees. It's not that impressive."

"It sounds nice. Is that what you do for a living?"

"Partly." Wilde was being cagey. I wasn't certain if that was his usual spiel or if I'd been too skittish earlier. "What do you do, Alex?"

"I'm hoping to get a job here." I glanced back at the bar, but the owner was gone. "I have an audition tomorrow."

"Audition?" Jace asked, annoyance flashing across his face.

"There's an opening for a dancer."

"You dance?" Jace sounded surprised.

"We'll see." I cracked a weak smile. "It depends on if you plan to break my kneecaps or something."

"No." His face contorted into confusion. "Why would you say that?"

"I don't know." The bitterness found its way to my vocal cords. "You sabotaged my interview this morning. The coffee spill plus the traffic made me late, and I missed it." I blinked a few times, glad the waitress had arrived with my food. "You have an obvious vendetta against dress shirts." Shifting my focus to the plate, I continued to speak while I disassembled the sandwich. "I know I shouldn't blame you. I just really need something to work out."

"You have an audition tomorrow, and you met us," Wilde interrupted. "Things are already looking up."

I glanced at him. "Wow, that's really optimistic."

"That's kind of what I do." Wilde removed a flyer from his pocket and handed it to me. I unfolded it awkwardly while keeping one hand on my fork. "I wanted to find a way to help people, and I started this movement."

"It's a church?" I looked up at him. "No offense, but I'm not particularly religious."

"You don't have to be. Some in the community are

searching for a higher power, but others are simply there because they need support or want to give back. Times are tough for everyone. We all struggle with our burdens. Finances, health problems, addiction. Everything in day-to-day life just seems so desperate, so heartbreaking." He gave me a sad smile. "Like seeing you have that freakout. I know your biggest problem isn't a stained shirt. You have troubles. That's why I want to help people."

"I appreciate it, but I'm not looking to join a church." I pushed the flyer back to him, but he shook his head.

"That's okay. I didn't mean to make you uncomfortable. I just wanted you to know there is help available. All you have to do is ask." Wilde studied me for a moment. "People confuse dignity with pridefulness. There's nothing wrong with having some friends to talk to when times are tough. It's okay to ask for a little help." He looked pointedly at Jace.

"It's true." Jace smiled warmly. "Tim helped get me squared away. I didn't have a place to live or a job. Now I have both. Our community is growing. This is a small town. People know us. They help one another out. If this audition doesn't pan out and you're still looking for a job, Tim might be able to help."

"I'll keep that in mind." I finished eating, my stomach protesting the last few bites, but I forced them down and tucked the flyer into my pocket. "I should get going."

"It was nice meeting you." Tim stood and shook my hand again. "Remember, we have a farmer's market and open house on the weekends. You should stop by sometime."

"Maybe I will." I glanced back at Jace. "Do us both a favor and watch where you're going next time. White linen shirts everywhere will thank you."

"I'll do that." He watched as I walked away.

After leaving the restaurant, I realized I had no idea what I was supposed to do. Jace sent me on this job interview because he and Wilde would be there, but it wasn't a job interview so much as begging for a job. The internet listing was wrong, or the owner didn't want to hire me. Either way, I didn't know if our intel was bad or if I'd gone off book in my attempt to carry through with the cryptic instructions. Why didn't we have an actual briefing and set agenda? Mark was right. The DEA was full of cowboys who played it off the cuff. That was fine when there was only one UC involved, but bringing in a secondary operative required planning and strategy.

I returned to the apartment. No one was inside, and nothing strange had been left. My eyes searched the rooms for signs of surveillance devices, but I didn't spot anything. Surveillance was keyed into the building security systems. The housekeepers were agents who would sweep for bugs and leave notes. However, none of that helped me relay a message to them. I couldn't exactly go into the hallway and hold up a sign in front of the camera because building security would also see it.

"What am I doing here?" I asked the room. "What's our play?" Narrowing my eyes at the smoke detector, I snorted. "Why do I get the feeling you don't even know?"

Acknowledging that I was now speaking to inanimate objects as if they were hidden spy cams, I decided it was time to call it a night. I had to get up early in the morning and stretch, watch internet footage of the saloon's stage show, and learn the steps. Damn, I hated dancing.

TEN

Arriving for the audition a half hour early, I was shown to the dressing room where a rack of costumes waited in the center. Most of them were low-cut corsets with big poofy skirts in the dusty browns associated with the Wild West. Being this close to L.A. and not too far from Vegas meant most of the dancers were struggling wannabe actresses or former showgirls. I didn't have a prayer for getting this gig.

I picked the simplest costume I could find and held it against my chest, secretly hoping it wouldn't fit to save myself the embarrassment of going through with the rest of this cockamamie plan. After changing, I left the dressing room, heading for the stage where the others were warming up.

I walked past one of the back offices, and the door opened. "Psst." Turning, I spotted Decker lingering in the dark. "Get in here." Once I was inside, he pushed the door closed. "What the hell are you doing?" he whispered.

"I don't fucking know. You told me to come here for a job. I'm following orders."

"Rule number one, you don't tell unnecessary lies. We had bad intel. The position was filled two days ago, so we would have found something else. You weren't supposed to decide to broadcast that you can dance. Tim's going to expect a performance."

"This is an audition. I won't make the cut, and that'll be it. He doesn't need to know anything more."

"He's here."

"What?" Shaking off this newest hitch, I shrugged. "Fine. I'll give him a show."

"How? There's no way you picked up a completely new skill set in the last eighteen hours."

Snorting, I shook my head. "I spent my childhood being tortured with classical dance lessons. I sucked at them, but this is different. It's steps and keeping time with the count. That's something I can do. I'll stay in the back and slink away when I don't make the cut. It's not that big of a deal."

"Don't screw this up." Despite his words, I heard the motivation behind them. Decker didn't want to lose eight months of hard work over something this stupid.

"In the future, I suggest you make it very clear what you expect. Cryptic messages and crossed signals aren't making things any easier on either of us." I glared at him. "And if you bump into me again, I'll knock you on your ass."

"Break a leg." He gestured to the door. "And to avoid any confusion, Tim doesn't know I'm here." He softened. "We'll come up with a fleshed out plan once we see how your audition goes before we proceed further."

"Thanks." Taking a deep inhale, I peered out the slats of the blinds, slowly opened the door a crack, and slipped back into the hallway. I needed to be focused on the routine, but one thought continued to echo in my mind. Why was Tim allowed at the audition? How much pull did he have in this town?

The warm-up was brief. The choreographer went through the routine once at half speed to show us the steps. Then he performed the routine again at a normal pace with the music. Hitting stop, he turned around and smiled at us.

"Let's see what you girls can do." He hit the music, nodding with the beat and counting us off.

It wasn't a particularly difficult routine. However, it did require flexibility, timing, and enough coordination so as not to trip over these ridiculous costumes. As we ran through, he began thinning the herd. I hadn't missed a step, but that didn't mean I had any actual talent. Yet, as he continued to dismiss more and more of the women, I wondered why I hadn't been asked to leave. We completed the routine for the third time, and he turned off the music. Four of us remained on the stage. I had no doubt in my mind that I had no business being there.

"Okay, ladies, give this one a try." He went through a second routine, this one with a few more intricate moves. Briefly, I wondered if we were trying out for the Moulin Rouge. We ran through the routine again, and he dismissed the girl to my left. Once she had cleared the stage, he smiled broadly at the three of us. "It looks like we've found some new talent. Sonya, you'll be lead. Rehearsals will begin this evening to get you ready for the weekend performance. Katy and Alice will be background dancers." He came closer, holding out a stage layout. "Katy will be here." He pointed to a spot close to the center. "Alice," he glanced up, and his eyes relayed what I already knew, I wasn't his top choice, "you'll be here." He pointed to the far corner, practically invisible to most of the diners due to the construction and shape of the stage. "Cast rehearsals will begin tomorrow afternoon. We perform a dinner show Thursday and Friday, and we have a lunch and dinner performance Saturdays and Sundays. Are there any questions?"

Sonya had several. While she prattled on about technical things, I edged off the stage toward a waiting bottle of water. The restaurant was nearly empty except for the hostess wrapping silverware. However, Timothy Wilde sat at one of the tables off to the side. After the choreographer finished with Sonya and congratulated Katy, he approached me.

"Make sure you have the steps down. You'll get the hang of it."

"Thanks." Forcing a smile on my face, I had to act like this was the greatest thing since sliced bread. The desperate woman from last night had been granted a reprieve.

A slow clap sounded behind me, and I spun. Wilde had left the table and was making his way toward me. I cocked a questioning eyebrow.

"Congratulations," he said. "It appears your luck is turning around."

"I hope so. Did you have anything to do with this?"

"Maybe." He gave me a knowing smile. "Everyone could use some help sometimes."

"I don't know what to say. Thank you. That seems so lame, but thank you."

"Don't thank me. You earned this. You made this happen. I just nudged the management in the right direction. Like I said, we need to help each other out." He placed another flyer on the nearest table. "Just think about it." Without so much as a goodbye, he walked away. Damn, he was smooth. We should probably add con man to his list of criminal attributes.

*   *   *

For the next month, Decker instructed me to remain aloof. We had weekly briefings at the command center to discuss strategy and plans. Wilde hadn't lost interest in the prospect of having me join his cult, but Jace didn't want me to appear too eager. My situation was supposed to be improving, not deteriorating, so I had no reason to run to Wilde for help. However, I did stop by his farmer's market every weekend. Tim had given me a tour of the co-op and his facility, and he stopped by the restaurant on Thursdays to watch the dinner show, despite the fact my dancing had not improved. If anything, it had gotten worse.

"This is ridiculous," I said, eyeing the DEA agents. Jace hadn't shown up yet for the weekly briefing, and my frustration had increased. I understood the reasons for a slow insertion and the need to avoid raising suspicion, but we weren't getting anywhere. "Lexington's background indicates her assets are frozen. She can't afford an apartment, not on what she's making at the restaurant."

"You have to be patient," Ben insisted. "Someone ran a credit report two weeks ago. I'm guessing the request was generated by Wilde. He wants to know your precise financial situation. He should see you as the long game. It's the best way to ensure your safety, Agent Parker." He cocked his head to the side. "Alex?"

"Parker's fine."

"Good to know. We need him to see you as an investment. That's why we can't rush. Lexington's savings account should be dwindling. After paying your bills this month, you'll barely have enough to scrape together for another month. I believe he knows this. He'll wait to make his move, but that's why we've had you show some interest. You're curious, and you're grateful. He helped you out when you needed it. He'll do it again, and in turn, he'll expect you to return the favor."

"He wants you to be grateful," Decker declared, entering the room and coming to stand at the head of the table. "Eventually, you'll be expected to repay his kindness." He blinked a few times. "I don't know what that might entail."

"Meaning?" I asked.

"We know he'll want access to your trust fund as soon as it's no longer frozen. Based on the legal intricacies and docket number we've planted, it'll be at least six months before the situation with your father's estate is resolved. At that time, he'll either create a situation that will require a financial contribution to his commune, or he might pursue a romantic engagement prior to that." Decker glanced at the others. "Have we made any progress identifying who cut the drugs out of Wilde's former followers?"

Carlo shook his head. "We're friendly with the LEOs. They'll let me know if they find something, but from what their CIs have said, it was probably the dealer who gutted the girls. Based on the coroner's reports, each of the women had a large amount of narcotics in their bloodstream. They were either dead or dying from an overdose when they were cut open. I'm guessing the balloons ruptured, and whenever the dealer found them, he cut out the stash and tossed the bodies aside."

"We see it a lot." Eve clicked a few keys on the computer. "What we need to do is unearth the connection between Wilde and the local dealers. Then we might be able to get someone to talk."

"What do you think I've been trying to do?" Jace

growled.

Normally, he was friendly and calm, especially when he was back amongst friends. I knew how difficult it was to turn off the undercover persona at times, but something was bothering him. I hadn't seen him very often in the field, but I knew something was off.

"Jace, what's up?" I asked.

"Nothing."

"Bullshit."

Five sets of eyes stared at me, utterly horrified. Apparently, no one had called him out before.

Decker inhaled deeply, pushing his shoulders back and bringing his eyes up to meet mine. An amused twitch teased the corner of his mouth, and then he focused on the rest of the team. "Tim's planning something. I don't know what. I can't pinpoint anything. I've been trying to stick close to him, but he's been secretive lately. I'm hoping it's the break we need, but I have no way of knowing."

"Surveillance hasn't picked up anything suspicious. We've been monitoring his movements. No one new has surfaced," Carlo offered. "We can get a second team to sit on him, if you think it'll help."

"No." Jace glared at me, as if to say 'see, this is why I don't say anything'. "The last thing we need to do is spook him. I'll keep on him." He looked at his watch. "I hate to cut this meeting short, but I should get back."

"Be careful," Eve said.

"Stay safe," Stella called.

"I'll catch you guys later." Jace headed out of the room.

Ben looked at his watch. "Don't you have a rehearsal?"

I sighed dramatically. "A hundred bucks to anyone who kneecaps me." I glanced around. "No takers?"

"No one told you to improvise, so you have no one to blame but yourself." Carlo smirked. "Don't break a leg."

"Ha ha."

Letting myself out of the office, I went down the hallway to the back entrance where I'd parked. This mansion was a giant maze, but I'd finally gotten the hang of it. After getting back into my car and running through all the checks to make sure I wasn't followed or being watched, I drove the twenty miles back to the tiny tourist trap town and parked in the designated employee spots. It was just another day of high kicks and shimmying for this working girl.

"Katy," I called, spotting her in the dressing room, "where's my costume?" The first couple of weeks had involved several practical jokes and a bit of hazing by the rest of the dance crew, but it had fizzled out.

"Ask the manager." She rolled her eyes and lowered her voice. "How stupid is it that we have to do every rehearsal in full dress? It's ridiculous. I worked at five different shows in Vegas, and we rarely did dress rehearsals."

"Yeah, it's crazy." Leaving the dressing room, I found the owner speaking to the choreographer in the hallway. "Excuse me. I can't seem to find my costume."

"Oh," Mr. Lowery, the choreographer, turned, "if it's not in the dressing room, it's probably still on the truck. We sent them to the cleaners. Dylan just picked them up. It's the white pickup out front."

Unfortunately, this wasn't a sign I was getting fired. Perhaps I should have mentioned the historical inaccuracies of the stage production and costumes or pointed out our dance number teased at the saloon being a brothel, which wasn't particularly family-friendly entertainment or educational. But with my luck, even that wouldn't get me booted from this place. Tim wanted me grateful. Making a mental note to have Mark run the financial history of this restaurant and its owner for any type of connection to Wilde and his cult, I once again stepped into the afternoon sunlight.

The white truck was the only one in the lot. A tarp covered the truck bed with a stack of plastic dry cleaning bags laying flat on top of it. However, I didn't spot Dylan or anyone else for that matter. Knowing Dylan, he was probably huddled behind the building, smoking a joint. I approached the rear of the pickup and lowered the gate.

Footsteps sounded behind me, but I didn't bother to turn around. "Hey, I just needed to grab my costume for rehearsal," I said, assuming Dylan had returned. "Do you need help dragging the rest of these inside?"

In response, something solid slammed into my shoulder blade, sending my body careening to the ground. Turning, I saw an aluminum bat coming at my face.

ELEVEN

The bat slammed into the pavement inches from my face. Cold eyes stared down at me from beneath a mask as he raised the bat again. He aimed for my shin. I scissored my legs in the nick of time. The aluminum crashed into the ground with a resounding metallic thunk. The reverberation must have jarred the assailant because it took him a moment to recover. In that time, I jumped to my feet. The man wore jeans, a grey zip-up sweatshirt, and a black mask, but he was no Zorro. He swung at thigh level, and I leapt backward. The bat struck the side of the pickup, breaking the taillight, but the assailant kept coming.

"Help," I screamed, fighting my instincts to engage this bastard in hand-to-hand combat. No one immediately came to the rescue, and I cautioned a glance toward the restaurant. "Screw this."

My focus remained on the bat. It posed a danger. It was a distance weapon. Getting too close would come with consequences. I had two options, fight or run. Running would be the safe choice. This stocky son of a bitch wouldn't be able to catch me, but if I got away, so would he.

"Can we talk about this?" I held up my hands while circling farther away from him. "If you want what's inside the truck, just take it. I hate that costume anyway."

"Alex?" a voice called from the vicinity of the building.

During that momentary distraction, the assailant barreled forward like a charging bull. I dove to the side, but he spun and swept the bat low. It skimmed my leg just below my knee. I dropped to the ground, hearing rushed footfalls echoing across the pavement. Help had arrived, but the attacker didn't give up.

He raised the bat again, determined to break my legs. I rolled over and kicked him in the stomach. He stumbled backward, glancing up for the first time at the sound of angry voices getting closer. Raising the bat a final time, he swung again. With no place to go, I slid beneath the truck, but my ankle got clipped by the edge of the bat while the brunt of the impact connected with the ground.

I screamed, perhaps out of surprise, pain, or as a way of reminding myself I was not supposed to be a federal agent. Help had arrived in the form of a stoned teenager and his cell phone. The Zorro impersonator ran, and I watched his escape from my position beneath the truck. He took off down the block, got into an old black muscle car, and drove off.

A second later, sirens sounded, and a police cruiser pulled into the lot. I remained underneath the pickup, wondering how I was supposed to play this. There was no clear connection between what just happened and our investigation into Wilde, but I didn't believe in coincidences. I couldn't help but notice the attacker had been intent on breaking my leg. The first hit was to get me on the ground, but after that, his focus was entirely below the belt. He must have really hated my performances, or he wanted to keep me from being able to escape. Neither thought was particularly comforting.

Two officers exited the cruiser. One immediately went to Dylan while the other crouched down next to the truck. I pushed my way out from underneath the vehicle. I didn't try to get up. My injuries weren't that substantial, but I needed to buy time to think this through. The officer offered a hand up, but I shook my head, propping myself against the front tire.

"Ma'am, are you okay?"

"I don't think so."

"An ambulance is on the way. What's your name?"

"Alice Lexington."

"Can you tell me what happened, Miss Lexington?"

"I came out here to get my costume. I dance in the dinner show." I jerked my thumb at the restaurant. "I had my back turned, and this psycho came up behind me and hit me with a baseball bat."

"Did you get a look at him?"

"Dark jeans, heather grey hooded sweatshirt, a black mask. He was white, five eight, five nine," I shrugged, feeling the sting in my back that I hadn't had time to process during the fight, "stocky build. I'd say around one eighty. He got into an old muscle car. Black. I don't know the make, but I can tell you it didn't have a front plate. He was headed that way." I pointed down the road.

"Wow," the cop smiled, "it isn't every day we get such a thorough description."

"Do you want me to describe the bat too? It was aluminum. Silver." I pointed to one of the areas that it had come into contact with the concrete. "That might be paint transfer." I cracked a weak smile. "I watch a lot of cop shows." It wasn't true, but it was a better explanation than saying I was on the job.

While I spoke to the officer, the choreographer and owner came outside. The owner was on the phone, probably with an attorney or the insurance company to determine if they were liable. The other answered questions.

Dylan had finished giving his statement, which wasn't nearly as in-depth as mine, and edged over to us. "You okay?" he asked.

"I hope so." I looked back at our bosses. "I don't know if I'll be able to dance tonight." I swallowed, making this my newest priority. "I can't afford this right now."

"It's cool. I'll talk to Mr. Lowery. I'm sure he'll give you the night off." Dylan's eyes went wide when he noticed the broken taillight. "Shit. Did you see what that asshole did to my truck? My dad is going to kill me." He looked at the officer. "Are you going to have to take it in as evidence or something?"

The cop gave him a stone-faced stare. "No. We'll take a few photos to include in the report. That'll be about it. You can pick up a copy and forward it to your insurance. They should cover the repairs, minus your deductible."

Dylan looked like he was about to protest but changed his mind. Without saying another word, he went into the cab, pulled something out of the glove box, and stuffed it into his pocket. It was his stash of weed, but I doubted the DEA would be interested in that, but he didn't want to leave it behind in the event the police impounded the vehicle.

A moment later, the ambulance arrived. The EMTs circled around to me. After the perfunctory flashlight in the eyes routine, they put me on a board and got me into the back of the rig. I had no intention of going to the hospital. If the cop ran my alias, it'd get flagged by the DEA and Agent Eckhardt would intervene.

"Y'know," I said to the paramedic taking my vitals, "I can't afford this. I don't have insurance."

"Don't worry about that."

A second car arrived. Jace got out of the passenger's side a second later. He peered into the ambulance, surprised to see me inside. Tim went straight to the congregation of employees and police officers, and Jace stepped up to the ambulance.

"Are you okay?" he asked, glancing pointedly in Wilde's direction.

"Someone wanted to make sure I couldn't dance. They must have seen the show."

"Are you going to the hospital?"

I gave a barely perceptible headshake. "I can't afford it."

The nearest EMT started to explain that I would be treated regardless of my lack of insurance or financial status, but I tuned him out. That wasn't the problem. We needed to figure out who this masked man was and how Tim knew to show up at the restaurant when he did.

Jace pushed his way into the rig, forcing the EMT to back away. "Can you give us a minute?"

"Only if you promise to talk some sense into her." The EMT stepped out of the rig.

I looked out the open doors, keeping an eye out for Wilde. Decker shifted his gaze outside briefly before turning back to me. "What happened?"

"Some asshole came at me with a bat. I'm pretty sure he wanted to break my legs."

"But you're okay?"

"I'm fine, but I don't think I'm supposed to be. He meant business. He didn't expect me to duck and cover. How do you want to play this?"

Decker worked his jaw, lost in thought. Without elaborating, he unhooked the strap holding me against the board. "Follow my lead. Do you think you can remember to limp?"

"I can do more than that." Standing, I looked down at the ankle the bat had come into contact with, but there was no obvious swelling or bruising. Without missing a beat, I kicked my foot sideways into the metal support, biting my lip and hissing. That would definitely bruise. With any luck, it might even swell. Jace's eyes flashed to mine, but he didn't say a word. His look said more than enough. "I might need to borrow a shoulder."

He nodded, stepping out of the rig and offering me a hand down. The EMT protested, but I waved his words away. I leaned against Jace's shoulder as we crossed the parking lot to join the group.

"Alex," Lowery said, "I'm sorry this happened. Is there anything we can do?"

"Can I have the night off?"

"Of course. If you need a couple of days, let us know. Whatever we can do."

The owner nodded, promising to help the police apprehend this asshole. The officers followed him inside to get the security tapes from the parking lot, and Lowery disappeared to tell the others not to postpone rehearsal on my account. Dylan looked at me uncertainly and offered to grab my belongings from the dressing room.

"Alice," Tim brushed a strand of hair away from my face, studying the way I favored my right side and leaned against Jace, "you should be at the hospital. Are you hurt?" He looked down, assessing my swelling ankle. "This could be serious. It could be broken."

"I don't have health insurance, and even with this job, I'm barely making ends meet. I can't afford the emergency room."

"I told her about that free clinic in the city. It's where I went when I dislocated my shoulder." Jace shifted his arm to support some of my weight. "I think she needs x-rays."

Tim nodded. "Alex," he soothed, crouching down a little so we were at eye level, "I know you and Jace didn't actually get off on the right foot, no pun intended, but he'll give you a ride to the clinic. I'd take you myself, but I'm leading a group tonight." My gaze had dropped to the ground, and he lifted my chin and stared into my eyes. "Is that okay?"

I nodded.

"Do you need my car?" Tim asked, shifting his focus to Jace.

"Alex said I can take hers," Jace replied.

Wincing, I closed my eyes and inhaled slowly. "Why is it you show up every time I'm in trouble?"

Tim smiled. "Perhaps I'm being sent where I'm needed, or it's serendipitous." Dylan returned with my belongings, and I pulled my keys out of my purse and handed them to Jace. "Everything will be okay, Alex. You just have to believe it," Tim insisted.

"We should go." Jace eyed Tim. "Shit. I'm leaving you in the lurch tonight."

"Don't worry about it. This is more important." Tim squeezed my hand. "I'll pray everything goes well."

Once we were out of earshot and away from the mark, Jace whispered in my ear, "Tell me you didn't really break your ankle for Tim's benefit."

"Let's hope my bones aren't that brittle."

He helped me into the car, waved to Tim and Dylan, and got behind the wheel. Once we were out of the parking lot and back on the interstate, I shifted in the seat.

"Don't you think it was incredibly convenient Wilde showed up a few minutes after the attack?"

Jace looked at me from the corner of his eye. "Not when he orchestrated it." He reached into his pocket and withdrew a burner phone. Dialing a number, he put the phone on speaker and stuck it in the cup holder. "Matt, the police just responded to an assault. They have a description of the assailant, but to save time here's what we know." He looked at me, and I repeated everything for Agent Eckhardt. "Find this guy and put him on ice. I'm positive Wilde put him up to this. We need to solidify that connection."

"No problem. Are you okay?" Eckhardt asked.

"We're fine. Patch me through to Eve." A moment later, she came on the line. "Hey, I need you to create a phony medical report for Alex. She has trauma to her left ankle. Come up with some diagnosis that will keep her from dancing for the next few weeks but isn't serious enough to require a cast or anything like that."

"Bone bruise it is," Eve said. "No dancing for the next month or two and strict adherence to RICE. Any particular medical office you want these records to originate?"

"Do you remember that free clinic we used as a drop?" Jace asked. "That's what we want."

"I'll get right on it. Are you on your way back?"

"Yep."

"In that case, you owe me a hundred bucks, Alex," Eve teased, disconnecting.

Jace gave me a confused look, but I didn't bother supplying an answer. It was pointless. We had more important things to discuss, and now that I had the boss all to myself, I wasn't entirely sure where to start.

"Did you know ahead of time this was going to happen?" I asked. "You were distracted during our briefing. You said Wilde would do something to further ingratiate Lexington to him. Did you know?"

"I wouldn't do that to anyone on my team." He turned and gave me a look. "Was that a serious question?"

"You're the shrink. Shouldn't you be able to tell? You had no problem ripping me wide open during our initial meeting. What changed?"

He gripped the wheel harder, rolling his shoulders back.

"You're angry because you were targeted."

"No, I'm annoyed because you knew something was up, you didn't share it with any of us, and even now, you still won't say why your panties are in a bunch." I sighed. "Believe me when I say that I get it. I get being a lone wolf, changing the play as you go and rolling with the punches. I also know it's hard to trust an outsider. But I've been here for a month. I'm not going away, and after what just happened, things are about to get serious real fast. So either tag me in or cut me loose. It's your choice."

"That's not it. It's not about trust or being a glory hog. Wilde has classic hero syndrome. He creates these situations in order to come to the rescue. Personality wise, I can tell when he's planning something, but I never know what it is. I didn't know he was targeting you. It's too soon, like he's desperate. I don't like it, but without any proof, I don't want to put the others on edge because they'll react differently if they expect something. That could compromise the op."

"You seem to forget you're not the only one in the field."

"You were on the periphery. I didn't expect this. Honestly, I feared another body would pop up." He inhaled deeply. "I hate not having any proof, just these gut feelings. It makes me crazy."

"Apparently, it's catching." I offered a smile and leaned back against the seat.

"I can tell. I don't know anyone who would make an injury seem that convincing. You're hardcore."

Flashing back to the look he gave me when I did it, I couldn't help but reassess what I saw in his eyes at that moment. "Do I scare you?"

"Your reasoning might."

"You'd do the same to nail this bastard."

"I've been at this for nine months. It's different."

"Maybe it isn't."

"We'll see."

TWELVE

"I need to tell Tim we're back," Jace announced when we entered my cover apartment.

"Have you always been his bitch?"

Jace snorted, running a hand through his shaggy surfer hair. "Pretty much. I did mention he has a savior complex, right?"

"I thought it was hero syndrome."

"Both, really." He pulled another phone from his pocket and dialed. After exchanging a few words, updating Tim on my health status, and attempting to voice a protest that didn't seem to go anywhere, he hung up. "Tim instructed me to stay here and take care of you."

"Wasn't that sweet? Do you think he's on to us?"

"Not a chance in hell. This is what he does. If he can't be somewhere, he sends one of his disciples to do it."

"Okay, Judas, you better do what you're told, but fair warning, I'm not much for being taken care of."

"Unfortunately, I don't have a choice. Tim said he'd call later and let me know when he can pick me up. He likes people to depend on him. It makes him feel powerful, needed, in control." Jace surveyed the cover apartment. It remained in an eerily similar state to when I first arrived. "You're careful. That's good. I take it you have your gun and ID hidden somewhere safe."

"Underneath the grate in the fireplace. The gas has been disconnected, so I figured there wasn't much chance it would burn to smithereens."

He nodded, not really listening to what I had to say.

"I'm gonna get cleaned up. Make yourself at home," I insisted.

Grabbing a pair of jeans and a t-shirt, I ducked into the bathroom. Stripping out of my grimy clothes, I turned in the mirror to see the swollen bruise that fell almost perfectly in line with the bottom of my left shoulder blade. That bastard with the bat needed to learn some manners. It wasn't nice to hit a woman. Eckhardt better find him and teach him as much, or I would.

After a quick shower, I returned to the kitchen. "What are you doing?" I asked, horrified at the sight of my full trash can.

Jace spun to face me. "You can't eat this shit. I just phoned in a grocery delivery. It'll be here soon."

"But that was my dinner." I pointed to the trash, fighting back memories of Martin and his obsession with cooking. "I didn't come to your house and throw out your dinner. By the way, where do you even live?"

"In a trailer on Wilde's property." The disgust on his face kept me from asking additional questions. "It's the best place to monitor our surveillance feeds after everyone goes to bed. It also keeps me close to the target, but it can be a little too close for comfort sometimes." He dropped his voice, closing the fridge door. "When the latest body was discovered, I wanted to storm across the lot and beat a confession out of him."

"But you didn't."

"Not yet." He rubbed a hand down his face. This op was weighing on him, more so today than I'd ever seen.

"Why do you hate takeout?" I asked, sifting through the containers at the top of the pile and contemplating whether anything could be salvaged.

"A couple years back I was sent to infiltrate some low-level dealers in a crackhouse. It was a poor area, and it was a shit job. No fancy cover apartment. No nothing. We slept on the streets and ate fast food for every meal. Occasionally, the food came from inside a dumpster." He cringed. "Now the only time I can stomach that shit is when the situation absolutely calls for it. I'm all about fresh foods."

"I get it." I pushed past him and opened the freezer, glad to see he hadn't cleaned that out yet. Removing an ice pack, I checked to make sure there was nothing inside that I really wanted and left the door open. "Have at it."

He looked inside, finding nothing offensive, and closed the door. "Does your ankle hurt?"

"No," I went to the couch, pressing the ice against my shoulder blade before leaning back, "but I'll have to wrap it before Tim arrives to make our story convincing."

"What's wrong with your back?"

"Nothing." I gave him my best *drop it* look, but he didn't seem to catch on. "That jerk took a practice swing before trying to kneecap me. Frankly, he should have gone straight for my legs. Amateur."

"How bad is it?" He closed the distance between us and reached for the hem of my shirt. "You should have said something when we were back at ops. We have a medical team on standby."

I slapped his hand away with more ferocity than was necessary. "It's fine."

He held up his hands. "Okay. I'm sorry. That was inappropriate. I just wanted to help." He took a seat across from me. "To answer your earlier question, Alex, I can't read you. Today proved that I have no idea what you're thinking or how you'll react. Case in point. But I'm also under the impression you don't know what to expect from me either."

"We're barely acquainted. We haven't exactly had much time to bond, unless you think twenty minutes once a week is supposed to provide great insight into how we function."

He checked his watch. "I don't know how long we'll have, but it's about time we rectify this situation. Do you play poker?"

I nodded.

"Get the cards. I could use a break from Jason Ellis for a

few minutes." He offered a friendly smile, reached into his pocket, and pulled out a handful of change, dividing it up on the coffee table. "Each coin is worth one question."

"Are you insane?"

"You have to win in order to ask that. Plus, it'll give us a chance to get to know each other's tells, how we bluff, how we think. It's a twofer. The only rule is the questions have to be personal. Asking about facts of the case won't help us bond."

I wasn't convinced, but I didn't have anything better to do with the rest of my evening, and if it put Jace in a better mood, it might be worth it. "Fine, but we're not playing strip poker."

"Damn, you're still hung up on trying to get me in bed, aren't you?"

"You're not my type." I swallowed the pang of loneliness and guilt and went to find some playing cards.

"Who is?" he asked, and I turned with a glare. "Right, I have to win a hand before I can ask."

I returned with the cards and settled on the floor, leaning against the couch with the ice wedged in the middle. Jace took the cards, shuffled, and dealt. Then he slid a stack of coins in front of me.

"Ante up."

Somewhere between that first hand, the arrival of the groceries, and Jace tossing together a large salad and broiling up some tuna steaks, we managed to break the ice. He might have been the first person I'd ever been partnered with that didn't drive me crazy. He didn't seem to be overly macho or competitive, and he wasn't a know-it-all, even though he knew a hell of a lot. Despite our initial interactions, his default setting was laidback. He was professional and serious when it came to work, and he didn't want anything to jeopardize the operation. But he didn't seem the type to micromanage either. He trusted his team to do what they did best.

He was single. No wife, no kids, and no permanent ties. That's why he didn't have a problem volunteering for these operations. The team was his family. After working extensively with addicts in rehab, he wanted to take a more proactive approach and applied for a position in drug enforcement. He'd lost one too many patients to overdoses to sit back and wait for it to happen again.

"Why are you here?" He held up a coin and placed it in the center of the table. "And don't feed me that line of bull about your partner transferring."

"Lucca did transfer."

"But that's not why you traveled three thousand miles to work a case you barely knew anything about. How could you just uproot like that? Didn't you leave behind family and friends?"

"You're allowed one question. I believe it was asked and answered."

"And I believe you don't want to talk about this."

I touched my finger to my nose and pointed at him. "Brilliant observation."

"Why not?" He lifted another coin off his stack of winnings and put it in the center of the table. "Did someone break your heart?" He added another coin to the pile.

"Jace, I don't want to talk about this. It has no bearing on who I am or how I work. It has nothing to do with anything."

He held up his hands and leaned back. "Okay. Does it have anything to do with why you were so willing to bust your ankle?"

"Oh my god, it barely even hurt. And since Tim's behind the attack, he needs to believe his thug was successful. If not, he'd just have him try again." My rationale was sound. There was no reason for Jace to question it.

"What are you going to do when he decides he wants to sleep with you or if he lays out a line of blow and hands you a rolled up hundred? How far are you willing to go? Do you know where the line is?"

I knew exactly where the line was. I'd crossed it, and it cost me almost everything. "I don't sleep with marks. I never have, and I sure as hell never will. I've worked drug cases before. I have no desire to use. I don't give a shit if the DEA allows it or not. I won't do it. I was dosed once. That was a horrible experience. As it is, I barely drink.

Another bad experience." I snorted. "My life is mostly bad experiences, so something stupid like taking a few punches or getting a couple of bruises to sell a story isn't a big deal."

He picked up another chip and tossed it into the middle of the table. "What's the worst case you worked?"

"I can't answer that. I honestly don't know. Ask me something else."

He was almost out of coins. I had already used all of mine, but that part of the game had been a lot more fun. I liked asking questions, not providing answers.

"Why'd you freak when I tried to look at your back?"

"Knee-jerk reaction."

He remained silent while the wheels in his head turned over all the things he'd recently learned about me. "Did you come here to escape an abusive relationship?" He pushed the rest of his winnings into the center of the table.

I burst into laughter. "No. He would never hurt me, not like that." Quickly sobering, I got lost in my own thoughts. "I don't even think it was intentional. He just created the distance as a last-ditch effort at self-preservation. It was like a page out of my playbook."

"Did he cheat on you?"

"No."

"Did you cheat on him?"

I stared at Decker. "I said we weren't talking about this. And no, I didn't cheat on him. I lied to him as a way of protecting him. Work happened, shit got real, and I made him get out of Dodge with the promise I would meet him."

"But you didn't."

"No. I needed him safe, so I could stay behind and handle the situation."

"Is he an agent?" Jace asked, and I shook my head "Prosecutor?"

"No."

"Tell me he isn't a defense attorney."

"Do I strike you as insane?"

He cocked his head to the side, clearly enjoying the twenty questions even though I was still trying to figure out why we were having this conversation when I kept insisting we weren't discussing what led to my relocation. "Local police?"

"No."

"Military?"

I blinked a few times, wondering why Jace was jumping to those conclusions. Agent, lawyer, and cop made sense. Those were the people I interacted with on a daily basis, but military wasn't. "Why would you think that?"

"You have a tough job. Whoever you'd be involved with would need to possess similar skills just to understand what we go through."

I laughed cynically. "And that my dear headshrinker is precisely why we're not together anymore."

"So he's a civilian? That complicates things. Medical professional?"

"I hate doctors, Ph.D.s included. And you ran out of coins a while ago." I looked at the clock, wondering what was taking Tim so long. Shouldn't he have phoned to say he was on his way by now?

"You still love him." Jace gathered up the cards and put them into the box. "You shouldn't be here. You should be at home, sorting things out."

"I'm where I need to be. He has to move on, and the only way that's going to happen is if I'm not around. He doesn't trust me. He threw me out." I blinked back my emotions. "He didn't speak to me for a month, and when he did, everything was different. He deserves someone who fits into his world and doesn't complicate things."

"What do you deserve?" Jace asked, his blue eyes boring into mine.

"I already got what I deserve."

THIRTEEN

Wilde never showed up last night, so Jace had to crash on the couch. I couldn't help but think we'd been compromised. Tim made a move against me, and the paranoid part of my mind decided it was to test my reaction. A woman with a privileged upbringing who fell on hard times certainly wouldn't react the same as a seasoned federal agent. I didn't run or scream or cry. Okay, I screamed for help, and then I circled the enemy. Thankfully, my firearm had been inside the restaurant, or things would have gone a lot differently. I'd probably be on a plane by now.

Rolling onto my back, I hissed. The blow from the bat had done some damage. I wondered if I had a fractured rib. It wouldn't be the first time, but it would make life more annoying than necessary.

The sounds of the blender working in the kitchen indicated my guest was awake, which meant I should get up so we could revisit the facts of yesterday before Wilde arrived. I didn't know when Jace and I would get another chance to discuss these things outside our weekly briefings, so now was as good a time as any. Yesterday, he'd been moody and useless on the Wilde front. Hopefully, he had his head on straight today. Getting up, I pulled on the same jeans and t-shirt from the night before and went into the kitchen.

"How'd you sleep?" I asked, noticing it was barely eight a.m.

Jace turned and smiled. He was a food snob and a morning person. The universe was having fun at my expense. "It's the first night I slept soundly in six months. I tend to monitor the surveillance feeds even though there are techs back at ops doing the same thing. I'll wake up several times just to make sure the signal is being transmitted and nothing's going on. It's stupid, but I can't stop myself." He scooted a glass filled with a thick, green concoction over. "You look like you could use this."

"I must look like shit. What is it?"

"A green smoothie."

"Y'know, I'm not color blind." Picking it up, I gave it a sniff. "What's in it?"

"Some fruits and vegetables blended together. Drink up. It's good for you."

Giving it a tentative sip, I was surprised it didn't taste the way it looked, which was a relief. Putting the glass down, I shrugged, wincing at the movement. Jace noticed but didn't comment. At least he was a fast learner.

"We didn't spend much time talking about Wilde or the case last night, but I have questions. Lots of them."

"Go ahead."

"Should we be worried Tim never came to get you?" I asked.

Jace shook his head, downing most of his smoothie in a single gulp while he removed some breakfast steaks from the fridge. "We're fine. The situation hasn't changed. I suspect Tim's trying to force us to like each other. He often says I should go with him to see your performances or make an effort to say hi when you drop by the commune on the weekends. It's imperative that you have close ties to those in his cult. That's how he lures in his members."

"Why does he want you to be a one man welcome wagon? He has two dozen followers. I've spoken to several who sell goods on the weekends. They've all been friendly, but no one's asked if I want to grab a coffee or anything. What makes you so special?"

"It's not me. It's you." Jace diced some vegetables, tossed them into the skillet with the steaks, and added some seasoning. "You didn't seek out the commune, and you've demonstrated skepticism in regards to his religious order."

"Should I have not done that?"

"Actually, that was smart. Your distrust is genuine. It's real, and he might have picked up on the deception. This way, you don't have to convince him to let you in. Instead, he has to convince you that you want to join. It turned the tables."

"And solidifies my cover."

"Precisely, and since I came to him desperate, alone, and in need of serious help, I'm the ideal candidate to woo you to the dark side. Plus, he treats me like a younger brother. He trusts me to serve his interests."

Jace's back story was simple. He'd gone through foster care, like Wilde, and when he turned eighteen, he had to find a way to fend for himself. He worked odd jobs, scraped together what he could to survive, but ultimately ended up on the streets. He was a drifter, searching for a place to sleep and something to eat. He was a nomad, traveling all along the Pacific coast for a decade until he happened upon the commune. Wilde secured him a job at a gas station and helped him with the down payment on the trailer and let him park it on the property, effectively putting Jace forever in his debt.

"Why doesn't he bring you in on whatever's really going on inside that place?" I asked.

"I don't know. He has control issues. Perhaps that's part of it."

"Or he doesn't trust you completely. Sure, your cover story makes you a kindred spirit, but it's not like you saved his life or took the rap for a crime he committed."

"There's one other thing you're forgetting. Not to sound sexist, but his flock is predominantly female. His victims are women. My gender makes me a potential threat. He could perceive me as competition. Another cock in the henhouse."

"If that's the case, why would he let you spend the night in my apartment?"

"Aside from the obvious fact that Alice has never been one of Jason's fans, perhaps he thinks your dislike of me would keep you from joining his cult and handing over your trust fund. He needs you to be comfortable with everyone, particularly when he wants to bring you into the fold and isolate you from the outside world. The attack yesterday is the first step in doing that. Now that you can't work, you'll be removed from outside influences and face additional financial hardships which should result in dire circumstances." The burner phone rang, and he checked the display. "Or maybe he just wanted me out of his hair in order to take care of business."

"Who is it?" I asked

"Matt." Answering the call, Jace listened for several minutes, not providing any hint what was happening. "Okay, find out what you can. We need to be certain it's the same guy. Use our connection with the LAPD, and make sure you update and forward the reports to Alex's handler. If they think it's necessary, the FBI will step in and get us answers faster. They might be able to put a rush on things, despite the backlog." He hung up, deleting the call from the phone before tucking it back into his pocket. "Based on the description you provided yesterday, Matt believes they found the man who assaulted you. He was killed in East L.A. late last night. It looks like a gang hit, but he didn't have any known gang affiliation. It would appear to be a random act of violence, except his car was found a hundred and fifty miles in the opposite direction, abandoned on the side of the road."

"Shit." I got up to pace. "That must be why Wilde was too busy to stop by. There has to be evidence linking him to the deceased. A ride like that would have taken all night. Wasn't he leading a group? Someone must have seen him leave."

"Surveillance places him at the commune last night. All night. We spotted him when he arrived, and he didn't leave again."

"What if there's another way off the property? Have you pinged his phone? If he placed any calls during the night, they would have bounced off different cell towers. We can use that to prove he wasn't home. We might be able to put him at the scene of the murder."

"Stella's working on it, but we have no proof. I don't think we'll get a court order for his phone records." Jace took the skillet off the stove. "Dammit." He slammed it down on the counter.

"Call Wilde," I urged. "Perhaps he'll let something slip if you catch him off guard."

"He has morning meals now. He'll phone afterward. I know it." He licked his lips, frustrated with the circumstances. "This shit keeps happening, and every time, it's just another fucking dead end. I know he's behind it, but I have absolutely no way of proving it. I don't expect this to be any different."

"It is different. You have me this time." I grabbed a sheet of paper and a pen and jotted down some notes. "Since Alice is going to be laid up, I can use the downtime to get on top of this murder. Barring the possibility it's not the same guy or it really was just a coincidence, there has to be something to find." I met his eyes. "I'll find it. I'm part bloodhound." He didn't seem convinced, so I gave him a playful wink. "That's why I'm such a bitch."

Rewarding me with a half-smile, he pulled some plates from the cupboard and put them on the table. "Guess we might as well eat."

He didn't say another word while he shoveled the food into his mouth, not tasting any of it. He was annoyed another murder occurred on his watch, and our plan might have been the impetus for some schmuck's death. He never voiced it, and I chose not to think about it. My conscience was already overloaded.

Once Wilde collected Jace, I'd be able to get to work. Even if this was my cover apartment, it allowed a modicum of privacy. The DEA had it swept for bugs every week, so I knew it was clean. As long as I was discreet and covered my tracks, I'd be able to research the case, contact Eckhardt for the latest updates, and run everything by Mark.

Whatever I couldn't access, he could. Maybe this wasn't a hundred kilos of coke or a dead drug mule. But murder was a heinous crime, and this asshole crossed state lines when he abandoned the car, making it a federal matter. Since he wanted to take the game onto my home court, he'd get schooled.

The phone chimed, and Jace glanced down at the message. "Tim's on his way. You better get ready."

I left the table, wrapped my ankle, brought a few extra pillows into the living room, and grabbed the ice pack out of the freezer. Then I hid my notes inside the fireplace grate and gave the place a quick check.

"You need to mention your stay here is temporary. The lawyers are concerned they have to sell off assets to pay the remaining debt before you stand to regain access to your trust fund." Jace gave me a pointed look. "Now's as good a time as any to clue Tim in on this fact. Remember, you're having a shitty day. You're scared. You're hurt. And you're pissed."

"Sounds like most days. But you don't want me to oversell it. If I do, how can Tim be sure I'll inherit anything? Perhaps luring me in is a waste of time."

"Don't worry about that. I know Tim. He's done his research. Ben planted enough evidence to make your win in court obvious to even a layperson. It's just a waiting game until your assets are unfrozen, which gives Tim a limited window of opportunity to swoop in and save the day. At the end of the month, you'll be evicted. Without any income, you won't be able to get another apartment in the meantime."

"And without liquid assets, I can't exactly move into a hotel for the long haul."

"Precisely. Everything will change once you're at the commune full time. Enjoy the freedom while you have it."

"I plan to use my remaining time to build our case against him."

"Good luck with that."

Before I could say anything else, the doorman buzzed to tell me there was a visitor. After giving permission for Tim to come upstairs, I took a seat on the sofa and propped my foot up on the pillows, dropping the ice on top. Jace put the dishes in the sink and opened the door as soon as Tim knocked. He gestured our mark inside, plastering a pleasant smile on his face, even though he wanted to kill him.

"Good morning," Tim greeted, friendly warmth seeping out of every pore of his body. "Are things looking brighter today?"

I rolled my eyes. "Definitely not." After spending a few minutes bitching about the doctor mandated break from dancing, I moved on to the talking points Jace and I had just finished discussing, concluding with a rambling list of Alice's growing fears. "I can't even think where I can go. I'll have to start looking soon, but I don't even know if I want to be here. It doesn't seem safe, not after everything that happened yesterday. I was attacked in broad daylight in the parking lot of a family restaurant. How screwed up is that? What if that guy comes back? What if they never catch him? I just don't know."

"Don't be afraid." Tim sat next to me. "The police will find him. I'm sure of it. Everyone at the restaurant is on the lookout. I told my friends about it. If anyone sees anything suspicious, they'll report it." He glanced at Jace before turning back to me. "I'm sorry we inconvenienced you last night. I just couldn't get away, but I thought you might be comforted to have a friendly face nearby in case you needed anything."

"We had fun," I said. "Jace made dinner, and we played cards. He even got up early and made breakfast. He's done a lot." I smiled at him. "Thank you."

Jace ran a hand through his hair. "Anyone would have done the same thing. It's no biggie."

Tim looked around the room. "This is a really nice place. I'm sure the money issues will be straightened out soon. Have faith." Abruptly, he stood. "We should get going, but I want you to promise me something, Alex." He waited until I met his eyes before continuing. "If you need anything at all or you start to feel overwhelmed or scared, you'll call me. Okay?"

"I will."

"Good." Tim squeezed my shoulder, and I fought to keep the cringe off my face. "Are you sure you'll be okay on your own?"

"I'll manage."

Jace cleared his throat. "I'll make sure to drop by in a few days to check on you."

"We both will." Tim went to the door, ushering Jace out ahead of him and giving me a final goodbye wave. He was an exceptional con man. Too bad we were on to him.

FOURTEEN

"I can't be completely certain, unless you put a Zorro mask on the corpse, but he looks like the man who assaulted me." I zeroed in on the photograph of the abandoned vehicle. It had been stripped, but it looked like the same car I'd seen the previous afternoon. "Who was he?"

"Vincent Harbring." Eckhardt read the name and address off the man's driver's license. "It looks like he resided south of here, much closer to the border, but not so far that it would be out of the question for him and Wilde to have crossed paths."

"Do we know that they crossed paths?" I asked, and Eckhardt turned to Ben.

Ben clicked away at a couple of keys, sending previous addresses and employment history to the big screen. He overlapped that with what we knew about Timothy Wilde, but there wasn't an obvious connection. That would have been too simple.

"What about Harbring's connection to the restaurant?" Eve asked. "From what we've gathered since Alex's arrival, Wilde's chummy with the owner. Plus, it's one of the only places he frequents in town."

"Maybe he's buddies with the choreographer too," I

said.

Eve shook her head. "That's doubtful. He has to know someone in management, if not you wouldn't have gotten any type of job. Wilde wanted you to get it, probably to see if the miracle would be enough to lead you to his commune." She narrowed her eyes at the screen and clicked a few more keys. "When that didn't happen, he moved on to plan B."

Stella made a tsk sound, shuffling through some paperwork. "The LAPD is investigating the shooting, but an eyewitness said it was a gang hit. Unless we can prove otherwise, we can't expand the scope of the investigation to include Wilde. If anything, our surveillance provides him with an airtight alibi."

"What about one of his disciples?" I asked. Decker's words echoed through my mind. "They'd do anything for him. Perhaps he sent one of them to take care of Harbring."

Eckhardt let out a groan. "Why do it? The man wore a mask. You can't be certain of his identity, and from what you said, Tim basically promised you that your attacker would be apprehended. Killing Harbring doesn't serve a purpose."

"You don't think Wilde was afraid Harbring would squeal if he was arrested?" Carlo asked. "Parker's description was spot-on. Wilde never would have expected that type of recollection. Maybe he panicked and cut his losses."

I let my eyes skim across the images and words until they became a blur. "Harbring has no known connection to the commune. That means he has to be part of Wilde's illegal dealings, assuming non-cult members are involved. This random, seemingly unconnected murder has to lead to something."

Stella let out a hum. "There is another possibility here."

"Don't say it," Eckhardt warned.

She ignored him, crossing the room to stand in front of us. "Harbring's death might be unrelated. It could have been a gang initiation." She pointed at the photo of the cars. "We've seen this before. Cars get jacked, driven across county or state lines, dumped, and stripped. Harbring might have been in the wrong place at the wrong time." She offered me an apologetic look. "You admitted that you aren't even certain it's the same man."

Letting the words roll off my back, I shrugged away the frustration. "Okay, say you're right, we should at least determine what brought Vincent Harbring to that neighborhood at that time of night. He didn't live there. He was far from home and in a bad part of town. He was up to something. Maybe he was looking to score or looking to deal. If your assumptions about Wilde's involvement in the drug trade are accurate, that's where you need to look." The DEA agents exchanged a few glances, making me acutely aware that I wasn't in charge. I didn't mean to take over. It just happened. "I'll get out of your hair and phone Jablonsky. If the local field office knows anything, I'll pass it along."

Eckhardt checked his watch. "Keep track of the time. You don't want to look suspicious if Wilde shows up at your place unannounced."

"Wouldn't Jace tip us off?"

"You have to keep in mind his cover has a day job, courtesy of Tim. We have surveillance on the commune, but if Tim leaves, we aren't always able to track him."

I continued out of the command center and made my way to the tiny space the DEA had been kind enough to provide for my use. Based on the dimensions, I had a feeling it had originally been a walk-in closet or a pantry, but I'd been in tighter spots. Lifting the landline, I dialed Jablonsky's office number and waited. Silently cheering when he answered, saving me from having to leave an awkward voicemail message, I filled him in on the last twenty-four hours. He'd already been read in by the DEA and had started tracking leads on his own.

"How are you holding up?" he asked.

"I'm starting to have doubts. Decker's been under nine months and has nothing to show for it. Why hasn't the op been scrapped? How is it they still have active warrants to surveil the commune?"

"Bodies are turning up. The obvious motive is drug

trafficking. Keep in mind the dead drug mules were part of Wilde's following at one point or another. He's the common thread, or that church is."

"It isn't a church. Not really. It's more like a women's shelter that has a weekly bake sale."

"You'll fit right in," Mark teased. "What's next? Cooking classes?"

"No." I didn't find his routine amusing. "The next play will be moving out of the cover apartment and onto Wilde's property."

"Just make sure you don't become his property."

"No shit." My mind chased after a few possibilities concerning the DEA's lack of progress and the dead body. "You've taught me to never believe in coincidences, so I'm having issues understanding why Vincent Harbring was killed. He looks like the guy who assaulted me, but with a mask, a positive ID is impossible."

"What about prints? Did he touch anything?"

"Just the bat, and he took it with him."

Mark's drawer slammed. "I'll see what turns up. In the meantime, keep your head on a swivel. This time, it was a bat in broad daylight. Next time, it could be a gun in the dead of night."

"Aren't you a ray of sunshine?"

"Parker, you're in southern California. You should be sick of sunshine by now. Don't turn into some West Coast hippie."

"I did drink a green smoothie this morning."

"I'm hanging up now. I'll let you know what I find."

After flipping through my notes and rereading the files I'd pulled concerning the previous victims, the cause of death, and evidence found at the crime scene, I was no closer to a solution than when I started. Wilde was meticulous. He was careful, and above all, he knew how to manipulate everyone and everything around him. That's how he gained a following and eluded the authorities. He probably tricked Harbring into committing the attack and then convinced him to make a delivery to that neighborhood, knowing what would happen. Perhaps he didn't have to orchestrate the hit.

Leaving the cramped office, I went back to the command center. "How many gangs operate within the vicinity?"

"Too many to count." Eve looked up from the analysis she was conducting. "We're considering that possibility as motive for the murder. Right now, your focus should be on determining Tim's connection to Harbring and how they communicated. We've run through Harbring's phone records. Nothing traces back to Tim. E-mail and internet history will take some time, but I'm guessing Tim's too clever to risk leaving a trail." She looked pointedly at the clock, as if to remind me of Eckhardt's earlier warning.

"I'm out of here. I have the burner you provided, so if you discover anything new or valid, let me know." I went out the door, almost making it to the exit before being stopped by one of the medics. "Blood draw or piss in a cup?" I asked.

He smiled good-naturedly. "Given the attack yesterday, the assistant director believes a needle stick can be easily explained if necessary. Is that a problem?"

"I'm not overly fond of needles, but it's not like I have a choice." I followed him back to the lab for the mandatory drug testing and asked for a quick check on my shoulder. Thankfully, nothing was broken, just bruised and tender. "I'll see you in two weeks."

By the time I made it back to the apartment, it was dusk. The streetlamps hadn't turned on yet, but they would any minute. I had to take a different vehicle to and from HQ since Alice wasn't supposed to be driving yet. I parked the nondescript sedan in a public garage several blocks away. Remembering to walk with a limp, I maintained a steady gait, not seeing much foot traffic around town. Cars drove past or idled at the stoplights, but not many people were hoofing it.

Crossing the street, I could see the high-rise apartment building looming at the end of the block. It was taller than the other buildings with a much more ostentatious architectural design. Even the buildings screamed out notice me. Rolling my eyes at the completely different approach to life, I continued toward home.

Passing an alleyway, I heard something rustling around near the dumpster. I slowed my progress, gripping my purse tightly in one hand. It contained my firearm, but before I could unzip the bag, a raccoon darted out of the trash. I took a deep breath, acknowledging that I was on the brink of paranoia, and continued past the opening. A few steps later, I felt a presence. The sound of footsteps urged me to turn around. Just as I began to turn, a masked man grabbed me by the shoulders and threw me against the wall.

He wore the same mask as the man from yesterday, but he was taller. It wasn't the same guy. Those thoughts delayed my actions, giving him time to stomp down on my ankle. I grunted and kneed him in the balls. Bringing my interlaced fists down on his slumped shoulders, I hoped he'd drop, but he didn't go down. Instead, he crawled backward, recovering from the hit to the groin, and pulled a telescopic baton from his pocket. Extending it with a quick flick of the wrist, he swung. I dove to the side. This guy wasn't aiming for my kneecaps. He planned to take me out.

Ducking beneath the next swing, I charged forward, ramming him in the stomach with my shoulder. The advantage for being that close meant his range of motion was limited. I attempted to subdue him with a proper hold, but he knocked me away before I could get my arms around him. He swung again, the steel glancing off my forearm and sending painful tingles through the limb.

A second blow landed against my side with enough force to knock me to the ground. He continued to attack, and I released a loud, shrill scream. His eyes darted around, checking that help wasn't on the way. I swept his legs out from under him with a well-placed kick. He sprawled backward, and I climbed to my feet and unzipped my purse.

I'd just gotten my hand around my gun when the doorman rushed toward us, his cell phone pressed to his ear. Building security was at his heels, and the assailant scrambled to his feet, darting into the street and getting clipped by a nearby car. The man rolled back onto the pavement, and the two security guards surrounded him while the doorman spoke to the 9-1-1 operator.

During the commotion, I tucked the gun back inside my bag. This wasn't the man from yesterday, despite the mask and similar clothing. This guy was taller and thinner. He didn't come in a vehicle. He had no quick escape route planned. Unlike his counterpart from yesterday, this guy easily surrendered. However, his attack was meant to cause maximum damage. His lurking outside my apartment building provided no comfort.

Wilde's words came back to me, and I couldn't help but think this was some patsy he had found to take the fall for yesterday. Tim wanted me incapacitated so I'd have to stick around. He also wanted to make sure my temporary home didn't feel safe. He'd accomplished his mission.

"Miss Lexington, are you okay?" the doorman asked. "The police are on the way. Do you need an ambulance?" He looked at the large welt on my arm, the only visible sign of the attack.

"No," I stared at the guy who was on the ground, clutching his side, "but he does."

Moving a few feet closer, I glared down at him. "Who are you?"

He didn't say a word.

One of the security guards glanced up at me. "I'm sure the cops will figure that out. Why don't you wait in the lobby? We'll keep an eye on him and make sure he doesn't get away."

"This way." The doorman held out his hand as if to usher me back to civility. "I heard about the assault that occurred yesterday from Mr. Wilde when he dropped by earlier. I can't believe the same punk came back to try again."

"Who said it's the same guy?"

"I'm sorry, ma'am. I just thought it had to be. Muggings happen, but normally, not right outside our door. I figured he must have been someone you knew, like an ex or a stalker."

"Great, now I'm being stalked."

"No. That's not what I meant. I didn't mean to imply—"

"It's okay. You're probably right. I don't know who this guy is, but he attacked me at work and now at home. He must know things about me." I took a seat on the oversized couch in the lobby. "It must be the same guy." Despite my words, I knew it wasn't. However, the police and Tim would try to convince me otherwise. I might as well get ahead of the game and buy into that theory. The only real questions on my mind were who was this new guy and how could Tim be certain that throwing him to the wolves wouldn't bite him in the ass.

FIFTEEN

After the commotion downstairs, I was glad to be in the privacy of the apartment. There wasn't much I could do. I had to stay in for the night, but there were things that needed to be done. First, I phoned Eckhardt and updated him. He would keep abreast of the situation and see what he could find. He offered to have agents sit on the apartment, but that was too risky. I could handle myself. Next, I did the only logical thing that Alice Lexington would do. I called Tim. Making my breath shallow and rapid so my voice sounded frantic, I told him about the second attack.

"Calm down. Take some deep breaths. In and out. Where are you?"

"I'm home. I'm okay, but he was here. At my house." Panic was an appropriate response, and I decided to stick with it. "How did he know where I lived? Who is he? I didn't recognize him. The cops took off his mask, but I've never seen him before. They said his name was Anton Shrieves, but I don't know anyone named Anton. I just...I...I need to get away from this place. It's cursed. This apartment. That shitty job. All of it. I need to go. I want my old life back."

"Shh. I hear what you're saying, and I completely understand. But you're upset and shaken. Making life-changing decisions right now isn't a good idea."

"No, it's a great idea." I opened and closed some drawers loud enough that he'd hear it through the phone. "I need to pack."

"Alex, right now, you're safe. You're in your apartment. The building has excellent security which is on high alert. For the moment, you should stay where you are. In the morning, after you sleep on it, if you're still adamant about leaving, we will help you pack."

"I'm going crazy. I don't want to stay here for another second, but I don't want to go out there either. I don't know what to do. Tell me what to do."

The smile was evident in his voice. He had me right where he wanted me. "We'll figure it out together, but running away won't solve your problems. You need to stick around to press charges. You don't want this lunatic to hurt someone else, do you?"

"No, but what if he gets released and comes back to hurt me. I don't even know why he wants to. He doesn't know me. I don't know him. I...I should go."

"Sleep on it," Tim insisted. "In the morning, I'll drop by and take you to breakfast. We'll figure it out together. I told you when we first met that my mission in life is to help people. I promise I'll be there to help you, just have faith, okay?"

Pausing dramatically, I didn't want to keep the protest up too much longer. "I'll try." It was the most diplomatic and indecisive thing I could think to say.

"Good girl. Now try to relax. Take a nice hot bath and get some sleep. I'll see you first thing in the morning."

"Thanks, Tim. I'm sorry to burden you with this."

"We all have burdens to bear, but when we help one another, everyone's load gets a little bit lighter. Good night."

Hanging up, I couldn't help but think that was a steaming pile of bullshit. Eckhardt would get word to Jace, and he'd be extra vigilant to pay attention to what was happening at the commune. However, it'd be more of the same. Surveillance never demonstrated anything of use, even though crimes continued to be committed. A disconcerting thought entered my mind. Timothy Wilde might be an actual psychopath, brilliant and able to manipulate the situation however he saw fit. I'd tangled with a few other men like that in the past, but none were as convincing.

*   *   *

"Take a seat. I'll get you a plate," Tim insisted. He'd shown up at seven a.m. to collect me. He didn't waste any time coming inside, but on the drive to the commune, he assessed the visible bruises from the scuffle last night. However, the conversation had remained light. He was in savior mode and had done nothing more than preach about the good in humanity, insisting that being around good people would make me feel better. Gathering enough hard evidence to put him behind bars would also do the trick, but I didn't volunteer that information. He led me to a long cafeteria table in one of the multipurpose rooms inside the main facility. "Sarah, this is Alice. Make her feel welcome."

The forty-something blonde woman offered a friendly smile and scooted closer. "It's nice to meet you, Alice."

"Alex," I corrected. "My friends call me Alex on account of my last name being Lexington."

"That's better than the jokes they used to make about my last name." She lowered her voice, like she was sharing a secret. "It's Guylas, but they liked to pronounce it *guy less*. Poor Sarah, she's so guy less." She rolled her eyes. "What can I say? Growing up can be tough."

"Don't I know it."

Although she continued making idle chitchat about breakfast and having farm-to-table meals at the commune, her eyes absorbed everything about me. Finally, she asked an actual question. "What brings you to us this amazing morning?" As she said it, her eyes came to rest on the apparent bruises.

"I had a rough night. Tim came to the rescue."

"He does that a lot." Another megawatt smile appeared

on her face. "Are you planning on joining us?"

Tim reappeared, placing a heaping plate in front of me. "Let's not scare Alex off yet. Transitioning to this life is a big step. I don't want to rush her into any decisions." He took a seat beside me. "She was attacked last night at her home. Right now, we just want her to feel safe and welcome."

"You poor dear." Sarah's face contorted into utter sympathy. "I'm so sorry. If you need anything, all you have to do is ask."

"Thanks." I picked up the fork and dug into the breakfast casserole as if I were famished. It was the best way to avoid speaking, and until Jace and I had a chance to confer, I didn't need to commit to anything. Without warning, Sarah got up from her place at the table and wrapped me in an awkward sideways hug. I inhaled sharply as she pressed into the bruises, but she didn't seem to notice.

Tim nodded to her. "Why don't you prepare one of the empty dormitories so Alex can rest if she chooses?"

"Right away, Tim." She gave him a hug and disappeared out of the room.

Shaking my head, I dropped the fork. "That's really not necessary."

He raised a skeptical eyebrow. "The bags beneath your eyes say otherwise." He pressed his lips together to hide his annoyance at my ungrateful attitude. "Of course, I won't force you to rest. I just thought you might want a place to lie down, should you stay for a bit."

"I'm sorry. I'm not accustomed to people wanting to take care of me."

"That much is obvious." He offered a playful smile, keeping things light and flowing. "Be honest. How are you feeling today? Have you given any more thought to what you want to do?"

I pushed the plate forward and wiped at the edges of my mouth. "I'm scared. My assets are frozen until the discrepancies concerning my father's estate are worked out in court. I can't afford another apartment. As you know, I'll be evicted soon. I can't work. I can't do anything. Life has been a living hell since I arrived." I glanced up at him. "You, Jace, and everyone here are the only bright spots I have, but I don't feel comfortable taking a handout."

"What are you going to do? Do you have another home or family to go back to?"

"There's no one. My family's gone. The few friends I have are across the country and aren't in a position to help. Honestly," I cast my eyes downward, looking ashamed, "we had a huge falling out when they learned about my frozen trust fund. They saw it as a betrayal because I always insisted on making it on my own, but I guess that wasn't true either." I sighed. "Perhaps I deserve this. I did this to myself. I've never been a very good person. Not really. Not like I should have been. I should have been a better friend, a better daughter, a better human."

"Everyone makes mistakes. No one deserves bad things to happen to them. Believe me, I've made my share of mistakes in the past too. We all have. No one here is perfect or beyond reproach, but that doesn't mean we aren't working to be better people now." He scooted the plate closer. "Finish your breakfast. You can at least have a meal before you hit the road."

I picked up the fork and forced myself to clean the plate. When I was done, I put the fork down and turned my full attention to Tim who'd been staring at me with utter fascination the entire time.

"Don't get upset, but if you don't get help from somewhere, how will you survive?" he asked.

"I have no idea. Maybe I'll sleep in my car for a few weeks or see if the lawyers have any way of releasing a small stipend to cover living expenses." Hunching my shoulders in defeat, I stared up at him with big doe eyes. "If it isn't too much trouble, maybe you can show me that dormitory."

A sly smile crept onto his face. "Sure." Leading the way out of the dining hall, he chattered about the facility. There were twenty dorms inside this building. Only the women used them. The few men in his flock had places outside the building. "I want everyone to feel comfortable and safe. I can't imagine anyone would act inappropriately, but as you might have noticed, some of the ladies I've helped have come from abusive backgrounds. They thrive in an all-female residential hall."

"Wow, it's just like boarding school. Is there a sign-in sheet and an enforced curfew too?" I winked, letting him know it was in jest. "On a more serious note, does that mean no one here is in a romantic relationship? Is dating against the rules?"

"The rules are that of common courtesy. Relationships are perfectly acceptable, but as you'll see, this isn't the ideal location to bring a casual hookup." He pushed open a door at the end of the hallway to reveal a tiny six by ten foot room. The twin bed and dresser took up almost the entire area. "Those who are in serious relationships don't live here. A few couples live in trailers on the property. In the future, I'm hoping to renovate one of the other buildings to house several apartments for our married and engaged guests." He glanced down the hallway, waving to Sarah who was on her way back to the dining hall. "Why don't you take a few minutes to see if you could be comfortable here and catch a few z's. Come find me when you're ready to go home. I doubt you're in much of a rush."

"Not really," I also didn't have much of a choice, "but I don't want to impose if you're busy."

"I'm going to lead a meditation class that you're free to join. After that, I don't have any duties until dinner. You may stay as long as you like." He cast another meaningful glance at me. "You could stay permanently."

"We'll see. I have a tendency to get claustrophobic from time to time."

Acknowledging my statement, he quietly left the room, leaving the door ajar.

Now what was I supposed to do? Finding myself with a sudden headache and slightly nauseous, I couldn't help but think the room was making me claustrophobic. Perhaps the lie held more truth than I realized. With nothing else to do, I walked around the bed, checking the room as I went. I peered beneath the bed, unsure what I hoped to find. Finally, I plopped down on the mattress.

The sheets were clean and a boring beige. The blanket

on top was a handmade quilt similar to a few I'd seen for sale at the farmer's market. Apparently, they also used the things they made. If this place didn't turn out dead bodies as often as handcrafted goods, it might have been a pleasant place to visit. Then again, perhaps it was slave labor or indentured servitude that kept the facility afloat.

After a few minutes of quietly waiting to see if anyone would pass the room, I got off the bed. The stabbing pain behind my eyes kept me from venturing through the compound. Instead, I closed the door, searched the dresser for any signs of a previous occupant, and went back to the bed. Curling onto my side, I couldn't imagine what triggered the migraine, but stress and lack of sleep would probably explain it.

I checked the time, deciding I'd venture out in a half hour and do some exploring while searching for Tim. While I waited for the minutes to tick by, my gaze went to the ceiling, and I studied the tiles. Two and a half across, four down. They had dark colored specks against the grey and beige details, but one of the specks looked like a hole.

Making an effort to appear to be trying to get comfortable, I sat up and took off my shoes. While I was placing them neatly on the ground, I looked up, seeing that my assessment was correct. That sicko had surveillance cameras inside the dorms, or the DEA had done a great job of bugging the place. But my money was on Tim. Perhaps we could splice into his system to have a better idea of what was really going on inside the commune.

Turning away from the fiber optic cable running through the hole in the tile, I rolled onto my side and stared at my watch. In twenty minutes, I'd give up on the pretense of resting and get the hell out of here. This place wasn't as innocent as it appeared, and I wanted to dismantle it before any more of Tim's followers became casualties of misplaced trust.

SIXTEEN

Once Tim dropped me off at the cover apartment, I spent the rest of the afternoon on the phone with Eckhardt. The LAPD wasn't any closer to finding a connection between Harbring and the Followers of Perpetual Light. The second attacker was in custody, but the arresting officers weren't in any rush to take my statement or work the case. They figured the longer it took to process Shrieves, the longer he'd be off the street. I didn't fear him. He was just a symptom of a much more sinister disease. Timothy Wilde posed the real danger. Even though I'd spent several hours with him, I hadn't learned much. Wilde was careful how he presented himself and his facility. Outsiders only saw the sanitized, friendly version. The camera in the ceiling hinted at the insidiousness that lay beneath the surface. I needed to go deeper.

"Alex, it's me." I opened the door, confused how Jace managed to get to my apartment without alerting the doorman. "I used the service entrance around back. I didn't want to risk tipping anyone off to my presence in case Tim has spies in the area," he said, reading my mind. He stepped inside and locked the door behind him.

"Is that paranoia contagious?"

"I heard about the attack, but Tim's kept me busy. I had a shift at the store, and then he made me run errands. It's almost like he wants to keep me away from you."

"Maybe he does. He brought me to breakfast at the commune this morning, showed me the dorms, and offered room and board for the low, low price of twenty-four hour surveillance."

"What are you talking about?"

"He has fiber optic cables in the ceilings to keep an eye on his flock. They aren't supposed to date or canoodle inside those tiny prison cells, but I guess he wants to make sure there aren't any rule breakers. He said men aren't allowed to sleep in the main facility, but he sleeps there. I guess you're right to assume he doesn't want any other cocks in the henhouse."

Jace smirked. "I'm glad you're enjoying my analogy." He looked around the messy apartment. "Did the attack happen here?"

"Out front. It wasn't the same guy. I don't care what the cops think or Tim insists." Self-consciously, I started to clear the clutter away. I'd spent the night awake, piecing things together and had scattered my work throughout the room while I'd been on the phone with Agent Eckhardt.

"We're on the same page. I won't waste my breath asking how you are, but we need to agree on the play."

"I'm ready to dive deep."

"In forty-eight hours, you'll move into the main facility. You'll need to pick up a secondary burner phone. Keep it on you at all times."

"I already have one." Going to the fireplace, I pulled

out the hidden bag with the two phones and my credentials. "Will this work?" I tossed it to him, and he scanned the internal memory. "It's brand new."

"Yep." He stared at the screen for several minutes, closed his eyes, mumbled something, and checked the screen again. "Memorization."

"Fantastic."

He snorted, rolling his eyes while he handed me his phone. "Don't write it down. Don't store it. Don't share it."

"I thought Eckhardt had it."

"Everyone on the team does, including you."

Repeating the digits several times in my head, I made sure they were committed to memory. It was stupid that I couldn't store the number, but Jace wanted us to be cautious.

"Normally, this would be for emergencies only, but since Tim limits the use of technology, this might be our primary source of communication when we aren't able to meet face-to-face. Make sure you always have your phone and keep it on silent if you're near anyone else," Jace instructed.

"Yes, sir."

He reached for a pen and a sheet of paper. After drawing a rough sketch of the commune grounds, he marked off the building locations. "This is my trailer, but if you're right about the surveillance, you won't be able to sneak away to meet me."

"How do you know your place isn't bugged too?"

He smiled, that infuriating self-assured look of his. "It gets swept every week, just like this apartment. I've always had issues with the heating and cooling system. It must be a lemon. The repair guy has to tinker with it on a regular basis. While he's there, he makes sure there aren't any bugs around." Picking up the pen again, Jace drew another diagram of where he'd planted cameras inside the facility. "Do you think we could splice into Wilde's system?"

"That's the plan. I already spoke to Matt about it."

Nodding, he pondered a few more things, flipping through the stack of notes and papers while he thought. "In the last seventy-two hours, Wilde sent two men to attack you. He had one of them killed and the other arrested, and he invited you to join his cult. He's desperate to reel you in. It's too dangerous to drag this out. You'll need to inform him of your plans by tomorrow morning. Tell him you need a day or two to pack and get everything in order. There isn't much room at the commune, so bring a week's worth of clothing, a blanket and pillow, a few towels, and minimal toiletries."

"Don't worry. I've seen my new room. It won't hold much, and I assume everything will be searched."

"That's probably a good assumption." He met my eyes. "Once you're there, it'll be harder to back out. Are you sure about this?"

"Absolutely."

"Okay. I just wanted to hear you say it. I'll do what I can to keep an eye on things, but from now on, you'll be closer on the inside than I am. So I guess I'll be your backup."

"Well, it's been nine months. You deserve a break." I laughed. "Does this mean I get to the call the shots from here on out?"

"We'll see." His eyes swept the room again. "I need to head back before Tim wonders what's taking so long. Be careful. You know what they say about the third time?"

"That you'll get lucky?"

"Not with this mission." He went to the door. "Make sure you stow everything out of sight before you leave. We're not taking any chances. He's already sent two goons to get under your skin. At this point, I don't believe a home invasion would be out of the question."

"Does that mean I'm supposed to phone him tonight with my answer?"

The lines in his forehead deepened, and he swept his hair back, something I'd seen him do when he was contemplating things. "This is your play. I'll back it either way."

I bit my lip, taking into account everything I knew. "Tomorrow morning. He knows he has me hooked. He can stand to lose some sleep in anticipation."

Decker nodded and disappeared through the door. As soon as he was gone, I flipped the locks and pulled out the other burner I'd used to phone Jablonsky. At this rate, I should label all three phones to avoid confusion.

After spending the next two hours updating Mark on the play and spit-balling ideas about Harbring, Shrieves, and the real reason Timothy Wilde was running a commune, I was out of ideas and intel. Once we hung up, I packed everything I had. It was time to clean house, especially if I had to entertain an uninvited guest later this evening.

After sealing the box and shoving it in the hall closet for pickup by the DEA, I nibbled on some leftovers and decided to call it a night. My headache never went away, but it wasn't nearly as bad. And since I was about to move into the lion's den, there would be no other opportunities for a good night's sleep in my future.

I'd just crawled under the covers and closed my eyes when I heard rustling. The noises grew louder until I was certain someone was inside the apartment. Then the sound of gunfire boomed through the enclosed space.

"Alex!" Martin screamed my name, and I shot up in bed.

Before flipping on the light, I grabbed my nine millimeter from beneath the mattress and crept out of bed. Aware that I was shaking and drenched in sweat, I knew it had been a nightmare, but the noises had been so vivid. Martin's pained, frantic voice reverberated in my ears. The dreams hadn't been this bad for some time. Something was seriously wrong.

I checked the attached bathroom and the closets before turning on the bedroom light and making sure the rest of the apartment was clear. The front door remained locked, as did all the windows. The box of intel remained inside the hall closet. Nothing had been moved. I was just insane.

Glancing at the clock, I rubbed a heavy hand down my face. It was three a.m. I'd been asleep for almost three hours. It was only a dream. Another stupid dream. But no matter how many times I repeated that to myself, I couldn't get Martin's voice out of my head. He was in trouble, and I wasn't there.

Disregarding every ounce of rational thought and violating the basic tenet of deep cover work, I picked up the burner I used to speak to Jablonsky and dialed the familiar number that I hadn't used in over six weeks. With the time difference, he should be up by now, preparing for a workout before getting ready to leave for the office. Then again, maybe he wouldn't be alone. Frankly, I didn't care. I just needed to know one thing.

"Hello?" Martin sounded tired.

"Are you okay?"

"Alex." He let out a lengthy exhale. "How dare you ask me that. It's six a.m. What the hell do you want?"

"I just need to know you're okay."

He snorted. "I'm not. If you call back around noon,

I'll probably be a little better because I'll be two or three drinks in by that point, but right now, I'm about as sober as I've been since you left. And it fucking hurts."

"I'm sorry." I shouldn't have called.

"Don't say it when you clearly don't mean it. Why the hell did you really call?"

Slowly, I inhaled, making sure my voice remained steady. "I had a nightmare. I heard you screaming my name. I thought you were hurt."

He let out an angry laugh. "Guess what. I don't have to deal with your nightmares anymore, sweetheart."

"You're absolutely right. I won't bother you again." I pulled the phone away from my ear, knowing I needed to press disconnect, but he stopped me.

"Wait. Don't go." It sounded like he was talking about more than just the phone call. I blinked back the tears, pressing the phone back against my cheek. "Alex?"

"I'm here."

"No, you're not." The pain in his voice was unbearable, and I knew that leaving had been the biggest mistake I'd ever made. "There's something I need to know. Why didn't you fight for us? You just stopped fighting. You gave up. You turned into the victim, and you let me use our relationship to vent my resentment. I know I fucked up. I was angry. I'm still angry. But you didn't fight back. You rolled over, and then you ran away. You ran away from me. From us. From everything. Did I push too hard? Did I push you away?"

"It's not your fault. You said you didn't trust me, but the truth is I don't trust you."

"Alex—" he began, but I shushed him.

"Let me finish, or I may never get this out. I owe

you an explanation or an excuse, whatever this is." The tears were falling now, but I fought to keep my voice steady. "I almost lost you, and every time shit goes sideways, all I can think about are the mercenaries and you bleeding out inside your office. When I lost my first OIO partner, I didn't think I'd ever find my way out of that black hole, but I didn't love him, not like I love you. If anything ever happened to you, I can't imagine I'd survive that. And now the fucked up thing is I'm three thousand miles away, and the only thought in my head is that if some asshole were to come at you, I'm too far away to do anything about it. God," I wiped my eyes, trembling, "I want so badly to find some way to fix this. I just don't know what to do."

His voice sounded strained. "You don't act like this with Mark or Nick or Derek. Is this really because of the shooting? And don't tell me it's different with them. Jabber's the closest thing you have to a father, and your cop friends might as well be your brothers."

"But it is different with them," I insisted, hearing Decker's voice in my head. "They've been trained. They have experience. They signed up for this shit. You didn't."

"So I should apply to the FBI or enroll at the police academy in order to get my girlfriend to come home?"

"It's not that simple."

"Why can't it be?" He blew out an angry breath. "Haven't I proven myself to you? Do I need to remind you that you came to me when you were in trouble? How about the time I saved you from that asshole who was going to shoot you up with a lethal dose of heroin?"

"Stop."

"What about the countless nights spent awake, dealing with your night terrors? Or that horrible night we spent on the bathroom floor?"

"Martin, why would you even want to be with me after all of that? This is your chance for a clean break. A good life. A normal life."

He laughed cynically. "Do you have any idea how many women I've dated? None of them meant a damn. I wasn't looking for a relationship. But then I met you, and you made me work for it. We went from strictly professional to friends, and finally, after a year, you agreed to give us a chance. I knew that was it for me. You were it for me. Now you want me to give that up and go back to nothing." He got quiet, and I pressed the phone closer to my ear, waiting for him to speak again. "I'm sorry that I wasn't it for you."

"You are." I squeezed my eyes closed. "You always will be." The words sputtered out, leaving me raw and exposed. "Look, I don't know how but I'm going to figure this out. There's something wrong with me, with the way I react to things, but I want you to know I'll work on it. I'll find a way to conquer this fear of losing you. It's so ironic and stupid, isn't it? I mean, I've already lost you. I did that to us. I did it to myself."

"It doesn't have to be that way. Come home. We'll work on this together. We'll get therapy, or I'll take self-defense classes or whatever you want."

"I can't. I'm not sure what I need or what we need. Not yet. But when this assignment's over, in the event you're still single, maybe we can talk. Just don't wait for me. Whenever you're ready to move on, do it. You deserve so much better. I just wanted you to know that I love you. And I want to fix this. I wish things were different. I wish I never sent you to London. I wish I never lied to you. And I wish I never left."

Pulling the phone away before he could say a word, I disconnected and ripped the battery free, removed the SIM card, tossed them separately into the trash, opened my door, and threw the garbage down the chute. I'd breached protocol. That conversation could cost me this mission or possibly my job, but I didn't care. The call didn't pose a risk. If it had, I never would have made it in the first place. Unfortunately, my mind was on Martin, and it needed to be on the game.

With the knowledge that he had no way of contacting me and I was out of spare burner phones, idiotic ideas, and unrealistic promises, I went back to bed and cried myself to sleep. Tomorrow morning, Alex Parker and her problems would have to remain on the backburner until Timothy Wilde was taken down. If that wasn't incentive to wrap this up quickly, I didn't know what was.

SEVENTEEN

"You look like hell," Tim said, entering the apartment. "I take it you didn't sleep well last night either."

I shook my head and stared at the kitchen tiles. Agent Eckhardt had shown up earlier with a few police officers. After taking my statement about the attack and learning the fundamentals about the second assailant, I knew we weren't any closer to making a case against Tim. Once the police were done, Eckhardt removed the questionable items from the apartment and promised they'd be placed in my office space at HQ. After that, I'd phoned Tim and asked for his help. His casual snooping wouldn't uncover anything, so I let him wander the apartment while I made lunch.

"There is limited storage space in the basement of the main building," Tim offered, "but it would have to be short-term."

"Thanks, but the apartment came furnished. I don't have much, just some clothes and the necessities. I don't want to put you out. Are you sure this is okay?"

"Alex, it's fine. It's better than fine. It's wonderful. We're like a large extended family. We'll benefit just as much by having you join us." He smiled brightly and took a seat at the kitchen table. "But you should know we all contribute. It's a commune. A cooperative of individuals. Not to sound too much like a socialist, but we work best as a community."

"What does that mean exactly?" I placed a plate in front of him.

"People volunteer to do different chores. Sarah made up the room for you the other day. Hannah and Dana cooked breakfast. Joseph cleaned up the kitchen and the dining hall afterward. We each take turns. No one expects you to jump in right away. Hopefully, your housing and financial issues will be handled swiftly, and you may choose to leave without participating. That's okay too."

"No, I'll help out. I'm no chef," I nodded down at the plate, "but I can wash dishes with the best of them. I don't care to pull my own weight."

"That's good, but promise me you won't do anything to stress that ankle. You need to get well so you can get back to work at the restaurant. I miss seeing your performances."

"I'm really not that good."

"You're incredible." For a moment, he oozed smarmy lechery.

Staring him down and making the sudden awkwardness in the room obvious, I cleared my throat. "Not really." I wouldn't thank him for the thinly veiled sexual remark. "You know, you didn't have to come all the way here to discuss this in person. I know how busy you are. I just wanted to make sure you hadn't changed your mind on the offer."

"I wouldn't do that." He stabbed at his plate, chewing thoroughly. "It's a lot quieter here with far fewer distractions. At the commune, there are always things to do and questions to answer. I wanted to make sure I devoted the proper amount of time to you." He dabbed at his chin. "Are you sure you didn't find the dorms too claustrophobic? You didn't stay particularly long. I thought you would have wanted to get some rest."

I wasn't sure what game he was playing, but I imagined he had watched the surveillance feed from that room. Did he realize I'd spotted the camera? Being undercover required walking a thin line, and I forced myself to become the lie.

"I was too wound up. There were a lot of things to think about, and for some reason, I had this horrible headache. I'm not sure what brought it on, probably stress, but it made it difficult to relax, let alone sleep. But the room was great. It will take some getting used to a shared bathroom again, but it's a huge step up from having to shower at the gym or wash up in a gas station bathroom."

"We wouldn't want that." He finished eating. "Thanks for lunch. You didn't have to reciprocate for yesterday."

"It's the least I can do." At this rate, the over-the-top pleasantness was likely to kill one of us. I pushed away from the table, getting ready to clear the plates, but he put his hand on my uninjured forearm. "I got it. I'm here to help you. What can I do?"

"There's nothing to do. I just have to throw my things in a bag, speak to the lawyers again, and I'll be ready to move in sometime tomorrow."

He went to the sink. "Perhaps you'd like someone to stay with you to make you feel safe tonight. You said you didn't sleep. Are you afraid of the man who attacked you? Isn't he in custody? When you phoned, you said the police had been here. Did something happen?"

"No, that creep is still in jail. They needed to ask me some more questions about the attack. I was afraid they'd want me to ID him in a lineup or something. Apparently, they only do that on TV. Building security was also questioned. I think the doorman was too. The officers believe they have a solid case and promised this asshole wouldn't bother me again." I moved to the window and gazed outside. "It scares me, though. The first time was broad daylight outside work. The second time was at night right there." I nodded out the window. "I don't think I've ever seen this guy before and I don't know how he knew everything about me. It's really unsettling."

"There's no way of determining what leads someone down a wayward path. I'm no detective, but maybe he saw you perform and became infatuated."

"I guess. It just frightens me." Quirking my lips into a slight smile, I laughed softly. "That is a huge reason why I'll be glad to be surrounded by a lot of other people."

"The commune is a safe environment. You have nothing to worry about." He finished washing the dishes and checked his watch. "My afternoon is clear. I don't need to be back until supper. You are welcome to join us," he said, seeing the hesitation on my face, "but I understand that you have a lot to accomplish." He gazed at the dark circles beneath my eyes, the visible bruises on my arm, and the bandage on my ankle. "Are you certain you don't want to get some rest? I'll stay if that will make you feel safe."

That was the second time he'd mentioned it. For some reason, he wanted to remain in my apartment while I was asleep. My mind went through the few possible motives for such an act, quickly dismissing altruism as his main reason. I didn't know if he hoped to score with or without my consent or if he wanted a chance to snoop. Snooping was the more likely scenario, but did that mean he was on to the operation or hoped to gain some type of access to Alice Lexington's wealth? Deciding to see how this would play out, I made an exaggerated stretch and yawned.

"I'd really like that. The cable hasn't been disconnected yet, so feel free to watch TV or meditate or whatever it is you like to do. I'm sure I'll be up by the time you leave, but if not, just lock the door behind you."

Smiling like he won an Emmy, he plopped down on the couch and picked up a magazine. "I'll be right here if you need anything."

"Thanks."

Leaving the bedroom door opened a crack, I crawled beneath the covers and stared at the sliver of living room. After Tim finished leafing through the magazine, he placed it back on the coffee table and stood up. He went to the bookshelf and then into the kitchen, vanishing from my line of sight. I strained to hear what he was doing, but I couldn't tell. Finally, he returned to the couch and turned on the television. When I grew bored of watching him, I got out of bed and thanked him for staying. As soon as he was gone, I shot a quick text requesting another visit by the maid to sweep for surveillance devices. With any luck, we'd find something, but I had never been particularly lucky.

*   *   *

"He wants to sleep with you," Jace hissed. "There's no other explanation for it."

"Maybe he wants to suffocate me in my sleep."

We were at a table in the far corner of the dining room. Supper ended almost an hour ago, but Jace was late on account of another shift at the gas station. I'd been living at the commune for three days. Last night was the second time Tim had entered my room in the middle of the night. The first time, he claimed he wanted to make sure I was settled, but last night, I remained completely still, pretending to be asleep. He stood near the door for almost twenty minutes before leaving. It had left me unnerved. Of course, the fact that I hadn't slept at all since my arrival was beginning to show. I'd managed a few brief naps in my car when I was supposedly meeting with the lawyers, but this couldn't last. And there wasn't a chance in hell I'd sleep when some psycho was getting his rocks off by sneaking into my bedroom.

I looked at the time. We had another twenty minutes before Tim finished leading a thoughtful meditation group. No wonder I was always skeptical of New Age trends. People like Timothy Wilde gave them a bad reputation.

Rubbing my temples, I looked down at the barely touched plate in front of me. Just the sight of food made me queasy. This mission was killing me.

"You're lucky you have a trailer and don't have to eat this shit."

"Another migraine?" Jace narrowed his eyes. "That doesn't make any sense. You don't have a history of migraines."

"I don't know what it is." I shoved the plate away, too tired to get up. "I think it's called life." I blinked a few times. "Don't worry, I'm sharp as a tack."

"So how has your stay been so far?" Jace increased his volume at the sight of a few women moving past the dining hall. "Has everyone made it pleasant for you?"

"Yep." I proceeded to detail my encounters with the women in the rooms near mine. I'd only spoken to six or seven, but I'd been invited to join them in pilates or hang out while they quilted. Since I was supposedly injured, I spent a lot of downtime in my room. They had let me borrow a few books, and with the constant surveillance, I had to appear to read them.

When the bulk of the Perpetual Lighters were meditating or conversing in a group sharing session, I started exploring the main building of the compound. There were three levels—the main floor, the basement, and a second story. However, I had been told the upper level was being renovated and off limits. It also housed Tim's bedroom. The basement was pretty cluttered, and as soon as I went down the steps, Wilde materialized behind me, suggesting I shouldn't take the stairs with my busted ankle. It was obvious I was being watched, and snooping wasn't encouraged.

"I'm hoping to check out the rest of the property tomorrow. I could use some fresh air," I concluded.

"I'll have to show you my trailer," Jace offered, nodding to a couple who entered the dining hall. "Hey, Vanessa. How's it going, Javier?" He called them over like any good Perpetual Lighter would. "Have you had a chance to meet Alex? She arrived two days ago."

"Three," I corrected. We'd done an introduction like this the day before in order to keep our clandestine debriefs under wraps. "It's lovely to meet you." I smiled at Vanessa. "Do you live in the dorms?"

"No, Javier and I share a trailer." She pointed to the right. "It's closest to the fence." She reached for his hand. "That was just another blessing of finding this place and being here."

I cocked an eyebrow, confused by her meaning.

Javier chuckled. "Meeting our soul mates. I had been here for a few weeks before Vanessa's path crossed with mine. It was pretty instantaneous. Tim gave us his blessing and arranged for us to share a home. He's really great."

"Yes, he is," I agreed, wondering how consensual their

original liaison had been. Perhaps I was jaded, but there were a lot of things about this place that didn't make much sense. I glanced at Jace, seeing the wheels turning in his head, but he held the smile. "It was lovely meeting you, but I have an early appointment. I should get to bed. Good night."

"Night, Alex. We'll see you around," Vanessa said.

"Hang on," Jace called, stopping me from retreating, "I'm heading out too. I'll walk you to your room." He said his goodbyes, grabbed the plate from my hand, dropped it in the return tray, and fell into step beside me. "We can't keep meeting like this. Someone's bound to notice sooner or later."

"I know."

He bit his bottom lip, scanning the area for stragglers. "After going to the restaurant tomorrow, why don't you stop by the gas station?"

"Okay, I will."

"Are you going to make it through another night?" he asked, and although I suspected the question was a joke, the look in his eyes told me it wasn't.

"No worries. I'm fine."

He gave me a quick hug, aware of the security cams in the vicinity. "I know when you're bluffing." He let go and went toward the front door while I went into my room.

Living inside the lion's den while being constantly watched was a lot more complicated than I ever imagined. There was no peace. I had to be on twenty-four seven, and admittedly, I was afraid to sleep. Who knows what I might miss or what Tim might try if I was out cold. The only bright spot was I hadn't detected any fiber optic cables or other surveillance devices in the community bathroom. I just hoped he possessed that slightest shred of decency.

EIGHTEEN

"Alex." Jace shook my shoulder, and I jumped six feet in the air. My hand went to my firearm, and he held up his hands, stepping backward and tossing a careful glance at the opened door behind him. "It's me." My gun hand didn't waver as I blinked the blurriness from my eyes. "It's okay. It's me," he repeated, slowly moving closer and taking the gun from my hand. "Shit." He rubbed his face. "This assignment must really have you twisted around."

Sitting up, I buried my face in my hands. "I'm sorry. Tim came into my room before dawn and waited inside until morning to make sure I was awake and ready to meet my boss at the restaurant. He's always there. He's always watching. I didn't realize how intense this would be. No one else seems to notice, or they think this is normal." I shook my head. "I need to find out. I'm going to get close to some of the women and see if I can get any of them to open up. Someone has to know something. He can't just be targeting me. He must have done this to them too. How can a predator like Tim convince so many people he's some kind of savior?"

"It's the game he plays. Can you honestly say you wouldn't be bending over backward to show your appreciation to this guy if you were in Alice Lexington's position?"

"Newsflash, not all women are prostitutes."

"I didn't mean it literally, but nine times out of ten, an unattached individual is likely to exhibit displaced emotions toward anyone who helps them out. You don't have to sleep with the guy, but you might bake him cookies or buy him a bottle of Jack. Isn't that something you'd normally do?"

Shrugging, I got off the cot and stretched. Jace had let me crash in the break room at the gas station. It had a cot and a table for the guy stuck working overnight. It wasn't particularly cozy, but knowing I had a DEA agent out front watching my back allowed me to sleep soundly for three hours.

"It's been four days, and I'm ready to crack. How did you do this for eight months on your own?" I asked.

"It wasn't easy, but I know it's harder for you. He won't let you sleep. The risk of being assaulted or raped is obvious with the way he lingers inside your room. Do what you can to get the other women to trust you. If someone is willing to talk, it'll give us a solid lead from which to work." He bent down, sliding his pants leg up to reveal a blade. "Take this." He handed me a small triangular dagger. "This is easier to conceal than a gun, and it'll be much faster than trying to get to your firearm if things go south."

"If I need this, any hope of determining his drug connection will go straight to hell, along with him."

"I can live with that."

After leaving the gas station, I returned to the commune. Tim and several of his followers were preparing for the farmer's market. The stands were being put into place, and the signs were being hung. Every weekend, like clockwork, they opened the commune to the public, hoping to make a quick buck and gain more potential followers. I was uncertain if the goods being sold were aboveboard, but I had walked the grounds and seen the honey collection, the gardens with fruits and vegetables, and several of the women knitting, quilting, and sewing. Artisanal items were extremely hip, and hordes of millennials swarmed every weekend, so there was a good chance that was the legitimate part of Tim's business. It was also possible he was using the farmer's market as a cover to distribute narcotics or to clean otherwise dirty money.

Ducking inside to avoid the spiritual leader, I went to my room. The door beside mine was open. Sarah was inside with Anika. Knocking politely on the doorframe, I smiled at the two women seated on the bed.

"Sorry to intrude. I just wanted to say hi." I hoped they'd invite me to join them.

"Come in," Sarah offered. "Have you met Anika?"

"I think so. Jace introduced us, right?"

Anika grinned. "Yep." She crinkled her nose playfully at Sarah, and I felt like I was missing the joke. "Are you going to finally give some of our sessions a chance?" My brief conversation with Anika had entailed listening to her rave about the benefits of Tim's spiritual classes, particularly meditation and talk therapy.

"Maybe. I'm still getting acquainted with everyone. I've always been shy and introverted. I'm not what you would call a joiner."

"Leave Alex alone," Sarah scolded. "She'll come around eventually. We all do. Do you remember how long it took before you opened up to the group? And now the others have to tell you to shut up so they have a chance to share." She met my eyes and scooted over on the bed to make room for me to sit. "Take your time, dear. We all find our inner light. It just takes some of us longer than others."

Anika reached out and combed her fingers through my hair, perfectly comfortable invading my personal space. Maybe she learned that from Tim. "You look worn out."

"I am. I keep having these weird dreams, like someone's in my room at night. I don't know. I probably sound crazy."

"You're just not used to the surroundings. That'll make anyone uncomfortable," Sarah said, getting up from her place on the bed. "You'll get used to it soon enough, and then you'll sleep like a baby. You know, you could talk to Tim about it. He has a lot of herbal remedies and healing teas that might help. When I first got here, I was a wreck. It really calmed me down." She gave me a pointed look. "Not to pester, but the guided meditation helped a lot too."

"I'll think about it."

Sarah nodded, moving toward the doorway. She was helping with dinner, and after saying goodbye, she left. Deciding I should leave as well, I moved to stand, but Anika grabbed my wrist.

"Where did you work?" she whispered.

"What?"

She released her grip and nodded at the faded scars that ran around both of my wrists. "I had a friend with the same scars. She worked in a S&M club in Vegas. One of her clients was particularly rough, and she quit. One thing led to another," she shook her head, "but it doesn't matter. That was a long time ago." She attempted to offer an encouraging smile, but I saw the dark cloud hanging over her. "It's good that you got out and found a safe place like this. It's hard knowing where to go or who to trust."

"I wasn't a sex worker. This isn't why I'm here."

She assessed me carefully. "Did your boyfriend do that? Was he into the rough stuff?" Her eyes went to the week old bruises on my arms. "You shouldn't let someone hurt you."

"I didn't." Seeing an opening, I decided to ask a question of my own. "Is that why you're here? Did someone harm you?"

She looked away. "I was told this is a good place to be. It's safe."

"What about Tim?"

"What about him?"

"Did he ever force you to do something you didn't want to do?"

She laughed it off like it was the most ludicrous thing she'd ever heard. "I understand it's hard to trust, but Tim's a good man. He protects us from the bad men. He would never let any harm come to us."

Remembering the surveillance cameras in the ceiling, I shook my head and smiled. "I'm sure you're right. I'm just being silly. Those dreams I've been having, I keep thinking he's sneaking into my bedroom, like he wants to hurt me. Isn't that crazy?"

"Yeah...crazy."

I didn't like the tone she used or the delay between the words, but Anika wasn't about to say more than she already had. Whatever life she had outside of these walls had been worse than three hots and a cot, even if the room and board were being provided by a murderous, drug dealing, sexual predator. Shaking my head, I couldn't help but think how fucked up this world was.

"Hey, Anika, if you ever want to speak one on one, I'm right next door."

"Sure, I'll stop by sometime, but you really should join us in group. We have so much fun talking about philosophy and the universe and whatever's on our minds. Sometimes it's the past or our problems, but it really is about opening our minds to enlightenment."

"Maybe next time."

Returning to my room, I grabbed one of the magazines I'd brought with me and picked up a pen. Pretending to work on the crossword puzzle in the back, I couldn't help but mull over the things Anika had said. As soon as I got the chance, I'd send Eckhardt a message to run a background on her. The fact that she noticed my old scars worried me. I trusted Tim's followers about as much as I trusted Tim, and my battle wounds didn't exactly fit in with my cover's privileged upbringing. It was possible the women were told to observe me and report back. The fact that I might have just tipped my hand sent cold chills down my spine.

That evening at dinner, Tim worked the serving line and made me a special plate. He noticed how little I'd been eating and wanted to make certain I was nourished. After finishing his work, he sat beside me and asked dozens of questions about my day, which made me even more uncertain of everything. I remained calm and played it cool. Knowing it was time I jumped into this new lifestyle with both feet, I asked about the various talks, groups, and activities that seemed to go on from morning until night inside the co-op.

As I expected, Tim enjoyed being the center of attention, providing extensive details on his prayer, meditation, and spiritual therapy groups. In addition to the more spiritual aspects, he led a group that discussed addictions and dealing with cravings and making amends. It sounded like he'd ripped off A.A. and added his own flare, but I didn't say as much. Alice Lexington didn't have a history of addiction. That was Jace's schtick.

Aside from active discussion groups and Tim's preaching, the co-op fostered an environment of fitness and well-being. There were pilates, yoga, and barre classes. They were all geared toward making sure the women stayed lean and didn't learn a damn thing about self-defense. It was hard not to assume he was using this to keep his drug mules and sex slaves healthy without giving them the tools needed to fight back, but perhaps that was just the cynic in me.

"I was hoping for some cardio kickboxing when my ankle heals," I said.

Tim frowned, shaking his head in disapproval. "Our priority is love and peace. Violent actions, even for the sake of exercise, negatively affect our moods and personalities. The point of this commune is for betterment, not destruction."

"Sorry, I didn't mean to offend you."

"It's okay. You're still learning. Is it safe to assume you are curious about our mission and are considering coming to some of our groups?"

"Perhaps. Is that okay?"

His eyes lit up, and a smile erupted on his face. "Indeed." He pushed away from the table. "Let me get you a copy of our weekly schedule." His eyes went to the barely touched plate of food. "Eat up. I'll be right back."

Fighting the urge to roll my eyes, I picked up the fork again. Maybe I wasn't curvy enough for his liking. Or he hoped I'd gain a few pounds so I couldn't fit into my showgirl costume. That would mean I'd be forced to stay here indefinitely. Regardless of his motivation, I didn't like being told what to do.

A few minutes later, Tim came back with a pamphlet detailing the daily sessions. It was an advertising tool that I'd seen displayed at the farmer's market, but I had never seen anyone take a pamphlet with them. Most people wanted to support the local community and go back to their lives without being dragged into a cult. At this point, I would have liked to go back to my life too.

Moving the plate farther away, I spread the pamphlet out on the table and asked interested questions. At some point, Jace entered the dining hall and took a seat across from me. He waited patiently for Tim to finish talking before interrupting.

"Hey, Alex." Jace nodded before turning his attention to Tim. "Courtney didn't put me on the roster for the booths this weekend, so what can I do to help out? I can get up early and finish setting up, but there must be something I can do during the day."

"We already put up the booths. I can use you on maintenance and clean-up," Tim decided.

"Is there anything I can do?" Since Jace was volunteering, I should do the same, especially since I'd just made a point of giving this concept of enlightenment a chance.

"I don't want you to stress your ankle, but we have tables and chairs set up. Feel free to enjoy the festivities, and don't feel obligated to volunteer. I don't expect you to repay me for my kindness, Alex. That's not why I invited you here."

"But I want to pull my own weight. We already discussed this."

"In due time. You've been here less than a week. You deserve some time to process everything that's recently happened in your life before you push it aside and fill up the space with other duties and obligations. This is your new beginning. Isn't that right, Jace?"

"It was for me." Jace looked around the room. "I guess I might see what's left in the kitchen before heading home. These long days at the gas station take their toll after a while."

"Help yourself to my plate." I pushed it closer to him. "I can't eat another bite."

"No," Tim interjected, and Jace and I both gave him a bewildered look. "I'm sure there's plenty left in the kitchen.

As always, feel free to help yourself to the fridge and pantry. It's not often you eat with us, but there's plenty for you here."

Jace shrugged. "This is fine. There's no reason to let food go to waste."

"I'll have to remember to request smaller portions." I attempted to sound ashamed, even though Tim had ladled a hefty helping onto my plate despite my protests.

"Nothing goes to waste. Whatever is left is added to the compost heap and provides nutrients to the soil. We put back to the earth what we take away, and it provides more bountiful harvests for us. It's the circle of life." He gave Jace a stern look. "You are no longer a scavenger having to pick off others' leftovers and wait for handouts in order to survive. Go help yourself to something fresh."

Jace raised his hands and backed away from my plate. "You're right. I'm sorry." He bowed his head, playing the faithful role of follower. Excusing himself, he got up and went to the kitchen.

Tim apologized for the interruption and continued giving me additional details about the various groups. It sounded exactly like what he had already said, and my eyelids started to droop. Apparently, his lectures worked as well as boring bedtime stories. No wonder Sarah had said he had tons of remedies for sleep issues. Or had Anika said that? Everything was blending together.

Blinking a few times, I tried to focus, but I couldn't keep my thoughts on track. I needed to get some sleep. It was still early enough to catch a quick nap while the rest of the flock was around to keep Tim busy. If not, I'd have to bust out of this joint to find some caffeine to keep me awake. Too bad the kitchen didn't have any stockpiled, but all stimulants were banned on the premises.

"When should we expect you to join?" Tim asked.

"Um..." My thoughts weren't flowing together in a coherent way. "Can we talk about this in the morning? I need some time to think. I don't want to get overwhelmed by trying too much at once."

"Sure." Tim folded the pamphlet and handed it to me. "I'll take your plate. Go on to bed."

Wondering if I'd mentioned anything about sleep, I shrugged it off and stood up. My legs felt heavy and stiff. I was having enough trouble getting them to move without adding a limp to account for my injured ankle. Passing Jace on his way back to the table, I mumbled good night and continued toward the dormitory. I was a few feet from my room when my knees buckled, and I collapsed in the middle of the hallway.

NINETEEN

I'm not sure how long I remained on the floor. No matter how hard I tried to get up, my body refused to cooperate. Given the feeling of sudden paralysis and the frequent headaches I'd been experiencing, I couldn't help but think I was having a stroke. The world blinked in and out, and part of me just wanted to give in and sleep. The fear of what would happen if I blacked out was the driving force that kept me awake. Eventually, I was able to drag myself toward my room. Using my numb arms and hands as best I could, I managed to sit up against the wall. My breathing was labored, and my heart was pounding.

Footsteps sounded at the end of the hallway, and Sarah called my name. She yelled to someone to get Tim and ran toward me. "Alex, what happened? Are you okay?"

Even my speech came out garbled. I let out an exasperated huff. Finally, I managed one word. "Jace."

"What?" She leaned closer and put her palm against my forehead.

"Get Jace," I breathed.

"Alice?" Tim asked, concern creeping into every syllable. He turned to Sarah. "What happened?"

"I don't know." Sarah scooted back, unsure what to do.

"I just found her like this."

"Breathe easy," Tim instructed. "Does anything hurt? Should we call an ambulance?"

I shook my head, wanting him as far away from me as possible. In my current state, I wouldn't be able to fight him off if he tried something, but I wasn't going to blow my cover either. "I just need a minute."

He looked skeptical and put his hand against my throat. I quivered, and he made soothing sounds while he checked my pulse. "Don't be afraid. You're amongst friends. No one will hurt you." He turned to Sarah. "She'll be okay. It's likely exhaustion and stress." He focused entirely on me again. "Try to relax." He looked into the tiny dorm. "I thought your claustrophobia might be an issue." He pressed his lips together, looking contrite. "That's why I've been checking on you so often at night." His words sounded feasible, almost making it seem that everything I suspected and thought was insane. Almost.

He lifted my hand, watching my fingers shake. "I believe you're having a panic attack. I've seen this happen before with a lot of new joiners. Once you calm down and get some rest, the dizziness and numbness will go away. Just try controlling your breathing. Take some long deep breaths." He demonstrated for a few breaths, but I wasn't playing along. "Sarah, will you make some chamomile tea? I'm going to take Alex to my room to lie down. I don't want to subject her to an enclosed space right now."

"No problem." Sarah ran off toward the kitchen.

"I guess it's a good thing you didn't eat much at dinner," Tim teased. Carefully, he slid one hand underneath my back and the other beneath my knees. He lifted me off the ground and headed toward the stairs. "Close your eyes. Everything will be fine in the morning." Despite his words, I was more terrified than ever.

Tim shouldered the door open to reveal a vast bedroom. A queen sized bed took up maybe a quarter of the room. The rest was partitioned off. I couldn't see much beyond the opening to a private bathroom. Gently, he placed me on the bed and smoothed my hair against the pillow.

"You'll sleep here tonight. And tomorrow you'll begin a

meditation class. You can't let yourself get this exhausted or worked up. No one here will harm you. The man who attacked you is behind bars. You're safe. The only thing dangerous here is your stress level." He ran a finger along my cheek. "Do you want to try some deep breathing?"

Forcing a slow, steady breath down my throat, I swallowed. "I'll be fine in my room."

He let out a relieved sigh. "See, you're already starting to bounce back. These anxiety episodes only last a few minutes. I know how terrifying they can be. I used to have horrible panic attacks," he prattled on as if I would buy into it, "but they stopped once I learned to look inward for divine guidance and strength. You'll learn the same, but in the meantime, I know you won't be able to rest in the dorms. There's no need to put on a brave face. We're here to help you. Unfortunately, exhaustion makes these episodes a lot more likely. We'll have to see about getting you moved out of that room and to a larger space. Or you might have to start sleeping with the door open."

My wrists and ankles ached from the adrenaline surge, but I was able to move my limbs again. Pushing myself away from him, I didn't quite make it to sitting, but it was better than nothing. "How can you be sure this is anxiety?" He didn't know that I was acutely aware of what actual panic attacks did to my body.

"Are you feeling better?" He watched as I wriggled my limbs back and forth. He pressed his fingers against my neck again, and I cringed. "Why are you so frightened? I won't hurt you. I've never given you any indication otherwise. You need to calm down." He climbed off the bed and went toward the door. "Sarah," he called, "we need that tea."

A muffled reply came from beyond the room, but I couldn't hear her words. Was Tim's room soundproofed? Adding that to my growing list of worries, I glanced around for an escape route or possible weapons, remembering the dagger concealed in my ankle wrap.

A few moments later, Sarah appeared with a tray and a steaming mug of tea. She handed it to Tim and smiled encouragingly at me. "That should fix you right up. It's incredibly soothing. I brought up the bedtime blend too, just in case Alex was still having trouble sleeping."

Fink, I thought, deciding I would scald myself with the hot liquid before drinking a single sip. Thankfully, Jace stepped into the doorway. "I heard Alex collapsed. Is she okay?" His eyes went right to mine, and I shook my head while Tim's back remained turned.

"It appears to be anxiety." Tim dismissed the worry quickly. "She needs rest."

"She needs a doctor," Jace hissed. "She could be having a reaction to the pain medication they prescribed for her ankle."

Tim's brow furrowed, and he turned to me. "What are you taking?"

"I don't remember what it's called."

"Where's the bottle?" Tim asked.

Jace stepped into the bedroom, closing the distance between us. "She tossed it out after dinner, and I emptied the trash into the dumpster. Look, the clinic is open twenty-four hours. At this time of night, we can be there in thirty or forty minutes. It'd be best to go back. They warned her adverse reactions were possible." He turned to Tim for approval. "She might be okay, but what if she gets worse when we're all asleep?"

"I can stay up with her," Sarah offered, but Tim shook his head.

"No. Jace will take her." Tim sat on the bed and stroked my hair again. "Is that okay? Do you trust Jace to take care of you? Remember, he stayed the night after you were attacked. I trust him. You can too."

I gave an uncertain nod, internally cheering.

Jace helped me off the bed. Stumbling out of the room, we made our way down the steps, taking a quick detour to grab some things from my room. We didn't dare speak a word until we were inside the car and away from the commune.

"Alex, what the hell's going on? Are you okay?" His fingers tightened around the steering wheel, and he stomped down on the accelerator. "Sarah told me some things that didn't make any sense."

Leaning back against the seat, I detailed what happened and the things Tim had said. "Maybe I was drugged, or I had a mini-stroke. I don't know." Hitting the seat release, I dropped into a reclining position and curled into a ball.

"That would explain why Tim was so adamantly opposed to me eating off your plate. You said he prepared your dish special. Was it out of your sight at any point?"

"Only when he turned around to add some fresh herbs."

"He could have added anything. Based on your symptoms and his thinly veiled attempt to get you alone in his room, I'm guessing he slipped you some PCP or one of the other date rape drugs." He glanced over at me. "How are you feeling now?"

"Tired. Queasy. A bit short of breath."

"Could be ketamine." Jace ran a hand through his hair. "I'll have the medics on standby for when we arrive at HQ. They'll do a drug test and get to the bottom of this. Had I known sooner, I would have kept a sample from your plate." Briefly, he made eye contact. "Would you prefer to go to a hospital?"

"No. Wilde did this, and I will be damned if we do anything that will jeopardize using whatever evidence we have against him."

"Okay." Jace dialed Eckhardt and updated the team. "Hey," he nudged me gently, "I'm gonna need you to stay awake."

"Why? Are you afraid of the dark?"

He laughed. "Definitely."

I sighed. "To be honest, I don't think I could sleep now anyway. I'm such an idiot. I should have known better than to eat anything inside that place. Remind me to take a page out of your book and stay away from the kitchen."

"It's not your fault. You really don't have much of a choice. Tim expects you to partake in meals. His offer was for room and board. He's been attempting to force you to eat every chance he gets." A thought ran through Jace's mind. It was the same one I had. "Maybe those headaches are being caused by something."

We fell silent, considering the vast possibilities. Finally, Jace killed the lights, pulled into the garage, and cut the engine. He had a remote to allow access, but that didn't mean a tactical team wasn't on standby next to the medical team.

Climbing out of the car under my own power, I took a deep breath and followed the medic down the hallway and into the lab. They performed a quick blood draw and some basic diagnostics to make sure this wasn't an actual health crisis. I was slipping my shirt back on when Decker entered the room.

"Shit," he cursed, and I turned to look at him. "Why the hell didn't you say something?"

"About what?"

"The week old bruises on your back and side. Are those from the second attack?"

"They're just bruises. They're healing. It's not like I have internal bleeding." My flippant remark was lost on him, but it didn't matter. "How long until we get the results on the drug test?"

"The standard test won't take long," the medic assured.

"I want a full drug screen and tox report," Jace ordered. "The standard won't cut it." He narrowed his eyes at the laboratory equipment. "I'm guessing you're going to find ketamine."

"We'll be thorough. In the meantime, Agent Parker, you might as well get comfortable. Now that we've run the test, it'd be best to flush this garbage out of your system as quickly as possible." He spoke to someone else about getting fluids set up in the break room. "We should have answers by morning, but until we know what we're dealing with, you shouldn't be out in the field." He turned to Jace. "It's your call, sir."

Again, Jace's hand went through his hair, and I snickered. Someone needed to work on controlling his nervous tics, and for once, it wasn't me. "Come on, Alex. I'll show you to our team's break room."

Once I was settled into a bedroom that didn't appear to have been touched since the original occupant owned the house, I made myself comfortable on the bed. Not wasting my breath to ask if anyone had bothered to change the sheets, I remained on top of the covers. After getting hooked up to an IV, I let my eyes close.

"I need to phone Tim," Jace said. "He'll want to know your condition. I'm going to say the doctor admitted you to the nearest hospital for observation, but you'll be released in the morning. Should he call the facility to ask about your condition, the call will be rerouted and one of our guys will reply accordingly." He hesitated for a second before taking a seat beside me. "We need to talk."

Opening my eyes, I didn't like those words or that tone. "I don't think I'm compromised, but it's possible my reaction might have set off some alarms. I wasn't thinking clearly. I just wanted to get as far away from Wilde as possible."

Jace held up his hand to silence me. "We'll go through an official debrief in the morning, but assuming your cover remains intact, the safest thing to do is pull you."

"You can't afford that." I searched his ice blue eyes for a solution, but all I saw was pity and fear. "You can't tell me that you didn't learn more tonight than you've learned in the last nine months. You need me."

"Dammit, Alex." He broke eye contact, finding the fluid drip fascinating. "If I had already gone back to my trailer... Do you realize.... Fuck."

"Yes. Yes. And yes." I snorted. "You could have just asked for a thank you instead of being so dramatic." He looked at me, and I smirked. "Thanks for saving my ass."

"It was luck. And that's the problem." He took to pacing the room. "We aren't positioned to provide backup. Even if we splice into the CCTV feed, our agents are outside the property lines. Crossing into what is considered a sanctuary due to the church status will not go over well, but more importantly, it'll take time to get a team inside to get you out. Our communication sucks. Our surveillance sucks. I can't guarantee your safety."

"No shit, Sherlock. That's why it's called deep cover. I don't expect a rescue. However, I did appreciate it."

"We need to come up with a better play."

"It's your op, Decker. Figure it out and tell me what you want to do."

Before he could say anything else, the medic came into

the room. "The assistant director wants a full screen on you too. It's likely you might have been exposed to the same substance."

"I'll be right back, Alex. We aren't through discussing this."

"Take your time. I need to make a call anyway." I reached for the landline on the nightstand. "Is this secure?" As soon as I was given the affirmative, I picked it up. Mark would be pissed I was calling this late, but if he arrived at the office in the morning to a copy of the incident report and drug test on his desk, he'd have my ass. Thankfully, the effects of whatever I'd been exposed to were fading fast. Now I just had to run damage control with my boss and Agent Decker and find some way of nailing Wilde to the wall. Perhaps I should add world peace to my wish list while I was at it.

TWENTY

"Sir?" an unfamiliar voice asked, and a groan resonated from my left.

Decker had fallen asleep on the bed beside me. However, he'd kept a respectable foot and a half between us. I flipped over to see one of the lab geeks in the doorway. Carlo was passed out in a recliner, and Eve and Stella were curled up on different corners of the sofa. Ben was at the table with half a dozen empty energy drinks in front of him, working on his tablet. Almost the whole gang was here.

"What is it?" Decker sat up and rubbed his face.

"The drug screen came back negative."

"What about Alex's report?" Decker asked.

"It was negative also."

I sat up, feeling completely back to normal. "How can that be?" If Wilde had used some kind of mental mojo to elicit that reaction, I'd kill him and start wearing a tin foil hat.

The lab guy flipped through the pages. "As you know, there are hundreds of substances that can cause various reactions and are practically undetectable. Based on the blood test we ran and some of the elevated markers we found in Agent Parker's system upon her arrival last night compared to the test we ran again this morning, it appears she was poisoned."

"Poisoned?" Decker asked, pointing out the absurdity of the statement.

The tech nodded. "Certain plants and herbs can cause temporary paralysis, difficulty breathing, and the other symptoms with which Parker presented. The effects were temporary, but continued exposure could result in an accumulation and possibly death."

"That doesn't make me feel particularly warm and fuzzy," I murmured. "What kind of plants or herbs are we talking about?"

"There are hundreds. It'd be easier to narrow down that list if we knew what you encountered."

Decker licked his lips. "Wilde grows a ton of herbs on the property. He could easily be growing something like this without anyone knowing." The conversation had woken the rest of the team, and he turned to Stella. "Legally speaking, are we able to get samples of his crops to test against Alex's labs in order to find the cause?"

"We'll need a sneak and peek, just to be on the safe side. I'll get on that right away." She left the room, followed by the tech.

Decker turned to me. "Are you good?"

"Yep. A little thing like a failed poisoning can't slow me down. Do you still want to pull me?"

He pressed his lips together, feeling everyone's attention focused on our conversation. "We need a safer way of executing this op. I'll be back. Stay here." Without waiting for a response, he went out the door, closing it behind him.

Eve made a humming sound as she stretched, and Ben shook each of the cans, hoping to find one that wasn't empty. From the amount of caffeine he'd ingested, it was a good thing the DEA had a medical team on the payroll. Climbing out of bed, I stretched, glad to feel normal again.

"Don't tell me you all live here," I said, breaking the silence.

Eve laughed. "Not even close. We got the 9-1-1 last night, spent several hours working on strategy, and crashed here. We rally together in crisis. Last night counted."

"You're one of us now," Carlo said. "You spent the night in this crazy converted bedroom. All you need now is to party in the hot tubs, and we'll trade out that gold shield of yours for one of ours."

"Thanks, but I'll pass."

"Suit yourself," he said.

The next two hours flew by as we strategized our next plan of attack and ran through all the new possibilities regarding Wilde and his followers. Now that we had some idea of how Tim might be manipulating his new recruits into trusting him and agreeing to whatever he wanted, it brought us back to the main question. Was Tim involved in the drug trade?

Decker hadn't found anything on the property. The dead drug mules had been part of Wilde's following at one point, but at the time of their deaths, they were no longer part of his cult and hadn't been for several months. However, since I believed Tim had orchestrated a hit on the first man who attacked me and set the second one up to be caught and imprisoned, he must have some way of instilling loyalty and garnering enough trust to ensure no one would rat on him. We just needed to figure out what that was.

A phone chimed, and Ben checked his message. "Eckhardt just texted. Anton Shrieves has an open warrant in Texas for murder. He got flagged when the local authorities ran his prints, and seeing that murder trumps assault, they've agreed to transport the prisoner back to Texas."

"Who is Shrieves?" Decker asked.

"The man arrested for the second assault on Agent Parker," Ben replied. "Didn't any of you read the briefing notes I typed up?"

Decker rubbed at the scruff on his cheeks. He was tired and frustrated, making him easily annoyed and short-tempered. "Not yet. Update our field office and have agents conduct an interrogation once he's settled into his new digs." He looked at the time. "Dammit, we have to get back. Stella, where are we on that warrant?"

She gave him a thumbs up. "We're a go."

"Okay." He turned to me. "Let's head out. I'll update you on our new strategy on the drive back."

As we made our way to the door, Carlo held out a stack of stapled forms. "Your hospital discharge papers, diagnosis, and recommended treatment. And to think, my mother was disappointed I didn't go to medical school. She should see me now."

"Thanks." I took the pages, leafing through them as we went. The actual blood test was real, minus the drug screening. However, Doctor Carlo wrote it off as an unknown drug interaction and effectively declared it an allergy to the pain medication. At least Wilde couldn't ask to see any new prescription bottles.

"Be careful," Eve called. I cast a quick glance over my shoulder. She nodded slightly and went back to the computer. It was nice to know Decker's team didn't spend their downtime eating junk food and discussing sports scores.

Once we were back on the road, Decker exhaled. Visibly, I could see him shift from Jackson Decker to Jason Ellis. He went from a serious federal agent to a laidback drifter in the blink of the eye and a swipe of his hair. That was one hell of a party trick.

"Alex," he drove with one hand on the wheel and the other fidgeting with the gearshift, "I owe you an apology. We've paraded you in front of Tim like a piñata, daring him to strike, so he'll continue to find ways of beating you down until he gets what he wants." He didn't take his eyes off the road, perhaps unable to say what needed to be said if he had to look at me. However, now wasn't the time to mince words, and I didn't need him to sugarcoat things. I wasn't a fool. I knew what Wilde wanted.

"He'll just keep hitting me with a stick until he gets to the sweet, gooey center," I retorted, going along with the analogy. "He wants to fuck me."

Decker nodded. "He also wants access to your trust fund once it becomes available. I don't know which is his top priority. Logically speaking, it should be the money, but his play last night was uncharacteristic. It was the act of a desperate man who appears to be in a downward spiral." He mussed his hair. "Something has him off kilter. He's becoming erratic. It's not safe for you to be alone with him in that facility."

"Alone? There are twenty other women inside that building. It isn't safe for them either." I shook my head and stared out the window. "I'll be fine. I'll take extra precautions. We've been too lax."

"It never occurred to me he could be using the dining hall as a way to drug his followers. Those other women he brought into his bedroom," Decker swallowed, slipping back to his real persona, "I let it happen. I didn't realize. Dammit." He slammed his palm against the wheel, causing the horn to beep.

"I don't know if it was consensual," I admitted, "but from the way Sarah and Anika and the others have spoken about him, I think they've all been duped into believing he is their protector. Honestly, in some ways, he might be."

Jace's icy glare came to rest on me. "How can you say that?"

"Things aren't black and white." I let out a bittersweet laugh. "Didn't you ask if I was capable of sympathizing with his followers? I guess you have your answer now."

"Alex, I don't have time for decrypting your thoughts. Speak your mind."

"These women have no family, no close ties, no connections to the outside world. That isn't Wilde's doing. That's their own doing, and it's probably a safe bet that most of them did it for a reason. Abuse is the most likely cause. Addiction would be a close second."

"You think they're damaged in some way and that's why they revere Wilde."

"You have the fancy training. What do you think?"

"With the exception of a few DUIs or minor drug-related offenses, none of the women have a criminal past. No one ever reported abuse or filed anything related to it. There's no record, which isn't at all uncommon." He glanced at me again. "But they don't behave like victims."

"Are you sure? You haven't been looking at them. You've been focused on Wilde. He offers them sanctuary. He promises safety, but he can control them by simply reinforcing familiar patterns without ever having to resort to violence. They might do things willingly, but it's because they want to keep him happy and make sure he's pleased with them. They don't want to anger him and risk repercussions."

"I did say it's almost like Stockholm syndrome," Jace said. "I didn't just pull that out of my ass."

"Yes, you did. Those big words are just psychobabble meant to make you feel smart."

"Well, that didn't last particularly long since I feel like a fucking moron. Thanks for pointing out the glaringly obvious fact that I've been overlooking."

"Anytime."

He scratched at his beard. "That changes everything." He shook his head again. "Why didn't anyone ever speak out about this in any of the hundreds of guided meditations and sharing sessions that I've attended? Wilde emphasizes openness. These are topics that should have been discussed. He always talks about rebuilding, breaking down a person, and making them stronger from the foundation up. The only openness has been in his group rehab sessions."

"Maybe the women have some classes you weren't invited to join. Or perhaps he tells them to keep it a secret. The other possibility is I'm wrong, but Anika noticed some of my scars. She said her friend had similar ones, but I think she was talking about herself. And the way most of them behave, especially around Wilde, I bet I'm right."

"I don't doubt it. I could kick myself for not realizing this months ago." He sighed heavily. "We can't continue this play. Your cover doesn't have the victim mentality. She's scrappy, like you. We can't change that now, and even if we could, it would be a bad idea." He tore his gaze from the road and met my eyes. "I never intended to use you as bait. It's making him unravel. The first thing we need to do is get Wilde back on an even keel."

"How?"

"We need to get you out of the dorms and make it clear you are not to become one of his playthings. Once that's done, his attention will shift to the other women and using you solely for your bank account. With any luck, that'll lead to busting open his drug emporium."

"It's an emporium now?"

Jace cocked his head to the side. "Maybe. It's hard to say. I've been slow on the uptake." He cleared his throat, getting back to business. He didn't enjoy having his mistakes pointed out, but he wasn't going to deny the validity of my suspicions for the sake of his ego. "Let's get back to the facts for a moment. Several women who had been members of Wilde's cult were found with their stomachs cut open and drugs in their blood. We believe they were acting as drug mules. Wilde was arrested over a decade ago for possession with intent to distribute. Somewhere between then and now, he accumulated enough liquid assets to purchase the land and start his co-op. And roughly twelve hours ago, you were poisoned. Just to be clear, that adds up to drugs and drug trafficking, right?"

"With a side of sexual abuse, possibly multiple counts of rape, and a chance of sex trafficking." I scowled. "Timothy Wilde is one nasty son of a bitch pretending he's one of the good guys. Believe me, when the time comes, I'm going to enjoy putting his ass behind bars."

"That makes two of us. But first things first. We're getting you out of harm's way."

TWENTY-ONE

"This is such a bad idea," I mumbled, but Jace ignored me, which he had been doing a lot more often recently, and placed his breakfast on the table. "Wilde is going to excommunicate you or worse. He'll never approve of me staying here."

Jace rolled his eyes and sat down. I'd never spent much time in a travel trailer and was surprised how roomy it was. I imagined something more along the lines of what I'd seen in various comedy films. This was a much fancier model with a walled-in bedroom, a small galley kitchen, bathroom, and living room with a tiny dining area. It was probably half the size of my apartment back home.

He devoured his food in record time, pointing his fork accusatorily at me. "Food's in the fridge if you're hungry. Make sure you eat here. You don't want to give Tim the chance to poison you again."

"No shit. I'm not that stupid." I opened the fridge and removed a container. Picking up a fork, I ate a few bites. "He must know we're back. He'll be knocking down the door any second. How am I supposed to play this?"

"I'll take care of it." He stood, placing his empty plate in the sink. "Tim should be busy with the farmer's market. Go inside and grab your stuff." He opened the cabinet and unlocked the hidden compartment inside, tossing an RF reader to me. "Make sure nothing's bugged. We're already playing with fire. We don't need to get burned in the event he's eavesdropping on our discussions."

"Yes, sir."

Jace narrowed his eyes. "Y'know, I'm starting to notice you have some issues with authority."

Raising my middle finger, I glared at him. "Anything else?"

"Yeah, when you're done inside, come back to the trailer and stay put until I return. There's a good chance Tim might be with me, so don't leave anything out in the open."

"That goes without saying."

He smirked. "I said it anyway. If anything happens, call me."

Nodding, I left my breakfast where it was and went toward the door. Jace was attempting to overcompensate after what occurred last night, but I was just as much to blame as he was, maybe more since it happened to me. Tucking the trailer key into my pocket, I crossed the expanse from the edge of the property to the main building and went inside. Voices filled the air, but the bulk of Tim's followers were working the stands outside.

A few women were preparing more baked goods to sell, but I bypassed them and went down the hallway toward the dormitories. My door was open, but the room appeared the way it had last night. Even if someone had searched my belongings, they wouldn't have found anything. I'd taken the essentials with me before leaving last night. Knowing my credentials and firearm had been secured, I tossed the few unpacked items into my duffel, grabbed my pillow and blanket from the bed, balanced them over the bag, and made my way out of the room.

I was several feet from the front door when Sarah came inside. Her eyes immediately zeroed in on me, and she let out a relieved squeal. Putting the large box down on the nearest table, she stepped in front of me before I could get out of the way.

"You're back," she said, noticing the bag over my

shoulder, "but you're leaving again."

"No, I'm not. I wouldn't do that without telling everyone. You've all been so kind. I'm just relocating to a larger space."

"What are you talking about? What did the doctor say? Did they find anything wrong?"

"It was an unexpected interaction from the meds they gave me for my ankle. It's also possible it might have been an allergy. They aren't completely certain what triggered that episode, but I'll be okay. The fact that I've been anxious and haven't been sleeping well hasn't helped, so on the way back, Jace offered to let me stay at his place." I didn't want to tell Sarah this. Knowing her, she'd run to Tim as soon as I was out of sight, but I didn't have a choice. There was no reason to keep it a secret. Everyone would know soon enough anyway. "Actually, Jace is talking to Tim about it right now to make sure it's okay."

She gave me a hug. "I'm so glad you're okay. I knew you would be. Tim wouldn't let anything happen to any of us." She released her grip. "Do you need a hand? I just have to refill this box and run it back to the stand, but after that, I can help you get settled."

"No, that's okay. I don't have much. I should probably wait for Tim to give his approval, but the doctors were adamant that I rest. And Jace didn't want me to be stuck in a cramped room right now, so he said I should go on over, even if it is only for the afternoon."

"He's so sweet, but if you need anything, give me a holler." She hugged me again. "I can't wait to tell everyone you're back. We've all been so worried. You're all that anyone's been talking about this morning."

Luckily, she disappeared into the kitchen before I had to say anything else. Returning to the trailer, I unlocked the door, scanned my belongings for any type of radio interference, and stowed my bag behind the sofa. Placing my pillow and blanket on the couch, I stretched out. Until now, I had never met a couch I didn't like, but I'd manage. I just had to wait patiently for Jace to return.

It didn't take long before the trailer door opened. Tim was on Jace's heels, but the cult leader didn't look perturbed by this unexpected turn of events. If anything, he was curious. Scooting over on the couch to make room for the men, I put my empty breakfast container on the side table and beamed a million watt smile at Tim.

"Thank you so much for taking such good care of me last night." I moved to get up, but Tim held up his palm.

"You don't owe me any thanks. I was doing what anyone would have done. Jace informed me of what the doctor said." Tim surveyed the interior of the trailer. "This is quite the improvement from that dorm, right?" He eyed Jace. "And you're certain about this?"

"Absolutely." Jace sat beside me, close enough that our thighs touched, and put his arm around the back of the couch behind me. "What can I say?" He tossed his hair back with a flick of his wrist. "You must have known this would happen when you insisted I spend time with Alex and get to know her. On the ride to the clinic last night, it was like I'd been struck by lightning." He grinned. "Dude, seriously, it all just clicked. The entire time I've been here, listening and learning from you, I never thought those epiphanies and breakthroughs you speak about would happen so suddenly. It just made sense, and everything became clear." Jace looked at me, his eyes told me to play along. "For both of us, right?"

"Yeah." I sunk into him, letting my head rest against his shoulder. I assumed he decided to sell us as a newly minted couple so Tim would agree to cohabitation, but if I'd misinterpreted, my gesture could be played off as something between close friends. "Everything just came together. It was kismet."

Tim took a seat at the table, opposite the two of us. "Alex, are you sure you're comfortable with this?" He chuckled, playing it off as a joke. "From what I recall, you wanted to have nothing to do with this guy."

Jace nudged me with his shoulder, hoping I'd say something to solidify whatever they'd already discussed.

"You've always sent him to help. It's like you're King Arthur, and he's Sir Galahad. You've been telling me all along he's one of the good guys, and when you told him to take me to the clinic, I knew it was true. He was there. He's always been there. You sent him to me when I needed him the most." I turned my gaze to Jace, daring him to do something to indicate what was going on.

Thankfully, he realized I was lost and leaned forward and gave me a quick kiss. At least, I knew where we stood. Doing my best to force a blush onto my face, I turned back to Tim.

"This is because of you. You led us to each other. You made this happen. You really do take care of us physically, emotionally, and spiritually. Thank you." If I had to continue this gratitude parade much longer, I'd hurl. But given Wilde's desire to be in control and worshipped as a savior, this would stroke his ego and satisfy his cravings long enough to slow that downward spiral. Unfortunately, it might also make Jace his next target.

"Don't thank me. The universe works through me." Tim stood, extending his hand toward Jace. Obediently, Jace gripped Tim's hand. "Do not forget the gifts you have been given." Although Tim's words were said pleasantly enough, all I heard was the warning behind them.

"We won't," Jace replied. "Now that Alex is settled, I'll get back to work."

"And I'll see you tonight for guided meditation," I said.

Tim smiled. "Excellent."

Once Tim let himself out, I released the breath I hadn't realized I was holding. Jace sighed, sinking back to the sofa. He rubbed a hand over his face and met my eyes.

"I believe that makes you my property now," Jace teased, and I slapped his arm. "At least he agreed. That was a clever move, crediting everything to him."

"I'm just following your instructions."

"Maybe that's why I found it so clever." He winked. "Now I have to go help out. I'll do what I can to answer whatever questions the others might have, but I expect your evening meditation will be anything but peaceful."

"Aren't you coming with me?"

He shook his head. "I attend the morning sessions before going to work at the gas station. Depending on my schedule on any given day, I usually catch up with Tim before or after dinner, but that's mostly one on one. Since you have to get close to the women, you'll need to live and breathe all of these classes and sessions."

"Obviously, one of us needs to be in the know on what's going on around here." I jerked my chin at the door. "You should run along. You don't want to anger our matchmaker."

"I'll try to keep that in mind." He took his phone out of his pocket and held it up. "This is my cover phone. You have the number. On the plus side, with this guise, we can use overt communication now."

"Hallelujah."

*　　*　　*

Jace and I weathered the hundreds of questions and well-wishes from the Perpetual Lighters. Our story was simple and straightforward. Tim led us together, and Jace's continued rescues made it clear we were meant to be. Thankfully, we were old news after three days, and life returned to normal or what passed for normal inside a cult.

As promised, I'd been attending three of the offered classes each day. Tim led guided meditation in the evenings and tranquility sessions in the mornings. Jace and I attended the morning session together before he'd go to work or pal around with Tim on various errands, but since my cover identity was on the mend, I spent my afternoons with the other unemployed women.

Given the physical restrictions of my faked injury, I took pilates classes on Tuesdays and Thursdays, and Mondays, Wednesdays, and Fridays were spent crafting. There were cooking and baking sessions lined up, but since I was no longer eating with the others, I needed to make sure I wasn't anywhere near the dining hall when meal time came. Avoidance of the kitchen wasn't too difficult, and given the twenty women on the property, there wasn't a shortage of someone wanting to play happy homemaker. Personally, I hoped that mentality was part of the brainwashing they had endured since joining Tim's rank and file, but realistically, that behavior was probably already ingrained in who they were.

My new "sisters" seemed warm and friendly, but they only made small talk. I was an oddity in the group. I was one of the select few in a relationship. That distinction made me an outcast, so I was cautious to push too hard.

Each morning, I learned what I could from whichever group member decided to share her story or recent difficulty in attaining tranquility. The theory behind it sounded like a bunch of bullshit, but I wasn't here to pass judgment on paths that led to enlightenment.

On the bright side, some of these fun facts could prove useful in the future. So far, I'd learned about Linda's recovery from meth, Dove's gruesome divorce, and Charlotte's fear and loneliness when her parents threw her out of the house after a pregnancy scare. This was real life for everyone else here. They wanted a safe haven, not a predator like Tim who wanted nothing more than to exploit them.

After getting into a stable groove, I began assessing the others, hoping to determine who was the most likely to know something useful and would be willing to share. Anika remained at the top of my list. She always stuck close to me, positioning her mat next to mine in pilates or sitting across from me when we worked on whatever popular craft would be sold over the weekend. Occasionally, I'd find her eyes drawn to my wrists. I'd been careful to keep the rest of my scars hidden from her. However, I'd been unable to get her alone, and the words we exchanged were always in relation to the group or the session we were attending.

Gaining trust was proving to be a slow process. I hoped to gain some insight while listening to the others talk. When another meditation class ended for the evening, I couldn't help but notice Sarah pulling Tim off to the side. Perhaps she had something private to discuss, but I had no idea what it might be. She hadn't said a word during meditation, but she seemed just as bouncy and bubbly as ever earlier in the day. Tim spoke to her in a hushed tone that didn't carry as I helped Linda gather the cushions and place them in the closet. By the time we had tidied up the room, Sarah was wishing us all a good night.

"Alex," Tim called, "may we speak?"

"Certainly." I smiled at Linda and crossed the room. "That was another excellent class. I always feel so much better afterward." Truthfully, there was something about the meditation and tranquility sessions that energized me. Perhaps I was just as susceptible to Tim's mind games as everyone else here.

"I'm glad you enjoy them and that you finally came around to what the Church of Perpetual Light has to offer. You've really committed to this. It's nice having someone new being so gung-ho about things." His eyes flicked behind me, and he offered a wave to Linda as she left. "I just wanted to ask how you like your new living arrangement."

"It's good."

His brows knit together. "Are you sure?"

I shrugged, unsure where this was going. "My entire life is so different now than it was a couple of weeks ago. This is probably still the adjustment period, but I'm happy. Jace is too, I think." I tried to look worried. "Did he say something to you?"

"Nothing negative. He's absolutely smitten. It just happened so fast, and since you were so staunchly independent before the attack, I wanted to make sure you were adjusting okay and not feeling trapped."

"Not at all. You and this place are the best things that have ever happened to me. I wish there was more I could do to repay your kindness."

"Just keep coming to classes, work on bettering yourself, and the rest will follow naturally." He gave me a lingering hug that felt awkward. "I'll see you in the morning."

"I'll be here."

TWENTY-TWO

After the meditation session, I was pumped. Perhaps it was the quiet and introspection that made me feel like I should run a marathon afterward as a means of escape. Every night, I'd return to the trailer and attempt to do something to fight off the stir craziness. Decker wasn't back from his cover's day job yet, so I pushed the sofa against the wall and used the free space to work out. After a hundred sit-ups, I tossed my sweaty t-shirt to the side and moved on to lunges and squats. Jumping jacks were a nice way to get some cardio in. When I lost count of how many I'd done and breathing became difficult, I did some stretches and planks. Finally, with more energy to spare, I moved on to push-ups.

The door to the trailer opened, and I turned my head to see Decker entering. He glanced in my direction and went into the kitchen. Finishing a set of fifty, I grabbed my t-shirt and used it to wipe the sweat off my face before pushing the couch back to its original position.

"Anything to report?" he asked, finding the inside of the fridge fascinating.

"Tim and Sarah had another weird interaction, but I have no idea what it was about. She's secretive. She doesn't talk about much of anything with the others, at least not when I'm around." I maneuvered next to him and grabbed a bottle of water. "Anika is still our best bet. She wants to talk to me. I just don't know what she has to say. We haven't exactly had any alone time. I should be able to corner her during the farmer's market this weekend. We'll see what she says then."

Decker grabbed a salad out of the fridge and turned to look at me, his eyes coming to rest on my exposed skin. "No wonder you said bruises were no big deal." His gaze flicked to my eyes. "You might want to make sure you cover up when you're in exercise classes with the others."

"Yep." Taking the hint, I pulled my shirt over my head. "I'll take a shower and then watch the surveillance feed while you get some shuteye." I glanced toward the bedroom. "You really should take the bed. I'm cool with the couch."

He shook his head, considered saying something, but changed his mind. "Matt phoned earlier. It sounds like we might be on to something, but he didn't say what. We can't risk a compromise, so we keep our messages short. But we should be able to sneak away tomorrow evening for an update. I told Tim I wanted to take you out on a proper date, so that will explain our absence for a few hours."

"Okay."

At least now I understood why Tim had spoken to me earlier. Perhaps he hoped I was unhappy with this arrangement and wanted to move into his bedroom instead, or he was trying to stack the deck in his protégé's favor to reward Jace for his obedience and commitment to the cause. It didn't matter as long as our covers remained intact.

After a shower, I changed into a different t-shirt and pajama shorts, noticing my hands shaking. Chalking it up to the difficult workout, I decided to put some protein and sugar into my body. Damn Decker and his stupid conscientious food mentality. His habits were ruining my palate for processed foods and convenience snacks.

After eating some leftovers, I took a seat on the sofa beside him. He had a tablet dialed in to the hidden cameras that had been planted on the property. Ever since Tim attempted to lure me into his room, we been vigilant to stop him from doing it to anyone else. So far, things had been quiet, but neither of us had been sleeping particularly well, choosing to trade out shifts to keep an eye on things. The cameras were motion sensitive, only activating when movement was detected in order to conserve battery power. Unfortunately, the darkened hallways limited the range and sensitivity of the motion sensors. The only excitement I'd seen on the feed was when one of the women got up to use the restroom. Other than that, the screen remained black.

"Don't you ever get tired?" he asked.

"Not really. This is the norm when I work undercover. It's high stress amidst a lot of tedious downtime."

"Is that why you've been doing killer workouts every night?"

"You're one to talk. I caught you doing burpees this morning. I've just been doing floor exercises and strength training. Face it, I'm totally slacking off, and I really miss running. Of course, that's out of the question since my ankle is supposedly busted." I batted my eyelashes. "Do you think we could justify purchasing a treadmill as a necessary expenditure for our assignment? If we come up with a feasible excuse, I'll file the paperwork with my agency instead."

"Even if we did, Tim would notice and become suspicious."

"This sucks." I rotated my shoulders, feeling my muscles starting to cramp. "I hate waiting."

"*You* hate waiting? Talk to me again in nine months."

Pressing my lips together, I didn't want to think about being stuck in this hellhole for nine months. How many bodies would turn up between then and now? How many kilos of narcotics would be smuggled in or out, and how many would die from overdoses related to drugs because of that? And selfishly, I wanted to go home. I wanted to see Martin, even though I had no idea how to fix things.

"I'm sorry."

Decker turned to me. "Tell that to the victims." He

sighed and rubbed his face. "Now I'm sorry. I shouldn't put that on you. I just hate that we came so close to having something to stop him, and it turned out it wasn't drugs. Not that I wanted you to be roofied, but if he was going to slip you something, why couldn't it have been some easily identifiable shit?" He brushed his hair back. "I've been collecting samples from the gardens. Every single thing I find growing, I take a clipping. I left them at the dead drop this afternoon."

"Is that why Matt called?"

"I hope so." He shook it off. "There's no reason to speculate or get our hopes up." He propped the tablet up so it was easily in view and turned to me. "Let's talk about something else."

"Like what?"

"What would be your perfect date? I'm only asking so we can come up with a corresponding cover story for this weekend. It'd probably be easier to gush, if it's something you'd enjoy."

"I don't know."

"Come on, Alex. Didn't your last boyfriend ever take you anywhere nice? What'd you guys do? Where'd you go? Was any of it particularly memorable?"

Seeing the past unfold, the galas, the charity functions, his insistence on getting me to dance, the restaurants, the bars, the exclusive clubs, and the private tours of art exhibits and museums followed by catered meals on rooftops, made my chest feel tight, and I fought to calm my broken heart. "Don't expect me to believe you've never been on a date. You were probably the high school quarterback. Just come up with something simple, tell the lie, and I'll swear to it," I said.

Decker held up his palms. "I didn't realize dating was a touchy subject. I wasn't asking about the man, just a date. Any date."

"My dating life has always been troublesome. That's something normal people do, and I'm not particularly normal. My personal relationships aren't necessarily healthy."

"What's that supposed to mean?"

"It means you get to decide on the details for any romantic event by which we allegedly partook."

Decker laughed. "Fine, but I'm going to get you to open up to me about your life one of these days."

"Not if I can help it. It's called a private life for a reason." Scooping the tablet up, I got off the couch. "Get some sleep. I'll be in the bedroom, waiting for you to take over sentry duty."

Closing the door, I sunk to the floor and listened to the shifting of the couch cushions while Decker got settled. Once everything was quiet, I turned the volume up on the tablet and hit the alert button. Knowing the device would chime should any of the cameras become active, I picked up the novel I'd been reading, but my mind was elsewhere. Returning it to the stack of books, I leafed through a few magazines, but all I seemed capable of was looking at the pictures. Eventually, I found a deck of cards and played solitaire until Jace knocked on the bedroom door.

"Anything?" he asked, nodding at the tablet.

"Nope." My eyes found the nearest clock. It was three a.m. "Are you sure you don't want to get a few more hours. I'm okay to stay up."

"If you fall asleep right now, you'll get almost five before Tim's morning message. Get some rest." He scooped the tablet off the end of the bed and left the room, closing the door behind him.

I dropped the cards to the floor and crawled under the covers. It didn't take long to fall asleep. And what felt like moments later, I jumped up in bed. Gasping for breath, I wasn't certain what woke me or why I was so afraid. Remnants of a reoccurring nightmare entered my mind. I sighed, dropping back to the pillow. I was okay. Everything was okay. Relax, Parker. Just breathe.

A few seconds later, Decker knocked on the door, cautiously opening it. "You okay?"

"Yep." I threw an arm over my face, blocking out the bright light that streamed in from the doorway. The bedroom itself had no windows. The main area had two small ones, one on either side, and from the looks of it, morning had come. "I just need a minute."

He lingered for several seconds, finally mumbling okay. Once the door latched, I removed my arm and opened my eyes, staring at the ceiling. This was hell. The monotony would have been bearable if we were making progress, but it didn't feel like it. It felt like we were playing house while Tim did whatever he pleased right under our noses. Today, I was determined to find some answers. This couldn't go on. I was already cracking under the pressure. My sanity wouldn't last nine more months. I had no idea how Decker wasn't *Loony Tunes* by now.

Our typical morning routine followed, a quick bite then off to see our favorite cult leader for the morning worship session. Tranquility lessons and sharing personal stories weren't exactly what I considered a religious experience, but that's how Wilde packaged it in order to apply for his tax exemptions. While Berta droned on about her past experiences in the corporate world, I zoned out, wondering why Tim would start a church in the first place. From what we knew about him, he was a dealer with a predilection for sexual assault. At least that was my hunch based on the dropped charges and whatever he hoped to accomplish by poisoning me and taking me to his bedroom. So why a church? Why not a crackhouse or a whorehouse?

Decker put an arm around my shoulders. I glanced up at him, following his gaze to the corner of the room where Anika was huddled all alone. Something was wrong. She looked small and frightened. Sarah and the others were at the front of the room. Perhaps they'd had a fight or disagreement, but since Tim preached peace and techniques to avoid conflict, that didn't make much sense. I didn't know what happened during morning meals, but whatever spooked Anika was far worse than some tiff over macramé lanyards or who got the last bacon strip.

Unfortunately, I was trapped until class was dismissed. The tedium became even more unbearable. I struggled to keep myself facing forward while monitoring Anika with my peripheral vision. She looked like a deer caught in headlights. I knew that look. She wanted to run. What happened that transformed her attitude overnight? The possibilities that popped into my head weren't pleasant, and I reminded myself we'd watched the surveillance footage all night. However, a single unpleasant thought came to mind. What about the blind spots?

"I'm going to talk to Tim," Decker whispered as soon as we were dismissed.

Nodding, I hurried away before anyone tried to speak to me. Painting a smile on my face, I fell into step with Anika and wished her a good morning. She mumbled a greeting back, but the passive indifference wasn't normal for her.

"Is everything okay?" I dropped my voice so no one else would hear us. The dorms were under surveillance, but I wasn't sure where all the cameras were hidden inside the facility.

"Of course. Why wouldn't it be?" She didn't meet my eyes and continued on her trek back toward her room.

"Hey," I grabbed her shoulder, watching her wince at the contact, "do you want to get out of here for a bit. Maybe we could grab a cup of coffee or tea. We could really splurge and get a cookie or pastry to go with it." I glanced around, making sure no one was nearby. "Jace doesn't keep any caffeine or processed snacks at the trailer. I know Tim feels the same way about those things. What do you say we be rebels for an afternoon?"

She narrowed her eyes, assessing me as if the offer might be intended to trick her. "You want to leave the facility?"

"We aren't prisoners. Granted, I don't have a job or much incentive to go out into the world, but Tim's made it clear we can go and come as we please. We'll be back soon. Plus, we're supposed to be working on those stained-glass coasters today, and my art skills suck. Perhaps some chocolate chip cookies will be just the inspiration I need."

A smile played across her lips, not quite making it to her eyes. "Let me grab my purse. I'll meet you near the front door."

"I'll be there."

On my way to the front of the building, I crossed paths with Tim and Jace. The two were lost in conversation but stopped as soon as they spotted me. Tim smiled, politely excusing himself a second later when one of the women beckoned to him. Decker moved closer, holding out his arms for a hug. Slipping into his embrace, I updated him on my plans for the morning.

"Do you think Tim did something to her?" Decker whispered in my ear. "We maintained eyes all night."

Shaking my head, I entwined my arms around him and turned my face toward his neck. "How did Tim seem? Any different?"

Decker released me. "I don't know." He blinked a few times. "I have a surprise for you this evening. I'm getting off work early. I want to take you somewhere special. I'll meet you at the trailer at five. Don't be late."

"I'll let you know if I will be."

He gave me a quick peck on the cheek, shouted a goodbye to Tim, and went out the door. I watched him leave, waving like a lovestruck idiot. When I turned around, Anika was a few feet away. She clutched her purse like it was a lifeline.

"Do you mind walking back to the trailer so I can grab my purse and keys?" I asked.

"No problem."

Luckily, we slipped out without anyone noticing. She fell into step beside me as we made our way across the dusty path. It was too early in the morning for this, but I wanted to know what happened, even if it meant taking advantage of her vulnerable state.

"I had this horrible nightmare last night," I volunteered, hoping to break the ice. "I have them a lot. That's probably the reason for the caffeine and sugar craving." I watched her out of the corner of my eye. "If you don't mind me saying, you look like you could use a bit of a pick-me-up too. Did you sleep okay?"

She didn't answer the question. Her focus remained on kicking a pebble along the path as we went toward the trailer. Finally, she said, "What was your nightmare about?"

"People getting hurt. Bad men trying to kill me." It wasn't exactly a lie, and it worked well with my cover's background and the goons Wilde had sent to kneecap me. "It's stupid, but I can't exactly shake the feeling of being afraid or alone." Unlocking the trailer door, I held it open for her. "Do you want to come inside? It might take me a few minutes to find my keys."

"Yeah, okay."

"Great. Make yourself at home."

"Jace won't mind?"

I gave her an odd look. "Of course not. I can do whatever I want. He said this was my home too, so I can have guests. I could probably draw all over the walls or paint everything pink if I really wanted to."

She giggled. "Maybe you should."

"Maybe I will." I laughed along with her. As she walked through the trailer, looking at the furniture and the roominess compared to the dorms, she started to relax. Deciding I should make a pretext of searching for car keys, I asked, "Do you have your own car?"

"I sold it years ago when I needed some quick cash. I managed without, and once I came here, there wasn't a need for one anymore." She peered out the window, and I suspected she was regretting that decision. Before I could ask how long she'd been here, she crossed the room and grabbed my wrist. "How did this happen? You said you didn't work in one of the dungeons, so what caused these scars?"

"Why do you want to know?"

She looked me right in the eye, determining if she could trust me. "Who are you?"

"Anika, it's me. What's up with you today? I'm Alex. A-lex, Alice Lexington. Seriously?" I gave her a bewildered look, but my heart raced. How could she be on to me? "And to think we haven't even had the caffeine or sugar yet. What's got you so crazy, girl?"

"I'm not crazy." She dropped into one of the kitchen chairs. "Rich women like you don't have bondage scars." I opened my mouth to come up with a feasible lie, but she cut me off. "Don't tell me your boyfriend liked the kinky stuff. He would have had the foresight to get the leather cuffs that wouldn't leave permanent marks."

"I'm not rich. My father was wealthy, not me. As soon as I was smart enough and old enough, I distanced myself from him and his wealth. Maybe you'd call it slumming it, but I hung out with a rougher crowd, surviving as best I could off barista tips and minimum wage. Shit happens. Shit still happens. I've been open and honest about who I am, but the dark spots in my past don't need to come to light. I'm not that person. I don't hang with those crowds. And I'm here, so I don't end up back there."

She set her jaw, mulling over the things I said. "In that case, I don't think you should be here." She wet her lips. "I'm not sure any of us should be here."

TWENTY-THREE

"That's all Anika said?" Decker asked, and I nodded. "Shit."

"She told me to meet her tomorrow. She wants to show me something she found, but she wouldn't even hint as to what it might be. I wanted to push so hard, but she's already skeptical. Maybe I could have done something more to convince her to confide in me. I don't know. She made me swear not to tell anyone about this, but I don't even know what this is."

"She could be a plant. Wilde could be on to you. Perhaps he asked her to find out what she could. You said she's been observing you since you joined the cult."

Looking down at my wrists, I didn't know what to think. "These are a couple of years old. I don't even notice them anymore, and she points to them like they're neon signs."

His gaze went to the faded scars. "Until you pointed them out, I didn't even see them. It just looks like you were using a hair elastic as a bracelet. Was she right that they're bondage scars?"

"In a manner of speaking." I stared out the windshield. "When I was private sector, my cover was compromised by a rat and I was tied up and tortured." His eyes shot to me. I was glad I wasn't driving so I could look out the window to avoid eye contact. "Don't worry," I added cynically, "I didn't break. I would have died before giving up anyone else. In fact, for a few moments, I wanted to die, and just think, then we wouldn't be here having this delightful conversation right now."

"Fucking hell," Decker exhaled quietly. "The only way she would notice those damn scars is if she's seen them before. What if it wasn't an S&M club? What if she's seen things at the facility? We need to separate her from the group and bring her in."

"How? You just said she could be a plant."

"We could grab her when she leaves."

"Except she never does. She doesn't have a car or any method of transportation out, unless someone offers her a ride. We didn't even make it to coffee this morning. I got her as far as the trailer, and then she ran back to her room after giving me that cryptic message." I shook my head, fighting away the frustration. "If she's so afraid of someone or something on the property, she should have been begging to leave."

"Doesn't that fit with the abuse mentality? She doesn't want to risk angering Wilde for fear he'll retaliate. It's very possible he's the one who caused her friend's scars."

"That doesn't explain why she was spooked at this morning's tranquility session. Something just happened, or she just found out about it. Either way, now is the worst time for us to be away from the co-op. If something's going down, we need to be close."

He didn't say anything, but I knew he agreed with my assessment. Unfortunately, this was only a hunch. Anika's fears might turn out to be nothing at all, or her story could be a trap. However, my gut said her terror was real, and I learned long ago to trust my instincts. Convincing myself that a few hours away wouldn't hurt since everyone at the co-op was getting the property ready for the weekend helped quell my nerves. With any luck, the rest of the team had hard evidence we could use to further our agenda and take this bastard down. At the very least, it was worth checking out.

We arrived a few minutes later and stepped into the

command center. "You two look cozy," Eve said. "Is this the honeymoon phase?"

"Zip it," Decker growled.

Eve gave me a look, wondering why Decker wasn't his typical friendly self. I shook my head, pressing my lips together in warning. She gave a curt nod and busied herself with gathering whatever reports she had collected in our absence.

Ben kicked off the floor, rolling his chair toward the table in the middle of the room. He placed his tablet on top and hit a few keys, broadcasting the data to the large screen. "While we wait for Matt and Stella, the lab's been working around the clock to run the samples you've collected. As you can tell, most are run-of-the-mill spices. We have our parsley, mint, basil, oregano, and thyme."

"We get the point," I interrupted. "Anything sinister?"

"Not sinister exactly. There were several varieties of kratom growing on the property." Ben raised an eyebrow. "I can't keep up if that's a schedule I narcotic or not. Stella's looking into it. If it is, it might provide enough evidence to conduct a raid."

"And throw the entire op into jeopardy." Jace shook his head. "If Tim's growing it, he'll defend it as a means to alleviate opium withdrawal symptoms. It's no secret that several of his followers have addiction problems. He'd play it off as being a Good Samaritan. With the right judge, everything would be tossed, including whatever else we find. I want something with teeth that isn't a legal grey area."

"Then please turn your attention to door number three." Ben clicked a few keys and a photo of a flowering plant, along with a molecular representation, filled the screen. "I believe we've identified the poison. Meet a member of the *Strychnos* family."

"Like strychnine?" I suddenly felt like we were chasing a Bond villain.

Ben smiled. "Yep, except that comes from a tree. This is a plant. It's not native to the area, but our climate is close enough for it to stay alive with the proper care. It produces a poison that causes muscle paralysis. As you probably remember, it impairs all voluntary muscle function as well as the diaphragm. That's why you were having trouble breathing."

"Is there an antidote?" Decker asked, studying the picture of the plant.

"One can be manufactured, but as long as breathing is maintained, the poison burns itself out after a while. The time it takes depends on the dosage. The only problem is it has to come into direct contact with the bloodstream. If ingested, it's harmless."

Decker narrowed his eyes. "That's not it. He dosed her food. We're still missing something. Dammit." Turning away from the table, he slammed his palm against the nearest desk. "Is there anything else?"

"That was it." Ben gave me another look. "Are you certain you didn't get scratched or jabbed before your body locked up?"

"Not that I noticed." I looked at Eve who was watching Decker with concern. "This morning, Anika was distraught. She didn't tell me what was wrong, but she seems to be aware of something unsettling happening on the property. Now isn't the best time for us to be away." I turned to Ben. "Tell me about the cameras we planted on the premises. Is it possible to traipse past one without setting it off?"

"Ideally, no. Realistically, probably."

Before Ben could go into the technical specifications, Matt and Stella entered the room. Carlo was two feet behind them. Decker dragged himself back to the table. I gave him a look, but his expression was unreadable. The last few times we'd been at headquarters, his frustration and annoyance had been an issue. Typically, he was relaxed. One could even call it chill, but being back here brought out the worst in him. I didn't like it. Seeing his team made him realize just how alone and in the cold he really was.

Stella dropped the paperwork on the table. "The assistant director approved a raid at your discretion. The kratom raises questions. However, the legality of the herb is currently being debated, so unless you have something more solid, the AUSA I spoke with warned we should tread lightly."

"We'll hold off for now," Decker said. "What else do you have?"

Eckhardt cleared his throat. "A couple of things. First, a gangbanger was arrested for Vincent Harbring's murder. The LAPD is pushing the kid hard for a confession. They identified the killer after pulling his prints from inside the abandoned vehicle. When officers arrested him, he had the murder weapon on him."

"He must have missed the crash course in gangbanging 101," I muttered.

Eckhardt snorted. "Based on nearby traffic cam footage, the kid jacked the vehicle, shot the driver, left him for dead, and took off. He delivered the car to a chop shop several blocks away, and someone else drove it across state lines. It was a shitty car, not worth the effort of chopping, but the gangbanger wanted it for a reason. Forensics found traces of cocaine in the trunk. We're thinking that's why Harbring got jacked. The gang wanted what was in the trunk. We're running a joint investigation with the police narcotics unit to monitor the chop shop for other drug related activity."

Decker rubbed at his stubble. "Good. That could be promising. Have we solidified Harbring's connection to Wilde yet?"

Eckhardt shook his head. "We're still working on it. In the meantime, we're offering the killer incentives for any information he provides that will help our current investigation. He's mulling it over with his attorney."

"Anything else?" Decker glanced at his watch.

"You're not going to like it," Carlo muttered, "but Shrieves supposedly hung himself in his cell a couple of hours ago. However, I have my doubts. The guy was wanted for killing a police officer during a routine traffic stop."

"Dammit," I swore, "this is worse than some outlandish conspiracy theory."

"Wait," Decker's focus went razor sharp, "get the details on the traffic stop. If Shrieves killed an officer for being pulled over, he probably had contraband in his vehicle. I want a full workup and profile on this guy—his known associates, any aliases, and prison stints. I want to know everything about him." He let out an incredulous laugh. "No wonder Wilde didn't care that he got arrested. He must have assumed the cops would take revenge or he'd off himself if caught, whichever the case may be." He blinked a few times. "Check for any connections between the dead drug mules and Shrieves, Harbring, and the gangbanger. We need something solid, and we need it fast." He pointed at the time. "We should get back. Call when you have something." Without waiting for me, he left the room.

"Do me a favor," I said, "run everything you can on Anika again. I know you already have profiles on the flock, but she mentioned Vegas and S&M clubs. She said she sold her car years ago because she needed cash. See if you can find out what kind of trouble she was in and how she got mixed up with Wilde. There's a chance we might be bringing her in, so we need to prepare for that contingency." I gave Eve a reassuring look and ran for the door. It was time we headed back.

"Do you want me to drive?" I asked, eyeing Decker who had yet to turn the key in the ignition.

He shook his head and started the car. "This is a shitfest. We have another body to credit to Wilde, and we're stuck chasing our tails."

"Tell me about the men who signed on to be Perpetual Lighters. Wilde recruits women, but there are four or five guys currently at the co-op. What's their deal?"

"They don't fit the same profile as the women. I've never seen Wilde actively recruit any of them. They just showed up at his doorstep, looking for a handout. At least that was more or less how I infiltrated the cult. I'd say they're all drifters, homeless, down on their luck. Three of them are recovering addicts. Before you ask, aside from petty larceny, possession, and public intoxication, they don't have criminal records. Nothing violent. No indication they were pushers. They were just bums. Statistically speaking, chances are they suffer from some kind of mental illness, but I've spoken to them. Whatever maladies they might have seem to be under control at the present." Decker sighed. "Perhaps they're self-medicating or all that sharing and therapy Wilde harps on actually helped them."

"Or it's bullshit. They could be part of his network. He brings them in and lets them get close to the women to ensure a level of trust and obedience. Then after some time, he sends them away and uses them to run the women as mules."

"I applaud that theory. To be honest, I had already considered it, but unless you can pull proof out of your ass, it's nothing more than conjecture." He rubbed a hand over his mouth. "How much faith do you have in Anika blowing this open for us?"

I didn't respond. Instead, I watched Decker fidget on the drive back. Something had him twisted up inside, and I wasn't completely convinced it was the case. We didn't speak much. I was lost in thought, attempting to weave the random pieces of the puzzle together into a logical narrative. I had plenty of theories, but none of them provided a means by which to gain evidence. Something damning had to be on the property. We needed to find it. Decker had done his best to search every nook and cranny since his arrival, but some areas were off limits. Now that there were two of us, our chances of snooping increased exponentially. The biggest obstacle was the surveillance equipment Wilde had hidden throughout the compound.

"The camera feed goes somewhere, and since Tim is anti-technology in order to prevent outside influence and news from affecting his followers, it's not like he has a computer bank out in the open. There must be some hidden parts to the compound that we just haven't found yet."

"Like I said, the entire upper level is a mystery to me. I've only been in Tim's bedroom once, and that was to rescue you."

Ignoring the condescending way he said the word rescue, I considered a few more things. "Are there generators on the property?"

"I don't think so. What are you thinking?"

"I'm thinking he'll be busy with the farmer's market this weekend, so if we cut the power inside, I can snoop around undetected while you keep him distracted."

"What if the cameras have a backup?"

"What if they don't?"

He stopped at a red light. "Find out what you can from Anika first. Then we'll take it from there." He blinked a few times. "Be honest with me," he shifted in his seat to look straight at me, "am I being too cautious? Is that why this investigation isn't going anywhere?"

"It's your op."

"Alex."

"Trust your gut. If you think we need to be careful, we'll be careful."

"That is not an answer, Agent Parker."

I stared at him, surprised he referred to me in such an official capacity, particularly when we were less than ten miles from the co-op. Normally, he'd be back to being Jason Ellis by now. Something was definitely wrong. "What's going on with you?"

He pressed his lips together and narrowed his eyes. "I don't know. I've been anxious since you told me about the conversation with Anika. If that asshole did something to her last night," he bared his teeth, scowling, "I should have done something to stop it."

My gut said it was time we blow this mother out of the water, but my brain came up with twenty-four reasons why it was important to be cautious. Anything that disrupted Wilde's perfect harmony would result in detriment to the men and women living on the grounds and whoever worked for him beyond those walls. Just bringing me onboard had resulted in two fatalities. Wilde was calculated and pragmatic. He would burn down every bridge before letting anyone get to him. That's why Jace had been so cautious.

"Anika's scared. All we know is it has something to do with Wilde. The sooner we get something on him, the sooner this stops. If he attacked her, it's probably because he didn't get to follow through with me." I hated to think someone had been assaulted right under our noses, and we were too clueless and blind to do anything to prevent it from happening. "You're right. We should wait to see what she says before we do anything rash, but if her story doesn't lead to something solid, I vote we take a more proactive stance in the future."

"Agreed."

TWENTY-FOUR

"Alex." The voice yelling my name was no longer Martin's. It sounded familiar, but no one was inside the house except Martin and the men hired to kill him. "Alex."

I jolted upward, gun drawn and pointed at the cause of the disturbance. Decker stood in the doorway, a Glock down at his side. He didn't make a move. He stared at me from the darkened doorway. Flipping the safety on, I tucked my gun into my hiding spot between the mattress and frame.

"Sorry." Shaking it off, I ran through the possibilities for Decker being in my bedroom. It was dark outside, so I hadn't overslept. "Do we have something on the feed? Is Anika okay?"

"She's fine. Nothing to report." He reached behind him, grabbing the tablet and placing it on the dresser beside his weapon. "There's been no movement inside the facility since I took over watch." I raised my eyebrow, waiting for a reason why he woke me up two hours after I went to sleep. "Are you okay?"

"I was better two minutes ago before you woke me up."

He cocked his head and snorted. "So that's why you were screaming?"

"Shit." I flopped down on the mattress, hoping he'd let it go and we could have this conversation at a later date, preferably never, but the creaking floor told me Decker planned on talking about this now. "I'm sorry I disturbed you."

"Don't do that. This isn't about me. It's about you." He moved around the room until he was in front of me, crossing his arms over his chest and leaning against the wall. "Is this why you volunteered for this assignment? Did you become too much of a liability at the OIO?"

"I am not a liability. It's called a nightmare, Jace. Get over it. Everyone has bad dreams."

He rubbed at the light beard on his chin. "Not a liability? What would have happened if you had fallen asleep inside the co-op? You would have blown your cover and possibly mine. Did you ever think of that?"

"Get real. I'm sure most of the women inside have nightmares. I was attacked by Wilde's goons. Twice. That warrants a few bad dreams."

He closed his eyes, fighting to control his words. "Yeah, and that's why I gave you the benefit of the doubt. But I have listened to you cry and scream every single night since you moved into the trailer. I have half a mind to pull you off this mission." Shaking his head, he set his jaw. "But we'd lose more by doing that than what we can gain. You should have disclosed when you realized what the op entailed. How long have the nightmares been an issue?"

"They aren't. I have it handled. Don't start some psychobabble bullshit. I don't want to hear it. I'm fine. Really." Flipping over, I hoped Decker would get the message and drop it. However, the former therapist wasn't about to do that.

He bumped the mattress with his leg. "From what I gather, you keep having the same dream. Am I right?"

"Yes." Growing even more agitated, I threw off the covers and sat up in bed. "Next question. And before you say I'm agitated, angry, or irritable, I'd like to point out that I haven't had a chance to sleep yet, so it's wholly justified. Frankly, shooting you might also be."

He chuckled. "At least you're familiar with the

symptoms of PTSD."

"I don't have PTSD. Do you want to know what I have?" I stared him down like a speeding train, daring him to ask but silently willing him to walk away. He nodded. "A broken heart."

He gave me a skeptical look. "It sounded more like you were begging for your life." His eyes moved to my wrists. "It would be completely understandable if you were remembering being tortured after Anika harped on that point."

I climbed out of bed and left the room, heading for the kitchen. I needed space to breathe. "Don't even. I told you about what caused my scars because it was relevant to the case. That's the only reason I mentioned it, and for the record, I haven't had *those* dreams in a long time."

Decker followed behind me, replacing his gun in the hidden compartment in the kitchen cabinet. Perhaps he feared I'd take it away from him and shoot him. Admittedly, that thought was growing in appeal by the second. I filled a glass with water, swished it around my mouth, and swallowed.

"I've seen your other scars, Alex. You've been in a few bad situations. I'm not faulting you for that, but we need to be honest with one another. I need to know where your head is in order to have your back. If this op is getting to be too much for you, I need to know."

Biting back the comment I wanted to make about Decker's head being up Tim's ass, I was too exhausted and frustrated to continue the fight. It'd be easier to tell Decker what he wanted to know instead of arguing with him over it. Draining the glass, I put it in the sink.

"My nightmares have nothing to do with any of the scars you've seen. I just miss someone back home."

"Your ex-boyfriend?"

I nodded.

He let out a disbelieving huff. "What does that have to do with a gunfight?"

"Our history is extremely complex. He was my first private sector gig. We weren't dating at the time. I'm not even sure we were friends. Shit went sideways." I blinked, hearing my voice hitch. "A group of mercenaries was hired to kill him. It was just the two of us against four heavily armed men. One of them snuck up on us, and Martin pushed me out of the way. He nearly bled out." I fought to keep my voice from shaking, knowing the exhaustion had heightened my emotional state. With my luck, Decker would use it as fodder for demonstrating how unbalanced I was. "It's so stupid. I was past this for a long time. We didn't even start dating until I made peace with it, and now all I can think about is that if someone tries to hurt him, I won't be there this time. And I keep having these fucking dreams about it, reminding me how badly I've screwed up."

"That's what you keep dreaming?"

"Yep."

The analysis went through his mind, playing across his eyes with more pity and sadness than I ever wanted to see. "What are you doing about it?"

I shrugged. There wasn't anything I could do. It was just how things were.

"Yeah, that's not gonna work," Decker said. "You have to get over this. Your focus needs to be here, not back home."

"I'm not compromised. When I'm inside that house, I am Alice. My subconscious just hasn't gotten the memo yet, and I can't control that." Deciding I was done talking, I headed back to the bedroom. I needed to sleep, and if Decker continued to be a pain in my ass, I'd barricade the door to keep him out. I had just gotten into bed when the mattress dipped down beside me. "What the hell are you doing?"

"Keeping you company."

"I can assure you that you won't be getting lucky tonight or any night. Ever."

He smiled. "Good. We're on the same page." He closed his eyes. "Damn, I really missed this bed."

*　　*　　*

Our morning routine continued as if nothing had happened a few hours earlier. Decker was working out in the main room when I padded into the kitchen in search of coffee. Of course, there was none to be found, and I glared at the box of tea like it was personally responsible for eliminating all coffee from the planet. Settling on juice and some leftover stew from a couple of nights ago, I took a seat at the table and watched Decker do a few dozen burpees, adding an extra jumping jack at the height of it just to make life interesting. When he was finished, he slurped down a few gulps of his morning smoothie and took off his sweaty shirt.

"Impressed?" he teased, tossing that surfer boy grin my way.

"I've seen better."

He pointed to the littering of red across his right pec. "I caught shrapnel from a frag grenade on a particularly dicey raid of a cartel stronghold. I was so close to the impact that some of the pieces went through my vest. You should see my leg."

"Did I ask?"

"No, but it's about time I share some of my history with you." He held the smile a few seconds longer before succumbing to my morning grumpiness. "Whether you like it or not, I need you to be completely focused. That includes your subconscious, so we aren't done talking about things. You need to accept it."

Ignoring my death stare, he grabbed a change of clothes and headed into the bathroom. In fifteen minutes, we'd be on our way to Tim's morning tranquility session, and I was anything but tranquil. Compartmentalizing my problems, I allowed my thoughts to return to Anika. I had no idea what she wanted to show me, but I needed to be prepared for anything. For all I knew, it could be a head in a box or a brick of coke. Checking my secondary phone, I didn't have any messages from the team, so they hadn't made any more progress in the last ten hours.

"Jace," I turned to watch him run a towel through his wet hair and shake his head like a dog, "what's the play? Are you going to keep Tim occupied?"

"The farmer's market should do that, but I'll stick close to him. Do you have any idea where Anika will be?"

"She didn't share much. She just said she'd see me

tomorrow. Please tell me you watched the feed last night after I fell asleep."

He nodded. "Everything was quiet." He checked his watch. "We should get going. Enable your phone's GPS tracking, and I'll keep mine on vibrate. Text a 9-1-1 if you run into trouble."

We headed into the main facility and endured another half hour of Tim's lecturing, followed by Abner sharing his story of how his inner turmoil led to drugs and ultimately drove his wife away. Now he had found inner peace or some sanctimonious garbage and realized he had been responsible for his own serenity. There was some discussion afterward, but I didn't pay much attention. I'd been searching the group for Anika. She wasn't in her normal spot or hiding in the back of the room. Perhaps she slept in or was making certain all the stands were set for when the gates opened in twenty minutes.

As soon as Tim dismissed us, I grabbed Jace's elbow. "I don't see her. She didn't come to the morning session. Has she ever missed before?"

"Not that I remember, but there's always one or two missing for the day. So maybe. Do you want to ask Tim?"

"No. I'm going to check the dorms in case she's in her room. If you see her outside, let me know."

He nodded. "I'll help Tim set up and welcome our customers," he said at a normal volume so the others wouldn't think anything of our whispered exchange. "You should take it easy. Do what you can, and come find me when you're ready. I'm sure we'll find someplace you can help that won't aggravate your ankle." He kissed my forehead and called to Tim.

Ducking into the cafeteria, I grabbed a piece of fruit from the basket and took a seat at the table. It was best to maintain the appearance of partaking in normal functions, despite the fact I hadn't eaten anything from the kitchen since the incident. As soon as the bulk of the Perpetual Lighters cleared out, I got up and went down the hallway toward the dormitories. Even though I no longer resided here, my presence wouldn't seem suspicious.

Knocking on Anika's door, I waited, hoping she would

answer. When she didn't, I knocked again, calling to her. Still nothing. "Anika," I turned the knob and pushed the door open a few inches, "are you in here?"

The bed was neatly made, and her belongings remained. Okay, so she wasn't in her room. Maybe she'd snuck out before we got here or during the morning session. After checking the communal bathroom and showers, I gave the kitchen and dining hall another look and checked out the multipurpose rooms in case she was conducting her own private impromptu yoga or pilates class, but I didn't spot her. In fact, I didn't spot anyone. The building had become a ghost town, and I fought my instinct to search for evidence. Instead, I went outside and across the grounds toward the stalls and tables. Anika said she would meet me here. I was probably just being impatient thinking that I'd get a chance to speak to her inside while everyone else was busy outside.

From the inside looking out, the farmer's market appeared much smaller and less intimidating than it did when I was still being courted to join the cult. There were a dozen and a half stands. Several of them sold produce, herbs, and the honey the beekeepers harvested. Another six stands sold various baked goods, beverages, and snacks. Several tables and chairs were scattered around for guests to sit and enjoy the sights and sounds while being brainwashed into thinking this was a magical, safe place. The other stands had various crafts and handmade items. It was all rather quaint and rustic.

I went from stall to stall in search of Anika. She wanted to show me something. That meant it had to be small enough for her to carry and conceal, or it was already out here. Somewhere. My gaze shifted to the fields. The entire property was roughly four acres, but with the various buildings and trailers, a lot of the space was already being utilized. The greenery was sectioned off into different gardens. I hadn't explored very much since my initial arrival.

The trailers were obvious. There were six in total. Each occupied by either one of the male followers or a couple. Briefly, I wondered if we'd need separate warrants for each unit since they were being used as primary residences for the occupants. The legal part of my brain already knew the answer. But whatever Tim had to hide wouldn't be inside any of them.

The main facility took up the bulk of the property, but there were three other reasonably sized buildings and two other structures. Why didn't Jace and I ever talk about this?

"Good morning, Alex," Sarah said. "In the event you're having a blonde moment, the farmer's market is behind you." She laughed, enjoying her own joke.

I spun, plastering a smile on my face. "Have Jace's highlights started to rub off on me? I accused him of using lemon juice, but he insists they're natural. Let's hope they aren't catching."

She giggled. "No, I was just kidding. What are you looking at?"

"Have you seen Anika? We made plans to hang out together and help out, but I haven't seen her this morning. I figured she must have come out here to get a head start and is wondering where I am. I don't want her to think I flaked on her."

Sarah's smile dropped. "I don't know where she is. I haven't seen her today. Did you check her room?"

"She wasn't there."

"Hmm, that's weird." Sarah turned around, surveying the crowd. "There's Tim. Let's go ask him. I bet he knows." Grabbing my hand, she pulled me through the group toward the corner where Tim and Jace were moving tables and chairs underneath a canopy. "Hey, Tim, do you know where Anika is?"

Tim turned, his eyes settling on me. For a split second, his expression was cold and angry. "She left."

"When will she be back?" I asked.

Tim inhaled slowly, forcing a sad smile on his face. "She won't be back. She decided she learned all she could from being here and wanted to go home and face her demons." He cast his eyes downward. "I'm sorry to tell you this. I was going to make an announcement at evening meals so I wouldn't spoil everyone's day. She asked me to say goodbye for her because she feared it'd be too painful."

"But I was just in her room. I could have sworn her belongings were still there," I insisted.

"You must be mistaken. She left early this morning. I drove her to the bus station myself. I'm sorry. I know you were close."

"We were all close," Sarah whispered. "She should have given us the chance to say goodbye."

Tim offered empty platitudes and encouraging words, but I couldn't help but shake the feeling he had done something to her. He must have known she was on to him, and he silenced her before she could talk. That might also mean he would be suspicious of me since I might have been the last person to speak to her.

"If you'll excuse me, I need some time alone to process this." I made my voice quake as if I were overcome with news of her departure. Stepping away, I went back to the facility, determined to find something pertinent in her room before Tim had the chance to erase her presence completely.

TWENTY-FIVE

Entering Anika's room, I resisted the urge to acknowledge the fiber optic cable hanging in the carved out hole in the ceiling tile. There wasn't a doubt in my mind Tim would watch the footage later. I couldn't afford to be compromised. Dammit, Anika, why couldn't you have talked to me yesterday? Pressing my lips together, I didn't want to think she was dead. Maybe there was a chance she escaped. Maybe she did go home.

Scoffing at the notion, I kept my face turned away from the camera and threw myself onto her bed. Sweeping my arms beneath her pillow and burying my face in it, I pretended to sob while feeling around for any hidden items. There was nothing under the pillow or between the mattress and headboard. Counting to a hundred, I slowly sat up, wiping at the nonexistent tears.

Keeping my face down, I got off the bed, smoothed the covers, and made hospital corners in order to check beneath the mattress. After tidying up, I went to the dresser and picked up the random knickknacks that had been left behind. She didn't have any personal effects on display, but I didn't think she'd leave without her belongings. Her toiletries and shower caddy were on top of the dresser, and the drawers contained her clothing.

I wasn't sure how to nonchalantly search the drawers, so I didn't even bother to conceal what I was doing. In the bottom drawer, I found a creased and folded photograph. A couple of women were in the picture with Anika, but before I could analyze the photo, someone cleared his throat.

Tucking the picture into my pocket, I didn't turn around immediately, hoping to force some tears to my eyes. I wasn't an actress by any stretch of the imagination. But my sadness came in handy, and when I turned, my eyes were wet. Tim was in the doorway of the room, watching me curiously.

"I told you her things were still here. Every drawer is filled with clothing and towels." I stood, picking up a tube of face lotion. "Why didn't she take any of it with her? How could she leave without saying anything? We had plans. I thought she was my friend."

He held out his arms. "I'm sorry, Alex. I know it hurts when people leave, but we should be happy for her. She came here to grow as a person, and she did. That's how she found her inner strength and why she wanted to return home. It was time." He hugged me against his chest while I resisted the urge to pull the dagger and gut the bastard where he stood. Real tears fueled by rage came to my eyes at the thought that within the last twelve hours he had probably murdered her. How many people was he responsible for killing? My body tensed, but he held firm. "It's okay. You can let it out."

"I'm angry, and I know I shouldn't be." Anger wouldn't bring me any closer to arresting this asshole, but it was a real emotion and one that was easier to play off. Pushing away from him, I squeezed the bridge of my nose. "This just caught me by surprise. Why didn't she say anything yesterday?" I searched his face, hoping to see the slightest hint of fear or worry, but there was nothing. "Is this my fault?"

"Why would you say that?"

"Yesterday, I asked her if she wanted to grab a cup of tea from one of the local cafes. It was as if the thought of leaving had never occurred to her, and I just kept going on about cookies."

He attempted to stifle a laugh, as if dealing with a precocious toddler. "I'm sure she didn't decide to leave the commune to indulge in limitless cookies." He ushered me out of the room, placing a guiding hand against my back. "However, it's clear from your mood that you are in need of some baked goods. We have chai lattes at one of the stands and strawberry scones hot out of the oven. Go outside and join the others. It'll make you feel better to be around people."

"Yeah, until they decide to abandon me too." That played along with Alice's issues. Unfortunately, Alex could also relate.

"Jace is outside. If anything, you can be certain he won't abandon you. And you know I never would."

"Why not?"

He gave me a quizzical look as if the notion was blasphemous. "You are my responsibility. I'm here to guide and protect you. And Jace is my most loyal follower. He would never act against my wishes or the mission of this church."

Cracking a small smile, I nodded. Caesar never expected Brutus to betray him either, but eventually, March would roll around. And just like Caesar, Wilde's empire would crash and burn around him.

Once outside, I felt as though every follower was watching me, expecting some type of insane reaction. Sarah was hunkered down behind one of the stands, bawling her eyes out. The news had already spread. No wonder everyone was awaiting my reaction. Keeping my head down, I moved toward one of the refreshment stands, feeling Tim's presence at my back.

"Hey," Jace bounded up to me, "are you okay?" His eyes darted to someone else, and I knew Tim was within earshot.

I pushed him away. "Anika left. It just sucks that she didn't even say goodbye. She left everything in her room, like she was in a hurry." I didn't have to say any more. He got the point. "But I'm determined to make today a good day."

"Here." Tim held out a cup of tea and a napkin with a scone.

Taking it, I smiled at him. "Thanks. I'll go grab my purse and pay for this."

"Nonsense." He shook the sentiment away. "It's the least I can do. After all, had I realized how upset you'd be, I would have tried harder to convince Anika to say her farewells."

My gaze moved toward Sarah's last position. "Actually, I know someone who could use this more than I can. Excuse me." Setting out toward the stand, I was glad to have found a reason not to eat the offered snack. Frankly, it was insulting Tim thought he could distract or cheer me up with food.

Taking a seat beside Sarah, I put the napkin and cup down beside her. "Tim thought it might help," I said lamely, "but I think it'd be best if we talk about things. Did you know she wanted to leave?"

Sarah shook her head.

"How long has she been here?"

"Three or four months. She was our newest addition before you." Sarah dabbed at her eyes. "I'm happy for her, but it makes no sense. She never mentioned wanting to leave. She always stayed here. She didn't have a job, and since everything was provided for, she didn't venture off the grounds. She was happy here. At least I thought she was."

"How'd she find her way to Tim?"

Sarah cleared her throat and composed herself. "I'm not sure. She just showed up out of the blue one day. The metaphoric orphan left on the stoop. From some of the things she shared in group, I think she was running from something."

"She lived in Vegas, right?"

Nodding, Sarah picked up the tea, but after taking a sniff, she put it down. "I'm not sure what she did there, but with the way she guarded the details of her career, I imagine it was something she didn't want known." The look on her face was one of distaste. "It didn't matter. This place is about starting over and finding your true self through enlightenment and Tim's teachings. We all have pasts."

"Then why would she go back?"

"To make amends. To reclaim her power. To be with the ones she left behind." Sarah's face contorted into a question mark. "I'm not sure. I can't imagine ever leaving here. I guess that's the goal, but this place feels right to me, at least for now." Her eyes zeroed in on mine. "You're planning on leaving, aren't you? Once you get back to work and are financially solvent, you're gonna leave us too."

"That was the plan." I stared off into the distance. "But it's nice being around people and feeling connected. I haven't had that in a really long time. That's why Anika's disappearance is so difficult."

"Yeah, but Tim's right. We should be happy for her. She's doing what she feels driven to do. It's what she wants, and we should celebrate it." She wiped her eyes. "No more tears. It's the weekend, and there's plenty of work to do and customers to greet." She offered a hand, helping me off the ground.

Determined to make the most of things, she set off toward the crafts table. I poured out the chai latte and ground the scone into crumbs before leaving that spot. The last thing I wanted to do was hang around here, but getting into my car and driving away would be far too obvious since the entire commune was outside.

Ducking away from the group, I returned to the trailer. I locked the door and took out the RF reader, scanning for any signs of radio signals or possible hidden cameras. Tim had made me paranoid. I didn't want to risk blowing my cover.

Once I was positive it was safe, I took out my secondary phone, scanned the photo, and sent it to the team, requesting identifications on the other women. Then I phoned Eckhardt.

"We'll issue a BOLO. In the meantime, I'll start with DOT cams in the vicinity. Wilde said he drove her to the bus station. The surveillance van didn't notice any activity, but maybe he gave them the slip. At the very least, it's a starting point. If he went anywhere, we'll find his vehicle in the footage and track it from there. Keep your fingers crossed. This will take some time and a lot of favors, but I'll get back to you as soon as we know something. Be careful."

"Always." Hanging up, I stared at the photo for a few minutes longer before pulling the hidden tablet out of the back of the cabinet and connecting it to the satellite antenna.

Wilde's attempts to prevent access to the internet and other current news sources resulted in the DEA getting creative. Frankly, I was surprised none of Wilde's followers had thrown a fit over their lack of Smart phones or other devices, but Wilde insisted these things polluted the soul. That's why the only phones permitted at the commune were hardlines and the cheap throwaway flip phones Jace and I had.

Gnawing on the thought of whether Anika had a phone, I searched old Vegas news articles from six months ago, looking for any hint of what Anika might have been involved with in her previous life. Once I hit the four month mark, I stopped reading. The papers were littered with homicides, sex crimes, and drug offenses. However, none of them involved S&M clubs. Whatever Anika was running from hadn't made it into the papers.

A key scraped in the lock. I ripped the antenna from the tablet, tossing both of the items into the false back of the cabinet and slamming it shut. Turning, I spotted the photo and dove for it just as the door opened. Jace cocked an eyebrow and shut the door behind him.

"What happened to sending a polite text announcing your arrival?" I asked.

"I didn't want to waste time." He looked at the item I was ineffectually concealing beneath my palms. "What did you find?" He took the photograph, flipping it over in the hopes of getting a name or date. "Anything else?"

"Everything is inside her room. She didn't leave."

"No shit. That son of a bitch must have realized she was on to him and did something with her." He put both hands on top of his head, fighting the urge to hit something. "This can't go on. Maybe the DEA should conduct a raid. The kratom gives us probable cause."

"What about the other buildings? Have you checked them?"

"That asshole has taken me on a guided tour of each of them. The two smaller sheds house farming equipment. The other three buildings are practically condemned. Once Wilde turns this place into a sustainable farmstead, he wants to renovate them to make additional housing, a separate dining hall, and some other shitty things. I don't know. I never got a good look around. He just made it clear that was his dream, and everyone was to stay out."

"Do they?"

"For the most part, except when we need to use them for additional storage, and that's under Tim's supervision. The doors are chained. I'm sure the lock would be easy enough to pick or break, but I don't think anyone has."

"Great."

"Alex, I'm not a moron. I've been here for what feels like an eternity. I've done my due diligence. I've checked everything I possibly can. I...," he blinked, scrunching his face as if in pain, "I can't outsmart this bastard. I've analyzed him, studied him, diagnosed his psychological issues, but I've yet to determine how he's trafficking in drugs or forcing these women to become mules. Take Anika for example. He managed to do god knows what with her, and we were a hundred yards away in this tin can." He slapped the wall with his palm. "Maybe a raid is exactly what we need. It'll throw him off balance, or the tactical team will find something I keep missing." His forehead furrowed, and he stared at the carpet. "I let him get away with this."

"No, you didn't." Thoughts of last night ran through my head. "We can share the blame." Considering something else, I picked up the phone and dialed Eckhardt again, putting him on speaker. "Did you have units sitting on the commune last night?"

"Yeah," Eckhardt replied

"Did anyone enter or leave the property yesterday?" Jace asked.

"Tim was mobile most of the afternoon, but in the evening, it was just you and Alex."

"Nothing after that?" I asked.

"No," Eckhardt replied, "but like I told Alex, he's given us the slip before. That's why we'll analyze DOT footage."

I looked at Jace. "Is Wilde under twenty-four hour surveillance?"

"He is, but sometimes he notices things and begins to exhibit paranoid behavior. He seems to have a sixth sense about eluding us and avoiding detection whenever he wants." He narrowed his eyes. "Matt, get a second team to sit on him. Wherever he goes, they follow. I don't care if he notices or not. We need to find that woman before she ends up dead."

Pressing disconnect, I gave Jace another look. "She's already dead."

"How can you be certain?"

"I just am. She possessed knowledge or evidence that could hurt Wilde, and everyone else that's been able to do that ends up dead. Anika will be no different." Grabbing my phone, I went to the door. "If whatever she had is on the property, I'm going to find it. I'll be back later. Run interference for me. And tonight, let's figure out how to make that blackout happen. I want unlimited access to the main facility tomorrow during the farmer's market. It's our best bet."

"And if that doesn't work, we're gonna raid this perversion of a convent."

"Deal."

TWENTY-SIX

I searched the main level of the facility as best I could. I even searched every tile in the bathroom for something hidden, but there was nothing. The multipurpose rooms, the dining hall, and kitchen all turned up nothing. I'm sure my actions were suspicious, but if questioned, I'd come up with a lie. However, no one was inside the building.

After rolling up the last of the yoga mats, I returned them to the equipment closet and knocked against the wall, checking for a false back. The corner sounded hollow, so I knocked harder. But I didn't find any removable panels or secret openings.

Stepping out of the closet, I left the room and turned right, but there was nothing but an open space designed to be a quiet place to sit, reflect, and read. Several couches and chairs were clustered in the opening. Knocking against the wall produced a solid sound. That made no sense. If this was the same wall, it should sound the same.

Returning to the other room, I went to the back and opened the equipment closet again. The resounding thump echoed, indicating something beyond that wall. I searched the floor and ceiling but couldn't find any indication of how to access the hidden compartment.

Thoughts of what could be walled inside filled my head. It could be anything from narcotics to bodies. Maybe Tim was literal about keeping skeletons in his closet. I gave the wall another hard shove, but it was sturdy. Maybe I was crazy. Maybe the echoing was from the confined space of the closet rather than an exterior space beyond that wall, but I doubted it.

"Alex?"

I turned, spotting Hannah. She stood at the entrance to the yoga studio, watching with piqued curiosity. I stepped out of the closet, pulling the door closed. "Guilty." I offered her a sheepish smile.

"What are you doing?"

"Nothing really. Since everyone's outside, I was hoping to make myself useful inside. I wiped down the tiles in the bathroom, reorganized some of the kitchen and pantry, and refolded the yoga mats. I just wanted to keep busy."

"Okay. I'll pretend I didn't notice you." She winked. "If you want to clean my room, I won't stop you. It's tough when people leave. I get wanting to keep busy and keep to yourself, but if you change your mind, I'll be working on dinner."

Realizing there wasn't enough time to search anything else and needing an excuse for my erratic behavior, I volunteered to help. While she took out the oversized pots and pans to prepare enough chow to feed a platoon, I sifted through the spices, pulling out the things she asked for while checking for anything suspicious. Of course, I failed to find any containers labeled PCP, ketamine, strychnine, or kratom, but it was worth a shot.

When dinner was almost finished and a crowd had formed in the dining hall, I ducked out of the kitchen. A group of ten had congregated near the front door. Among them were Tim and Jace. They were discussing Anika's departure. I edged closer until I was beside them.

Without missing a beat, Jace put an arm around me. Apparently, several of the women were not taking the news particularly well. I listened to the questions they asked and the perfunctory lies Tim told. The story never changed. Eventually, the crowd disbanded as the scent of dinner wafted throughout the first floor.

"Are you two coming?" Tim asked.

Jace shook his head. "We brought home leftovers from dinner last night. I thought we'd do something romantic at the trailer, but that was before the news spread." He looked at me. "Would you rather stay here among friends?"

Shaking my head, I leaned into him. "I just want to go home and mope. Is that selfish?" I glanced at Tim, expecting some type of enlightened inner peace mumbo jumbo to pass his lips at the suggestion, but he didn't say a word. He wished us a good night and went to join the others.

Jace and I didn't speak until we were locked inside the trailer. "The news has created quite a buzz," he said. "Others have left while I've been here, but it's never been this abrupt or unexpected. Whatever Anika had must have really freaked out Tim for him to react without having a plan in place."

"Or he had a plan, but my snooping ruined it. He probably would have removed her belongings and forged a goodbye note if he had the time." Fishing out the phone, I checked for any messages or missed calls. Nothing. I dropped the device on the table and plopped into a chair beside it. "Do you have blueprints of the main facility?"

"Tim had it custom renovated, and while the law requires such things to be kept on file, I've never seen them. Stella's gone through building records, but the schematics and the actual buildings don't line up."

"Can we get the city planner or a building inspector out here to check the codes?"

"Tried it. Do you want to guess what happened?"

"Wilde killed him."

"No. He paid him off. Apparently, Wilde helped this guy's cousin get a car on the cheap, so the commune got a stamp of approval."

"I didn't realize the small town mentality existed this close to a major city."

"Welcome to the sub-suburbs, babe." He shook his head. "That's what I like to call this Podunk hellhole." He rubbed his face and took a seat at the table. "Did you find anything?"

"Maybe. How are we coming on creating a power outage?"

He picked up a pen and drew a rough sketch of a map on a napkin. "The fuse box is here. The electricity comes in here. During the day, it won't be obvious the lights are out, and with everyone outside, we should have some time to look around. The only problem will be whenever they run out of baked goods and need to bring out another batch."

"We'll take our chances." After telling him about my search efforts and the questionable wall, we decided it was time to perform a thorough search of the entire facility. "I'll take the upper level. Tim never said I couldn't go up there, and we don't want to compromise your cover. He trusts you. He told me as much. And you've sacrificed way too much to screw yourself over by getting caught."

"Fine," Jace relented. "I'll see what I can figure out about that closet. Do you think a sledgehammer would be obvious?"

"A little bit."

He cracked a smile. "Dammit."

*   *   *

Waking up with my head on Decker's shoulder, I let out an agitated sigh and pulled away from him. We had too much to do. I didn't want to waste any time or energy on last night's sleeping arrangement. The very literal sharing of a bed was the least of our problems.

"Jace, it's morning."

He blinked a few times and scratched his chest, sliding our notes and the tablet off of him. We'd fallen asleep strategizing the best way of not getting caught. Simply flipping the electricity off would be too obvious, so Jace had researched a few foolproof ways of overloading the circuits. With everyone out of the facility, they wouldn't notice, and it would give us a chance to look around without big brother watching our every move.

We raced through our morning routines and arrived a few minutes late for Tim's morning tranquility session.

From the quirked eyebrow and licentious look Tim gave us as we snuck in, I knew what he was thinking. And I didn't like it. After going off on a tangent about our recent loss from the collective, he concluded by encouraging his followers to strike up conversations with the patrons at the day's market, hoping to replenish our ranks and improve someone else's life. I didn't like the recruitment spiel, but whatever roll Anika played in his grand scheme might be important. Perhaps she had millions stashed away from winning it big at one of the casinos.

"Alex," Tim called as everyone clamored out of the room, "may I speak with you?"

"Of course." Crossing to him, I smiled at some of the women as they went past in groups of two and three. "What can I do for you this morning?"

"You're in a chipper mood. It's a welcome improvement from yesterday." He glanced at my partner who was speaking to four of the women near the door. "I imagine Jace has made you feel less alone and abandoned."

"Yes, he has. I overreacted yesterday. I was just caught by surprise. I don't deal well with surprises. Most of the surprises I've had lately have been bad."

Wilde held the grin, but his eyes searched for something. "Well, I enjoy surprises, like finding out you did several chores yesterday while everyone was busy outside."

"I needed the peace and quiet to reflect. I was planning on doing a bit more cleaning today. I hope that's okay."

He continued to smile, and I wondered if his cheeks hurt from doing that so often. "That would be delightful." Without another word, he went out the door, whispering something to Jace on the way.

That conversation was intended to make it known that he hears all and sees all, but that wouldn't scare me away. Exchanging a few pleasantries with some of the remaining women, I made my way back to Decker. His look said it all. I didn't want to know what Tim had said to him.

"Are we good to go?" I asked as soon as the rest of the women disbanded.

"Green lights, babe." He looked disgusted and rolled his

eyes, shaking his head to let me know we would discuss it later. "I'll be helping set up, but I should be done in about an hour."

"I'll be here."

After he left, I went into the cleaning closet and pulled out a mop and broom. Then I set to work on the floors in the dining room. After that, I'd continue sweeping the rest of the main level until the power cut out. The broom was an easy cover and a good excuse for why I would be upstairs, and since the entire facility had tile floors, I could take it with me when I went exploring.

Forty-five minutes later, Jace found me sweeping near the front door. He wrapped his arms around my waist and huddled close to whisper the plan in my ear. After checking that we were alone, he went into the kitchen to overload the circuits. Thankfully, his trick blacked out the entire building and not just that one room.

"I'm heading upstairs." I hoisted the broom off the ground. "If you need help down here, send me a text."

"Just be careful and don't work too hard."

Dashing up the steps, I made quick work of the lock and slipped inside Tim's bedroom. My eyes scanned the area for signs of surveillance equipment. Wilde was smart enough not to risk being caught by putting himself on camera, but at the same time, he was paranoid. There was no telling the lengths he might go to feel secure. Pushing this fact aside, I started in one corner of the bedroom. Any second, we could be discovered, so I had to choose speed over thoroughness.

The suite was partitioned off into three different sections. The sleeping area contained a bed, two nightstands, and a dresser. This was the area I'd been given access while in an impaired state. From the way Sarah had entered the room and the stories Jace had told, several of the women had been inside. The usual sex related paraphernalia filled the nightstand drawer. The dresser contained clothing and nothing else. And the bed was just a bed. Surprisingly, I didn't even find a dirty magazine under the mattress.

The bathroom was no different, but the medicine

cabinet contained several unlabeled bottles. Removing a baggie from my pocket, I took a sample from each. Replacing everything, I checked the toilet tank, beneath the vanity, and every other place that could be used to conceal contraband. When I failed to find anything else, I entered the third area of the room.

"Shit." I didn't come prepared for a computer. I took a seat behind the desk, flipping open the laptop while I searched the drawers. The log-in screen requested a password. I sent Jace a text for assistance and continued the hunt, but Wilde didn't have a list of passwords hidden inside the desk or anything overtly damning either.

The phone chimed, and I read the message. *Leave it for now. We'll get help from the team. They'll crack it remotely.*

"Great." The rest of the room was decorated in a minimalist fashion. There was very little furniture, practically no clutter, and not a damn thing that indicated Tim was anything but a peace, love, and tranquility kind of guy. "Fucking A."

After making sure nothing appeared to have been disturbed, I ducked out of the room. I gave the door handle a quick jiggle to make sure the lock reengaged before continuing down the hallway. There were three other doors. The second door I tried led to another bedroom that was being used for storage. Several plastic containers lined one wall. Each was filled with linens. Several yoga mats and exercise gear took up the back wall, and the rest of the room was filled with stacks of folding chairs, random pieces of furniture, a few small tables, and some TV trays. I snapped a few quick shots, in case any of it meant something to Jace, and continued on my way.

My phone vibrated. *Twenty minutes and counting. Are you almost done?*

I shot off a quick reply while I opened door number three. Making sure the door shut, I stared at the row of filing cabinets. "What do we have here?"

I picked the locks on the drawers. The first drawer I opened contained legal documents regarding the property, permits, and exemptions Wilde had filed. Deciding none of that was particularly important, I scanned the rest of the drawers in that cabinet and moved on to the next one. Inside were folders for each person at the commune. They were organized by date of arrival.

My folder contained my estimated net worth, several photographs, my known employment history, a list of likes and dislikes, and every other tidbit Wilde needed to manipulate me. The most disturbing thing inside was a set of images taken at night when I was alone in the dorms. There were several of me in bed, and I was thankful I never changed in that room.

The next folder I opened was Anika's. I took photographs of every page before moving on. Flipping through the stack, I found Jace's file. It was thicker than the others. I skimmed it to make sure he hadn't been compromised or Tim had grown suspicious. It looked like Jace was in the clear, so I tucked the file back inside.

My phone chimed again, and I read the new message. *A group is heading toward the house. Get out of there.*

Asking that he buy me a few more minutes, I took a photo of the interior of the cabinet so we'd be able to read the names off the tabs to solidify a better plan for next time. Then I unlocked the final filing cabinet. All but one of the drawers was empty. The filing cabinet contained a rolodex and a ledger. Clicking photos of a few of the pages, I hoped this would be something. Then I exited the room and went to the last door.

Alex, get out now.

Quickly, I opened the door, prepared to take a quick peek and make a break for the staircase. However, I froze in the doorway. At first glance, it appeared to be another bedroom, but the sheets were rumpled. I couldn't help but think the stains on the rug and bed were blood. Creeping closer, I noticed the closet door was cracked open. Moving toward it, I eased the door open and stared down a steep set of stairs. Where did they lead?

Twenty seconds.

I raced out of the room and down the hallway, grabbing the broom on the way. I was three steps down when the power came back on. I skittered to a stop, sweeping the broom back and forth on the step while wiping sweat from my brow.

Jace came into the entryway, relieved that I had reappeared in the nick of time. Two men were right behind him, talking about the circuit breaker. Jace looked at me. "What are you doing up there?" he asked nonchalantly.

"Sweeping."

"Come down and take a break. I want to show you something in the trailer."

TWENTY-SEVEN

"That was too close," Jace snapped.

We'd already spent the last forty-five minutes discussing what I had found upstairs. He hadn't had nearly as much luck determining what might be beyond the equipment closet in the yoga studio, but it was a safe bet that it was probably the staircase. At least we had some idea of where to focus our efforts in the future. This gave the investigation hope. However, I'd been kicking myself for not being more prepared. We could have learned so much more if only I had started with that staircase, moved on to the rumpled bed, and then the file room.

"It was worth the risk," I said. "I should've gone down the steps."

"This is my op." He forced his volume to remain low in the event anyone was eavesdropping from outside the trailer. "When I tell you to haul ass, you do it."

"Yes, sir."

Scratching at his beard, he flipped through the photos I'd taken, rereading the information from Anika's file. Copies of everything had been sent to the team, and they were working the leads. The ledger was written in code. The few pages I'd snapped photos of didn't give us much to go on. The rolodex was also coded, but even if we deciphered it, a couple of names weren't likely to prove useful. We needed everything.

"Tell me about that last bedroom again," Jace insisted. "Not the steps, the state of the room."

"The bed was unmade. The sheets were this faded grayish lavender color, but they were speckled with brownish stains. The area rug surrounding the bed had similar stains." My mind went to dark places. I wanted to castrate the perverted cult leader.

"Blood?"

"That was my assumption. I don't know. I should have taken a sample, but I didn't have time."

"What about the walls? Any spatter on them?"

I shook my head.

"Since you're not sure it's blood, there isn't enough of it to think a murder took place in that room. We need to determine where that staircase leads and who or what Tim is keeping inside that hidden room."

"Call in the fucking cavalry. Didn't Stella say we had enough for a raid?"

He tossed his phone on the table. "The assistant director changed his mind. The punk who murdered Harbring has been chirping up a storm. The DEA is now functioning under the assumption Wilde is working for the Sinaloa cartel. Our objective is no longer to take out a big fish in a small pond. It's to use that fish as bait to catch a whale."

"When the hell were you planning to tell me this?"

"I just did."

"Great." Grabbing my phone, I pocketed it and tucked my gun at the small of my back, making sure my sweatshirt covered the bulge. "I'm leaving. One of us should see about running down leads. Text me when you grow a pair."

Storming out of the trailer, I went to my car, glad that everyone was distracted with closing up shop. I got behind the wheel and pulled out of the parking lot, following the line of customers exiting the property after a day of shopping. I was a few miles away before I realized I had nowhere to go. Parking in a garage, I dialed Eve.

"Do you have the profiles I asked for?"

She exhaled slowly. "I've made the identifications and compiled the information you requested on Anika Thatcher, Carmen Chavez, and Natalie DuBois, the other two women in the photo. Anika and Natalie were college roommates. They were practically inseparable, but after graduation, Natalie went on to get her masters and became a journalist. Anika worked odd jobs to pay her tuition, inevitably ending up working in a skin club. I imagine that's where she met Carmen."

"What happened to Carmen?"

Eve let out a mirthless laugh. "Someone wants to jump ahead to the end." She exhaled again. "A lot of questionable things went down at this S&M club. The police answered routine calls. The women were badly treated. They'd be chained up for hours on end, neglected, beaten, and the management let it happen. They only cared about catering to the dark desires of their clientele. The police would shut them down, but they'd pop up again with a different name or in a different location. At some point, a fire broke out. Four women were found dead in shackles."

"Shit." The papers hadn't mentioned any of it, but someone was probably paid to keep a lid on things. That explained why Anika was willing to give up so much freedom to Wilde, and it made me fear what else was happening at the commune for her to have been so panicked prior to her disappearance. "Please tell me you've located her and she's safe."

"I'm sorry. Matt's working on traffic footage, but there are no indications anyone else entered or left the property that evening or the following morning. Are you certain she didn't run away?"

"No." Scenes from that bedroom played out in my mind. "We'll be lucky if we ever find her body."

"Alex, you don't know that."

"Yes, I do."

Hanging up, I knew I needed to return. Regardless of the DEA's objective, I owed it to Anika to determine what happened and get justice for her. Her life had been rough. She came to Wilde looking for a new beginning, and she met a horrible end. I couldn't let that happen to anyone else.

Deciding it was time to take matters into my own hands, I dialed Jablonsky. My boss would know what to do. Mark listened patiently, searching his desk and furiously scribbling down notes.

Finally, he said, "This isn't my call. Do you have a plan?"

"Besides grabbing Tim by the balls, shoving my gun down his throat, and forcing him to confess to everything, I haven't figured out much beyond that."

"For Christ's sake, don't do it, Parker."

"That was a joke. Sort of."

"Is now a bad time to remind you that I didn't want you getting mixed up in this shit? The DEA has its head so far up its own ass they can't tell right from wrong. God forbid they take a small win instead of a giant front page victory. Look, I'll make some calls and see what I can do to get them to shut this down. In the meantime, color within the lines. What does Agent Decker have to say about this?"

"I don't know. Things were getting heated, so I left."

"Apparently, that's your new party trick," Mark retorted. "Get back to work. Unfortunately, he's all you got. So make the most of it. I'll do what I can from my end, and Parker, stay alive."

"Will do."

After hanging up, I returned to the commune. The last stand was being dismantled and placed in one of the structures for safe keeping. Jace said the buildings didn't house anything sinister, but I was beginning to doubt my DEA counterpart. Sending the polite text of my imminent return, I crossed the lot and unlocked the trailer.

Jace had Eckhardt on speaker while they discussed the vast turns the investigation had taken in the last two days. While they spoke, he'd alternate between making notes and puttering around the kitchen. I wasn't sure exactly what Jace's system was, but it seemed to be working. Deciding to stay out of his way, I took a seat on the sofa and listened to the conversation while compiling a list of possible leads and evidence that needed further exploration.

When the call ended, Jace hovered over me. "Don't do that again."

"What? Leave in the middle of a fight, or take too long to follow your orders?"

"Both." He offered an apologetic smile. "To be fair, I would have done the same thing. But too many people have already been killed on my watch. I don't want that to happen to you."

"It would have been my fault. And let's be real. Unless Wilde comes at me with a poisoned dart, I can take him."

"Now who's being arrogant?"

"I'm just being truthful."

Before he could say anything else, the timer dinged. Jace returned to the kitchenette and removed a baking sheet from the oven. He tossed the two burgers from the skillet onto plates and scooped the fries next to them. "Peace offering, if you're hungry." He put the plates on the table.

"I didn't think you did burgers and fries."

"Not from those drive-thru joints. But it seemed like the type of thing you'd scarf down while working through dinner." He looked down at his notes. "We'll definitely be working through dinner."

"In that case, you should have made more fries." I picked one up and took a cautious bite. The baked wedge wasn't soppy from the deep fryer, but it hit the spot. "Where should we begin?"

He cut his burger and speared it with the fork. "Let's start with finding a way to bypass Wilde's security system in order to gain access to the upper level. I believe everything we need to build a case is housed on that floor, including his connection to the cartel." He chewed thoughtfully. "I'm on your side, Alex. I want justice for Anika, everyone he's manipulated, and the ones he's used or sold out. He's a killer. We need to stop him. If we find Anika's body or proof that he poses an imminent danger to his followers, we will shut him down. You have my word. Can I count on you?"

"Can I count on you?"

He chuckled. "Damn. You really do have trust issues."

Our priorities were clear. We needed to be ready to explore upstairs whenever the opportunity presented itself.

Based on previous experiences, our next chance would be the following weekend, but since Wilde spent most afternoons out of the building, we might be able to access the upper level sooner. Ben was working on creating a program that would hack Wilde's computer password and copy his hard drive. With any luck, we'd be set to move forward on that front by tomorrow. Carlo and Eve were experimenting with tech. Without cutting off the power supply, we could use a few gadgets to temporarily deactivate the surveillance devices. They'd determine the most pragmatic option, but a jammer or shortwave EMF burst were our best bets. However, we'd have to watch our time, and it could also short out our equipment. In terms of exploring the hidden passageway, all we could do was hope to be ready for whatever we encountered.

Once we had the basics down, Decker moved the conversation to our shifting set of facts. Vincent Harbring was targeted by the Southside Giants for running drugs in their territory. Harbring had been warned to stay off their turf, so when he showed up that night after assaulting me, the Giants had no choice but to show him they meant business. They sent Paolo Raza, their newest recruit, to do the dirty work as an initiation. The kid was only twenty, but unlike most in that life, he didn't want to spend the next two decades behind bars. He had given up the chop shop as part of the drug biz. The owners had been taken in quietly and were cooperating in providing detailed information about the competition in exchange for some leniency. However, the intel had yet to be verified.

"What about Anton Shrieves?" I asked. "Have we established any connection between my second assailant and the drug trade?"

"No one's said a word to me. Stella's on top of that, but it's all speculation. The police never recovered Shrieves' vehicle, so we don't know what he might have been hiding when the officer pulled him over. We can't even connect Shrieves to Wilde at this point. Once we break into Tim's files, that might change."

"I hope so."

"Me too." Jace jotted down another note next to one of

his bullet points. "Matt thinks the dead mules connect to the cartel. He's hoping someone from the Southside Giants will recognize them or be able to point us in the right direction. The team's been scouring their background histories for links, but we haven't found any that connect to the cartel or gangs operating in the area."

"They connect to Wilde, and although we can't prove it, this entire operation is predicated on the assumption he's running drugs independently or at the whim of the cartel. The question remains how do we prove it if we can't get access to the evidence?"

That had been the problem for the last nine months. "Today shifted the tides. We know something's there. We're going to figure out what it is and how to get to it without tipping off Tim. He's careful, Alex. If he so much as suspects you were up there looking around, he'd do whatever was necessary to protect himself and his business."

"We'll be careful. I'll be more careful," I corrected.

"Good." He cleared the table. "Do you think Anika went looking around upstairs and stumbled upon the truth? She said she wanted to show you something. Apparently, there's plenty upstairs for you to see."

Shaking my head, it didn't feel right. "The doors were locked, and whatever she had was small enough to carry. Maybe she discovered he was growing illegal substances."

"I didn't recognize any of them, and kratom's a hot-button topic at the DEA right now. It has to be something else." He dropped the last few dishes in the sink. "At night, some of the guys go outside, light a fire, and smoke a joint. Maybe I should join them. Perhaps they'll have something interesting to say."

"What does Tim think about that?"

"He knows it happens, but he doesn't acknowledge it. Marijuana's a grey area, especially in California. With all the dispensaries, it's hard to say it's wrong, especially when half the people in the commune have been given prescriptions for it at one point or another. He doesn't want to come down hard against it and alienate anyone, but he doesn't want us using anything that alters our state of being or acts like a crutch instead of finding a true and honorable path toward enlightenment."

"Meaning?"

"He doesn't like it when his followers depend on something else to bring them peace and tranquility. He specifically urged me to avoid falling into the same trap as them, but he could be afraid of what I'd learn."

"Should you risk angering him now?"

"Probably not, but I can say I wanted relationship advice from the guys. That would go along with Tim's earlier directive."

"Which was?"

"To keep you comfortable and sexually satisfied."

"What a sicko." Tim wanted to control our intimate relationship. "In that case, you better go talk to the other men about our problems because I am far from satisfied." I jerked my head at the door.

TWENTY-EIGHT

By the time Jace returned, I was in bed, staring at a blank screen and daring someone to walk past one of the cameras and activate the feed. Since I'd been living in the trailer, the only camera that ever activated was the one near the bathroom. I had a feeling the others were no longer functioning, or the darkened corridors inhibited their use.

"Did you ever see Wilde sneaking into my dorm?" I asked.

"No, but if he stuck to the opposite wall, he might not have been in range."

"Or the cameras don't work. Weren't we going to splice into his security cams and piggyback off that feed?"

"Eve nixed that idea. The setup would be obvious. We'd be compromised."

The mattress dipped down, and Jace curled around me, placing his hand against my side where my shirt had ridden up. He leaned over to see the tablet, and I dropped it to the bed.

"Jace, get off of me. You reek like hot trash." I peeled his hand off my skin. "Are you high?"

"I didn't inhale. So if I am, it's a contact high. Those are still fun though."

Turning my head, I glared at him. "I'm not playing." His gaze rested on my scars. I pushed him backward and tugged my shirt down. "Are you straight?"

"Alex—"

"Are you straight?" I asked more forcefully.

He backed away, getting off the bed. "Yeah. I'm good." He took up a spot near the doorjamb, finally respecting my space. "I did some searching, but I didn't find anything. I told the guys you lost a bracelet, but no one's found anything outside. I'm guessing whatever Anika wanted to show you was with her when she disappeared."

"Probably." I searched his face for signs he was intoxicated. "Did you search the dumpsters while you were out there?"

"And the compost heap." He grabbed a change of clothes and headed for the bathroom. "I'll take a shower. Why don't you get some sleep? I'll take first watch."

"Fine, but there's no reason to watch. We have teams outside the fence who will notify us if anything happens. I don't believe the cameras work. You might as well get some sleep too. Who knows when we're gonna move on this. We should be sharp."

Agreeing, he ducked into the bathroom, and I turned off the bedroom light. But I couldn't sleep. I kept thinking about Anika and the other women under Tim's spell. I had gotten to know all of them by name, but I didn't know their stories. Reaching for my phone, I flipped through the photographs of Anika's file, finding several lists Tim had compiled. Aside from likes and dislikes, several pages were dedicated to secrets she had shared. These dated back to her college days, including things like the frat boys she slept with and the exam she cheated on. It also included intimate details about her life as a sex worker. Tim had blackmail on all of his followers. No one could leave without risking exposure.

Jason Ellis and Alice Lexington's files contained similar things, but I hadn't divulged much to Tim. And the things in Jace's file were part of his cover, so I hadn't given any of it much thought. But Tim spent time cultivating close personal relationships with everyone. I doubted it was for altruistic reasons.

I sat up, scrolling through the photos again for the image of the file folders. Tim had to have something on Anton Shrieves and Vincent Harbring. However, if he had folders on them, they weren't inside the filing cabinet. I cursed again, flopping backward onto the mattress.

For the next hour, I tossed and turned, contemplating what Tim might have on everyone, what transpired in that spare bedroom, and where the staircase led. Somewhere in the midst of my contemplation, Jace knocked on the bedroom door.

"Can't sleep?" he asked.

"No." I turned on the lamp and sighed. "What about you?"

He shook his head. "I can't get the case out of my mind. Do you want to watch some TV?" He held out the tablet like a peace offering. "It normally helps numb my brain enough to send me into a coma for a couple of hours. There are times I'd kill for an actual television, but Wilde is adamantly opposed to them."

"He's afraid his followers will wise up and decide there's more to life than an eight by ten cell and three meals a day."

"Those dormitories aren't even eight by ten." Jace came into the room and sat on the far edge of the bed. "If you don't want me in here, we can go in the living room."

"We're both adults, and I hate that couch."

"Just the couch? Or maybe me too?"

"I'm ambivalent toward you." I cracked a smile. "It's why you needn't worry about me jumping your bones."

"Ooh, big word." He tapped the streaming app and handed me the tablet to make a selection. "We can talk about it if you'd like."

"I wouldn't."

"Figured." He fell silent, but it was a heavy, oppressive silence. After scrolling through several pages' worth of shows, I found a sitcom from the nineties and hit play. We watched the first episode and half of another in complete silence. "Mindless television isn't going to do the trick."

"Then buy a dirty magazine and lock yourself in the

bathroom."

He lay back in bed and put his arms behind his head. "You get really uncomfortable when you think I'm going to try to have an honest conversation, and you do whatever you can to deflect and derail. You hate getting close to anyone. So you say these things to get me to leave you alone or leave the room."

"So you got the message. You just choose to ignore it." I powered off the tablet and put it on the dresser. "If you want the bed, I'll sleep on the couch. I don't mind." I got up to leave, but he grabbed my wrist.

"I'd like you to tell me about when you were shot."

"What?"

"C'mon, let's trade war stories. I told you about the frag grenade. It's your turn."

"Tonight's not the night to do this. Too much is going on with the case."

"I know. And if you fall asleep, your nightmares are bound to wake us both up. So let's talk about it before it happens. You said your current nightmare only started after you took this assignment. What about before? You mentioned you used to have other nightmares before this. Were they due to the various scars?"

"Don't you think Wilde's been breaking me down enough?"

"I'm not trying to break you down, Alex. I'm trying to get you to open up about your past. It's the only way you will ever be able to move beyond it. I promise that once it happens, the nightmares will stop, just like they did when you came to terms with being tortured and almost dying." He stared at my wrists. "That's why you don't even see the scars anymore, but the ones on your back and side, those you hide and conceal. Why?"

"They don't fit with my cover."

"And they're fairly fresh, at least in your mind. Look, it might be easier to sneak upstairs and get a look around if one of us was sleeping in the main facility. You're the only one who can do that, but it can't be like it was when you first arrived. You were exhausted and likely to slip up and make a mistake. I need you solid. That means you have to suck it up and face your demons."

"And you're just the therapist to help?"

"Actually, no. I'm not your therapist. I'm more of a friend, which means I don't have to wait for you to reach some kind of revelation on your own. I can point shit out and let you figure out how to deal with it. Won't that be fun?"

"Not particularly." But I wanted the nightmares to stop. I didn't want to spend another night watching Martin almost bleed out, not after what I'd seen in the upstairs bedroom or what I imagined must have happened to Anika. "Okay, but don't screw me up more than I already am."

"Is that even possible?"

*   *   *

The days blurred together. The only constants were the morning and evening sessions with Tim. Everything else was erratic. Tim hosted various recruitment functions over the course of the next few weeks, making his schedule even less predictable. He'd come and go throughout the day at random intervals, and his followers milled about the main facility, working the program even harder than usual. From morning until night, each of the multipurpose rooms remained in use with different group activities and enlightenment quests. The dining hall ran nonstop. Even though Tim had said the kitchen was open twenty-four hours, I had never seen so much activity in and out. It was as if this was intentionally orchestrated to prevent another trip upstairs.

The team had run tests on the samples I'd taken from Tim's medicine cabinet, but they were legal herbal supplements. Fortunately, Ben had given us a USB drive. As soon as we plugged that sucker in, data would be uploaded, opening a backdoor into the hard drive that would enable us to monitor Tim's usage in real time. Carlo and Eve finally decided on a device that would disrupt all electronics within a ten foot radius. Any camera feed would get snowy, and everything from cell phones to radios would short out while the electromagnetic pulse was activated. It could raise suspicions, but with the comings and goings, it was the fastest and easiest means of bypassing Tim's security measures without drawing undue attention to ourselves by powering down the entire facility.

Most days, Wilde dragged Jace along to run errands and bolster community support for the co-op. From the way Wilde pitched the Church of Perpetual Light, one would think he was hurting for membership and funds. According to Jace, my cover's case would be coming up on the docket sooner than originally planned. It would encourage Tim to ask for a sizable donation. However, his desperation seemed to be about more than money. I wondered if eliminating Anika had caused some kind of unforeseen harm. It was impossible to tell, so Jace did his best to remain close to Wilde. Except for the few days Jace had a shift at the gas station, he spent more time with the religious leader than his fake girlfriend. I might have pointed out once or twice that Jace was Wilde's bitch when the shrink turned drug enforcement officer was being particularly annoying, but he laughed it off as a well-known fact.

My cover's phone rang, and I glanced at the number. "Hello?"

"You have an hour until he returns," Jace whispered.

"Okay. I'll see what I can do."

I tucked the electronic disrupter in my pocket and palmed the USB. The only caveat was I had to deactivate the disrupter before booting up the laptop. Hopefully, I was correct in believing Tim didn't have a camera in his room.

After exiting the trailer, I entered the main facility. A pilates class was in full swing, and an addiction meeting was being held in the adjacent room. The kitchen was alight with activity as Hannah and her clique experimented with recipes for the weekend bake sale. Several others were meditating in the various quiet spaces.

Moving to the bottom of the staircase, I spotted two people within visual range, but their eyes were closed. Hoping they would remain that way, I flipped the switch, causing the lights to flicker and go out. In broad daylight, the change wasn't noticeable. The two Perpetual Lighters didn't notice.

Tiptoeing up the steps, I crouched down and picked the lock to Wilde's room. I went straight to the computer, keeping my head on a swivel in case someone was in the room. Powering off the disrupter, I waited thirty seconds, like Ben instructed, before opening the laptop and pressing the power button. I plugged the USB in the side, entered a few commands in the dialog box, and waited for the download bar to fill. Then I texted Ben for confirmation.

We're in, he replied.

Unplugging the USB, I hit the power switch and closed the laptop lid. After reengaging the disrupter, I slipped out of Tim's room. I should have plenty of time to explore the file room or the hidden staircase, but a voice from below stopped me in my tracks.

"Alex?" Sarah called.

From the sound of her voice, she was on the staircase. Tim's door had shut, so I couldn't hide. Even though the cameras were on the fritz, I'd been made. I needed a feasible lie, and I needed it now. Slowly edging toward the staircase, I looked down to find her big brown eyes staring up at me.

"Hey, have you seen Tim?" I furrowed my brow and flipped the device off before taking another step. "I looked everywhere, but I can't find him. I needed to talk to him about something personal."

"He doesn't like us to go upstairs without his permission. You need to come down from there."

"Right." I shook my head as if I knew that and had forgotten. "Sorry. It was just really important."

"What is it?"

"It's about Jace."

"Is everything okay?"

"I just really wanted to talk to Tim in private. Do you know where he is?"

"The last time I saw him, he was on his way out with Jace."

"Great," I replied sarcastically. "If you see him before I

do, can you ask him to talk to me when he gets a chance? He's been so busy lately. I feel so disconnected, but he always knows what to say or do to ground me."

"No problem." Before I could escape, she cleared her throat. "I was actually looking for you. A few of us thought it'd be best to clean out Anika's room and donate or repurpose the few things she left behind. Do you want to help? Her departure hit you hard. I thought if there was something you'd like to keep as a memento, you should get first pick."

"Thanks, but you were closer to her. I shouldn't interfere." Having unfettered access to Anika's room might uncover whatever piece of evidence she had to show me.

"Nonsense. The two of you were instant friends." She grabbed my hand and led me down the corridor to the dorm. "Go ahead and get started. I'll grab a couple of bags so we can separate her belongings into different piles."

Less than an hour later, we finished sorting the items. I had checked inside everything from her makeup compact to the pockets of her jeans, but nothing surfaced. Whatever she wanted to show me was long gone.

However, I used this as an opportunity to get closer to Sarah. I didn't want to risk starting a budding friendship with any of the other women after what happened to Anika, but Sarah seemed particularly close to Tim. She might know more than the others. From what Jace had said, she had been at the co-op a long time. She was the only one who still seemed miffed about Anika's disappearance.

"How long have you been here?" I asked as we took the bags out of the room.

"To be honest, I've lost track. It's been a good while."

"Yeah, I can tell. You're really close to Tim. I don't know if I ever got a chance to thank you for coming to my rescue a couple of weeks ago, but if it weren't for you and Tim, my nerves would still be shot."

"And Jace," she chirped. "You can't forget him."

Her tactics to wheedle details out of me were obvious, so I decided to go with a lover's quarrel as the premise behind my need to speak to Tim. "Apparently not." I stopped her in the middle of the empty hallway and lowered my voice.

"Tim really likes Jace, and he knows him better than anyone. I just need some reassurance that we're doing the right thing."

"About what?"

"Jace is great. Really. But we moved in together so quickly. I don't know if he offered because he was being nice or if he really likes me. And if he does like me, was he just pretending to be a knight in shining armor in order to get laid? Guys have done that before. I don't think that's the case, but it could be. What do I know about Jace other than he's a clutz who ruined two of my shirts?"

"That isn't true. You know him better than that." Her voice adopted a knowing quality. "But what do we know about anyone for that matter? There are very few people you can actually trust."

"Even Tim?"

She didn't fall for the bait or speak ill of her leader. "No. Tim's as he appears. He's genuine, and he cares. That's why he's working so hard to keep this place afloat. The bills are piling up. It happens sometimes, so we work extra hard to make our bake sales and farmer's markets extra productive. He won't let anything happen to us. He always has a backup plan. You can trust him, and you can trust Jace because Tim does." She took the donation bag from my hand. "I'm needed in the kitchen. You're welcome to join."

"That's okay. I'm not that great at cooking. Thanks for the advice. I really needed some female perspective. Can we keep this between us? I don't want Tim to mention any of this to Jace when I'm just being silly and paranoid."

"I guess, but you should talk to Tim about your insecurities. He's great at helping with problems."

Or causing them.

TWENTY-NINE

"It's done. As soon as Tim turns on his computer, we'll have access to his files and keystrokes. He must be one of the only people left on the planet who doesn't use wi-fi."

"He's paranoid. It's a miracle he even has a computer. From our research, he's been off the grid for so long, I'm surprised he was willing to compromise himself in that manner." Jace scratched at his jaw. "He's hardwired which gives him a false sense of security. As long as he stays plugged in, we're in business. Did you encounter any problems?"

"There was a snag. Sarah must have seen me go upstairs. She came looking."

"Shit." He paced back and forth. "If she tells him, he'll check the camera footage, see that they were on the fritz, and realize you're a plant."

"Maybe not. She doesn't know I was in his room. I told her I was looking for him. I wasn't in there that long. I think we're okay."

He stopped midstride and stared wide-eyed at me. "Is that a gamble you're willing to take?"

I nodded.

"Fine, but you are staying away from upstairs from here

on out." He held out his hand. "Give me the EMP generator. I'll flip it on and off at random intervals to make him think it's faulty wiring. He already heard about the power outage from the weekend, so he might buy it."

"Now who's paranoid?"

Before Jace could respond, his phone rang. He answered and put it on the table. "You're on speaker. What do you have for us, Matt?"

"The geek squad is hard at work downloading Wilde's files. His hard drive is mostly blank, but his internet history is another story. Eve and Carlo are parsing through the websites he frequents, and Ben is monitoring his current session. In case you were curious, Wilde is researching soil conditions to increase crop yield. It's really exciting stuff."

That fact made me want to slam my head into the table, and from the look on Jace's face, he had the same desire. "You shouldn't have bothered making the call," I said, defeated.

Jace held up a finger, silencing me. "What else do you have?"

"Another body turned up. Her stomach's slashed open like the others, but we're having trouble making an ID. Her fingers were badly damaged, and her teeth were knocked out. Facial rec is a tad challenging. She was found in the desert on the side of the road, about fifty miles from the border. A trucker called it in, but he didn't stop. To top it off, the birds and wildlife did a number on the body."

"Do we think it's Anika?" I asked.

"Hair color's a match, and preliminary reports indicate she's in the proper age range. But we can't be sure," Eckhardt replied. "The assistant director is allowing the locals to work the case until we know for certain if the deceased is another of Wilde's former followers. I just thought you should know."

"I want to see the body and the crime scene. If it is Anika, I'll be able to recognize her. That'll save some time on waiting for the DNA results, and it'll give us jurisdiction faster, preventing more of the evidence from being contaminated or corrupted." Jace rubbed a hand down his face and stared across the room, not seeing any of it. "Where are the remains?"

"They've been moved to the state's main forensic processing facility," Eckhardt said.

"Fine. I'll phone for approval, but you should expect to see me tomorrow. Also get the team mobilized. While I'm gone, I want you close enough to back up Alex if the situation escalates."

"Affirmative," Eckhardt replied, and Jace disconnected.

Without giving me a chance to say anything, he picked up the phone, dialed a number, and shut himself in the bedroom. I dropped into the nearest chair, unsure of what to do. The news of another body shouldn't have been shocking, but it felt like a sucker punch. Today should have been a win, but it was another devastating loss.

When Jace opened the door three minutes later, he resembled a downed fighter determined to get up and kick ass. Leaving the bathroom door open, he lathered his face and picked up a razor. "I'll leave in the morning. Can you cover for me?"

"No problem, but what excuse do I use? You're a drifter. It's not like I can say you have a sick aunt."

"Tell Tim I wasn't feeling well and wanted to sleep in. I'm supposed to work at the gas station anyway, so he won't be expecting to see me the rest of the day. I should be back by tomorrow night."

"Okay. In the event he drops by the trailer, I'll say you went to the clinic."

He nodded, stepping back into the bathroom to finish shaving away the stubbly beard that drove him crazy. When he was done, he wiped his face on a towel and returned to the main room. "How did another body turn up? We're all over the DOT cams. We have two vans outside this place. One of them is sitting on Wilde. It's not like he called someone to pick up a body." He zeroed in on me. "Do not do anything stupid while I'm gone. He has some way of getting people out of here without anyone noticing, and after today, you're on thin ice. Perhaps this is stupid. It's not like I'll be able to tell much from a mutilated carcass."

Recognizing the running commentary as a version similar to my internal dialogue, I blew out a slow breath. Someone needed to be logical. "Why'd you volunteer? What do you hope to gain by going? Be honest."

He shrugged. "I haven't seen any of the bodies or crime scenes up close and personal. But this is personal. Anika was going to help us, and we didn't help her."

"She didn't know that."

"No, but I want to help her now." He deflated, taking a seat across from me. "I know Wilde. I know what makes him tick, how he acts and reacts, and right now, he's in panic mode. He's spinning. I think he fucked up. At the very least, he thinks he fucked up. That means there could be something on the body or at the scene that ties the dead girl to him. It could be something inconsequential, but it might be the nail in his coffin."

"You think it's whatever Anika wanted to show me?"

"I do, or I'm letting hope cloud my judgment. I guess we'll find out tomorrow."

*   *   *

Jace left before daybreak. He dressed in black, kept to the shadows, and made his way off the grounds without anyone noticing. A few blocks away, Eckhardt picked him up. They were going to drive to the crime scene, and Jace would take a chopper to the ME's office to save time. Assuming everything went according to plan, he'd be back late that evening and everything would continue like clockwork.

I attended the morning tranquility session alone, finding a spot near Sarah. Securing our budding friendship might prevent her from disclosing my activities to our spiritual leader. At least, that was my hope. The morning session wasn't the usual lecture followed by a personal account. Instead, all twenty-two attendees were forced into a large circle around Tim, who insisted we share our deepest anxiety. I didn't like the change in our typical pattern, but I played along. When it was my turn, I came up with something fitting of Alice Lexington's current dilemmas. As was par for the course, Tim and the others contributed some type of reassuring comment or helpful suggestion to minimize said anxiety. Luckily, he didn't draw any overt attention to Jace's absence, and since the session ran almost twice the normal length, those who had employment were in a rush to leave, providing a perfect means of escape.

To avoid more questions, I returned to the trailer and waited for confirmation from the surveillance team that Tim was on his way into town. Once he was gone, I went back to the main building. Sarah and Hannah had constructed an assembly line for the weekend's bake sale. I took a spot among the seven other women. Thankfully, the conversation remained light.

After the group disbanded, I returned to the trailer, hoping to avoid running into Tim. Truthfully, I wanted to avoid his evening preaching, but I couldn't decide if that was a good idea. Had I thought faster, I would have volunteered to check out the body and crime scene. Jace was only a DEA agent. What did he know about murders and crime scenes? Plus, I could have used a break from the damsel in distress mentality and the sicko wolf in sheep's clothing. Damn, now I was thinking in idioms. Didn't that indicate I needed a break?

Someone knocked on the trailer door. I glanced at my phone, making sure I hadn't missed Jace's returning home text. Opening the door, I was confronted by the wolf. He didn't bother to smile or hide behind any of his usual pleasantries. He just stared expectantly at me, waiting to be invited inside.

"Hi," I stepped backward, thankful I'd spent most of the afternoon tidying up and hiding everything of importance, "what are you doing here?"

"After hearing your confession this morning, I thought it would be best to speak in private." He stepped into the trailer, his eyes shifting throughout the room and to the opened bedroom. "Jace missed our morning tranquility ritual. Is there a problem? Are you two okay?"

"He wasn't feeling well. His stomach kept him up most of the night. I told him to stay in bed and rest." I entered the kitchenette and filled two glasses with water.

"What a shame. He could have benefitted from hearing your fears this morning." He took a seat at the table, diverting his eyes from my ass when I turned back around to place the glass in front of him. "Thanks."

"Jace spends a lot of time hearing my fears. I'm sure he's familiar with them by now."

Tim took a long, slow sip, turning the glass in his hand and studying it. "Is that so?"

"Yeah. When you two found me, I was pretty broken. I'm not completely back together yet. My ankle's still busted, just like my finances."

"How's that going?"

"The attorneys are hopeful it'll be resolved soon. They've been working to get this expedited. We'll see what happens. Honestly, I think they're in a bigger rush to see this thing through than I am. I guess it's because they don't get paid until my assets are unfrozen."

"Why do you always assume the only possible motivation for helping out is self-serving?"

"Isn't it true most of the time?" I snorted. "It's sad that everyone isn't like you."

He nodded at the compliment. "You've doubted Jace lately." It wasn't a question, so I didn't bother denying it. I didn't believe for a second he determined that from the crap I said this morning, but that was the game he wanted to play. And it probably worked with most of his other followers. To fall into line with his doctrine required a certain amount of naiveté and gullibility. Or maybe it was blissful hope and denial. At this point, I had no idea what motivated his followers to stick around and remain loyal, but his omnipotent commentary only solidified their resolve that he was in some form or fashion a savior. "Has he given you any such reason to reach those conclusions?"

"No. I'm just scared."

"Of?"

I focused on the glass. "Falling for someone and depending on them. What would I do if things fall apart again, especially this time? I don't have anywhere else to go. I like it here. If he realizes I'm not a good person and that I'm not good enough, then what?"

Tim bought my story hook, line, and sinker. "That won't happen because you are a good person and so is Jace. Regardless of any romantic entanglement or dissolution, you will always be welcomed here, and so will he." Tim looked around the room. "Why don't you join us for the evening meal since he's at work?"

"Actually, I wanted to make him some soup and wait to eat with him."

"That's a good girl." He stood, holding out his arms for a hug. After a brief embrace, he left.

Closing the door, I watched from the window as Tim returned to the main building. Then I scanned the trailer for any planted surveillance devices. Wilde had stopped by for a visit to feel me out. He must have known I had been upstairs, and he was hoping to determine if I posed a threat. With any luck, I passed with flying colors. However, the last thing I wanted to do was discuss this with Jace. I'd already been chewed out for nearly getting caught. If he heard about this, he'd probably pull me off the mission. I'd already invested a few months of my life. I wasn't going home until the bastard was behind bars.

Deciding I needed to make soup in case Tim stopped by again, I ransacked the fridge and cabinets for ingredients. I just finished chopping vegetables when the phone rang. A pit formed in my stomach. Jace shouldn't be calling. He should be sending a courtesy text saying he was on his way inside.

"What's wrong?" I asked in lieu of a greeting.

His exhale didn't help calm my nerves. "It's not her." Although I could take a small amount of comfort from the fact it wasn't Anika's body, I realized what the implications were. "It's one of his other followers. I know it. I'm going to stay until we determine who it is. She looks familiar. It shouldn't take that long to run the names of the followers who left. The ME is trying to salvage one of her fingers so we can perform a comparison. I should be back sometime tomorrow."

"All right."

"Is everything okay? The surveillance team said Tim was

at the trailer."

"Damn, you're dialed in," I teased. "Yeah, he stopped by for a quickie while my old man was at work."

"Alex, what did he want?"

"Nothing. He wanted to know where you were this morning and make sure everything was okay. I said you were sick last night and slept in. When you don't show up tomorrow morning, things might get more interesting."

"I want you to get out of there as soon as you can. Duck out after the morning ritual and go to the restaurant. It's been a while. Touching base with your boss is a great excuse to avoid having to feed Tim more lies. I'll make sure a team stays on you in case any more goons with clubs try to break your bones."

"Thanks." I held the phone for a moment, wanting to say something encouraging. "Go get that ID. We're going to nail this son of a bitch. I know it."

The smile was in his voice when he said, "I do too."

THIRTY

.

Jace hadn't checked in today, and I couldn't shake the bad feeling I had. I spent most of the day outside the co-op, but upon my return, I'd been jittery and anxious. Putting that nervous energy to good use after pacing for thirty minutes and doing an hour long workout, I hooked the tablet to the satellite link, visited the list of sites Wilde frequented, and researched the previous six deaths, finding several similarities in the wound tracks and their toxicology reports.

It wasn't uncommon for balloons to rupture, but I couldn't help but wonder if the supplier was using substandard latex or if the structural integrity of the balloons were already compromised. Sending an e-mail to the team to request an analysis of the remaining shreds of the damaged vessels recovered from the bodies, I hoped they might be able to trace the chemical compound to a manufacturer and figure out where the balloons had been purchased. Truthfully, it was a fool's errand, but I wasn't sure what else the bodies could tell us. Everything had been processed. Dirt, fibers, and trace elements didn't indicate any pattern or point to a suspect.

"What about natural supplements and herbs?" I asked the empty room, scanning the reports again. From everything we knew about Wilde's farming practices and his online research, I didn't think anyone could leave this place without having some type of herbal substance in their bloodstream. If we could trace that to the dead mules, we'd have reasonable cause for searching the compound for drugs. However, months had passed between the time the women left the cult and when they were found dead. My theory wouldn't work.

I didn't like where my mind had gone. Tim was doing a lot of heinous things to his female followers, but maybe he wasn't directly involved in the drug trade. Perhaps the women escaped him, only to be preyed upon by a supplier linked to the cartel. Scratching that thought, I knew we had to stick to the facts. The fact was Tim had a record involving drugs and sexual assault. The leopard didn't change his spots. He just got better at hiding them.

My phone beeped. Jace had returned. Maybe he brought good news with him. Tidying up the mess I made, I placed my random notes in a pile and unplugged the tablet. Before I even left the bedroom, the door to the trailer opened. Since Jace was alone, I hefted the stack into my arms to place back in the secret cubby in the kitchen.

Jace gripped the edge of the doorway, struggling to hoist himself up the steps. He was pale and sweaty. Even when he was in complete drifter mode, he didn't look this bad. Slowly, he pulled the door closed behind him and stumbled to the couch, collapsing sideways onto it.

"Are you okay?"

"Sorry, I'm late." He rolled onto his back and put an arm over his eyes to block the overhead light. "Did Tim get suspicious?"

"I haven't spoken to Tim today." I put the items away and locked the door. "You don't look so good."

"I don't feel so good. I think I have the flu."

"I thought you were checking out the crime scene. Don't tell me you took off for a night of partying?"

He pulled his arm away from his bloodshot eyes. "Don't I wish. The crime scene and the body were six hours from each other. The commute was a total time suck." Suddenly, he pushed himself up. "Bathroom." He crossed the room, barely making it before getting violently ill.

My stomach turned, but my constitution was strong enough to resist becoming susceptible to the suggestion. When he came out, I pointed to the bedroom. "Take the bed. You're sick."

He didn't protest. He just moved into the other room and dropped face first onto the mattress. While I went into the kitchen to get something to settle his stomach and keep him from dehydrating, he kicked off his shoes and got under the covers.

"I have to stop being such an overachiever," he said when I came in with a cup of tea. "It takes real commitment to go to the lengths of contracting the flu just to sell a lie. I guess I wanted to be just like you."

"It's not a lie anymore." I edged away from him. "And for the record, if I get sick, I'll kill you."

"Noted." He closed his eyes, exhausted and miserable. "I should update you on the situation." The thought made him turn a shade greener.

"Unless it's something that can't wait, we'll go over it tomorrow. Did you have the medical team at HQ check you out?"

"There wasn't time. I wanted to get back before Tim started asking questions that you couldn't answer."

"How considerate." Leaving the room, I returned with the bucket from under the sink. "In case you need this." I placed it on the floor beside him. "If you need anything else, yell. I'll be in the other room. But there isn't a chance in hell I'm cleaning up your puke, so don't even ask."

He let out a pained exhale. "Okay."

Leaving the room, I gave the couch a tentative glance. I had too much to do, and sleeping on that uncomfortable excuse for a sofa wasn't going to help matters. Rolling my eyes, I set up shop at the kitchen table and pulled out the gear and notes I just stowed away.

I spent the next few hours analyzing Wilde's web history. Ben had been kind enough to forward it to me, so I read page after page of farming procedures and practices. While some of the articles had scientific value, it was the comment section that caught my attention. Wilde posted on several of the pages under an indecipherable handle.

His messages related to the articles and appeared innocuous. However, this could be how he was transmitting encrypted messages.

He used several words repetitively, and he often listed quantities. In some instances, it was crop yield. Other times it was acres, fertilizer amount, and nutrient ratios. Sitting back, I simplified the repetitive words, assigning each one a letter. Next, I wrote down the corresponding quantities, leaving off the unit of measure. He could be talking about kilos. He could also be talking about how much nitrogen to add to the soil.

Performing a search for the same set of words and values, I hoped to hit on something. Of course, Wilde's posts filled the page, but the farther down I went, the more obscure the search results became. Realizing this wasn't getting me anywhere, I logged into the DEA's database to see if they made any busts that corresponded to the numbers in any of the posts. I started with the oldest one I could find.

At some point, my eyelids became heavy, and I decided to give up on the endeavor. Scribbling down the last entry I checked, I put the tablet and uplink into the false back of the kitchen cabinet and reviewed my notes again. We were missing something. What was it? I rested my head on my arm, and reread the page, but the words no longer made sense.

The sound of running water woke me. I opened my eyes and stared at Jace who was rinsing out his mug in the sink. He didn't look nearly as sickly as he did last night, but he wasn't firing on all cylinders either. Lifting my head off my arm, I straightened, regretting having slept at the table, and decided it was Decker's fault for getting his flu germs on the couch.

"How are you feeling?" I asked.

"I kept down the tea you gave me last night. And I just finished a cup of soup. We'll see how it goes." He rested his hips against the counter. "Didn't you say you were going to sleep on the couch?"

"I changed my mind. I wasn't sure how long it would take for the flu virus to jump off you and infect the sofa cushions."

"I didn't realize you were a germophobe. That wasn't indicated in your file or in any of your previous behaviors." He pulled out a chair and sat down. "I'm pretty sure that's not exactly how it spreads either. However, you'll be pleased to know I disinfected the bathroom this morning."

"Great." I stretched my shoulders and back, nostalgic for one of Martin's massages. "Since you're feeling better, why don't you tell me how your trip went?"

"It was brutal. The latest victim was torn apart. I'm hoping she was dead before it happened. A lot of the damage was due to predation, but the knife marks were obvious. The fingerprints turned into a bust, but we matched the wound track to the other dead women. Whoever gutted them used the same knife." He bit his bottom lip. "I know our latest victim was one of Wilde's former followers. There haven't been that many women who have left, maybe ten in the last nine months. That's counting Anika. I have the possibilities narrowed down to two, possibly three, based on build and what was left of her facial features. The team will start there for the ID. We should know something soon." He checked his phone to make sure he hadn't slept through a call.

"Didn't you say you weren't leaving until you found something solid?"

"I did." He scanned the photos on the device, holding it toward me. "Recognize that? It's part of one of the informational flyers Wilde hands out at the farmer's market. It had some writing on it. Our techs are working on an analysis, but it's the closest we've come to connecting this to Wilde's cult."

"Where'd you find it?"

Jace's sad smile turned into a deep frown. "It was partially buried in the desert, fifteen feet from where the body was discovered. Stella already said any decent defense attorney could have it thrown out as circumstantial. It isn't our lynchpin, but it gives us every indication we're on the right track."

I looked down at my notes, remembering some of my wayward thoughts before falling asleep. "The only way we're going to seal this deal is by getting upstairs, copying his records, and finding out where that staircase leads. So what the hell are we waiting for? How many more bodies have to turn up before someone gives us the go-ahead? If the DEA is happy dicking around, tell me, so I can get approval from my superiors. I'm not going to sit on my hands any longer, Jace. Let's get this ball rolling."

"I agree. We only discovered the existence of these files less than a week ago. We're monitoring Tim's computer activity and tracking his contacts. The ball is rolling. We'll get those files soon enough. Trust me."

"Can I? Sometimes it doesn't seem like I should."

He grinned. "You're so full of shit." His eyes crinkled at the corners. "There's no way in hell that's true. You'd never say it if you really thought it."

I shrugged, getting up to make some tea. It was the closest I'd get to caffeine, and I really needed the jolt. "Maybe I would."

"You're frustrated and annoyed. Probably tired too."

"Exhausted."

He chuckled quietly. "Which is why you chose to work all night instead of sleep. I'm just a little unclear as to your motivation. Is it because you're driven by some unhealthy obsession with justice, or is it because you want to go home?"

"Neither. It's because I'm tired of your pestering ways and psychobabble annoyances. Plus, I had to pick up your slack since you decided to go on a little vacation."

"Then you must be thrilled I caught some kind of stomach bug."

"Not really, but it seems to have left your system pretty quickly. Are you sure it wasn't food poisoning?"

"It could have been. I really don't know. I started feeling off yesterday morning. I was sick most of the day, which made investigating pretty pointless, but it fizzled out after I got back last night. Maybe it was a twenty-four hour bug."

"Let's hope so." I looked at the clock, realizing we were late for the morning ritual. "I should head out. Are you staying here?"

He shook his head. "Tim will expect to see me,

particularly when I haven't been around for two days. I don't think I've ever gone more than a day without seeing him. I never had that long of a furlough. It's nice having someone to watch my back."

"I don't take flattery well."

"Yeah, I noticed. You don't take most things well."

"No, I don't."

THIRTY-ONE

Things around the co-op continued to be erratic, but Jace was back to himself by the next day. The team identified the dead woman as Melanie Shaw. She had left the Church of Perpetual Light seven months ago. Before joining the ranks of the enlightened, she had been an investment banker. A few bad personal investments had reduced her amassed wealth from ten million to a million. An SEC investigation into her private and professional trading cost her her job. A very public divorce wiped out another fifty percent of her assets, and Tim took the rest. Jace remembered the announcement that she had left, supposedly to reconnect with her ex-husband, but he didn't remember seeing her leave. Agent Eckhardt and the LAPD liaison spoke to the ex, but he hadn't seen Melanie since the divorce. And he had an alibi for her TOD.

"When's the team going to bust through the fence and start asking Wilde about her disappearance?" I asked. "We have an ID. She never went back with her husband. Tim's the last person who saw her alive. It's logical. It makes sense."

"It does. But Wilde has an alibi for her estimated TOD."

"Of course he does. Why wouldn't he?"

Jace rubbed the stubble on his cheek. "Do you want to know who his alibi is?"

"You?"

"You can't even begin to comprehend how much this sucks." He sifted through the printouts and notations that had been piling up in our hidden compartment. "Farmer's market starts in an hour. If Tim's suspicious of you snooping upstairs, he hasn't let on to me. He checked the circuit breaker a few times, so I'm hoping the random power disruptions saved your ass because in an hour we're breaking into that room and scanning every file we find."

"We? Didn't you ban me from the upper level?"

"Stop being a martyr. My orders aren't intended to punish you, and you know that. That being said, you will listen and obey. If I tell you to get out of there, you get out of there. Is that clear? There's no *give me five seconds*. We go when I say we do. Or are we going to have a problem?"

"No problem, sir."

He smirked, hearing the disdain in my voice. "Go outside and help Sarah with the baked goods. Once the table is ready and customers come in, slip away and meet me in the dining hall."

"Aye, aye, captain."

"Now you sound like Scotty from *Star Trek*."

"But I didn't even use a Scottish accent." Bumping the table with my fist, I met his eyes. "I'll see you soon."

As usual, the farmer's market was a busy event. The townsfolk and hipsters from the inner city and surrounding areas stopped by to shop for artisanal, farm fresh offerings. The honey was always a big seller, as were the fresh herbs, baked goods, and various folksy trinkets. I doubted any of the patrons realized this co-op was a cult in disguise. Even when Tim started preaching and passing out pamphlets, they thought he was just one of the vendors setting up shop.

Once the table was set, I snuck back to the main building. Jace was eating an apple in the dining hall while watching Hannah and Dana hurry about the kitchen. I took a seat beside him, relaxing against him when he put an arm around my shoulders.

"Why are you eating that?" I asked in a lovesick tone.

"I had to do something."

Dana stepped out of the kitchen.

"Do you need help?" Jace asked.

She took one look at the two of us, blushed, and shook her head before scurrying back to the kitchen.

"I'm surprised none of the women have tried to kill you yet. In case you didn't realize it, I was a hot commodity before you took me off the market," Jace whispered.

"Sure, you were." I watched as Hannah traded out the unbaked goods for the freshly made treats. As soon as the timer was set, they marched out of the kitchen, armed with pastry boxes brimming with croissants, muffins, and cookies. "Ready?"

He strained to hear the sound of the front door before standing up. "Let's move."

Before we left the dining hall, he activated the mini EMP, shorting out the lights and the ovens. The ladies would be pissed. We continued out of the room, toward the rear of the building. Taking a left, we went up the stairs and down the hallway without missing a beat.

"File room." I pointed to the door as we moved past it. I didn't bother pointing out the storage space. Leading the way to the end of the hallway, I knelt down, pulling my lock picks from inside the ankle brace. "Time me." After twenty seconds, the lock popped, and I pushed the door open an inch. Stepping inside, I made sure we were alone. "Clear."

Jace pushed the door closed behind us, scanning the room for signs of a struggle. The spots remained on the rug, but the bed had been made. He went past it, moving toward the only other door in the room. Removing the gun he had hidden beneath his untucked shirt, he twisted the knob and opened the door. The staircase led into a dark abyss. Pulling a tiny flashlight from his pocket, he turned to me. "Wait here."

While he went exploring, I studied the room and searched the furniture. A few minutes later, he returned, tucked the flashlight away, and wiped his palms on his pants. He went to the bed and pulled down the covers. When he revealed the sheets, he looked up at me. The stains were gone.

"They had the same specks as the rug," I insisted. While he remade the bed, I knelt down, photographing the spots. He joined me, using his knife to cut a piece of the stained carpet for further testing. After placing it inside an evidence bag and stuffing it in his pocket, he helped me search the rest of the furniture.

"The stairs lead to a series of tunnels," he said, not bothering to glance up. "The ground is dirt, and so are the walls. There's minimal lighting. Reinforced frames support the structure to prevent a collapse. I don't know where they lead, but they must run beneath this building. Last week, I checked the basement, but there were no hidden rooms or trapdoors."

"Shouldn't we explore them?" I asked, but he held out an arm to stop me from passing.

"Not today, Indy. The files are our priority. Those tunnels lead somewhere. I'll have the surveillance units scout for their endpoints." He closed a drawer. "This could be how Wilde manages to come and go without anyone realizing it. This is a total game-changer." He finished searching the dresser. "We need to move. Did you find anything?"

Using an empty plastic bag, I held up what looked like a metal shoehorn. "What is this?"

Jace came closer to examine the item. "Some kind of laryngoscope," he guessed.

"That's better than what I was thinking."

He tilted his head, examining it from another angle, and snapped a quick photo. "Anything else?" he asked, and I shook my head. The rest of the drawers had been empty. "Let's go."

He cracked the door open and peered into the hallway. As soon as he was certain we were alone, he stepped out first to make sure the mini EMP deactivated the camera and signaled for me to cross the hall and unlock the door to the file room. Once the door unlocked, we proceeded inside in a similar fashion. Jace looked around, in awe of the volume of potential evidence.

The two of us made quick work of the locked drawers,

prioritizing Wilde's ledger and rolodex. After that, we moved on to the files he kept on his followers. Jace was a whiz at scanning the pages with the handheld scanner. While he did that, I gave the other filing cabinets a more thorough search, checking for anything hidden or valuable amongst the financial and legal records.

While we hurriedly worked to process everything, time flew by. A noise from downstairs stopped us in our tracks. Jace checked his watch. "Shit." He looked at me. "We need to get this cleaned up and get out of here." He finished the last page of the file. He had gone through two-thirds of the folders while I had made a similar dent in the financial and legal documents. Closing the drawers as quietly as possible, he checked to make sure we hadn't left anything out while I made sure all the drawers were locked. Then he reactivated the EMP and opened the door. Muffled voices sounded from below. Jace crept into the hallway. "Come on," he whispered.

While I thought it'd be better to remain where we were, inside a locked room, it didn't exactly provide much of an escape route. We needed to get back downstairs before the rest of the group returned for supper. Jace hugged the wall, gesturing that I remain behind him. Our gear was safely tucked away, but just being upstairs was considered a violation.

"I need to check on something. Get started. I'll be there in a sec," Tim said.

Frantic, Jace swiveled his head, searching for another way out. We were trapped. "Get the door open. We'll take the tunnels."

Dashing back toward the door, I pulled my picks free, willing my fingers to tease the tumblers into place. The footsteps on the staircase grew louder. We didn't have enough time.

"Come on. Come on," Jace kept repeating. When he heard the third step from the top creak, he hauled me to my feet, pressed me against the wall, and shielded me from Tim. "One of us needs to get out of this with the evidence. In the event he doesn't buy our excuse, make sure you get everything and get it back to the team."

"Fuck that." I grasped his shoulders and hooked my legs around his waist. "Oh, Jace," I moaned loudly, making our presence known, "oh god, right there." He buried his face in my neck, gripping my back and knocking his forearms against the wall with a repeating, thudding echo.

"Ahem," Tim said from the other end of the hallway. He wasn't pleased his newest couple was copulating a few feet from his bedroom. I wasn't sure if it was because he wasn't getting some or because we were upstairs, but his annoyance was obvious.

"Shit," I cursed, dropping my legs.

Jace smirked, pressing his forehead against mine while he pantomimed zipping his pants and we both pretended to adjust our clothing. "Damn, you're good."

"You say that every time, babe." Adopting a humiliated grin, I held the look for when Jace stepped away. "Oh shit...Tim...I...," I sputtered, covering most of my face in my hands. "We...I...shit."

"Tim," Jace was serious, practically stoic, "I'm so sorry. We were downstairs, and we really needed some privacy, y'know. Everyone was outside. The lights were on the fritz, and it was kind of romantic. One thing led to another, and I thought we wouldn't get caught." At least that part was true.

Tim gave us both a hard stare. "Fine." He focused on Jace. "This wasn't exactly what I meant when I gave you instructions." Jace bowed his head, understanding that this was punishment. Then Tim turned to me. "Really, Alex, I would have thought you'd have more self-respect than this. Does the thought of being caught make you hot?"

I stared at the floor. The thought of finding evidence against Tim made me pretty damn hot. "A little," I said in a meek voice. "It won't happen again. Please don't throw me out."

He waved us both off like we were nothing more than a nuisance. "Return to the trailer until you remember the point of this church is to establish inner peace and reach enlightenment. Your actions were rash and far from what I would expect from either of you." He took a key from his pocket and unlocked his bedroom door. "Now go."

"We're sorry." Jace ushered me past the doorway. "It'll never happen again."

He looped an arm around my waist when we made it to the ground floor, pressing his lips against my temple as we made our way toward the exit. No one interrupted or stopped our escape.

"Tim is furious," Jace said as he unlocked the door. "I don't like this."

"I'm sorry." Perhaps my plan wasn't the best. I'd used that particular move with mixed results several times in the past.

Jace went to the pantry, removed the false back, and swept for bugs. Then he emptied his pockets and uploaded the data from the scanner to the DEA server so the team could analyze it. "You have no reason to be sorry. We didn't have another play." He rubbed his mouth. "I'm sure he bought it. But once he starts thinking about it, it won't make a ton of sense."

"Maybe I'm a freak." I handed him the memory card from my device. "Blame me."

"That wouldn't be very gentlemanly." He began the upload and lifted the evidence bag we collected. "He can search the entire upstairs, but we were careful. Everything should be the way it was." Once the upload completed, he placed everything into a second bag, sealed it, and phoned Matt. "I need a dead drop pick-up at the gas station. We'll go now and leave it in the usual place."

He hung up, locked the gear back in the pantry, and checked his weapon. A quick run to the convenience store wouldn't make matters any worse. After tucking the collected evidence inside a brown fast food bag and folding it over several times, Jace dropped the bag on the ground beside the trash can. Then we entered the store.

"Grab whatever you want," he said. "I'll pick up the essentials."

While he scanned the aisles for whatever reasonable excuse we needed for our departure, I grabbed a few magazines and puzzle books. Brilliant green eyes stared at me from a glossy cover, and I stopped dead in my tracks. Picking up the business magazine, I ran my fingers against the outline of Martin's face. He was the featured article for starting a new tech movement. He probably had the cover framed in his office. Hell, he probably handed out autographed copies too.

Adding the magazine to my purchase pile, I grabbed a couple others to mask the real reason for the purchase and met Jace at the register. He smiled at me, adding toilet paper, light bulbs, batteries, condoms, and a box of fruit bars to our order. We must have been in desperate need of at least one of those things. On our way out, we passed Eckhardt, who was wiping a spilled slurpee off his shirt and tossing the used napkins into the trash. I caught sight of him in the side mirror, picking up the brown bag. Maybe things were turning around today. We had gained a lot. Now we just had to wait for the team to analyze it.

THIRTY-TWO

It was getting late. Jace decided it'd be best if we avoided the evening ritual and the main facility. Since we were being shunned for our bad behavior, we should wait to be invited back to the collective. A bit uncertain of where to start now that we had obtained so much intel, Jace pulled out an aerial view of the compound. While we waited for dinner to heat, we discussed the possible purposes of the hidden tunnel.

"You've never seen any openings on the property?" I asked. "What about large drainage pipes or city access tunnels to gas lines or sewers?"

"No, nothing like that." He looked up with a straight face. "Have you noticed any alligators or rats roaming around?"

For a moment, I didn't understand the question. Then I realized he was making fun of my thought process. For all intents and purposes, this was a rural area. There weren't gas lines or sewers. The co-op had a septic system and electricity. It was amazing we even had running water. "No, but the next time I take the subway, I'll let you know."

He grinned. "You do that." After putting away the maps, he moved dinner to the table. "You weren't kidding about the files. The team will work that around the clock. I hate that I didn't finish, but after this afternoon, we can't afford to get caught again. You've already been spotted up there twice. I don't know if Tim believes in three strikes, but you shouldn't push it."

"We could always take the tunnel out."

"We don't know if it leads out." Whatever Jace was thinking, he didn't want to share it. "I hope we have something actionable. You copied everything from the ledger and rolodex, right?"

"Yes, sir."

He grimaced. "Why do you do that? I'm only asking for verification. I'm not questioning your intellect or abilities."

"Well, my secondary response would have been to say 'I thought that was your job,' but you might not realize it was a joke." I speared a beet with my fork and popped it into my mouth. Chewing was a nice way to avoid conversation.

"In other words, you're questioning my intellect and abilities. I see how it is." He watched me throughout dinner. When we finished, he leaned back, leaving the dishes on the table. "Why do you do this?"

Before I could ask what he was referencing, Wilde knocked on the trailer door. "I'll get it." Opening the door, I offered Tim a polite smile. "Would you like to come inside?"

"No, thank you. We missed you at supper and the evening ritual." He looked into the trailer. "I can see you're having supper here. I don't want to intrude. I just needed to speak to Jace for a moment."

I stepped away from the door, turning to find Decker a few steps behind me. "Tim," he moved closer, and I backed into the kitchenette, "we really do regret our hasty actions earlier." He took a step out of the trailer, pulling the door closed behind him.

I couldn't hear what they were saying, but I had a slight visual from the kitchenette window. Leaning over the sink, I pretended to busy myself with the dishes while I maintained eyes on Jace. Wilde was dangerous, and while it would have been incredibly stupid to do something right outside the trailer, I didn't put it past him.

The conversation continued for ten minutes. Finally, Jace held out his hand, and Wilde pulled him into a one-armed hug. He released him, waved goodbye, and went back to the main building. Jace waited several moments before opening the door and coming inside.

"Did you kiss and make up?" I asked.

"I guess so. Wilde wanted to make sure you weren't upset or embarrassed about earlier, and he clarified his previous instructions. I should keep you satisfied, just as long as it doesn't jeopardize the integrity of the church. Apparently, you're scandalous."

"Then why is Wilde willing to keep me around?"

"He wants to make sure I impart upon you the dire financial blight the Church of Perpetual Light is facing. Within the next month, you stand to gain a considerable amount of money. He wants to keep you happy until then because you're a cash cow."

"Did he call me a cow?"

"No." He licked his lips, lost in thought over Wilde's odd apology. "He wanted to clear the air, and he wanted to make sure I was aware of the stakes and was acting in the church's best interest. Tim wanted to remind me of all the things he has done, and that no matter how wonderful you might be, you haven't been the one to support and provide for me and put a roof over my head. He even took credit for putting you in my path."

"He should only know."

Jace snorted. "Feel free to tell him once he's been taken into custody. Until then, it's best he continues to believe I'm his loyal puppet."

*   *   *

I screamed. Decker grabbed my arm before I could reach for my concealed weapon. He held me tightly against his chest while I fought and bucked against him. "Alex, you're safe. It's me. It's Jace. Take it easy."

I stopped fighting and curled into his arms, letting him absorb the tremors that coursed through me. At least this wasn't the usual nightmare.

"Shh. Easy." He loosened his hold, but I didn't pull away.

Images of dark tunnels and Wilde's followers being kept in cages while being tortured and drugged ran through my mind. I had no basis for thinking any of it, but it felt real. The scary part was my dreams sometimes came from my subconscious thoughts. I hated to think that was the conclusion my mind had reached concerning this case. Those dormitories were like tiny cages, the entire facility a prison. As for the torture, it didn't take a genius to figure out Anika's mention of it connected the two in my mind.

"Damn you," I muttered, "now I'm psychoanalyzing myself."

He laughed. "It's about time." He ran a hand through my hair. "Are you hoping to pick up where we left off in that hallway, or do you want to see if you're strong enough to break my ribs after you elbowed me?"

Steadying myself, I pushed away from him. "Neither. I was hoping you'd get the point that sharing a bed is a bad idea and you'd stop falling asleep next to me."

He ignored the comment. "I've noticed your nightmares haven't been as pronounced or disruptive when I stay here while you sleep. If it's not my presence, then that means talking about these things has been helping." He pretended to hold a pen and paper, channeling his inner Freud. "So tell me, what was this nightmare about? Was it the same reoccurring dream?"

"No."

He quirked an eyebrow. "No? Well, damn, I guess you're cured."

"That implies there was something wrong with me in the first place. For the record, there wasn't. This was about Wilde and the tunnels. I dreamt he was holding the women prisoner so he could drug and torture them." I looked past him, finding other things in the room to focus on. "I know. It's entirely on the nose." My eyes came to rest on Martin's magazine cover. "I want to get back to HQ to see how things are progressing."

"It'd be nice to brief the team on what we found and get an update on the progress they're making. We'll go after the morning ritual." He reached for his phone, setting it to send a delayed message to my number at a predetermined time. "You can say your lawyers need to meet to discuss the case. And since I'm supposed to be doing my part to make sure you remember how great the commune is, I'll offer to go with you." He glanced up. "You can go back to sleep now."

"Thanks, but I'll pass." Climbing out of bed, I grabbed the stack of magazines and headed into the living room. "I'm going to chill out and catch up on current affairs. I'm starting to miss the outside world."

After skimming some Hollywood gossip rag, I dropped the periodical on the floor and leafed through a lifestyle magazine while Decker observed me. After twenty minutes, he got bored and decided to fit in an early workout.

"I'm going for a jog," he declared after changing into shorts and a long sleeve shirt. "I haven't done that since you moved in, but I used to do it all the time. Tim won't think anything of it." He stretched his calves against the doorframe. "I'll see if I can spot any type of tunnel opening. I'll be back soon."

"Take your phone, just in case."

He nodded, slipping out of the trailer. Letting out a breath, I picked up the business magazine and flattened out on the couch. My back was spasming, probably from trying to twist away from Jace. Deciding that focusing on a different set of problems might help, I flipped to Martin's article. I'd read it last night while Jace was asleep.

As usual, Martin gave a good interview. Charismatic as always. The focus was on business, but I couldn't help but dwell on the brief comment concerning his bachelordom. Perhaps he had disregarded my insistence that he move on and date. Or he hadn't found Miss Right yet, or he was keeping a lid on his relationship status. Too bad a part of me hoped he was waiting for me. Memories of our last conversation popped into my head, and I hugged the magazine to my chest. I was pathetic.

By the time Jace returned, I had moved to the floor and fallen asleep with the magazine against my chest. The sound of the shower woke me, but I was too achy to move.

When he came out, he helped me up.

"Back spasm," I explained, yawning. "It'll pass. I just need to stretch it out." I chuckled. "Tim probably has a class for that."

"Are you sure it isn't from all those intense workouts or sleeping at the table?"

"Probably."

He gingerly felt along my back for any obvious knots. "Maybe a hot shower will help. If not, they can give you something at HQ."

"Like coffee." I smiled, ignoring his much more serious response. Fueled by that thought, I dressed and waited for our return to the saner world.

Tim was pleasant, our indiscretion forgiven. The morning ritual focused on turning inward to address outward stressors. He spoke about relationships and the difficulty in maintaining them. That was when I realized all the men at the commune were paired off. Obviously, that was an easier feat since they were outnumbered four to one, but it gave me a strange feeling. Before Jace and I allegedly connected, he wasn't the only single man in the group. Now they were all in relationships. Another oddity was there were no same-sex couples. Obviously, Tim's recruitment was biased. He only wanted women who would be attracted to him. And from the beaming faces around the compound, I couldn't help but think this was nothing more than a harem.

My phone chimed, and I politely ducked away from the group. Pretending to take a call, I waited several minutes before returning in time to be dismissed. Tim waved off a few of his flock in order to approach us. After I filled him in on the staged phone call, he wished me luck with the lawyers, insisting Jace should go with me.

Something was nagging at Jace, but given the early hour, my aching back, and my disrupted sleep, I wasn't in the mood to pry. Frankly, avoiding conversation seemed perfectly acceptable. Jace tended to talk a lot, and if we weren't working through theories or evidence, he was wheedling his way into my psyche. In truth, his efforts were helping. Unfortunately, it also made our coexistence rather stressful at times.

"Last night, Tim asked if we were using protection," Jace said out of the blue. "That's why I bought the condoms. He'll ask the clerk about our purchases."

"You've gotta be kidding me."

He shook his head. "He's done it before. Should any of the women get pregnant, that would jeopardize everything. A baby would become the priority. Not the church. And certainly not Tim." He tapped against the steering wheel. "Have you noticed the other male members now have female companions?"

"Yep. What's up with that?"

"I'm not sure. I have this sick suspicion Tim discouraged them from choosing partners, so I would get first dibs. But until you, my interaction with the other women never went beyond the occasional friendly flirtation." He checked the mirrors and switched lanes. No one was following us, but it didn't hurt to be careful. "I believe he wanted me to choose someone like Sarah, who is committed to the cause and will never leave the facility. Now he's afraid. That's why he's been so lenient about our intrusion upstairs."

"He has big plans for you."

"I think so." He switched lanes again, turning onto a different road that would lead us to the tricked-out mansion. "I need to figure out how to play this to our advantage. If he'll share his side business with me, we'll have a real shot at grabbing him and stopping whoever his connection is. The first thing we need to do is have Ben move up your hearing date. We need to get the assistant director to sign off on the money. The sooner Tim gets a big payday, the sooner I'll be able to prove my loyalty to him and his cause. From there, we should be able to move on this."

"Great, just make sure you don't sell me out to be his next drug mule."

He chuckled. "You should think about that the next time you almost shoot me." He glanced at me from the corner of his eye. "Although, I should have expected the elbow to the ribs when I blocked you from reaching your weapon." I didn't say anything, and he tapped my leg with the back of his hand. "How's your back?"

"Oddly enough, it's fine now. It miraculously healed after entering the hallowed grounds of the commune."

THIRTY-THREE

The information overload was taking a toll. Jace was the only member of the team who slept well last night. From the number of empty soda cans and energy drinks, I was surprised Ben and Carlo hadn't gone into cardiac arrest. Stella hadn't moved since we'd entered the room. She might have been asleep with her eyes open. Eve was tackling the ledger and rolodex, cross-referencing the two to try to crack the code. Wilde had written everything in some form of shorthand that was proving impossible to decipher.

"Where are we on the carpet swatch?" Jace asked as Eckhardt burst into the room with the evidence bag in hand.

"It's blood, diluted with a mix of saliva and stomach acid." Eckhardt offered me a nod. "That tool you photographed is used to assist in retrieving swallowed contraband. Typically, an individual would tie off the ballooned item with some dental floss or string, swallow it, and later retrieve it. It's common in prisons, but as any corrections officer can tell you, the retrieval doesn't always go smoothly. The package can get stuck on the way up."

"That explains the blood." Jace blinked a few times.

"Any idea whose it is?"

"No match to any of the dead mules," Eve volunteered. "And since it's so degraded, by the time we sequence the DNA and run it through the database, it'll be a waste of a few weeks. It's too damaged to give us a viable match, and that's assuming the victim is in the system."

"That's also assuming the person smuggling the contraband is a victim," Stella said, snapping out of her trance. "I've done nothing but read these files. I don't even know where to begin. Tim knows so much about his followers. He could easily steal their identities, empty their bank accounts, and control every aspect of their lives. But I'm assuming they willingly gave him this information, which isn't punishable."

Jace frowned. "He has hidden cameras in their rooms, probably throughout the entire facility. It's an invasion of their privacy."

"Would they object if they knew?" Matt asked. "It sounds like they'd be willing to do anything for this guy."

"Is that because he has dirt on them?" I asked.

Stella sighed. "It's the chicken and egg. The good news is we have this information now. I'm updating our dossiers and backgrounds for his followers. From there, I'll do a quick assessment to find the weakest link and start knocking down doors to their past lives. With any luck, a few have a significant someone who will want to help us get them back. If we can separate one of them from the group, we'll have a better idea of how these people are really being treated."

"Shouldn't you already know that?" Jace asked. "Isn't that what I've been reporting for the last ten months? Does anyone here need a reminder that Wilde poisoned Alex? We know how these people are being treated."

"But we don't know why they're willing to put up with it," I said. "Is it loyalty or fear?"

"Probably both." Jace updated the room on the shift in Tim's attitude toward us and the need to move forward with solidifying our roles within the co-op. He concluded by saying, "I'm gonna speak to the assistant director. I appreciate the work everyone is doing. Keep it up."

Once he was out the door, I gave Matt an uncertain look. "How are things actually going?"

"We're making progress. Everything we've said is accurate. Our best bet is still infiltrating Wilde's operation once we learn his true agenda. All of this intel is great, but it isn't leading to an underground drug network or the person responsible for cutting open six mules. Jace is getting tunnel vision. It happens sometimes. I don't blame him. His focus has been on Wilde for so long he forgot we have to draw a connection."

"It'd be easier if we had an outside link." Carlo swiveled away from the computer, drained another can of soda, and burped. "Honestly, we're close to finding one. Those farming boards and posts aren't about soil conditions or equipment. I've read the articles and the messages. Given what we know about the property and the climate here, his questions and comments aren't feasible. They aren't even in the ballpark. Either he's the most incompetent hobbyist farmer ever, or he's talking about something else. We've been tracing IP addresses to RW locations."

"RW?" I asked.

"Real world." Ben clicked the mouse. "We have a dozen or so that check out as legit agriculturalists, but three users are posing a problem. They've been rerouting through various servers throughout the world, bouncing us from Canada to Africa to Russia. I'm deep diving to see if I can get an actual location or name. Some of my connections on the dark web might be able to assist."

"Did you get clearance for that?" Stella asked.

"Sure," Ben replied sarcastically.

Jace returned with a piece of paper. He gave Ben and Stella an odd look, sensing he missed something. Shaking it off, he handed the paper to Carlo. "We'll need to move up the estate hearing to the end of this week. Once that happens, we'll need documents ruling in Alice's favor and unfreezing her trust fund. I'll want her father's business assets to remain contested for now, so Wilde has a reason to keep her on the hook. In the meantime, make sure the court docket reflects the new date and time for the hearing." He spun toward Stella. "Figure out the earliest timeline in which she would have access to the money after the ruling. We've been authorized the usual amount, so I want those funds drafted into the account at that time. Make sure everything is completely traceable because she's going to wire it to Tim as a thank you."

"When is this happening?" I asked.

"At the end of the week."

"That soon?" It seemed suspicious to me that everything was happening at once, but I had been living on the property for over a month. It wasn't that soon.

"It'll coincide with your absence," Jace said. He reached into his pocket and handed me a note. "You need to call your handler at the OIO. Your flight's already been arranged."

"The hell it has." Assuming Jablonsky was pulling me, I stormed out of the room before Jace could pick up on anything besides my annoyance. Fearful of what might have turned up during the OIO investigation, I didn't know what was waiting for me at home. All I knew was we were on the cusp of a breakthrough, and I couldn't leave now. Slamming the door to my office, I picked up the phone and dialed Mark's cell. "What the hell's going on?"

"Parker?" he asked, his voice garbled by a mouthful of food. "Whatever happened to starting a conversation with 'Mark, I miss you. How's tricks?'"

"It's not the 1950s. Why are you pulling me?"

He snorted then coughed as he choked on his lunch. Finally, he managed to say, "What the fuck are you talking about?"

"Decker moved up my cover's court date to coincide with my absence."

"Oh," he coughed a few more times, "the prosecutor's office needs your testimony on that terrorism case. The bastard's defense attorney had the trial date moved, and since you were lead, the AUSA wanted you here to testify. They understand the situation, so it'll be done in a closed court. Everything should be handled within one day. Didn't you get my message?"

I snorted at the post-it. *Being sent home. Call OIO.* "Not the important part."

"Numbnuts," Mark grumbled. "I'll pick you up at the airport Friday morning. You'll arrive at eight a.m. my time. Enjoy the red-eye. We'll get you back on a plane Saturday morning. You should be back with those idiotic cowboys midday Saturday. I'll see you soon."

*　　*　　*

As soon as we returned to the co-op, Jace went into total game mode. While I worked on stress management techniques by taking a Tai Chi class with several of Wilde's flock, Jace spoke to the big man himself. Their interaction wasn't meant for my ears, but for all intents and purposes, Jace was a double-agent. He informed Wilde that I would be out of town for the court appearance. My legal team was putting me up in a hotel for the night, but they were hopeful we'd be getting a verdict the same day.

Tim was elated. He made that fact known when I arrived for the evening ritual. Pulling me aside before he began preaching, he spoke on how privileged it was to get to know me and how he hoped nothing would change. He made sure to point out every positive thing he'd done since our first meeting at the restaurant. Then he dedicated his evening's lecture to giving back to others less fortunate. He concluded by pointing out the church was suffering, and we needed to focus our efforts and band together to make the weekend sales and recruitment even more successful.

For the rest of the week, Tim nudged me in the right direction. He'd been extra attentive, asking about my ankle and plans for returning to work. He tried inserting subliminal messages into our conversations to encourage me to quit. My ankle should have been nearly healed by now, so I told him I'd been giving it plenty of thought. Despite Tim's connection to the restaurant, the business appeared clean. Going back to work would have been a waste of time, but I couldn't exactly say that. Instead, I told Tim I didn't want to commit to anything until I learned of the court's decision.

To prove he was onboard, Jace spent more and more time in Wilde's presence, going so far as to eat morning meals with the others. He and Wilde became inseparable, but after the evening ritual, Jace would turn his attention to me. We'd make googly eyes at one another and disappear out to the trailer after the other followers became uncomfortable with our PG-13 level of affection. One evening, I saw Tim give Jace an encouraging nod as we made our way toward the exit.

The team continued to process the data and run down leads. However, Tim's constant presence had made contact difficult. Phone calls to our DEA numbers had ceased for fear that Tim would discover the secondary devices. And since Wilde had been frequenting the gas station where Jace worked, we hadn't been able to use the dead drop either. The surveillance vans remained. A few agents scouted the outer perimeter of the facility, hoping to unearth the tunnels, but quite literally, nothing had surfaced.

"Dammit." I threw a few magazines into my bag. There was nothing inside the trailer that I needed to pack. Most of my clothing and other personal effects were locked up at HQ. "I shouldn't be leaving now. With the weekend approaching, we could have created an opportunity to explore the tunnel."

"You can run interference while I check it out Sunday," Jace suggested. "I'm sure Tim will be all over you once you return with the good news." He picked up a few rolls of paper towel and tossed them into the duffel to make it appear like I'd packed for my overnight excursion. "The team will reroute any potential calls to your hotel." He put the word in air quotes. "Tim might phone to find out how it went or to offer an inspirational word."

"Great."

"Just be prepared for the possibility. Although, I can probably run interference by telling him we spoke." He exhaled and assessed me. "You're testifying in a high profile case, right?"

I nodded.

"There might be media coverage. It doesn't matter if it's on the other coast, it could be broadcast here. The good thing is Tim limits access to outside news sources, but do your best to make sure they don't post your mug all over the media outlets."

"It's a closed court. I won't be identified by name. Nothing will become public. It should be fine. If you're stressed, you should talk to Tim or take some of his stress reduction classes. Might I suggest Tai Chi?"

"I've already served my time. I had eight months of that shit. And from what I can tell just by observing you, they don't work. You go to them twice a day, and you come back here wired like a jackrabbit. You've spent over an hour each night working out this week. Clearly, they do nothing more than wind you up."

"That's just a side effect of being in such close proximity to Tim." Glancing at the clock, I needed to leave. "Watch your back while I'm gone."

"I will." Jace handed me the duffel. "Have a safe trip. I'll see you Saturday. Don't forget to bring back the paper towel. We might need those to wipe up Tim's mess."

THIRTY-FOUR

SSA Mark Jablonsky waited at the airport for my arrival. I actually slept on the plane a lot better than I slept in the trailer. Admittedly, it was nice to be home. That damn California sunshine was driving me crazy.

"How was the flight?" Mark asked, eyeing the suitcase I rolled behind me.

"Not too bad. I couldn't review any of my notes for court because that material is here. I'm sure the prosecutor isn't pleased with this fly by night arrangement."

"So true. They're actually waiting for you at the federal building. From the way the case has been progressing, you won't be testifying until this afternoon, so from now until then, you'll be prepped."

"Are they bringing Lucca in on this?"

"He's already here. Damn, I never thought I'd see the day that you admitted to missing him." We made our way out of the airport and to the SUV. In the cup holder was a green concoction. "I thought I'd bring you breakfast. Kale smoothies, right?"

"You're out of your fucking mind if you think I'm drinking that."

"But it's your favorite."

Maybe I'd have a cab take me to the federal building. The taxi might have a strange stench and the driver might not speak English, but it wouldn't come with this type of harassment. Picking up the cup, I held it out to Jablonsky. "If it's so great, why don't you take a sip?"

"No, I stopped special and got that for you."

I pulled out my phone to check messages. At least this trip meant I didn't have to maintain radio silence. Finding several messages from Eve, I absently took a sip from the cup without thinking. Gagging on the bitter sludge, I put it back in the cup holder. "You're evil. What the hell is that?"

"Something I found in the crisper drawer of my fridge." He tossed the cup out the window and reached into the rear cup holder. "Let an old man have his fun." He placed a large coffee into my empty hand, and I inhaled deeply while reading my messages. "How are things with the DEA?"

I shrugged. "They have an odd way of investigating. We discovered a staircase two weeks ago. Last week, Decker realized it connected to underground tunnels, but we haven't explored the tunnels. We have no idea what's down there or where they lead. I don't understand his reticence. Everything is always delayed or taken over by the locals. The only reason this op is taking so long is because they're too careful. Didn't you tell me they were cowboys?"

"Did anyone give you any explanation why they aren't charging ahead?"

"They don't want to risk compromising our covers or spooking the mark. Originally, we believed Wilde was running his own drug operation, but something changed. The latest intel suggests he's linked to the Mexican cartels. Maybe *the* Mexican cartel."

"That's why they're being careful." Jablonsky chewed on his bottom lip. "They aren't too worried about this schmuck. They're worried the investigation will lead to something with real teeth and a lot of reach, so they're waiting to build a case against the big fish." He sighed. "God, you're cursed."

"Tell me about it." After making a note to get back to Eve after my court appearance, I stowed my phone, closed my eyes, and sipped my coffee. Life could have been this easy, but I had to throw a wrench in the works. "I saw Martin's magazine cover shoot."

"Yeah." Mark was going to make me work for this.

"It's probably a great way to score. Is he trolling the clubs with a few extra copies on hand?"

"That would explain the case of magazines he had delivered."

"Only one?"

Jablonsky snorted. "Isn't that enough?" He turned into the underground parking garage. "Is there a point to your musings?" He parked the car and met my eyes. "Go ahead. Ask whatever is on your mind. You have five minutes until you're bombarded with work. So now's your chance."

"Has he moved on?"

"Marty's an alpha male. He's wealthy, charming, and good looking. It wouldn't take much, even though he doesn't have a lick of sense when it comes to interacting with those of the female persuasion. Didn't you tell him to move on?"

"Yep."

"Then I wouldn't worry about it." He led the way to the elevator. "I picked up the clothes you wanted for court. They're hanging in my office. Go upstairs, get changed, and get to work. After you have your day in court, I'll take you to dinner. Maybe you'll even bother to ask how I'm doing."

"How are you doing? Is everything around the office quiet? Have there been any new revelations?"

"Everything's running smoothly. Things are pretty good. If you get a chance, you should ask Lucca how he's enjoying D.C."

"I'll do that."

Following Jablonsky to his office, I grabbed the garment bag from behind his door and took the elevator down to the locker rooms. After changing, I went in search of the AUSA. The prosecutor was waiting in one of the conference rooms. Several file boxes were on the table, and Lucca was seated beside them.

"You started the party without me?" I asked. I nodded to the AUSA. "Alexis Parker reporting for duty."

He glanced up, preoccupied. "Agent Parker, sorry for the inconvenience." He slid a box closer to one of the chairs. "These are copies of the evidence and files relating to this case. Please review them. It's been several months, but you will be asked about the role you played. It's best if you refresh your memory." His phone buzzed. "Excuse me."

The door closed, and I gently kicked Lucca in the shin. "What? No hello?"

"Parker," his face remained neutral, but he was hiding a grin, "it's nice to see you again, even if you stole my case." He dropped the folder to the table and looked at me. "Maybe I should thank you for saving me from that boorish DEA agent." He glanced out the glass door, keeping an eye on our babysitter. "Seriously, what were you thinking, volunteering to get involved in that mess? You sat behind a desk for weeks on end, never complaining about being pulled from the field, and then you go and do something as stupid as this. Why?"

"Someone needed to do it, and you left. I wanted a fresh start too."

Something passed over his features. "This isn't my fault. And for the record, running away makes you look guilty. Thankfully, there was no discernible connection or any evidence to support such a claim. And if there was, it must have vanished."

"Eddie," I began, but he let out a sharp shh seconds before the door opened.

For the next several hours, we read the files, answered questions, and discussed our roles in the investigation. Around noon, the AUSA moved us from the OIO offices to the federal courthouse. With the constant in and outs, I didn't get a chance to ask Lucca any questions or explain what had happened. It was bad enough we had to give testimony on this case. It had been brutal, and I'd come pretty close to a breakdown. Lucca had seen everything firsthand. He'd voiced several complaints and concerns regarding my performance. The defense would want to bring all of that to light. However, regardless of the amount of dirt they kicked up, there was no denying the defendant was involved in terrorist activities that resulted in several dozen casualties.

After being sworn in and testifying as to my role, the scope of the investigation, and the procurement of evidence, I was cross-examined. By the end, I had a splitting headache. They'd put me through the wringer, but the facts were on our side. The case was solid. Everything had happened by the book. There were no exceptions, and given the atrocious acts that occurred, it wouldn't have served justice to let this shithead off on a technicality, had there been one.

"Do you need a ride back to the federal building?" Lucca asked. "Or would you prefer going straight to a bar?"

"Mark promised to take me to dinner. I can't afford to get blitzed. My flight leaves in sixteen hours. But a ride would be nice."

We walked to the car, exhausted by the ordeal. "You know, you're one hell of an agent." Lucca unlocked the doors, and we climbed inside. "I believe in you, Parker. Today served as a perfect reminder of that." He started the engine, waiting for a break in traffic to pull out. "Jablonsky asked that I keep him updated on the oversight investigation into this field office. Your resignation and reinstatement garnered some attention, but there was no paper trail or any indication you had ties to crime lords. However, the police investigation into the nightclub fire turned up a photo on traffic cams from a few blocks away that put someone with a striking resemblance to you within the vicinity. No positive identification was ever made. There's no reason to believe the vehicle in question or its occupants had anything to do with what occurred. None of the police file into the nightclub fire ever made it into any official OIO investigation file, and it never will."

I blinked, overcome by everything. Lucca was the most strait-laced, by the book agent I'd ever met. If he had done something to protect me, he shouldn't have, but I was eternally grateful. "Thank you."

"Was it self-defense?" He didn't ask if I was involved, which meant he already knew.

"In a way, but it was mainly defense of another. Several

others, actually."

Before I could launch into any details, he nodded. "I knew you had a reason. I know you. You'd do anything to save someone else, but you should have reported it."

"I didn't follow protocol. When I confronted him, we didn't have legal grounds to stand on."

"I wish I had known you were going through this. It explains a lot about your behavioral changes and attitude. How are you holding up?"

"I'm okay." I laughed. "Actually, I'm not. The night of your going away party, I broke up with Martin, volunteered for this fucked up assignment, and now I'm back in the same damn situation. We don't have evidence that furthers the agenda of the op, but we found a lot of shit that adds up to some very questionable things. Bodies keep turning up, but we don't have proof the cult leader is involved. At least not yet. Everything is circumstantial. I need to call Eve and see what she's found." I paused. "Sorry, I'm probably breaking protocol by telling you this."

"You're not. Jablonsky read me in. Being in D.C. comes with certain perks. I've been researching possible connections and passing the data along to the DEA. I'll keep my ear to the ground in case the state department or customs hears any rumblings from the Mexican government."

"Thanks, Lucca."

"Don't mention it."

He dropped me off at the federal building, and I detoured to my desk. Picking up the phone, I dialed Eve. Her messages didn't make a lot of sense. I wanted to find out what was happening. Since Decker had limited outside communication, I'd have to brief him upon my return.

"I can't imagine it's a coincidence. I don't really get it, but there has to be something to it, right?" Eve sounded as though she'd broken into Ben's stash of energy drinks.

"Slow down. You said you found a link between Melanie Shaw and Anika. Obviously, the connection is Wilde. So what are you talking about?"

"Their stays at the commune don't overlap. Melanie left before Anika joined. But they have a mutual friend. Natalie

DuBois."

"That name sounds familiar."

"It should. She was in the photo you found in Anika's belongings."

I leaned forward, typing in the name. "She's a reporter for one of Nevada's biggest newspapers." Keying in the name of the paper, I scrolled through the pages dedicated to the writing staff. DuBois was on an extended leave of absence to conduct research for a series of articles she planned to write. No additional information was given. I closed the page to perform a background search. "How did she know Shaw?"

"She basically ruined the woman's life. She wrote a scathing exposé on insider trading, the dark side of financial management, and the downfall of the financial elite. Part of her story covered Shaw's mismanagement of her clients' funds, her own funds, and the resulting SEC investigation. There were some direct quotes from Shaw, so she must have interviewed her. Shaw lost it big, so she wasn't facing hard time for swindling or embezzling. From what I read, it sounded like DuBois sympathized with her plight."

"DuBois knew Shaw and Anika, and they both ended up seeking out Wilde when things went pear-shaped." I mulled over the possibilities. "Someone needs to have a talk with Ms. DuBois."

"Matt's on his way to her last known address. We contacted her boss at the paper, but he hasn't seen her in several months. She called him a couple of weeks ago, promising a huge break in the story she was working on, but he wouldn't tell us what it was. I'm under the impression he doesn't know. From the way he made it sound, she does quite a bit of freelance and was being scouted by major news outlets. It sounds like he was desperate to keep her, even if that meant letting her call the shots."

I squeezed my eyes closed. The headache I'd had since the afternoon was getting worse. "We need her financials. Have you come across her name in any of Tim's files?"

"Nope. You might also find it interesting that none of

Tim's former followers have a folder inside that drawer. The records you and Jace found are only on current members. If he was keeping intimate details to use as blackmail, why wouldn't he still be in possession of them?"

"He probably moved them to a different room." My mind drifted to the storage area in the spare bedroom. "Is there anything else I should know?"

"We're still working on analyzing everything. You'll get a full update tomorrow before you return to the commune. Have a safe flight."

After hanging up, I made my way to Mark's office. Hovering in the doorway, I gripped the frame and blinked a few times. He glanced up, his brows scrunching together.

"Are you okay?"

"Do you see an axe through the center of my skull?"

He chuckled. "No. You probably just need something to eat. Did the prosecutor's office even offer to buy lunch?"

"We didn't have time." I looked down the hallway toward the bullpen. "Time flies. Maybe I'll just grab something on my way home, drop my useless luggage off, and sleep in my own bed."

"Don't be ridiculous. You've been away for three months. You can't turn in early. Shouldn't you be on California time? That would make it feel like," he checked his watch, "five o'clock to you. Come on." He shut down the computer and locked his office. "We'll go to that greasy spoon near your place that way if you want to duck out early, you can."

On the ride to the diner, Jablonsky chattered about current investigations, his attempts to remodel the bathroom, and the basketball games he and Martin had seen. I zoned out, wanting the blinding pain in my skull to stop. By the time he parked a block from the diner, I was nauseous.

We took a seat in one of the back booths. Mark didn't make a move for the menu. Instead, he checked his watch again.

"Do you have a hot date?" I asked.

"No, but you do."

Dropping the menu to the table, I narrowed my eyes.

The headache must have made me delusional. "What?"

"It's been three months. Marty's dying to see you. He said you called a month and a half ago. Not to put too much emphasis on the fact that unauthorized communication is banned, but you wouldn't have done that without a good reason."

"Mark, I can't. I can't do this now."

"Too late." He stood, waving to Martin who had just stepped inside the diner. "I'll pick you up at eight thirty in the morning for a quick briefing at the OIO before you hop a plane. I'd suggest you get some sleep. You look like shit. But this might be more important." He smiled encouragingly. "Go get 'em, tiger."

He walked toward the entrance, clapping Martin on the shoulder and whispering something to him before leaving the diner. My heart skipped a beat when James Martin started walking toward me. Honestly, I might have been having chest pains. Pair that with the headache and queasiness and I had grounds to go to the ER.

"Alex," his voice broke my heart, and the look on his face ground the broken bits into dust, "you're back."

"For the next fifteen hours." There was so much to say, but none of it felt right. "I didn't expect to see you."

"God, you're so beautiful." His eyes searched mine. "How are you? The last time we spoke," he inhaled, rubbing his mouth while trying to come up with something to say, "I didn't realize... Have you come up with anything?"

"Not yet." I tore my eyes away from him. Seeing him was boring a hole through me. "I didn't mean to imply that you should wait. I wouldn't do that to you."

He leaned back in the booth, watching as I fidgeted with the menu. "Actually, that phone call set some things in motion. It made me realize quite a bit."

"Oh?" The room was too warm. A layer of sweat broke out on my skin.

"I've been seeing someone."

A sharp pain shot upward from my low belly through my abdomen. I was going to be sick. "That's great. Really, it's wonderful. I'm happy for you."

He smirked in smug amusement. "Are you sure you don't want to use a few more positive adjectives to convince me of that fact?" He leaned forward. "Admit it. You want to get back together. You practically said as much on the phone. Until you called, I had no idea how upset you were. You really would change what happened if you could." He blinked a few times. "That's all I needed to hear."

My stomach lurched. I didn't know how much longer I could sit here without becoming ill. "I'm trying to figure this out. To figure myself out. I need to find a way to let things go. I've done it before, but when it comes to you, I fail every time." I forced my eyes to meet his. "It's good you're seeing other people. I wish you the best." Another pain shot through me. This conversation wasn't helping matters. I pushed myself out of the booth. If I didn't leave now, I'd be spending the rest of my night in the diner bathroom. "I have to go."

"Alex, let me finish what I was going to say. You can't keep avoiding this conversation."

"It's not that. I must have caught Jace's stomach bug. We'll catch up the next time I'm in town. I promise."

He grabbed my hand before I could move away from the table. "When are you coming home?"

"I don't know." Another painful cramp shot through me. I bent forward, squeezing my eyes closed.

His hand brushed against my cheek, and he frowned. "You feel warm. You're not making up an excuse, are you?"

"No, I'm not."

"Let me take you home."

I wasn't sure I'd make it the four blocks to my apartment on foot. Even the five minute car ride might be pushing it, but it was a better option. Following him out to his sports car, I willed myself not to get sick and ruin the leather interior. He stopped the car at the front entrance to my apartment, and I bolted out the door and up six flights of stairs. The key stuck in the lock. I abandoned it, dashing toward the bathroom. The good thing was there wasn't much in my stomach, but that didn't prevent me from tossing up plenty of bile and acid. My throat burned, and I lay against the tile floor, knowing another round was imminent. When I got back to California, I was going to murder Decker. It had been two weeks since he came home with a stomach virus, but somehow, he managed to give it to me at the worst possible time.

Martin entered through the open front door and placed my keys on the counter. Then he came into the bathroom and held my hair while I got sick again. After several repeat performances, the pain in my stomach eased. That was around the time the shivers started. Leaving me on the bathroom floor, he went into my bedroom and returned five minutes later.

"I changed the sheets and turned down the bed," he said.

"You didn't have to." I pulled myself off the floor, rinsing my mouth in the sink. "Thanks for the ride home." Dismissing him, I stumbled into the bedroom and crawled onto the bed horizontally, burying the front half of me under the blankets. My back was exposed, but I didn't care. I just wanted warmth. Moving would expose me to more of the cold sheets. I started drifting, but footsteps in the doorway made my eyes flutter open.

"Why don't you lay back?" Martin asked.

"This spot is warm. I'm fine right here."

"The hell you are." He kicked off his shoes. "I'll make you a deal. I'll share some body heat if you rest like a normal person." He tugged the blankets free from around my arms and legs, and I shivered again, happy for his warm arms pulling me toward the top of the bed.

"You shouldn't be here. You'll get sick."

"I don't care." He tucked the blankets tightly around us. "I won't leave you, Alex."

THIRTY-FIVE

My sleep was broken. I had to change twice because I sweat through my clothes, even though the air felt frigid. At some point, Martin became concerned that I was dehydrating and woke me to drink some water. That, in turn, led to another trip to the bathroom. Until this thing was out of my system, it was pointless to try to keep anything down.

After a couple hours of sleep, I awoke to the morning sun, a firm chest beneath my cheek, and strong arms around me. "What time is it?" I asked, my voice scratchy and my throat sore.

"It's a little after seven."

"I have to get up. My flight's in a few hours."

"I spoke to Mark a few minutes ago and told him what's going on. He's rescheduling your flight. Alex," he said patiently, "you're too sick to travel."

Struggling to sit up, I felt dizzy and weak. My entire body ached. "I don't have a choice. Decker needs me." Deciding a bit more rest couldn't hurt, I gave up on getting out of bed.

"Decker," Martin asked, a hint of jealousy in his voice, "is that the same guy who made you sick in the first place?"

"Yep."

"Are you together?"

I snorted, feeling an unpleasant ache in my stomach and ribs. "He's my partner. My work partner." Old muscle memory had my forehead against Martin's neck without a second thought, but I remembered he wasn't mine. I tried to scoot away, but he held tight. "You really shouldn't have stayed. This virus strikes when you least expect it. And believe me, you don't want it. Your girlfriend probably won't be too thrilled about the fact that you spent the night either."

He didn't say anything. He just ran a hand through my hair. At this point, even my skin hurt. Last night, the bedclothes felt like razor blades, but that had subsided. Everything was just sore and achy. I dozed off for a while until Martin nudged me awake.

He whispered in my ear, "Jabber's here."

"Mark?" I asked, confused and foggy from sleep.

"We're in here," Martin called, and Jablonsky entered my bedroom. "She had a rough night. You seriously can't expect her to go back to work like this."

Jablonsky glanced at the pile of damp clothing on the floor before studying me. "I'll make sure she's okay." He looked at Martin. "It's Saturday. You have a prior engagement. Get going."

Martin shook his head. "This is more important."

"Don't argue with me. It isn't, and you know it. Alex will be fine. We'll get some fluids into her and maybe let the medics take a look. I'll make sure she's cleared before we let her go anywhere." He jerked his chin at the door. "Now get going. You can't afford to be late."

Gently, Martin wiggled his way out from beneath me. "Give us a minute." Once Mark left the room, he knelt next to the bed. "I'll stay if you want. You just have to ask."

I shook my head. "You have something to do. I don't want to ruin it. I'm okay." I looked at his sweat-stained shirt. "You might want to change. A few of your shirts are in my bottom drawer."

He stripped off the shirt. His chest looked broader and his arms thicker. His torso appeared even more chiseled than before.

"Someone's been working out more than usual," I noted.

"I needed an outlet." He pulled a shirt from the dresser and put it on. "I think you'll be pleased with my choice."

Suddenly, the obvious dawned on me. "You stayed here all night."

"I guess I did."

"Why?"

He leaned down and pressed his lips against my forehead and whispered in my ear, "It's because I love you."

Before I could say anything, Jablonsky was back in the bedroom, ushering Martin out of the room. He was gone before I even had a chance to say goodbye. My body, my mind, and my heart were wrecked.

Jablonsky took a seat on the edge of the bed and lifted one of my eyelids. "Martin told me about the night you had. He thinks it's the stomach flu. Is this the same thing Decker had two weeks ago?"

"Yes."

Mark chewed on his thumbnail, the wheels in his head turning. "Are you sure?"

"Yeah."

"How long was he away?"

"Two days." I pulled myself into a sitting position. "What are you thinking?"

"I don't think you're sick. I think you're going through withdrawal. When's the last time they ran a drug screen?"

"It's been three weeks, I guess. We were supposed to do it last week, but we were so busy bringing in evidence and getting our ducks in a row, it didn't happen. But I'm clean. Decker's clean. You know me."

"Then humor me and submit to a full drug panel."

"Even if you're right, you won't be able to find anything left in my system after last night."

He picked up my clothes. "We'll see. We can always analyze your sweat." He made a face. "Go take a shower. You stink. Then we'll get business out of the way, and I'll get on the horn with the DEA and see where to go from here."

*   *   *

After a banana bag and some clear broth, I was feeling a bit better. With any luck, I'd be able to graduate to soup by dinnertime. Jablonsky had put a rush on the results, but there was nothing particularly conclusive. The test showed trace amounts of cocaine, amphetamines, and a few other nasty things, but they were so minuscule they didn't register as positive. Frankly, it could have been a blip with the equipment. However, that information had given Mark an idea or an excuse, so he accompanied me on the late afternoon flight.

Before our departure, he phoned the assistant director. The DEA knew what to expect. At this point, I didn't have a clue.

Leaving the airport, we headed straight for HQ. When we arrived, Jace was waiting for us. He didn't look pleased by the change of plans, and I wasn't sure how any of this would play out with Wilde, who had every reason to be suspicious of us.

"Alex," Jace said, "how are you feeling?"

"Probably about the same as you did. I'm still thinking this is a stomach bug, but my boss is convinced it's withdrawal."

He rubbed at the scruff on his cheeks. "Our drug tests have been negative." He thought for a moment. "Let me grab them. He might be right."

"Of course, I'm right, kid," Mark said, joining us with the DEA's assistant director in tow. "Since you stopped eating on campus, it must be in the air. This shithead figured out how to create an inhalant to keep his followers calm, happy, and remove their will to leave." Jablonsky laid the toxicology reports on the table, saving Decker a trip to retrieve them. "When I ran a test on Alex earlier, she had trace amounts, but they were too far below range to test positive on a quantitative test. They might have even been too minor for a qualitative test. However, I'd say this obvious increase," he pointed at the discrepancies from before I joined the cult and after, "is worth investigating further."

"Son of a bitch." Jace took the words right out of my mouth. "We didn't even consider that."

"The levels were too low," Ben said. "And yours weren't nearly as linear as Alex's." He pulled the results up on the computer and created a line graph. "The exposure can't be from living in the dorms. The amount increased after she moved out."

All eyes in the room turned to me. "Your results are more consistent, showing an obvious accumulation."

"The meditation classes." My gaze shot to Jace. "It's the damn aromatherapy diffuser. Tim turns that thing on for every morning and evening ritual. I've been doing two a day, almost every day, plus whatever afternoon sessions I feel like attending."

"That's gonna come to an end," Jablonsky muttered. "I don't know what you people do, but we don't approve of our agents getting dosed at the OIO."

"We need to get a sample," Jace said, ignoring Mark. He turned to Stella. "If Jablonsky's right, does that give us grounds?"

"It should. If that tests positive, we'll be able to prove he's connected to drugs. We'll get warrants to search every nook and cranny of that place and find what he's hiding."

"Even the tunnels?" I asked.

She smiled. "Even the tunnels."

"And an arrest warrant for that asshole," Eckhardt chimed in. "We can squeeze him. From the evidence we've already obtained, we have grounds for multiple counts of blackmail, coercion, and possible identity theft, not to mention conspiracy to commit or accessory to murder. He's looking at life with the number of counts. We might be able to flip him with the promise of a deal, get to his cartel connection, and do what we can to shut them down, at least on this side of the border."

Decker eyed his team and nodded to Jablonsky. "Anything else, sir?"

Mark checked his watch, glancing up at me. "You good, Parker?"

"Yep."

"Okay. My return flight leaves in a couple of hours. I'll

use that time to review what you've done so far." He stared at Jace. "Don't let anything else happen to my agent."

"I won't," Jace promised.

"Then get back to work," Jablonsky ordered, giving me a quick wink. "And get your ass home soon."

I followed Jace out of the room. Thankfully, he told Tim I was having car trouble. It was a nice excuse and one that would give us the ride back to work out any logistics.

"We should continue on our current course of action until we know more. The money has been flagged. Later today, you will share the verdict with Tim and tell him you want to donate to the church. I've already told him your trust fund will be unfrozen on Monday. He'll want to go to the bank that morning. We have electronic trackers ready for the cash transfer. Whenever he uses it, we'll know. We'll trace it and figure out with whom he's in bed."

"Okay."

My silence caused concern. Jace shifted his gaze to me. "I can pull over if you need me to."

"It's not that. Did Eve fill you in?"

"Yeah. DuBois sublet her apartment, but the tenant wasn't home. We've made a few calls to her closest relatives. We're waiting for a call back, but we will find her."

"How are we coming along on locating the access points to those tunnels?"

"I've been all over the property. There are no cellar doors or manhole covers or anything that indicates an entrance. The surveillance teams have scouted the area around the perimeter. The drones have used infrared scans, but they haven't found anything either. Perhaps he tunneled straight down to China. I should have listened to you when you said we should explore. At least we'll get our chance if this new lead pans out." He watched me from the corner of his eye. "How'd Jablonsky realize it was withdrawal and not the flu?"

"I don't know. At first, I thought it was stress. A day in court will do that to a person, but you know how things progress from there."

"Don't remind me. Here's a horrible thought. Whenever

we finish this op, we'll get to go through the entire experience a second time."

"Don't say that."

"It's probably too late for me. I've already been back on the sauce for two weeks. You might have a chance to avoid it though."

"That's easier said than done. How do I appease Tim while avoiding every class and function at the commune?

Jace shrugged.

With plenty to chew on, I remained silent for the rest of the ride. Jace spoke about what he'd already said to Wilde concerning my hotel accommodations, the court proceeding, and the reasons for my sudden generosity. It was simple, straight to the point, and nothing that garnered further scrutiny or require follow-up questions. But I had plenty of questions I wanted to ask Wilde.

THIRTY-SIX

When we arrived at the compound, the Perpetual Lighters were pulling in their unsold wares and making sure the tables and stalls were secure. I went in search of Tim, hoping to keep him distracted while Jace took a sample of the oil mixture used in the diffuser. I didn't spot Tim among the group, but the smell of the baked goods and leftover bagged lunches turned my stomach.

"Hey," Hannah bustled toward me, holding a tray of uneaten scones, "you look green."

"I got sick on the plane. Traveling sucks."

"You're home now. How was your trip, minus the air sickness?"

"It was eventful," I looked around the emptying field, "but I want to share the news with Tim first. Can you point me in the right direction?"

"He was on his way inside. Come on, I'll walk with you."

We headed toward the main building, joining half a dozen other people lugging in chairs and boxes. Once inside, Hannah returned to the kitchen to serve supper. I wandered the hallways. Inside the multipurpose room, Jace was speaking to Tim. They were beside the aromatherapy equipment. I wasn't sure if Jace had taken a sample yet.

"There you are," I called. "I turn around for half a second, and you were gone." I gave Tim a smile while I slipped my arm around Jace's back and leaned into his shoulder. "And you're just the man I was looking for. Do you think we can speak after dinner? I have another favor to ask you."

Tim's brow furrowed. "We may speak now if you like."

"Go ahead, babe." Jace slipped the empty collection vial into my back pocket. "Talk to Tim. He'll be able to put things in perspective. I'll give you some privacy." He pecked my cheek. "Meet me back at the trailer."

"I heard you had car trouble." Tim said.

"Yep. My car was towed to the shop. It must not have liked the airport parking lot. They'll get to it on Monday. It's not a big deal. Actually, it would have been if it wasn't for you. Everything I have right now is because of you. I have a home, a boyfriend, a sense of security and safety. I'm not afraid anymore, which goes back to the favor. Originally, my stay was supposed to be temporary, but I was hoping," I looked up, giving him puppy dog eyes, "that you'd let me become a permanent member." He opened his mouth to speak, but I held up a hand. "Before you say anything, I would like to donate to this place. What you do is amazing. And regardless of your answer, I want to help you help others like me." My internal voice cringed. I sounded like one of those ads on TV with the sad music and the starving children or neglected animals. Perhaps I was laying it on too thick, but everyone in this place was over the top. "Ever since the judge handed down the verdict, I couldn't help but think my father's money shouldn't define me. I should be better than that. I should make my own way, without his help. I didn't want it when he was alive, and I sure as hell shouldn't want it now. It's a safety net, but I don't need it anymore."

"Are you sure about this?"

"Yes. Surer than I've ever been." I laughed, covering my mouth at the outburst. "You were right again. You said I'd be begging to stay."

"I'm not sure I used the word begging." He narrowed his

eyes. "You know you're more than welcome. That isn't contingent on any type of donation."

He was shrewd, making certain this negotiation couldn't be deemed any sort of contract or blackmail. If any of his followers were to challenge their decisions in court, Wilde would have an argument in his favor.

"I know, but I want to give."

"That's very generous. We'll deal with business tomorrow or Monday. Right now, dinner is being prepared. Is there anything else, Alex?"

Inhaling slowly, I made a show of internally debating before saying, "I don't want to go back to the restaurant. The work is okay, but after the attack, I really don't want to risk attracting any more weirdos." Like the one in front of me.

He smiled. "You've been contributing to the church and helping out with chores and sales. That's all I ask." He held out his hand, ushering me toward the door. "Now go be with Jace. He's missed you terribly."

Deciding to show some phony gratitude, I took a page from Sarah's book and gave Tim a big hug. Palming the vial a second before throwing my arms around him, I flipped the cap with my thumbnail and dropped my right hand, dipping into the open dish at the top of the diffuser. "Thank you."

He squeezed me tightly and sniffed my hair. As soon as I was free, I stuck my hands into my pockets and bounded out the door as if a weight had been lifted off my shoulders. Hopefully, the test results would be as positive as my cover's attitude.

Opening the trailer door, I stepped inside. "We got it." I held up the tiny glass tube with the silicone plug. "When can we deposit it at the dead drop?"

Jace phoned for a time. "Matt's on his way. I'll run to the quickie mart and pick up some seltzer for your stomach. Sounds good, right? Stay inside until I get back."

"That won't be a problem. I'm leaning toward spending the rest of the night in bed."

"It'll take a couple of days to get your strength back. Take it easy. You might have earned it."

By the time Decker returned, I was ready to fall asleep. He stayed on the couch, offering me the same consideration I had given him. It was a relief to have my own space. After spending the previous night in Martin's arms, having to share a bed with another man, even in an entirely pragmatic and platonic sense, would have been difficult.

Pushing thoughts of Martin and the things he said out of my mind was the best course of action right now. Instead, my mind wandered through the Anika/Natalie/Melanie connection, but the only thing I could come up with was Natalie must have helped Tim recruit new talent. Too bad we had yet to find the connection between the two of them. Could it be bad luck or a coincidence?

In the morning, I joined Jace for breakfast. He made soup to keep my tummy happy. While I sipped from the cup, he chuckled to himself. Placing the mug on the table, I waited for him to share the joke.

"Y'know, I owe you a huge apology. So much of your," he bobbled his head from side to side while hoping to find a diplomatic way of saying things, "inner turmoil can be explained away by our exposure to these controlled substances. Even my mood swings might have been a result of withdrawal from Tim's aromatherapy blend."

"Apology accepted."

Despite my words, he continued on the same trajectory. "The insane workouts, especially after evening ritual, your depression, muscle spasms, difficulty sleeping, disrupted sleep, even your nightmares are all symptoms of these stimulants. I'm sorry I blamed you for not disclosing."

"I told you I had it handled."

An errant thought crossed his mind. "Yeah, but you dealt with it before." Apparently, he was reconsidering the apology.

"Fine. Take all the credit you want. I already admitted I came here broken and depressed, but my issues weren't going to compromise the op." I stared at him over the rim of the mug. "You know me pretty well by now. I wouldn't risk myself or someone else over something that stupid."

He nodded. "I'll give you the benefit of the doubt that

those things were exacerbated by narcotics exposure, and the apology stands." He tapped a few keys on his phone and pushed it toward me. "We have confirmation Wilde's doping his followers. Stella's working on the legal paperwork. Eckhardt and the assistant director will coordinate a multi-team raid. They're hoping to do it this evening after lights out to minimize resistance and potential casualties."

"That's smart and fast."

"If that's what you call ten months in the making. They'll message us when they are prepared to move in. The teams in play know we're here. They know the location of our trailer. We'll join them after they breach. Keep your gear on you, and be ready to move at any time. And make sure you don't tip anyone off. No odd behavior. Understood?"

"Do you think I'm a noob?"

"I'm just making certain everything goes off without a hitch. There are very few things we can control. Our actions and reactions are the beginning and end of that list."

"Yes, sir."

"It still sounds sarcastic."

"That's your problem."

"Touché."

With a plan in place, we just had to wait out the clock. It was another day of hocking honey and artisanal goods. Thankfully, the weekend event kept everyone busy. Aside from 'accidentally' oversleeping and missing the morning ritual, none of the other daytime enlightenment sessions occurred on weekends. I kept busy by running to and from the kitchen, replenishing trays of cranberry scones that were selling better than the hotcakes. The Sunday morning crowds enjoyed a leisurely brunch before browsing the stands, so that meant extra hands were needed on kitchen duty and cleanup.

By late afternoon, the slump hit. Jace and I cozied up together at a table beneath one of the large tents. Vanessa and Javier decided to take a break and join us. They made idle chitchat about some renovations they wanted to make to their trailer.

"Remind me to ask Tim if we can put some of our belongings in one of the storage sheds," Javier said to his girlfriend. He looked across the field at one of the structures. "We pulled some extra tables and chairs out of there on Friday when we were setting up, but even with everything inside, there was plenty of room left."

"That's weird," Jace mused. "The last time Tim asked me to help out in the storage shed, we had to maneuver around a lot of yard equipment."

"Maybe he moved it into a different unit," Javier said.

The rest of the conversation turned into a blur of home repair's greatest hits. Unexpectedly, my phone vibrated. Jace raised an eyebrow. The team wasn't supposed to make contact, so who could be calling Alice Lexington?

"It's the lawyers. I'll be right back." I got up from the table and headed toward the fence. The number came up blocked. I answered, afraid of who would be on the other end.

"Hey, is Jace nearby? His phone goes straight to voicemail," Eckhardt said.

"He is. What's up?"

"We've made progress. Can you talk?"

"Not really."

"Then listen. We found info on Shrieves and Harbring in the ledger. We aren't sure what it means, but we have hard proof Wilde knew the men who assaulted you. Eve's working on cracking the rest of the code. Depending on what she finds, tonight might involve several other agencies. I wanted to make sure you were prepared for that possibility. Our people know you, but outsiders won't. Use caution and keep your IDs with you."

"Thanks." Hanging up, I went back to the group. "It was just my lawyer, reminding me my trust would be unfrozen at midnight. Apparently, he wants to get paid."

Jace put an arm around my shoulders and nuzzled my ear. I giggled, and he turned up the flirtation until Javier and Vanessa went back to work. Then he whispered, "Who the hell was that?"

"Matt. He tried calling you first. They found a

connection between Tim and the assailants, but that might mean other agencies get involved tonight. He wanted to make sure no one mistakes us for the rest of the group."

Soon after, the sun eked closer to the horizon, and we helped break down the booths and tables. I hoped the hipsters had gotten their fill. After the raid, this place would be shut down permanently. However, I couldn't help but wonder what would happen to the Perpetual Lighters. If they truly believed in Tim's message, this would be devastating. Most of them relied heavily on the financial support the co-op provided. With any luck, they'd find a way to bounce back. But the cynical part of me doubted it. I didn't want to think about the lasting repercussions. After all, they were just disposable pawns in Tim's game. Short-term this might appear to be a haven, but long-term this was hell. By shutting him down, we'd be saving these people from a gruesome fate. I just hoped we weren't condemning them to a life of additional hardships.

After cleaning up, Tim announced he'd be holding a bonfire after evening meals to celebrate the success of the weekend sales. Realistically, he wanted to celebrate the large donation I was making to him. Jace assured me these events happened periodically, and we need not worry about the distraction. It was basically the same evening ritual but outdoors and with hot cocoa.

Since I was under strict orders not to do anything out of the ordinary, Jace and I attended the bonfire with the rest of the flock. Tim gave a long-winded speech on practicing gratitude. After about twenty minutes of speaking, he concluded the evening ritual by encouraging us to enjoy the sense of community around the fire, the crisp night air, and the warm cocoa.

Jace and I milled about, exchanging small talk and pleasantries with the others. Tim kept us in his sights, making his approach as quickly as possible. Unlike our previous conversation, he didn't question my generosity. This time, he dictated when we would meet in the morning. He wanted the money before I could reconsider.

After assuring him I would meet him first thing and we would go straight to the bank, he eased up on the commands. I excused myself to get a refill. On my trek back to the main facility, I heard an echoing clang in the distance. My body went on high alert. I strained to hear additional sounds. No one was nearby. The closest building was one of the locked structures. From this distance, I couldn't tell if the lock was in place, but with Tim and the others back at the bonfire, they weren't the cause of the noise. Perhaps there had been a gust of wind, or something inside had fallen over. Then again, maybe I was nuts.

After standing in the open longer than I should have and not hearing a repeat of the sound, I continued to the main building. Refilling the mug with leftover cocoa from the farmer's market, I couldn't help but wonder if anyone was still in the main building. Snooping was strictly off limits, especially when we were so close to an official raid, but a few dorm rooms had their lights on and doors open. Obviously, some of the Perpetual Lighters weren't fans of the evening ritual or hot cocoa.

Returning outside, I watched the silhouettes of the group in the distance. They hunkered around the fire. Since everyone was occupied, I decided to take a little walk and enjoy the evening air, just like Tim had said. My destination was the locked structure. It wouldn't hurt to make sure the lock was secure. After all, Javier said they were using the sheds as storage. Maybe someone left it open.

As I got closer, the clanging started again. Something metal knocked against a pipe. The door was locked, so I pressed my ear against it. It didn't sound like the clanging was coming from inside, but I felt a distinct vibration against the door. Since this wasn't my op, it would be best to share the find with Decker. If anything, the tactical teams could do a thorough sweep for the cause. Just as I was walking away, a woman screamed.

THIRTY-SEVEN

"Shit." I pressed my ear against the door, but I wasn't positive the sound had come from inside. *Make a decision, Parker,* my mind screamed. Tossing the mug into one of the nearby shrubs, I circled the shed, hoping for brilliance to strike. When I couldn't find an inconspicuous method of entry, I raced back to Decker.

The small group seated with him looked up at my approach. One of the ladies asked, "Should you be running on that bum ankle?"

Decker turned, a stern look on his face. "Alex?"

"I thought I saw a coyote." My eyes conveyed urgency.

"It was probably just a shadow or a dog." He laughed, but he knew something was wrong. "Why don't you show me this coyote?" He turned and winked at the ladies. "We should wrap things up. It is getting late. Alex is probably already dreaming." They laughed and bid us good night. I started out at a fast gait, but Decker snaked an arm around my waist, forcing me to slow down. "What's wrong?"

"I heard sounds from inside that shed. A woman screamed." I willed him to burst into a run. "It's locked. Combination only. I could break it off, but that would attract attention."

Decker glanced back at the group. Some of them were heading back to the main building. "I'll do it. Cover me."

Positioning myself between him and the approaching crowd, I hoped the dark would mask his presence. He pulled his concealed handgun from beneath his sweatshirt and used the butt of the gun to pound against the lock. It took four tries before it broke away from the door. He glanced back toward the group. No one appeared to be looking in our direction.

"Go," I hissed.

He slipped inside, and I eased farther into the shadows. After a few seconds, I ducked into the shed after him and pushed the door closed. It was pitch black inside, and I froze. A second later, his cell phone screen illuminated a tiny area, and I remembered to breathe.

"Don't turn on the overhead," he whispered. "They might notice the light beneath the door."

Pulling out my phone, I held it up and looked around the enclosed space. Farm equipment, several boxes, tables, chairs, and a few odd lawn ornaments filled the space. Decker sifted through the mess, searching for any indication a woman had been inside, when I heard the same clanging noise again. It was coming from below us.

"What the hell?" Decker knelt down, brushing hay and dirt to the side. Standing, he walked around the room and tapped his foot in the hopes of finding some kind of trapdoor. "One of the tunnels from the main building must run beneath here."

"Whoever screamed is below us." The clanking grew more frequent. "Is the team in position to move in?"

He dialed Eckhardt, holding the phone to his ear. They weren't quite ready to breach. However, we didn't have time to wait. Whoever was beneath us needed our help now.

"Delay Tim as long as you can," I said. "I'll take the tunnel down and see what I can find."

"You have no idea what's down there."

"Neither do you." We didn't have time to argue. "Wilde trusts you. You know him better than anyone. You can detain him longer than I can. Fucking arrest him if you run out of ideas. The tac team should be on their way."

"I'll be right behind you. In ten minutes, we'll have twenty DEA agents storming this place."

Another shrill scream sounded, and my heart leapt into my throat. "She doesn't have ten minutes. Do what you can."

Bursting from the shed, I ran back to the main building. The group that had been on their way inside had already made it in. I slowed my pace, entering the compound. They clustered around the kitchen, talking and cleaning up. Slipping past them, I hit the stairs and took them two at a time, racing down the upper hallway and to the locked bedroom. Not wasting time, I kicked the door open, splintering the jamb. If Wilde made it past Decker, he'd know immediately someone had been here, but I couldn't worry about that now.

Leading with my gun, I went to the closet, opening it to reveal the hidden staircase. Pulling the chain on the light, I went down the steps, wishing for a flashlight. When I hit the dirt floor, I chose to move to the left. After several yards, I noticed a string of cheap mining lights along the top of the tunnel. Feeling around for a switch, I flicked it on, lighting up the path in two different directions.

"Great."

Taking a moment to orient myself, I made another left. The tunnel broke off into another three sections, but I continued leftward, believing that would lead to the area beneath the shed. The clanking sounded again, almost like an SOS.

I hurried forward. At the end, the lights came to an abrupt end. The tunnel sloped upward, so I kept my left hand against the wall while blindly aiming my nine millimeter in front of me.

The barrel of my gun knocked into something solid. I ran my fingers against the wooden barrier. Finding a handle, I pushed it down and slipped into a room. The tunnel led to a basement. It was damp and musty. A single standing reading lamp was turned on in the corner. Something moved to my right. I aimed my gun.

"Drop the weapon," I snapped, and a serving spoon

clattered to the ground.

The woman who had been banging against the water pipe turned her head and looked at me. "Alex?"

"Anika?"

She blinked. Her eyes homed in on my gun. "No." She shook her head. "That's not my name. No. Please, no." She scrambled as far back as she could.

"Hey, it's okay." I lowered the gun, realizing she was handcuffed to the pipe. She had been trying to break through by beating on it, but it hadn't worked. "I'm a federal agent. I'm going to get you out of here." Scanning the room for signs of danger, I didn't spot much of anything. It was just a dark empty void, like Tim's soul. Removing a handcuff key from my inner pocket, I released the cuff. "Are you hurt? Who did this to you?"

"I don't know." Her arms showed signs of track marks, and her eyes were glassy.

"We'll get you help. Right now, we have to get out of here." I scanned the room. Taking the tunnel back wouldn't work. "Do you know where we are?"

She rubbed her eyes, sniffing and blinking. "Underground. A basement." She blinked again, scanning the room as she tried to recall details. "I don't know how I got down here. Sometimes he brings food from there." She pointed to the doorway that I just used. "And sometimes, it's like he just appears out of thin air. He's like a ghost. He moves through the walls."

"Okay." Waiting for the co-op to be cleared out might be our safest bet, but I wasn't entirely sure where we were. Anika was anxious and distraught. Her breathing sounded harsh in the quiet. I crossed the room, noting several used needles in the trash can. Several vials were in the garbage, but they weren't labeled. I checked my phone. I had no signal. So much for calling in the cavalry.

"How long have I been here?" she asked.

"Longer than you should have. It's been a few weeks." She hadn't moved from her place on the cot, even though she was no longer cuffed to the pipe. "We searched for you, but we didn't know you were still on the property. I'm sorry we didn't find you sooner."

"It's okay." She sounded dazed.

"Do you remember the last time Tim was here?"

She squinted. "It felt like a few minutes ago, but I'm not sure." She pointed to a cup on the floor. "He brought me that."

I knelt down, finding an almost empty cup of cocoa. The cup was still warm, so it couldn't have been that long. "Did you drink this?"

"Yeah." She gasped a few times, trying to get enough air down her throat. "I didn't have a choice."

Finding a door painted the same color as the drab walls, I banged against it, realizing the door pushed inward, not outward. That would make it harder to break down, especially since there was no knob or handle to use to open it. But if I could remove the hinges, we'd be in business. "Hand me that spoon."

She lifted it off the ground, uncurled her legs, and stood up. Half a step later, she was on the floor. Dashing back to her, I checked her racing pulse. She was babbling about inner peace, but I didn't think she was overdosing. It was the crap Wilde fed his followers. He'd probably been dosing her with the same poison he'd used on me. Her symptoms were about the same. She didn't have control of her muscles. Her breath was labored, but from what I recalled, as long as she kept breathing, she'd be okay.

"Anika, hey, I need you to relax. You're going to be okay. We're going to get out of here."

"Not... my... name."

"What?"

She didn't answer. Speaking was too difficult. Removing my weapon, I left her on the floor and estimated where the lock would be. The sound of gunfire would attract attention, but that didn't matter. The raid would be commencing any minute. I was no longer afraid of attracting attention. Anika needed help, and Tim needed to pay for his sins.

The bullet worked its magic, and I pulled the door open. I was greeted by a dark, dusty staircase. Heading up the stairs, I kept my head on a swivel for signs of danger. I was halfway up the staircase when the lights came on.

Pressing against the banister, I aimed at the top of the stairs, unsure of what to expect. Maybe Decker had found us. Instead, I heard a meek, scared whisper coming from above.

"Hello? Is someone there?"

Edging closer to the voice, I wasn't positive this wasn't a trap. However, I didn't expect to see Sarah peeking her head into the building. She looked frightened, like she didn't want to get caught doing something she wasn't allowed to. I moved up another two steps, keeping most of my body obscured while I checked the rest of the cavernous room for other signs of life.

"Alex?" she glanced around, following my gaze. "We're not supposed to be in here. How did you get in? The door was locked."

"Where are we?"

She furrowed her brow. "Don't you know?" She gave me a concerned look, glancing behind her before stepping inside. "This is one of the buildings Tim plans to renovate. We moved the tables out of here today so he could move forward with the contractor. It's a surprise. We aren't supposed to see it yet. It's off limits." She took another few steps toward me. Seeing the gun in my hand, she screamed.

"Shh," I vaulted up the steps and put my hand over her mouth, "be quiet. I won't hurt you."

"Why do you have a gun?"

Not wasting time, I went to the door and eased it open. We were in the easternmost building, facing away from the main facility. From the silence outside, the DEA hadn't breached yet. Or they were using stealth tactics. Reaching for my phone, I dialed Decker.

Decker didn't answer. Hopefully, that meant he was keeping Wilde busy. In the meantime, I sent a 9-1-1 to Eckhardt with our location and Anika's condition. "Sarah, I need your help. Come with me." I pulled my badge from the inner pocket of my jacket. "Anika's in trouble. Until my people get here, we need to make sure she keeps breathing. Tim isn't who you think he is."

"You aren't who I thought you were. I trusted you. I

thought we were friends. What does the government want with the church? We're a peaceful people. Tim's all about enlightenment and inner peace. What are you doing here?"

"We are friends." I didn't have time for this. She stormed toward the door, trying to push past me, but I grabbed her shoulder and pulled her back inside. "Trust me when I tell you that you're much safer in here, at least for the next few minutes."

"Why? What have you done?"

Before I could answer, another clank sounded from the room beneath us. I needed to check on Anika. But I couldn't leave Sarah unattended, or she'd run straight to Tim. "Come with me. I found Anika. She never left. She's hurt." Sarah didn't look like she was willing to budge, so I added, "Please."

She huffed at the inconvenience and utter betrayal, but I pushed her ahead of me down the stairs. "Anika," Sarah said, searching my eyes, "how?"

"Tim lied." I crouched down next to Anika. "He's been drugging her and keeping her prisoner."

Anika's eyes went wide. She tried desperately to pull herself off the floor. I sensed her fear and turned just as Sarah tried to jab one of the needles into my neck. I deflected her arm, knocking the syringe to the ground. Without hesitating, she ran for the tunnel entrance and disappeared.

"Shit." I couldn't leave Anika helpless on the ground, but I couldn't let Sarah get away either. My gaze went from one doorway to the other, hoping help would arrive. After what felt like an eternity, Decker appeared at the tunnel entrance.

"Alex?"

"We could use some help here." I moved over as he came up beside me. "Did you see Sarah? She's working with Tim."

He shook his head, feeling for a pulse. "We breached the compound. Medical teams are beyond the perimeter." He lifted her off the ground. "Let's get out of here."

"What about Tim?"

"When I left him, he was en route to determine the

cause of the commotion. Matt should have him in custody by now."

"Okay. Get her to safety. I'm going back for Sarah."

"Be careful."

Racing toward the tunnels, I had no idea where Sarah might have gone or where any of the paths led. The tunnels branched out in several directions. She could be anywhere. Following the string of lights, I moved to the right. If Decker hadn't run into her, I had to assume she detoured elsewhere. Guessing she flipped on the lights as she went, I followed the lighted paths with my nine millimeter leading the way. Several alcoves were carved into the tunnel, leading to small underground rooms.

I leaned around the corner, checking the third alcove. I'd seen bricks of cocaine, bags of herbs, and a lot of cash. I didn't know what else was down here, but that was the DEA's problem. A rustling sound caught my attention. I bypassed the next opening and headed up another slope. Sarah was inside the next room, scraping against the wall in search of a hidden doorway.

"Stop right there," I ordered. "Turn around and put your hands on your head. Slowly."

She glanced at me over her shoulder. "Does Jace know the truth?"

"You'll find out soon enough. On your knees."

"That bastard. Tim wanted to share all of this with that ungrateful asshole. I told him to be careful. That we didn't know anything about Jace, but he swore I was paranoid. It looks like I was right." She slapped her palm against a panel on the wall and pushed against the doorway with all her might. A beep sounded twice. Before I could tell if she had gotten the door open, a blast launched me into the air. My body collided with the tunnel wall. I heard a loud crack, and then I was covered in rubble.

THIRTY-EIGHT

That bitch set off a failsafe that collapsed part of the tunnel. I imagined she had gotten the door open. If not, she just killed herself. The constant shaking and rumbling made me wonder how many other charges were placed throughout the underground labyrinth. Clawing through the dirt and rock, I moved toward the dust mote that floated a few feet from my face. I could see light and refused to acknowledge I might be trapped. That wasn't an option.

The ground vibrated. I feared the buildings above the tunnels would succumb to the collapse as well. It was difficult to hear anything over the ringing in my ears, but I thought I heard shouting from somewhere above me. Filled with renewed hope, I poked my head through a break in the debris. Pulling myself forward, I army-crawled out of the dusty mess. My leg snagged on something, but I ignored it and kept going.

Two tactical rifles appeared in my face, but Eckhardt called them off before I had to open my mouth. I nodded my thanks to him. Getting up, I hissed, finding a small piece of broken rebar protruding from my thigh. Before I said anything, one of the men wrapped it tightly.

"Where's Decker?" I asked.

"He isn't with you?" Eckhardt sounded surprised.

"We split up. He took Anika to safety, but we had another bogey. She's one of Tim's followers. She set off the explosion. Her name's Sarah. Blonde. Mid-forties. She must have had an escape route. I don't know where the tunnels lead, but we need people covering all the buildings on the property. She was trying to get inside one of them when the blast went off. She either escaped, or she's buried back there."

"We're on it," Eckhardt said.

I looked back at the partially collapsed tunnel. "I need a radio." Taking one from the nearest tac member, I glanced at the men. "Is Wilde in custody?"

"No. We haven't located him either. Where are you going?"

"To make sure Jace didn't do something stupid."

"Like you're about to do?" Eckhardt challenged, and I gave him a shrug. "You heard Agent Parker." He tossed a flashlight in my direction and tugged on the collar of his vest. "We have another suspect. Sarah, blonde, mid-forties. Find her and detain her." He waited for them to march past, toward the collapsed portion of the tunnel. "I'm with you."

Nodding, I headed back into the main tunnel. The light beam bounced off the walls. The string lights had gone out with the blast, but we were able to maneuver and crawl through parts of the opening. Hitting the radio, I requested an update on Anika and a location on Decker.

Decker had carried a woman out of the compound. She was with the medical team, but he had gone back inside. The last anyone knew, he was headed for the main building.

The passageway back to the main building had completely caved in. There wasn't even a tunnel left. Praying Decker wasn't beneath the thousands of pounds of dirt, I let my light bounce off the rightmost path I had declined to explore earlier.

The radio chirped, and I froze, listening to a message that a woman matching Sarah's description just surfaced in the southernmost building. She was being detained, along with the rest of the Perpetual Lighters. Eckhardt radioed back an affirmative, followed by a request for confirmation Timothy Wilde was in custody.

"Negative," the disembodied voice answered. "We're still sweeping the buildings."

A few drops of blood were in the center of the path. A few feet later, there were another few drops. Someone was injured and moving this way. I held the flashlight beneath my nine millimeter and ran down the tunnel's path as more rumbling echoed through the dirt walls.

Coming upon another split, I saw a light down the left path. Decker turned at my approach and let out a sigh of relief. "You're okay?"

"Yep." I focused on the end of the tunnel. "Where's Tim?"

Decker ground his teeth, his grip tight on his firearm. "Hiding like the pathetic rat he is." He turned the focus of his light skyward, making hand gestures so I could see them. There was another opening ahead, and Tim had ducked inside. "Above ground is covered. This is the only way out." He pointed to the blood specks on the floor. "We had an altercation, but he got past me. I should have shot the asshole. I tracked him here, but the tunnels started caving in. He said if I got any closer, he'd make sure the entire facility collapsed into the ground. I think he's bluffing, but I'm not sure."

"Sarah detonated the first explosive."

"Sarah?"

I nodded. "Your team has her in custody. We just need this asshole." I jerked my chin toward the opening. "Any ideas?"

Decker narrowed his eyes, staring at the space ahead of us. "I don't believe he's suicidal. He's too narcissistic for that, but this is a no win situation for him. He might do it." He took the radio from my hand, asking for orders on how to proceed.

The DEA wasn't sending anyone else into booby-trapped tunnels. As it was, they were evacuating the grounds in case the earth had been destabilized by the explosions. We were instructed to pull out as soon as possible, which was probably part of Tim's plan. He figured he'd bluff his way out of this and disappear into another hidden tunnel.

"Jace," Eckhardt stepped between us, "you know this man. You've done the research and put in the time." He put a reassuring hand on Decker's shoulder. "What's the play? Can we take him alive?"

Decker rubbed the back of his hand over his mouth. "Yeah. We can. Alex, his mind has been so focused on manipulating you, if you speak to him, it will be just enough of a distraction for us to take him."

"Fine. Is he armed?"

"I don't believe so," Decker said.

I took a few steps forward. "For what it's worth, you didn't suck as a partner."

"That's not funny."

"Sure, it is." Winking, I moved toward the opening. "Tim? Hey, Tim. It's Alex." I turned my head, making sure Decker was edging along the wall toward the room with Eckhardt behind him. "I'm having some issues right now. You might be too. Maybe we should talk them out. Isn't that what reaching enlightenment and inner peace is all about?"

I didn't get a response, so I continued my approach. When I made it to the doorway, I assessed the situation. Tim was in the middle of the room, scanning the walls for some unforeseen escape route. Something was in his hand. It looked like a television remote. I wasn't certain it wasn't. He didn't have any visible weapons, so I made a show of holding up my hands and holstering my gun. I left the flashlight on, placing it on the floor near the doorway, making certain the light bounced toward the left wall. Cautiously, I entered, moving so Tim would have to turn away from the door to face me.

"Are we still going to the bank tomorrow?" I asked.

He stared in utter disbelief. "You did this. You and Jace. You did this."

"No, I didn't do anything. I have nothing to do with this. I'm here to help. I was sent here to help. Isn't that what this entire place is about?"

He stared, as if I were off my rocker. "Don't twist this around. This place helped a lot of people. You can't deny that." But I saw the darkness in his eyes. He knew it was a front. A bogus lie he used to prey on victims. He moved closer to me. His free hand moved toward his pocket. In the shadows, it was hard to see movement, but the moment he pulled a blade, Decker grabbed him from behind and forced him to drop it. However, neither of us could pry the detonator from his other hand. Another whoosh of hot air exploded from the side wall. The blast launched us across the room and into the wall.

The three of us went down, covered in dust and powder. The explosion itself didn't expand beyond the room. Decker got to his knees, slamming Tim's face into the dirt while he cuffed him. Eckhardt had been thrown from the room, but he shook himself off and helped Decker wrestle Tim into submission. By the time we cleared the room, another tactical team responded to the newest explosion, despite their orders to evacuate.

"On your feet." Decker passed Wilde off to the men with the DEA emblazoned vests. He gave me an uncertain look, wiping a layer of white dust off my cheek. "We'll need decontamination and hazmat." He looked down at my leg. "And some patching up."

"We'll get a station set up," Eckhardt said, radioing in the request. "It looks like a shower for you, too." Matt turned to another member of the team, telling them to grab a sample from the explosion site before we evacuated. We wouldn't be able to explore the tunnels again until they were deemed safe. "It looks like you might be ending this case on a high note."

Decker glared. "That's not funny." He and I were both covered in white dust, and given the cocaine bricks we'd found in the other rooms, we couldn't rule out the possibility.

After a decontamination shower and an analysis of the samples collected, the powder was a mixture of dirt and dust from the tunnel, along with cocaine, methamphetamine, and various herbs. Although it was possible to become intoxicated through skin contact, the concentration had been low.

I went to the hospital with Anika, and Decker stayed behind to take care of matters dealing with the raid. After having the piece of rebar removed from my leg, I made my way to Anika's bedside. She was resting. I took a seat beside her and started on the paperwork. A couple of hours later, she opened her eyes.

"Feeling better?" I asked.

"Where am I?"

"You're safe, Anika."

She practically laughed in my face. "My name isn't Anika. It's Natalie. Natalie DuBois." She narrowed her eyes. "I don't imagine your real name is Alex either." She glanced at the FBI badge clipped to my belt. "You're a federal agent?"

"Alexis Parker," I introduced myself. "We have questions for you, Ms. DuBois. First, I'd like to ask what happened to the real Anika Thatcher?"

Natalie sat up and took a sip of water. "Anika's fine. She's been staying at my apartment while I've been away."

Anika had been a sex worker. After witnessing her friend Carmen be abused inside a sex club, she had shared that information with her college roommate. Natalie began investigating the management and found a connection between one of the owners and Timothy Wilde. The name rang a bell, and she remembered Melanie Shaw mentioning the Church of Perpetual Light during their interview. At that point, Melanie had just discovered the church and hadn't become a full-fledged member.

After more research, Natalie realized several former working girls eventually escaped to Tim's commune only to disappear months later. A couple turned up dead, suspected of trafficking in drugs, so Natalie decided to get an inside scoop. "It was stupid, but I couldn't think of a better way to get the real story. So I impersonated Anika. I didn't realize he was drugging us. One of my contacts sent me a message, telling me Melanie Shaw was working as a mule. I didn't believe it, but one morning, I found Tim outside, burning files. One of the pages must have blown away because I found it near the fence. It was a photo of Melanie. She didn't look so good." She blinked, swallowing and looking away. "Something was written on the back."

"What?"

"*Send another one. This one is used up.*" Natalie stared at me. "That's what I wanted to show you, but Tim must have realized I knew something. I ended up having Dana mail it to my work address before Tim broke into my room and dragged me down those stairs."

"We'll need permission to go through your mail at work."

"You can search anything you want. I want that bastard to fry."

Promising to make that happen, I returned to HQ. Decker and I never bothered to post a photo of the woman we knew as Anika, which explained our mix-up. Luckily, the rest of the team was on the ball with their identifications. The next twelve hours involved a lot of paperwork, evidence processing, interviews, and interrogations.

Sarah and Tim kept quiet, asking for lawyers and refusing to answer any questions. The DEA called in favors with every nearby agency to help process the bust and make sure none of Tim's other followers were involved.

For what felt like the next several days, I ate, slept, and showered at HQ. At least the mansion had ample space to accommodate our needs. By the fourth day, we broke Sarah. She confessed to her involvement, admitting she spied on the women and shared their secrets with Tim. She knew he was working for the cartel and had connections with dealers in Vegas and L.A. She had a background as a chemistry teacher and had been processing the drugs and herbs, experimenting to find new mind control substances and methods of introducing the chemicals into the unsuspecting Perpetual Lighters. The drugs were meant to make Wilde's followers feel better after their sessions, further promulgating the theory that by obeying Tim, they would reach enlightenment. For all her hard work, Tim had cut her into the business, giving her forty percent. The two were in a relationship, and that served as additional incentive for her continued obedience and cooperation.

Some of the female followers were sold to the cartel. It was no secret the types of things the cartel did to them. Some inevitably became drug mules. Others weren't as lucky. In exchange for leniency, Sarah provided names and dates of the transfers. With any luck, a few of the women would be recovered, but at the very least, there were a dozen cartel members to bust. It wouldn't put an end to the problem, but it would help.

Tim refused to give up anything, but once he was informed Sarah squealed, he had no problem turning the tables. He blamed her for masterminding all of it. He was just a figurehead. She was the brains. No one believed it, but there might have been some truth to the matter.

After spending a few days recovering in the hospital, Natalie took us to her office at the paper. During her investigation, she had deduced Wilde had friends at the various illegal skin clubs. Whenever a girl was in trouble, be it drugs, a rough pimp, john, boyfriend, or money problems, they'd make sure word got out about the commune. If the lady was desperate enough, she'd take a chance. After all, she was already in a bad situation and probably figured how much worse could it get. Several who answered the ad ended up dead within a matter of months.

"We'll work that angle," Decker said. "It'll be slow going, but I think I can get Wilde to come around. As soon as he accepts his empire crumbled, he'll be more likely to help us take down a large chunk of the cartel too."

"What about the two men who assaulted me?" I asked.

"That will come to light at some point. We know they're connected. The names are in the ledger. It'll just take a bit more time to piece it all together. We know Harbring was dealing in the wrong neighborhood. It's a safe bet Shrieves was transporting drugs as well. We'll start there and work through it," Matt offered. "If we need you for something, we'll give you a call. But since the undercover sting is over, you can go home."

"That's been the goal this whole time."

"I thought you wanted to run away from home," Decker said. Matt quietly excused himself, giving us some privacy to say our goodbyes. "You can never make up your mind, can you?"

"That is my biggest flaw. I just don't know how to fix what's already broken."

"You never answered my question." He stared at me for a long moment. "Why do you do this job? It's making you miserable. You let it be your top priority. You let it control every aspect of your life. It doesn't have to be that way. You walked away before. You know there's more out there. You don't have to keep doing this."

"How can you say any of that when you're out in the cold for years at a time?"

"Because I choose to do this. I had everything and decided I didn't want it. I want this. But I don't think you do. Stop being afraid to go after what you want. The only thing you can control is yourself. The sooner you accept that, the happier you'll be."

"We'll see." I extended my hand. "It's been nice working with you, Agent Decker."

THIRTY-NINE

Since returning home, Mark had been letting me crash at his place. He was afraid I might be facing another bout of withdrawal and wanted to offer support, or he didn't want to feel obligated to help me up six flights of stairs when I had a hole in my leg. I'd flown back on a Thursday. Friday I filled out the necessary paperwork at the OIO. The office was still eerily quiet. Ever since my reinstatement, I felt like an outsider, but with Lucca gone, that feeling had increased tenfold. I'd been welcomed back by my colleagues and friends, but I couldn't shake Decker's parting words.

Saturday morning, I blinked awake. Mark was in the kitchen, growling about something. Rolling my eyes, I buried myself deeper under the pile of blankets. I needed to go home. I just didn't want to think about the last two times I'd been in my apartment.

The doorbell rang, and I put the pillow over my head while Mark answered it. After a few moments, I heard a muffled, "Make yourself at home. I have to make a quick run to the office." Assuming he was talking to me, I removed the pillow from over my face and decided to take advantage of the quiet to get some sleep.

"Alex?" Martin asked, moving into the living room.

I opened my eyes. "I must be delirious." However, he didn't vanish. Instead, he edged closer and took a seat at the end of the couch, unsure where I ended and the blankets began. "What are you doing here?"

He jerked his thumb toward the door. "I needed a favor, and he told me to come over. I didn't know you were here."

"I got back Thursday. I haven't even been home yet. Just the office and here."

"Are you feeling better?" Martin inched closer, brushing my hair from my face. "I've been worried about you."

"I'm okay. I wasn't sick. It was withdrawal." I shook my head. "It changed the shape of the investigation and got me home faster. And you don't have to worry about catching the stomach flu."

"So you're back for good?"

"For now."

"What does that mean?" He looked around the room. "Why are you staying here?"

"I don't know what it means. I don't want to confuse things for you. You said you were seeing someone. You shouldn't have spent the night taking care of me when you have other priorities now."

"Alex," he tried to interrupt, but I was on a roll.

"No, it's okay. If she makes you happy, that's all that matters. I need to figure out what my life is going to be like without you in it. Maybe I'll do more of these deep cover things. Or maybe I'll quit my job and go back to the P.I. thing. I'm not sure, but I can't let this job define me, not after what happened in that club. It's like I have this huge secret, but so many people know the truth or suspect what happened. I let it destroy me and define me, and I realize it doesn't. They don't see me differently, and I don't need to see myself differently." I laughed, realizing I had reached some kind of enlightenment during this assignment. "I guess I didn't need to hide that from you either. I should have trusted you wouldn't see me as a monster. It just took me this long to realize I'm not a monster or a killer, even though I've killed."

"I never would have thought that. That's not why I

avoided you or why things became strained between us." He leaned in closer. "It was because you sent me away when I wanted to be with you. You lied to force me to leave. I knew it, but I still went. That part was on me."

"It doesn't matter now. Maybe I won't make the same mistakes in the future. Perhaps I'll take Decker's advice and only date within my species. Then I won't have to worry as much."

"You'd still worry."

"Probably." I blinked away the tears. "I'm sorry I didn't realize these things soon enough to save us. For what it's worth, I wish I hadn't forced you to go when you wanted to stay with me."

He narrowed his eyes, a smirk playing across his lips. "You really think I moved on in three months? I spent twelve just getting you to agree to go on a date. Have you ever known me to give up on a fight?"

"But you said you were seeing someone. Who is she?"

He practically burst into a fit of laughter. "First of all, she's a he." Not expecting that revelation, I didn't say anything. "And second of all, he was my therapist. After two weeks, I fired him. I wanted to understand why my girlfriend left, and he wanted me to focus on the part I played in the dissolution of our relationship and to consider the possibility that I might have control issues." He sighed dramatically. "Clearly, he didn't understand the real root of the problem."

"That we both have control issues?" I teased, and Martin smiled. "So you're not seeing anyone?"

He leaned forward. "I'm seeing you." He glanced toward the front door. "Depending on how long Mark stays away, I'd like to see a lot more of you."

"Full disclosure, there's less of me to see. I tried to take a piece of rebar home as a souvenir and thought it'd be smart to embed it in my leg."

That didn't stop Martin from insinuating himself between the sofa and me. He wrapped his arms around me and kissed me. "What are we doing?" he asked, nuzzling my neck.

"I don't know." I honestly had no clue. "I'm not sure

we've figured out how to fix our problems."

"But you seem different. It's a start." His hand slipped beneath the covers, finding its way underneath the hem of my shirt. He ran his hand along my abdomen. "I'm different now too. I have a surprise for you."

"Oh yeah?"

"Yeah." We started to kiss. "You'll see."

"I can guess what it might be." Hearing a key in the lock, I put my palm on his chest. "We can't have sex on Mark's couch."

"Why not?"

"Because he's home." I gave him a playful push. "And he's Mark. And we're ... us."

He nodded, sitting up and adjusting himself. "Yeah. I gotcha. We need more time to sort this thing out. I'll think about what you said and let you know what I decide." The sudden shift was like whiplash, and I gave him a confused look. "We'll talk about this tonight."

"What's tonight?"

He stood up, moving toward the front door as Mark entered. "You'll see."

*   *   *

That evening, I attended the police gala as Jablonsky's date. What he failed to mention was an entire table had been purchased. Detective Thompson had brought a date. Detective Derek Heathcliff was solo, but he was smart enough to put his jacket on the empty chair and come up with a lie as to where his date went. Detective Nick O'Connell and his wife, Jen, were seated across from me, but there were still two empty seats at the table, conceivably for Lieutenant Moretti and his wife.

Nick and Derek asked about my recent absence, so I gave them vague details about the case. Derek was drinking more than usual, but he seemed to be bouncing back from the last debacle we had faced. Nick and Jen kept eyeing me, as if they knew a secret and weren't willing to share. Mark was nursing a whiskey sour and scanning the room. His tense posture and alertness had me on edge, so my eyes immediately locked on Martin the moment the elevator doors opened.

He stepped out with a statuesque redhead by his side. She laughed politely, placing her hand on his forearm before moving off toward a group and exchanging air kisses with a few of them. Martin didn't stay near his date. Instead, he searched the room for our table and sauntered over. A few hours ago, that bastard had me convinced he wasn't seeing anyone.

Martin greeted Mark, leaned over the table to give Jen a friendly hug, nodded to Derek, and shook hands with Nick. Thompson and his date had disappeared to the bar. In usual fashion, Martin put his hand on the back of my chair and sat beside me, brushing his lips against my cheek.

"You're radiant," he cooed, slipping a hotel room key beneath my napkin so carefully I didn't think anyone saw him do it. "Maybe we can continue our conversation from this morning."

"Maybe."

Jen smiled brightly, glad to see the two of us were on speaking terms. "It's nice to see you again, James. I'm glad you're off the crutches."

"Crutches?" I turned to him.

"I tweaked my knee. It wasn't a big deal. It was just a couple of weeks."

"That's what you get for rappelling down a wall at that speed," Heathcliff muttered from the other end of the table, and my eyes shot to him as if I were watching a tennis match. "You passed the course. You didn't have to try to break the record."

Martin glared, giving Heathcliff a look I'd never seen before.

"Oh for god's sake," O'Connell huffed, "just tell her already. She's going to be pissed about it anyway, but drawing it out will make it worse."

"Make what worse?" I asked.

Martin swallowed. "As you're about to find out, I made a sizeable donation to the police department. Our friends in blue could use the funds." The philanthropic reasoning wasn't going to work on me, and I continued to stare at him. "I also convinced them to allow me to be a civilian ride along, so to speak. I went through the same training courses as ESU. For the last six weeks, ever since you called that night, that's what I've been doing. Weapons, tactics, emergency response, and first responder training. It was abbreviated, obviously. And Jabber got HRT to agree to let me run their course also."

"Why?"

He turned in his chair to face me directly. His green eyes bore into my soul, and I thought I'd break. They must have taught him advanced interrogation techniques too. "You said it was different with them. That you didn't worry because they were trained and knew how to handle themselves in tight spots. I'm just as capable, Alex. My scores prove it."

Before I could say anything, someone went to the podium to make an official speech. I sat through it, listening to the usual accolades and rhetoric that went along with these types of events. It was a charity function to raise funds for the police force, and they thanked Martin for his large donation. When he got up to give a speech to share his positive experiences with the city's police department and firsthand impressions of the vigorous training the men and women in uniform go through, I turned to Mark with a questioning look.

"You can watch him run the course," Mark whispered in my ear. "I recorded his last run with HRT. If you want, I can even pull a few strings so the two of you can go head-to-head."

"Why would you encourage this?"

Jablonsky snickered. "He can handle himself, and I'm not sure there's any other way of proving that to you. He doesn't want to give up on you. And I don't believe for a second you want to lose him either. The man proposed. And no one buys a rock like that if they aren't committed."

I stared, remembering that I asked him to return the engagement ring. "But..."

"But nothing. Say thank you and stop overthinking things."

After Martin returned to the table, we quietly excused

ourselves and headed upstairs. It was time we had a talk without any interruptions. Our last two exchanges had been civil. I hoped we were done fighting. I wanted to move forward, not harp on the past.

Martin opened the door, holding it for me to enter. I wasn't surprised to see the flowers and chilled champagne. That was classic Martin. "You told me you trusted Nick and Mark because they had training, remember?" He stared at me. "You can't hold that against me any longer." I didn't say anything, and he moved a few steps closer. "You said you'd find a way to fix this. So I've been doing everything I can to make some of that easier for you. I won't be your doormat. I won't let you dictate my actions or behaviors. You can't change me, and I know I can't change you." He pressed his lips together. "This morning you sounded like a different person. You reminded me of the woman I met. The one who was coming to terms with herself and her decisions. I fell in love with that woman."

"I'm glad I remind you of her."

He smirked. "You look just like her."

I took a seat at the foot of the bed. "You should know, I was sort of seeing someone too. My partner was a shrink before joining the DEA. We talked a lot about everything. I want things to go back to the way they were. I don't want to do this without you."

"This?"

"Life."

"It can't be the way it was. You can't do this ever again. I mean it. If some shithead wants to blow us to kingdom come, we face him together." He stared at me for a long moment. "I know what you did to save me. To save Heathcliff and Mark and the rest of us. That broke something inside of you. Promise me, you'll never sacrifice yourself again. We'll find another way." He stared at me for a long moment. "And don't say it if you don't mean it."

"I promise."

He closed the distance between us. "Good because I want to put my kickass rappelling skills to good use."

"You're insane. That training is hardcore. No wonder you bulked up. Do any of your suits even fit anymore?"

"They're a bit snug, but it was worth it." He pressed his forehead against mine. "We need to take things slow. We're starting over, so no moving in together. And if you ever feel like I'm punishing you, talk to me. I'm not perfect." He chuckled. "And I have no intention of letting you fall back into bad habits either. I don't think we can separate work from our relationship. It defines so much of who we are. We'll have to talk about it and find a balance."

"Are you sure you want to do this?"

He pushed me backward against the mattress. "It's the only thing I've thought about all day. Plus, third time's a charm."

DON'T MISS THE NEXT INSTALLMENT IN
THE ALEXIS PARKER SERIES.

WHITEWASHED LIES IS NOW AVAILABLE
IN PRINT AND AS AN E-BOOK

ABOUT THE AUTHOR

G.K. Parks is the author of the Alexis Parker series. The first novel, *Likely Suspects,* tells the story of Alexis' first foray into the private sector.

G.K. Parks received a Bachelor of Arts in Political Science and History. After spending some time in law school, G.K. changed paths and earned a Master of Arts in Criminology/Criminal Justice. Now all that education is being put to use creating a fictional world based upon years of study and research.

You can find additional information on G.K. Parks and the Alexis Parker series by visiting our website at
www.alexisparkerseries.com

Made in United States
North Haven, CT
20 April 2023

35690857R00200